AN OATH OF DOGS

"All of Wendy Wagner's s... us element: tremendous hea... nt example of this – with an ex... ...oration of philosophy, theology, an... ...ight at the heart of what it means to colonize a strange world. Wagner's characters are compelling and true. *An Oath of Dogs* combines echoes of Vernor Vinge and Sherri S Tepper with Wagner's own unique vision for the planet of Huginn and those who are trying to survive the planet, and each other."

Fran Wilde, award-winning author of Updraft *and* Cloudbound

"A compelling tale of corporate intrigue and biology, set on a thoroughly imagined world. Perfect for any fan of eco-science fiction and world building. A really great read."

Pat Murphy, award-winning author of The City, Not Long After *and* The Falling Woman

"Wagner's exquisite world-building takes Manifest Destiny to the stars. There's a dark Romanticism here, and it asks big questions about humanity and the cosmos. *An Oath of Dogs* is smart, dangerous, and impossible to put down."

Darin Bradley, author of Totem

"*An Oath of Dogs* nails the rough-hewn feel of a frontier town, then mixes it up with intergalactic corporate intrigue and alien biology. It's like Lake Wobegon mashed up with a Michael Crichton thriller, as unlikely a melding of cultures as the world of Huginn itself, creating a story that mashes massive questions of religion and ethics together with the joy of science and discovery."

Ferrett Steinmetz, author of the 'Mancer series

Skinwalkers
Starspawn

WENDY N WAGNER

AN OATH OF DOGS

ANGRY
ROBOT

ANGRY ROBOT
An imprint of Watkins Media Ltd

20 Fletcher Gate,
Nottingham,
NG1 2FZ
UK

angryrobotbooks.com
twitter.com/angryrobotbooks
Best friends

An Angry Robot paperback original 2017
1

A catalogue record for this book is available from the British Library.

ISBN 978 0 85766 666 6
EBook ISBN 978 0 85766 668 0

Set in Meridien and Big Noodle Titling by Epub Services.
Printed and bound in the UK by 4edge Limited.

Dedicated to Dale Wagner,
who once told me that everything a novel needed
could be found in Ash Valley, Oregon.
As usual, Dad, you were right.

PART I: THE CORPSE WORRIERS

I was taught that people could choose to do evil and that they were free to make that choice. But I never believed I would. I didn't believe – could not believe – anyone who knew love and kindness and the laws of God could possibly choose evil. I did not understand what that choice could look like.
        – from MEDITATIONS ON THE MEANING OF EVIL
                                by MW Williams

CHAPTER ONE

Duncan's murderer shoved him across the bench seat until the open glove box filled his field of vision. One of Olive Whitley's drawings was in there, crinkled under the weight of Duncan's favorite wrench. He wanted to get up, to look anywhere else, to get himself someplace safe. But his hand only scrabbled weakly against the cheap fabric of the seat. He could hear the bubbles popping in his lungs as his airways filled with blood.

The other bastard, the one who'd picked up the bolt gun and cleaned off the prints, said something. His voice was too low to make out clearly.

"Then hide it in the woods." Duncan's killer gave Dunc's leg a shove. "The deep woods – someplace no one will go." He pulled himself up into the utility vehicle with a little grunt. The door slammed shut. "You brought this all on yourself," he said, his voice conversational, as if he was just making small talk at the Night Light over pool. "You shouldn't have come out here, Duncan. Huginn is no place for a limpwristed treehugger like yourself."

Duncan coughed a spray of blood that spattered across the UTV's dash in a fine mist. Dark blood, not bright arterial stuff.

He felt a little surge of hope. Maybe he wouldn't bleed out after all. He wished he could move his arms and pull the bolt out from between his ribs.

The utility vehicle jolted forward, shaking his body. "What the hell were you thinking going out there to Sector 13? You got that data line installed. You had no reason to go back."

"Fuckers," Duncan managed to choke out. The horrible burning in his chest sent a burst of pain deeper inside him. He gagged on blood. He had a great deal more to say, but his body wasn't about to oblige. What he knew about the company and the woods would stay unspoken now.

"Don't worry. Nobody else is as snoopy as you. And nobody's going to find you. I don't think anyone's going to look too hard – not the sheriff, and not your old fuckbuddy, either." He was probably right. Not many people asked questions like Duncan did, and nobody listened to the answers carefully enough.

The UTV lurched and jolted on the rough road. Branches shrieked as they scraped across the vehicle's roof. The door vibrated as something slammed into it. They had to be headed out toward Sector 13. Duncan wished he could look at something else besides the goddamned glove box. Olive's picture was ruined – the spatters of his blood obscured the details of the little creatures she'd drawn. He was going to miss that kid. She could see the world around her, really see it, the way most people didn't even want to.

The bumping and thudding slowed until the UTV eased to a stop. The other man climbed down out of the rig, and for a moment it was just Duncan and his blood spatters and Olive's drawing. The colors wriggled and danced, the bright pinks and luscious yellows he'd never seen in anything living before he'd come to Huginn. If there was one thing he regretted about his life, it was that it had taken him so long to get to this stupid, wonderful moon. He thought about trying to pick up the drawing. Olive had wanted him to keep it.

Then the passenger door flew open and his armpits were seized. He slid out of the vehicle and hit the ground, hard.

His killer grabbed his arms. Duncan tried to twist away from him, but he didn't have the energy. He could barely breathe, although he could smell the woods all around him. The bright perfume of crushed button ferns brought a familiar sting to his nose.

He was going to die in the woods alone. The thought made him go cold.

"Wodin's coming up." The man grunted as he yanked Duncan over a fallen horsetail tree. He was skinnier and shorter than Duncan, and Duncan felt a perverse pleasure in the man's struggle. "Going to be full dark in about an hour. Lucky for me, the dogs don't usually come out until Wodin's high, and I'll be back in town by then."

Duncan made a little whimper.

"That's right. The dogs. Jeff Eames said he saw the dogs on his farm last night. That's not that far from here, really. They say a dog can smell blood up to four kilometers away. You think that's right?"

The skinny man dropped Duncan's arms, and Duncan fell onto his back. The broad limbs of a horsetail tree spread out above him, the candelabra arms nearly blocking out the sky. Full dark might not be for an hour, but it was plenty dark under the trees.

"I hope they don't find you, Chambers. We've all seen what the dogs do to the dead."

He walked away, his fancy cowboy boots jingling with every step. Duncan listened for the chiming to fade. Finally, the silence seemed complete, and he found the strength to push himself closer to the tree, where the up-swellings of its roots lifted his head a bit. It was harder to breathe now. He guessed he only had a minute left, maybe two. At least he could see the forest around him.

A leather bird dropped down beside him. Its eyeless face stretched toward him, its nostrils vibrating as it drew in his scent. The creature's soft clicking, the sound of a scorpion's feet on dry stone, made his skin prickle. Another landed next to it.

He choked on blood, coughed, gagged. The nearest leather bird rushed at him, its belly splitting open to taste the air. The yellow stinger inside shot out.

Duncan Chambers closed his eyes. Somewhere in the distance, a dog howled.

The cold drained out of her slowly. For a few seconds, Standish couldn't remember how to breathe, and then she gasped and choked and coughed up cryo liquid. Her abdominal muscles ached.

"There, there," the attendant murmured, the same soft-voiced woman who had intubated Standish on the other side of sleep. "It'll all come out in a second. Just breathe." Her hand was too warm where it gripped Standish's bicep. Standish wanted to wrench it off and sit up on her own, but she didn't have the energy for extraneous shit. Breathing was enough.

Then the fog cleared from her brain and she sat up fast enough to rip the monitor from her temple. "Hattie? Where's Hattie? My dog?"

The man sitting in the opened tube beside Standish gave her a sharp look. Half a dozen other passengers were rising, rubbing their still-cold throats, rotating their stiff necks. A second attendant, a painfully thin man with a handlebar mustache, opened the last tube in the room and frowned across at Standish.

The female attendant checked the display beside Standish's cryo tube. "You're getting too excited. Please lower your voice."

"Where the fuck is my dog?"

"She's still asleep. There's a different process for animals." The woman smiled with only her mouth. A set of tired lines stood between her eyebrows, and her skin looked parched. Space skin. When Standish had worked on Goddard Station, her skin could never get enough moisturizer.

Standish pushed the attendant out of the way and stood up, her legs wobbling. Her stomach twisted on itself. "I'm gonna throw up."

"Drink your slurry." The attendant handed her a plastic tube with a straw jammed into it. "And sit down before you fall down."

Standish toppled back on her butt. The padded cryo tube stuck to the backs of her bare legs. She fumbled the straw into her mouth.

"You've been asleep and frozen for more than a year, and now your body is restarting itself. Please try to breathe deeply and sip your slurry. I'll let you know when you can collect your pet."

"I need my fucking dog. Right now. So if you don't get her, I will."

The woman ignored her. Standish cleared her throat, which had turned from ice to dry flame, and tried swallowing more of the soupy stuff. It tasted like artificial cherry and vitamin tablets. "Hey, where are my things?"

"You just sit tight. I'll be back in a few minutes to help you with your things. I've got lots of passengers to wake up, Ms Standish."

The woman hurried out of the small room. Standish could hear her heavy footfalls in the corridor beyond. Standish eased herself to her feet again. She leaned on the bank of cryo tubes and took a sip of her fake food. She had to find Hattie.

"Persistent type, aren't you?" The man in the tube beside her took a last rattling slurp of his slurry. He had managed to drip some down the front of his hospital gown.

"Piss off." She shoved off the bank to propel her wobbly legs toward the numbered doors set into the wall. One of those lockers had to have her stuff in it. She threw open the first door. A pink carry-on: not hers.

"You've got a perky little ass, you know that?"

Standish ignored him. She opened the next locker, and the next. The one beside that held her bag, her ticket information tucked neatly into the front pouch. She pulled that out first, checking for Hattie's storage information. They'd put her in cargo over Standish's protests. There'd be no gravity down there. Fuck.

She tossed her gear on her empty cryo tube and stripped. She put on her clothes and boots as fast as she could manage, her fingers and legs quaking the whole time. They said cryo did a number on the body, and they didn't exaggerate. She had to swallow down her slurry more than once.

"All right, I'm off to get my dog," she announced. The slob was still sitting on the padded couch in his cryo tube, holding the slurry pouch as if it could hide the meager boner he'd popped while she was changing.

Standish propped her boot up on the edge of the tube. "It's the twenty-third century, not the tenth, shitface. If you come near me or anyone else, I'll throw you out an airlock. Do you understand?" She forced the toe of her boot into his crotch until tears welled up in his eyes.

She threw her bag over her shoulder and strode out into the hallway, flipping him off over her shoulder.

Beside the elevator bank, a view screen showed the hulking shape of the gas giant Wodin and its two attendant moons, Muninn and Huginn. The ship would enter orbit around Huginn soon, but even from this distance she could see the white swirls of clouds over the turquoise seas, the colors of a child's marble about to be swallowed by the great maw of space. She tore her eyes away from the screen and forced a deep breath. It was just a picture, she told herself. She was perfectly safe.

She jabbed at the call button and squeezed her eyes shut. She had never needed Hattie so badly before. There was so much space all around, every bit of it hungry and ready to swallow her. She couldn't breathe. She heaved up red slurry and watched it spatter on the beige plastic floor.

She fell to her knees. A hand touched her back.

"It's all right, Ms Standish. You should have just stayed in your berth."

She heaved again, but there was nothing else in her stomach. She wouldn't cry, though. Her stomach hurt, her head hurt, but there was no point crying about it.

Something wet and cold pressed against her cheek. She shivered.

"Ms Standish, I've brought you your dog. You should have told us she was a therapeutic animal."

She turned her head and got a faceful of Swiss shepherd tongue, stinking of multivitamins, a little dry, but definitely Hattie's. Standish wrapped her arms around the dog's neck and pressed her face into the thick white fur.

They would be on Huginn in a day and a half.

The leader looked back at the rest of the pack, their bodies taut arrows of pure intention, drawn to the cemetery by forces stronger than even the compulsion of their alpha. He could feel it too, his own flesh pulled achingly toward the freshly turned earth. One of their own was there, waiting for them. He couldn't stop the pack if he wanted to.

But he didn't want to. How could he want to? This was what it meant to be a pack: running together between the great trees and under the open sky, cool grit beneath his paw pads. There was a part of him, a part that he didn't like to look into, that had different ideas about living. He ignored that part. He was a dog. For him, the world was the tantalizing shift of the senses and the pure bliss of instinct obeyed. He leaped forward, his paws striking up pebbles that resounded against the hollow trunks of the horsetail trees.

The pack bayed with full voice as they surged out of the woods. It was a clear night; the planet's light rippled on their sleek coats and wet muzzles. One of the smaller dogs leaped over the nearest headstone, his back arched high and smooth, an echo of the stone's shape. The pack leader put a burst of speed into his paws and caught up with the smaller creature.

They were all big animals with thick coats and the disparate pieces of mixed breeds. A husky tail, a ridgeback hackle. The broad chest of a mastiff. They could have been any kind of dog, every kind of dog. The idea of a dog made real by sound and movement and the certainty of shadow. The pack leader slipped past a brightly painted cross that stood higher than his muscular shoulder and stopped at the edge of the naked clay soil.

The other dogs crowded around, overspilling the boundaries of the fresh grave, their paws sinking into the dirt. The alpha barked.

They began to dig.

For a few minutes all was silent, save for the patter of falling dirt and the deep breathing of the intent beasts. But then another scratching began, loud and frantic. A faint whine ran beneath it. Their packmate was suffering in there. The dogs dug faster.

Their nails scraped on wood, solid tight-jointed horsetail planks, but they didn't slow. They dug with skill, as if well practiced. One of them growled to itself. The others ignored it.

The damaged wood splintered beneath the collected weight of the pack. As if on cue, the dogs leaped out of the shallow grave, and with a tremendous flurry of barking, the top of the coffin exploded outward, a massive gray wolfhound bursting free. The rest of the pack circled it, barking, licking, pawing, delighted to puppyhood by the creature's presence. The alpha barked excitedly.

For a moment they tumbled and romped, content to have the pack reunited again, and then a different kind of instinct compelled them to action. Their nostrils quivered as they caught an irresistible smell. The pack leader fell behind as they trotted across the graveyard, steering clear of the ornate crosses and blue figurines marking the graves. They did not bark now. The jubilation had gone out of the group.

When they found the second patch of fresh dirt they began to dig. The pack leader watched them, uneasy. He sat down on his haunches and rubbed his dirty muzzle on his leg. He wanted to dig. He wanted to feel the cool soil press against his paw pads just as his packmates were feeling it. The delicious smell tugged at his nostrils, and a thread of hot slaver ran out of his mouth. He didn't know why he held back.

They didn't dig for long. At this end of the graveyard, there were fewer crosses to avoid, almost no statues of blue-clad women to be careful of. Their paws tore up the damp clods of clay and shredded the flimsy pressboard below. This time no muzzle strained up out of the ground. One by one, the dogs quit digging and fell in around the pack leader, watching the grave in silence. Finally, the largest of the dogs backed away from the grave, dragging a limp, linen-wrapped form behind it.

The package was the size and shape of a four year-old child.

The pack leader threw back his head again, and his howl cut through the night, a thin keening wail. In the houses on the shore of Canaan Lake, people stirred fitfully in their beds. In the farmyards, animals cried out in fear or huddled deeper inside their hutches. And in the horsetail trees along the highway, the things the colonists called birds buried their heads beneath their leathery wings.

The small shadow of the moonlet Muninn edged across the planet's face. The dogs raced out of the cemetery toward the lake, dragging their burden behind. The only evidence of their passing was a long strip of filthy cloth and two empty graves, and Frank the Caretaker had dealt with worse.

Only humankind has this instinct to name things and thus dominate them. What would this world be like if we had not called them horsetail trees and leather birds, names spun out of our experience as creatures of Earth? The names we gave them were themselves metaphors to make our relationship with this world consistent with our relationship to our home planet.

– from THE COLLECTED WISDOM OF MW WILLIAMS

CHAPTER TWO

The automated doors of the spaceport wheezed open and Peter stepped through them, slowing to stomp his boots on the vast black floor mat. A "Caution: Wet Floor" sign had been fixed permanently at the far end of it. Boots cleaned, he took off his glasses and tugged out his shirt tail to polish off the moisture. They were I+ glasses, but he'd turned them off when he'd left the office; the connectivity issues just weren't worth it.

In the nearest row of chairs, a couple was bickering. The woman was thin and angry. The man's cheek showed the fractal scars of a silicate explosion. Leaving Huginn, then. Probably tired of trying to get by on the salary the lumber mill paid. Neither of the two spared an eye for the toddler sitting at their feet, idly unpacking a rolling suitcase.

Peter looked around for the new communications manager. He had no idea what she looked like. A tall black man waiting by the baggage carrel caught his eye, gave him a friendly nod, and returned his attention to his handset. Mark Allen, the company's head of forestry, and thus, Peter's boss. He was even wearing a suit to greet whichever company honcho was arriving on the next shuttle. Maybe Peter should have changed out of his field gear.

His eyes roved over the other people inside the small waiting room. A few families, a handful of obvious spacers looking uncomfortable in nearly a full g, and a good-looking woman standing at the ticket counter, her hand resting on the head of a big white dog.

A dog. He hadn't seen a dog since his last trip to his grandmother's house. They were common enough on the rest of Huginn, but not in Canaan Lake.

He thought of the muddy bone he'd dropped off at the police station this morning and had a mental shudder. No, dogs weren't common in Canaan Lake.

He jammed his hands in his pockets and studied the arrival boards. As usual, half of them were burnt out.

"Are you Dr Bajowski? The guy at the ticket counter said you were from Canaan Lake HQ."

He whipped his head around. The good-looking woman with the dog was standing beside him, her hand out. There was an odd quality to her smile, as if perhaps the right side of her face was made out of stiffer skin than the other. He realized he was staring, and freed his hand from his pocket to shake.

"Kate Standish," she said. Her cropped hair stood up in messy spikes, and under her black leather-looking jacket, she wore what looked like a man's white tank top. "You look more Mexican than Polish."

He released her hand quickly. "So there've been some changes while you were in transit. There was an accident, and well, long story short, you've been promoted to communications manager. Congratulations, Kate."

"Standish," she corrected him. "What happened to Duncan Chambers?"

Peter let his eyes crawl from the woman's boots up to her face. She didn't look like a spacer – she didn't have the attenuated frame or the translucent hide that came from life under artificial lighting – but using last names was a spacer convention. On her, it seemed like an affectation.

"I grew up on Earth, but I served at Goddard Station for five years," she said. "That's why I'm not seven feet tall. I guess I deserve that look for the Mexican comment."

"Yeah," he said, drawing it out into two syllables. He couldn't read her, couldn't get a fix on her personality. Prickly, that was for sure. And the dog had come closer while they were talking. It watched him with what seemed like a friendly expression. "Is that your dog? Can you have a dog on a space station?"

"I got Hattie after that stage of my life. Dogs and low-g don't really go together. Can we get my luggage? And explain about Duncan? I was looking forward to working for him."

He pointed out the baggage drop at the far end of the building. There was no good way to tell her about Dunc. She kept glancing over at him, and he wondered if he looked as uncomfortable as he felt. "There was an accident," he began, but a piercing giggle cut him off. They both turned to see what made the noise.

A grubby kid, probably two years-old, maybe younger, raced at top speed toward Hattie and grabbed hold of her soft tail. Hattie stood patiently.

"You can pet her," Standish said.

"Don't touch that thing!" The toddler's mother snatched up the kid. It was the angry woman he'd seen earlier, the one whose husband had the scarred face.

"She's perfectly trained," Standish answered before Peter could open his mouth. "And she has a docility chip – she couldn't bite if she wanted to."

The woman said nothing but backed away, staring at the dog.

"Jesus. What's wrong with that bitch?" Standish grumbled.

Peter gave the woman a friendly smile and turned back to see Standish hauling her bags out of the baggage trough. He wanted to ask her more about the dog, which was sniffing his crotch, perfect training or not. He turned his body away from the inquisitive snout. "Can I take one of your bags?"

"That would be great. The company said my lodgings are furnished, so this is pretty much everything I own. You've got the coffee pot in that suitcase, so be careful."

He led her toward the exit and stopped on the black mat. Outside the rain drilled down hard enough to ricochet off the pavement, giving the illusion that water shot up from the ground at the same time it fell from the sky. The water hazed the air in silver sheets.

"Do you have a rain coat?"

"Somewhere in my bags. Do you think I'll need it?"

He gestured at the glass doors ahead. Through the curtains of rain, the parking lot was a black field surrounded by the green fingers of young horsetail trees. Standish stared outside a long moment, and then reached out to the dog and curled her fingers around its red leather collar.

"Didn't they warn you about the rain?" They obviously hadn't told her about dogs. He wasn't sure how to break the news.

"They said–" She broke off and cleared her throat. "They said it rained a lot. I guess I wasn't prepared for how wet it really was." She knelt to rifle through a pack and came up with a sturdy jacket. "I guess there's a difference between hearing it and seeing it."

"Well, hoods up. My rig is the closest – that white company UTV." He stepped out from under the wide awning, but Standish didn't move off the black mat, staring outside. The dog leaned comfortably against her leg.

"Kate."

She blinked at him.

He corrected himself. "Standish. It's just a few meters to the car."

She took a small step forward, then picked up her pace. Peter threw open the passenger door and slid her suitcase across the backseat. She slung her pack past him and motioned for the dog to jump in after it.

Peter ran around to the driver's seat. He didn't look at Standish as they settled into place, concentrating instead on drying his glasses and finding his seat belt, but he could hear her ragged breathing, as if she'd run a klick instead of just the few meters across the parking lot.

He risked a glance at her and saw she was shaking. "Are you sure you're OK?"

"A-fucking-OK."

"OK." He started up the rig and pulled out onto the highway. Maybe they could just not talk until they got to Canaan Lake. It might be better. She put her boot up on the dashboard and fiddled with the laces.

Then he remembered he still hadn't explained about Duncan. His heart sank. "Yeah, so about Duncan Chambers. He... This sucks. You're going to have to be the new Duncan."

"What?"

"Dunc's dead." Saying it like that made Peter wince. "He went out one night about a month and a half ago, and he never came back. By the time we realized something had happened, it was too late. Huginn's a wild place. If you forget that you could be in real danger."

"Jesus. You're sure? I mean, couldn't he have just gone back to Earth?"

"His passport was never activated. Anywhere. He liked to hike, so..." He cleared his throat. "Anyway, search parties looked for him for a week before the weather got too bad." Peter had kept looking for weeks afterwards, but he didn't need to tell her that.

She sat for a minute without talking. The left side of the road went bright as they passed a long swathe of clear-cut hillside, the pale yellow soil raw and naked between the strips of greenery. Then she blurted out, "Songheuser made this place sound so magical. Like everything's something out of Wonderland. Giant ferns, pink caterpillars. Fungus that'll dance to music. I should have known it was too good to be true."

"Well, there's some bad stuff – red death puffballs, for example, which will rip your lungs into goo within twelve hours – but you can learn how to avoid it, by and large."

The UTV rounded a corner and Peter braked hastily. "Plus, it's still pretty much Wonderland."

Standish's mouth fell open. "What are those things?"

Three creatures the size of sheep, roughly the same design as a potato bug but tinted the colors of rainbow sherbet, made their slow way across the road.

"Greater trudgees. We call this 'rush hour in Huginn.'" He pointed ahead. "They like the highway because of all the exposed rock. See where they're going?"

She rolled down the window to follow his gesture. She stared at the rock field beside the highway, which stretched at least fifty meters before the rocks began to form the slope of a steep hill. Nearly every centimeter had been claimed by rock-eater lichen. Its orange and pink tendrils wrapped the rocks like a net, clashing with the chartreuse spots of Devil's bogey and the shimmering rainbows of Huginn's puffball. A few trudgees were already making their slow nibbling way among the rocks.

"Wow." She scrambled to kneel on her seat so she could lean out the window. "So many colors. It's hard to believe."

"Fungi and spore plants fill most niches around here. The chemistry behind all the colors is complicated, but Songheuser is hoping to identify the pigments and use them in new dye technology."

She flopped back into her seat. "You don't sound like you approve."

He brought the UTV onto the highway. "If they cultivate the mushrooms in a contained facility, I think it's a good idea."

"You're very careful with your words, aren't you?" She rolled her window up. The worst of the condensation had cleared, but now dense stands of horsetail and fern hemmed in the road, and there were no colors to point out. "What do you really think?"

"I think harvesting these fungi in industrial quantities could cripple the local ecosystem," he answered, with unanticipated force. "Rock-eater lichen breaks rock into nutrients vital to plants, and the other fungi are critical recyclers. With this much precipitation, nutrients are leached from the soil faster than plants can absorb them. If we want to keep harvesting horsetails – and let's face it, horsetail lumber is Songheuser's biggest moneymaker on this planet – then they'd better find a way to help the fungi *grow*, not rip it all out."

He paused for air and realized he was talking too loud and too fast. "Sorry." He had to get smarter. After all, Kate Standish worked for Songheuser, too.

"Sorry you have thoughts and ideas that you care about?" Standish shook her head. "I owe the company a lot, but I came here to get away from all that apathetic bullshit back on Earth."

"Well, people there don't have much."

"Because people live in cans down there, that's why. Back on Earth, all those cramped cities – how can you care about any of it? I didn't. The only good thing I ever got on Earth is Hattie."

Peter scratched the back of his neck. "There's something you should know about Hattie."

The smile faded from Standish's face.

"Most folks in Canaan Lake aren't fans of dogs. In fact,

there aren't any li–"

"I checked," she cut him short. "Dogs aren't illegal. Farmers are even looking for breeding bitches. Hattie's fixed, of course, but she's perfectly legal."

"There's no law," he said. "There's just a local thing about dogs. They run away." He hesitated. "Or get lost. But mostly they run away and go wild."

They rounded a corner and eased aside to let a log truck pass. They'd made good time cutting through the gentle hills around Space City, and now they were nearly to Canaan Lake. He slowed the UTV as the highway rounded the steep flanks of Mount Hepzibah.

"They 'go wild'?" Standish snapped. "You mean people just turn their dogs loose in this kind of country? For Chrissake, that's the stupidest thing I ever heard. What could a dog even eat on this planet? Every goddamned thing is poisonous."

"There's livestock. Huginn has the largest population of sheep, cows, and goats in two star systems. The Believers of the Word Made Flesh have turned this area into a major agricultural center, and their people are pretty damn possessive of their livestock."

"I forgot," she admitted. "I'd read about the farms and the Church, but I never thought about the animals. I don't get it, though. I know Believers, Bajowski. I got Hattie from a Believer breeder – there's hardly anyone on Earth raising dogs besides the Believers. They're dog people."

"Not here," he said. "Canaan Lake's not like Earth, or anyplace else. The people who live here do things their own way."

They passed by the sturdy wooden gate of a farmhouse. Peter watched Standish study it, craning her neck around until they had passed out of sight. He was used to the way Believer farms looked on Huginn: the unpeeled horsetail trunk fences, the severe white houses, the pole barns. It reminded him of pictures of Amish country in Pennsylvania. The ornate and colorful crosses painted on the barn doors only added to the image.

She turned back around in her seat and stared at the battered toes of her black boots. "It's *nothing* like Earth," she murmured. She must have never made it to Pennsylvania.

He slowed the vehicle further. In a minute, Cemetery Hill would pop up, and she ought to see it. If anything would underscore the strangeness of this place, it was the graveyard.

"Look." He eased the UTV onto the shoulder of the road.

Cemetery Hill stood tall and proud, one side bordering Canaan Lake's posher neighborhoods – such as they were – and its other climbing up from the highway. Its steep flanks stood neatly terraced and landscaped, and gray cement paths alternated with green grasses imported from Earth. It was the colors that set it apart from any cemetery back on Earth.

"Holy shit," she breathed.

He'd had the same response the first time he saw it. He'd been to a cemetery or two – he'd buried his grandmother, after all – but those cemeteries were crowded little places with strict rules against headstones. The Believers had retained the headstone tradition, or resurrected it, perhaps, and they had given it their own strange touch. At the head of every grave stood a me memeter-high slab of stone with complicated artwork and lines of Biblical verses. Small blue statuettes, something like the figure of the Virgin Mary, sat beside several of these lavish headstones. And at the foot of every grave stood a hand-painted cross, the blond horsetail wood emblazoned with red and blue and yellow designs. Ordinary settlers had much plainer crosses and headstones, but it was clear to Peter that the Believer colonists had influenced even these burial plots.

"So many crosses," she said. She rolled the window down again and stuck her head out.

"At least one on every grave," he said. "The wind blows them down, but the Believers come out every couple of months and replace them." He'd found a broken cross laying in his yard one morning, and he lived in company housing all the way down by the lake.

She pulled her head back inside. "Why have so many people died here?"

"Most of the graves belong to Believers," he explained. "They allow basic surgical techniques and even some drugs, but they won't go to the hospital in Space City. If someone seriously gets hurt, they don't always pull through."

"Stupid." She frowned. "Who's that up there?" She pointed toward the top of the hill where a man was digging.

"That's Caretaker Frank." Peter twisted around in his seat to offer Hattie his hand to smell. He gave her ears a rub. She was such a pretty dog, and so well-behaved. "Remember what I said about dogs running wild?"

Frank planted his shovel and trudged toward a wheelbarrow covered in canvas. He pushed the wheelbarrow closer to where he'd been digging, and dumped the load, canvas and all, into the hole. Peter wondered if the bone he'd found by the lake this morning belonged with it.

"What about them?"

"It doesn't seem to matter what people do, they can't keep those dogs from digging in the graveyard. It's the smell, I guess. Something to eat."

Standish rolled up her window. "That's sick."

He nodded and started up the UTV again. Up ahead, the slate-colored waters of Canaan Lake appeared. Soon he'd be pulling into the driveway of the shabby house she'd inherited, like her job, from Duncan Chambers – the man who'd brought him to Huginn, his ex-lover, his best friend for fifteen years. He glanced at Kate Standish, quietly watching the town appear, her left hand stroking the big white dog.

Duncan had said he thought Peter would like her.

Time would tell, he supposed. He held back a sigh. Damn, he missed Dunc.

Standish moved from window to window, closing the curtains and slapping shut the blinds. The bathroom lacked such amenities, but at least a dense stand of ferns pressed up against the side of the building. It was surprisingly comforting. Hattie took a deep sniff of the toilet's base and made a whuff.

"Are you hungry, Hattie?"

The dog pricked up her ears. To minimize air sickness upon landing, the attendants had closed off the dining areas six hours before the shuttle hit Huginn's atmosphere, and between the wait and the drive from Space City, it had been a long time for the dog to go without food. After the winding roads and open spaces, even water sounded vaguely horrible to Standish. But Hattie might want lunch.

Standish left the bathroom's pleasant green view and sank down on the battered couch where she'd dropped her pack. The furnishings were the same style as the exterior: disinterested corporate cheap. Every house on the lake shore was the same squat plastic box, probably shit out by the same construction printer as every other company town. Standish had been working off-planet for more than a decade. She'd seen enough to know that even the brand new space stations looked scuffed and unloved. She zipped open the pack, took Hattie's heavy plastic bowls and a packet of dog chow out of the top layer, and sighed.

"At least the last guy could have decorated."

She tucked the bowls under her arm, forced herself up from the sagging couch, and trudged into the tiny kitchen. Her legs and back *felt* like they'd been immobile for a year. The attendant who'd greeted her on this side of the wormhole had promised that electric stimulation applied in the last two weeks of the journey would help her muscles defrost more effectively, but clearly there was only so much technology could do.

Still, she was on Huginn. After a year of application hassles, nearly a year's transit via wormhole and long-distance ships, she was here on this big green moon. She rolled her shoulders and made a mental note to find some resistance bands or weights. She liked the sense of lightness that came from living at just under one g, but it wasn't doing her bones any favors.

Hattie pawed at Standish's leg, reminding her of her task. She turned on the tap and filled the dog's bowl with water that wasn't recycled or reclaimed and didn't stink of iodine, plastics, or chlorine. Real water. And outside her window was greenery, not more humanity.

Standish grabbed her craft bag and plopped onto the floor, inwardly giddy. She could hear Hattie lapping up water in the kitchen. That was the only sound – not sirens, not someone in another apartment snoring or fighting or fucking. Just Hattie.

A grin crept across her face. She felt good. Her backside might hurt from the drive and her stomach might be churning from cryo, but she felt *good*.

She reached for her hand unit and thumbed it on. Not a lot of signal in here, but enough to make a call. She jabbed the first number in her contacts list.

The screen jiggled a moment and then resolved into a woman's beaming face. Her hair was gold today, the beaded braids clicking and clacking around her deep-brown skin. She tossed them back, but they immediately tumbled forward around her eyes. "You made it!"

The sight of her best and only friend never failed to soften Standish. She stretched her fingers out to the screen, the closest she could get to putting her arm around the other woman. "Thanks to you, Dewey. You backed me every step of the way." She balanced the hand unit on her knees so she could pull out her latest crocheting project.

Dewey pressed her fingers to her own handset for a minute. "Yeah, well, I knew you'd like this place. It's not like working on a space station. Things are clean. People care."

There was a subtext to her words, and they both knew it. Each was silent for a second, the past suddenly present. It had taken Dewey an hour to get the medics to come to Standish after the crawler accident, and it ate at her as badly as it did Standish. Nothing was direct on a space station. Nothing was personal. Those tin cans operated just like Earth, but with twice as much red tape and half as much air.

"I'm sorry I couldn't meet you at the spaceport. I can't believe your ship got scheduled to arrive at the same time as the Muninn launch."

Standish leaned closer to the screen. "What's Muninn like?"

"It's got no atmosphere, but scientists still want to live there. Luckily, there are some *fine* scientists to be found on that rock." Dewey's eyes widened. "Girl! I just realized! You haven't seen my new tatas!"

Standish laughed as the screen pulled back to reveal Dewey's deep-cut pink tee, the front stretched over a phenomenal rack. "Nice! They're better than mine!"

"Even my *fakes* were better than yours, Kitty." Dewey laughed and brought her face back into focus. "But seriously, I owe these to Huginn. You know how long I've been waiting to see a decent cosmetic surgeon. That's the perk of living in a successful colony."

Space stations had acceptable medical facilities, but they were low on frills. Plastic surgery was a luxury for everyone up there, no matter how much a difference it made in people's lives.

Standish patted her leg and Hattie came to sit beside her. "I just wanted to thank you for bringing me here. It's amazing."

"It's great, isn't it?" Dewey hesitated, then took a breath. "You sure you'll be OK here? I know how big changes can throw off a treatment plan."

"Dewey–"

"No, seriously. You were really starting to pull things together back on Earth. I don't want this to set you back."

"Look, the agoraphobia is practically a thing of the past. Hattie has saved me." Standish glanced at the dog. "Speaking of, I'd better get her a walk. I think she's suffering."

"You keep her next to you all the time." Dewey raised her voice. "Hattie, you hear me? You stick to my girl like you're her other half."

Standish hung up, laughing. Dewey was always overprotective. But she was onto something about Hattie. Sometimes Standish felt like she and the dog really were two halves of the same whole – a whole immeasurably better than the broken thing that was Standish.

Hattie whuffed. Standish rubbed the sleek white dome of her head. "Let's take you outside, you good dog."

The dog trotted out of the kitchen to stand patiently at the door. Standish put away the yarn, reached for her raincoat, and hesitated. There was no curtain over the plexiglass window in the door, and the greens and grays of the world outside stood at attention. Her chest constricted a little at the sight. It was a small open space, but still space.

She squeezed her eyes shut. Her shrink back on Earth had warned her that these moments would come frequently the first few weeks on Huginn. She reached for Hattie and pulled her close, breathing in the faint corn chip smell of her.

Standish forced open her eyes and gripped the doorknob. "Come on, girl."

They stepped out into the open air. The gray clouds pressing down on her felt comforting, but the drizzle had a bite to it. Standish made it to the shingled beach of the lake shore before she gave in and put on the raincoat.

Hattie squatted to do her business. Standish risked looking past the dog toward the lake, which spread itself in dark, silken folds the color of steel.

Canaan Lake ran like a long wavering gouge in the forested hills. At this time of day, the gravitational pull of Wodin had shifted the bulk of the lake's mass toward the east side, exposing the beach all the way out to the muddy lake bottom. On the far side of the lake, the hills climbed straight out of the water toward the clouds.

She could do this, Standish reassured herself. She could stand outside under the gray sky and look at the lake like anyone else and think about the weather and the town's inhabitants. It wasn't easy to draw in a deep breath, but she was still breathing and she was still standing outside and she was still patiently waiting for Hattie. She hadn't had to run back to the house and hide under the bed.

"Excuse me? Miss?"

Standish whirled around. "What do you want?"

The boy's smile wobbled. The homespun linen of his clothing and the flat straw hat pushed back on his head announced his background: Believer through and through.

"Crap, I'm sorry. I'm just… shit, I'm sorry, kid."

He glanced from Standish to the dog and back, and then his eyes went round and he swept the hat off his head. "Excuse me, ma'am."

"It's OK. I'm the one who bites, and I swear I'll be good."

"You're the new communications manager? At Songheuser?"

"I am. Kate Standish. And this is my dog, Hattie."

He stared at the dog a second, then swallowed. "Yes'm. They said a new lady was coming." He cleared his throat. "I don't know if you've made plans already, but the old communications manager, Mr Chambers, he always bought his produce from our farm?"

"Produce?" Standish shook her head, confused.

"Oh, nothing fancy. We grow salad greens, potatoes, apples. Cabbage and Brussels sprouts year round. Most of the other farms are growing about the same things. But you won't find better potatoes, ma'am, and that's the truth." He paused a moment, and then was compelled to add: "Mr Williams has plums on his farm, but they aren't in season yet."

Standish blinked at him a moment. Potatoes. Apples. She had always bought such things in a tin. Freeze dried, if she was off-planet. She hadn't eaten fresh food since she'd left her parents' house.

"It's all right, ma'am. I understand if you want to order from another farm. I'll just be on my way." He turned away, his head low.

Standish put out her hand, then pulled back. She wasn't sure about the Believer protocol for inter-gender touching. Maybe it was immoral to people like him. She would have to look into Believer manners. "No, please. I'd love to order my produce from your farm. I was just… thinking about my bank balance. I'm not sure when payday is, you know."

The boy grinned over his shoulder. "Oh, I'll come by on the 16th. It's the day after Songheuser cuts paychecks, so that's when everybody in town pays their bills."

"Everybody?"

"Sure. If it weren't for Songheuser, even the churches would have a hard time staying afloat." He clapped his hat back on his head. "I'll bring your first produce box tomorrow, ma'am. I'm sure glad to add you to our list."

"Thank you–" Standish broke off. "I don't know your name, or the name of your farm."

"Jemison. Of the Leavitt family farm." He paused. "I'm glad you said you wanted our farm box. You know, we're the only ones in Canaan Lake that keep dogs? I don't imagine anyone else would have come to ask you if you wanted produce."

Standish's mouth went open, but he had already climbed onto an ancient-looking bicycle and begun pedaling away before she collected herself enough to find words. Bajowski had tried to warn her, she realized. Hattie really wasn't welcome in Canaan Lake.

April 23rd –
Last month's Prayer Breakfast brought in the final thousand dollars we needed to finish paying our passage on the *Roebuck*. Well, that and a huge donation from the Indochinese Branch Headquarters. I don't care where the money came from – I'll just be glad to see the lines smoothed out from Matthias's face. He even smiled the other night. Praise to be to God! I hate seeing him like this.

There are enough funds now for all eighteen families to go to Huginn. When I took the news to our last meeting, everyone cried and threw up their arms and embraced each other. Pappy Morris picked me up and threw me in the air, and Orrin – Pappy's oldest son, and one of Matthias's best friends – fell out of his chair laughing.

While Matthias and Elder Perkins have been sorting out our funds, I've been focused on matters closer to home. It hasn't been easy, selling off all our livestock. Most of the local Believers are either coming with us or are strapped for cash. All our neighbors and kinfolk have been scraping up their last dimes and pennies to send us to the stars. Matthias will be greatly disappointed by the amount of money I've earned us. I had to give our sheep and dogs (except for my Soolie, of course) to my parents. They are getting old, and I know they couldn't manage cows, or I would have sent them some.

It's easy for Matthias to be excited about this trip, but it isn't so easy for me. His family is long gone, those still alive as distant in their hearts as their locations. But my parents are alive and well. My brother and his wife – still Believers, unlike Matthias's sister – live only a few hundred miles away at the Seattle center. They are cheering for me, but they are sad, too. I will never see them again. I may never *talk* to them again. It might be years before communications are settled between Huginn and Earth, no matter what Songheuser Corporation says.

I do not trust Songheuser. I know they are eager to open up Huginn to all kinds of mining and harvesting, but I don't see how our people fit in with their plans. They say we will provide valuable nutritional support for their workers. Well, I suppose every community needs farmers. But I have never seen an operation so concerned with the bottom line. They have no faith, not a one of them.

But I do. I might be nervous about our trip, but I remind myself that I am in the hands of God. Were we not told that we must be fruitful and replenish the Earth and subdue it? Huginn may not be Earth, but it is a new land, and we owe it to God to treat it as we would this planet. He made it just as He made the Earth.

Sometimes I *am* excited, Diary. We will be among the first colonists on the new world. My feet will step where no human's ever have, a place made by God for our discovery. How blessed am I to see such a miracle?

Empathy and common sense are the realm of the dog. They can communicate well enough with their postures, their scents, and their simple vocalizations that they function effectively not only as pack animals but within their adopted pack of humans. It is a sign of the dog's pronounced social intelligence.

Of course, social intelligence is not the only kind of intelligence. The human mind can process a vast and varied number of subjects, slipping between modes of thought with ease.

Still, to the mind of God, our own cognition is as limited as a dog's is to an ordinary man's.

– from THE COLLECTED WISDOM OF MW WILLIAMS

CHAPTER THREE

The beach was still dark, and from here the town's lights were yellow squares of brightness. But it was later than it seemed: dawn took a long time coming here, the sun's light competing with Wodin's shadow. There wasn't much time to enjoy the morning before Standish needed to go seek out her new office. First day on the job. Wasn't *that* nerve-racking?

Standish stooped to give Hattie a treat. She brushed her damp hands off on the back of her pants and stretched tall. Her last shrink had suggested yoga, and little as she liked admitting it, all that vinyasa-pranayama-chakra balancing nonsense seemed to help with the anxiety. She was glad she'd gotten up early to squeeze some in, especially after the dream she'd had last night. She rubbed her hands on her pants again, remembering the way they'd gone white and shaggy in her dream.

The creepy-ass dream.

Hattie sniffed at some green stuff caught between a couple of rocks. Smell was so important to her, such a critical component of her experience of the world. Standish usually found such notions mysterious, but in her dream last night – her most vivid dream in years – she had moved in a world defined and shaped by smells. She had felt so much more alive in her dream body, with its combination of dog parts and human parts, a body made equally of herself and Hattie. Just thinking about it made her feel weird and itchy now.

She shook out her wrists as if she could shake off the sensation. Her conversation with Dewey had triggered the dream, she supposed. And the change to a new planet, ever-so-subtly different from Earth in a thousand ways, was probably challenging her brain and making it more sensitive to all its senses.

But now wasn't the time to wonder about adapting to Huginn. She ought to get moving. It would suck to be late to work on her first day, and she didn't even know where to find her new office.

And it would be *her* new office, hers and hers alone. Communications manager! She'd never been in charge before. She wasn't sure whether to curse Duncan Chambers for dying or be excited for the pay raise.

She left the beach and squelched her way up the road leading between blocks of identical houses, pushing down the queasy fingers of agoraphobia. There were no sidewalks, and the side street had turned to mud. It was a relief to turn onto the solid pavement of Main Street and follow it toward the mill, which began just past the block with the second bar (the Night Light, according to a sign shaped like a candlestick) and the cafe with the log cabin facade whose parking lot overflowed with battered utility vehicles. A tall chainlink fence surrounded the mill's buildings and machines. Only a slender glass-faced skybridge connected the town to its biggest employer. It hung over the street like a disfigured umbrella.

The mist became a pelting rain. Standish huddled beneath

the skybridge, not sure where to go. Her office could be in either the tall, industrial building on the mill side of the street or the white-and-glass box connected to the umbilicus of the skybridge. A trip to either building meant a dousing in this weather.

"Kate Standish?"

She turned to face the business office and the man standing under the awning of the glass-fronted building. He wore a security guard's blue uniform, the sleeves rolled up high enough to show off his biceps. His smile was more than welcoming as he opened an umbrella and came to her side.

"You must have studied my dossier," she teased. Flirting she was good at; she might not be looking for friends, but fuckbuddies were always welcome.

He chuckled. "That's my job, isn't it? But in a town this small, every new resident sticks out like a second thumb." He led up the stairs and then pushed open the front door of the office building. "They're expecting you."

She followed him inside. She had to squeeze into the lobby space – a narrow room with a scuffed horsetail wood floor that probably cost a cool two mill back on Earth – where a table burdened with coffee things and pastries took up most of the space, and chattering people filled the rest. The smell of damp clothing fought with burnt coffee for domination.

"Kate Standish! So glad you're here!" A petite and very sharply dressed black woman pumped Standish's hand. Her hair stood out in a short orange frizz around her head. "Niketa Shawl. HR."

"Niketa organized this," the security guard drawled, leaning in toward Standish's ear. The room was almost loud enough to merit the closeness.

A man with a big gut slipped between Niketa and the older redheaded woman at her side. Standish recognized him from her interview, although he either looked younger on camera or had aged terribly in the last year. "Joe Holder, Head of Operations. It's good to see you here on Huginn. If you have any questions about the place, I'm in the office right next door."

Her department head had the office next door. Well, at least she knew where to find him when she needed to ask for a day off.

Other names, other faces all pressed themselves forward. Even in the chaos, she noticed Peter Bajowski wasn't there. Someone urged a cup of coffee into her hand. Twice someone stepped on Hattie's tail, and then spent too long apologizing. Standish bit into a pastry and tasted real butter, a flavor out of her childhood and thought forgotten. Everyone was smiling at her, paying attention to her, eager to talk to her. She knocked back a quick gulp of coffee and choked.

"You OK?" Niketa leaned in, her bright eyes concerned.

Standish wiped her mouth on the back of her hand. "Just getting choked up from all this welcome wagon excitement." She could see Niketa trying to work out whether or not Standish was being a bitch and reminded herself HR was in charge of benefits and staff housing. "I'm just really looking forward to starting work. Especially since the position has changed since I applied."

"Good." Niketa gave her another measuring look. "Good. Well, Joe and Brett will get you settled in. I'll have paperwork for you later."

Then people were saying goodbye and refilling her coffee cup. A second pastry appeared in her hand just as Joe Holder and Brett, the security guard, waved her toward the staircase. Her knees felt wobbly, probably because of too much coffee and too much friendliness. She held the pastry in her teeth and gripped the handrail tight.

The hallway below had the homely smell of cleaning supplies and burned popcorn, and every surface looked worn, as if scrubbed within an inch of its life for the course of fifteen or twenty years. There was nothing shiny to be seen. Clerestory windows let in some light, suggesting that in the time she'd met the office, Wodin had taken its big shadow and gone to bed for the day.

"Gonna clear off this afternoon," Joe announced. "Won't be long until the dry season, and then you'll see why we stick around the rest of the year."

"Dry season?" In the endless damp of the previous day, she had almost forgotten there was one.

"It's only about five weeks, but it's the best five weeks of the year," Brett agreed. "Sunshine all day, every day."

"Dry clothes, blue skies, and the sun twinkling on the lake? This place is paradise." Joe chuckled.

"Sounds... wonderful." She hadn't counted on open skies so soon. This was going to be harder than she'd expected, even with Hattie's comforting presence.

"Here we are," Brett announced. He stepped forward to unlock the door. The little placard on it read "Kate Standish, Communications Engineer." A clean spot above it suggested a similar placard had only recently been removed.

Joe frowned at it. "Should read 'Communications Manager,' of course. We'll get that fixed right away. There was just so much to do after Duncan... well, you understand."

The door swung open. Brett passed Standish not a key card, but an old-fashioned metal key. She tried to remember if she had ever used such a thing.

"Power outages," he explained. "Hardly anyone wants to get locked out of their office."

"Or in it," Joe added. The comment had the rehearsed quality of a joke, but he didn't laugh. He had stopped just inside the doorway, staring at the set of wooden pegs set into the wall. A battered hat hung from one, a set of binoculars from another, and beside them the kind of heavy rain jacket oldtimers called a "tin coat." "God, I should have cleaned out this place."

He looked pale and unhappy. Standish felt a surprising surge of feeling for the man. It was an unenviable position, dealing with the dead.

"I'll do it," she said. "It'll help me get to know the place. Is there anyone I should send his personal items to?"

Joe shook his head. "No family. Peter Bajowski took care of most of Dunc's things. They went way back. Friends on Earth, even."

Peter Bajowksi had been friends with Chambers. She filed that away for later. She turned a slow circle, looking around the office. A tiny desk sat in the corner, utterly bare and still showing the dull gloss of freshly printed plastic. A couple of uncomfortable plastic and wire chairs had been dragged in front of a much larger wooden desk, which hulked in the middle of the room with every surface covered in papers and tools and snippets of wire. She had her work cut out for her, she could see.

Joe cleared his throat. "All your sign-ins should have been sent to your hand unit by now. A fella came from Space City last week to catch up on some of the work orders, but I imagine there are plenty of service requests backed up already. The door to the motor pool is just down the hall, if you want to drive out to any maintenance requests. But we told folks not to expect you for a day or two. Give you chance to find everything."

"Thank you." Standish couldn't look away from the desk. It was daunting, completely daunting. And if the desk was like this, what would the tool shed look like?

"Anything you need, you just ask." Brett shot her a wink. The men left her to the disaster of her office.

Standish sank into the padded desk chair. Hattie sat down at her feet. A dust bunny clung to the black tip of her nose, giving her a disheveled air.

"I've got to get you a dog bed in here. This afternoon, all right?" She dug in her pack for the food and water dishes she'd stowed away.

The door opened.

"I've got all your paperwork, Kate."

"Standish. Please."

Niketa Shawl gave a charming shake of the head. "I'll catch on in no time." She folded herself into the chair beside the desk and began setting out stacks of paper. "We keep hard copies of everything, just in case. Here's your tax info, housing details and repair line info, motor pool instructions – sign here, please – security details, oh, and a map of Space City, if you ever head out there. Which of course you will, because Canaan Lake only has a clinic, and all your regular health care will be handled in the city. I threw in a list of psychiatrists, too, so you can get your meds set up right away. You've got a good supply right now, don't you?"

Standish thought of the past-dated box she'd tossed out before she landed at the spaceport. "Sure."

"Good. We will need a note from your new psychiatrist within sixty days. You remember that from your hiring session back on Earth."

"Of course."

"Then that's all set. You can drop the paperwork into my mailbox by the kitchenette." Niketa sprang to her feet. "I just know we're going to love having you on board, Ka... Standish."

"Good catch."

Niketa smiled. "See you soon, then!" She hurried out the door, as if she had a thousand other employees to badger about their tax or health insurance situation. Maybe she did. Songheuser was a big company.

Standish waited for Niketa's footsteps to fade away before

kicking the toe of her boot into the side of the desk, knocking over a stack of junk and bursting open a drawer. "Corporate b.s. is the same across the galaxy." She eyed the top of the desk. "How am I supposed to work like this, Hattie?"

She finished opening the drawer she'd kicked. It looked as if technology had gone to die in there. Who still used pens or a stapler or fricking paper clips? She shook her head and opened the next drawer. White plastic boxes filled it. She pulled out one, which proved to be full of smaller boxes, each containing scraps of wire separated by grade. She opened another bin and found neatly sorted boxes of plastic connectors, frowning. The kitchen cupboards in her house had been just the same, the different snacks sorted and labeled, everything in its own careful place. The disaster of the top of the desk seemed strangely out of character for Duncan Chambers.

But what did she know? Maybe he'd had some kind of personality disorder, compulsively neat at one moment and messy the next. Or maybe his substitute had messed up the desk as they tried to figure out Chambers' filing situation. Her first order of business was to get all the junk out of her way before it drove her insane.

Given her assignment to find a new shrink, the thought felt like a stab of dark humor. She grabbed a handful of papers and carried it over to the smaller desk. Scraps of paper dropped like snow from the heap.

Hattie curled up in the corner and watched Standish with unhappy eyes. She didn't like disorder any more than Standish did.

Standish stooped to rub the dog's ears. "Don't worry, Hattie. All of this is going to get sorted out in a couple of days." She picked up a paper scrap that had landed by Hattie's paw. The bold handwriting caught her eye.

To do: conduit, sector 13. Enough for school project? Che

Part of the "e" and the rest of the word were gone.

She turned slowly, still holding the note. "Sector 13." Behind the desk, a large, simplified survey map showed the area, the town and farms strung out along the side of the lake and the creek that fed it like beads on a winding string. Sector 13 was just about the ass-end of nowhere, an undeveloped tract tucked behind a stretch of Believers' farms. There ought not be any kind of conduit out there; from the general map, there weren't any houses or farms or even cell towers out there. The company hadn't even put in any access roads. She checked the bookshelf and found a binder full of more detailed maps, but Sector 13's was missing.

"Jesus Christ, Hattie." She put the binder away and sank into the desk chair. "It's a good thing Duncan Chambers got himself killed before I arrived, because otherwise I would have had to do it. What a disaster."

Hattie stretched and wagged her tail and laid back down. Standish watched her a moment, envious. Then she picked up a stack of papers and began flipping through them, doing her job.

Peter slammed the hood of the UTV down over the fresh battery pack. He had six hours of charge in there, and if he wanted to make it home tonight, he'd need to keep an eye on the levels. The forest canopy in Sector 12 was dense enough to defeat solar panels.

"Bajowski!"

He didn't recognize the voice, but the anger in the man's tone was palpable. With an inner wince, Peter turned to face the speaker. The face was vaguely familiar, his Mesoamerican heritage stamped as strongly as Peter's own. Songheuser had offices throughout Earth's solar system, but its presence was strongest in the North American Trade Federation.

As familiar as he looked, the man was a stranger to Peter.

Peter squared his shoulders. "Can I help you?"

The man slapped his palm down on the hood of the cruiser. His arm cut off Peter's path to the left, pushed him up against the driver's side mirror. "Yeah. You give my kid's bones to *me*, you stupid son of a bitch."

"Whoa." Peter flung up his hands. "I don't know what you're talking about."

"You turned in a bone to the sheriff yesterday. Now it's in an evidence locker, instead of the ground. Why the fuck would you do that?"

"What else would I do with human remains? I don't know who they belong–" Peter broke off. He did know who that bone belonged to now that he was staring up at this man's face. "You're Luca Alvarez's father. Oh, shit."

The man turned his face away. His shoulders sagged. "Yeah. My little boy."

It had been an ugly thing, that accident. The little boy tried to follow his father to work. Hanging off the back of the logging crew's crummy in the dark before dawn, nobody saw him. Nobody knew he wasn't safely at home until Matthias Williams brought the tiny crushed body into town on the back of his wagon. "I'm so sorry."

Alvarez blinked, hard. "Songheuser paid for four days of night guards in the cemetery. I couldn't afford anything more. Would have stayed up there myself, but I gotta go to work. You know what that's like, knowing I let my little boy get dug up by dogs?"

Peter didn't want to think about it, but he couldn't keep the image out of his head: the tiny body wrapped in its shroud, the dogs ripping at the fabric. The boy had only been dead a week – long enough for rigor to subside, but not long enough for his face or body to have lost its shape and humanity. Deputy Wu had told Peter the bone he'd found was probably a human femur, its surface stripped clean. Peter could all too easily imagine how it got that way.

"I'm sorry," Peter repeated. "I didn't know that had happened to Luca's grave. I just wanted to do the right thing."

Alvarez looked at him, his eyes fever-bright. "You know, Frank's gotten back about half of him. Do you think he only has half of his body up there in Heaven?"

Peter reached out to the man, but Alvarez stumbled away. "I don't think it works like that," Peter said, although Alvarez showed no sign he heard.

Peter opened the door and stared inside the truck, his heart heavy. He had no words of comfort for the grieving man.

"Dogs eating dead kids. This place just gets more and more fucked up," he muttered to himself. Shaking his head, he tossed his bag onto the passenger seat. A sandwich, his hand unit, and a stack of notes tumbled out.

He gave the notes a hard look and then tapped the starter code into the UTV's ignition. The spidery handwriting on the battered papers evoked the image of the man who had written them. Peter steered out onto the main road, only half-aware of his actions. Most of his mind was focused on the past, on the man who had disappeared a month and a half ago.

"What were you doing out in Sectors 13 and 14, Duncan? And why is the company so interested in those sites right now?"

He shook his head. He shouldn't talk to himself, even if no one was around to catch him. The utility vehicle gave a little jolt as it left the smooth pavement of Canaan Lake proper and rolled onto the little-maintained access road headed into the far end of the valley. The first and oldest road built on Huginn, it looked its age. On a larger or older vehicle, the road's jolting could throw Peter's back out of alignment.

Peter couldn't help but wonder if the Alvarez kid's accident could have been prevented by more regular road maintenance. He knew plenty of adults who could have barely held onto the back grill of a crew cab or UTV moving down this road. That someone had died didn't surprise Peter.

The thought felt disrespectful, and he immediately regretted it. But he still found himself scowling at the pole fence running beside the road. It was hard to get maintenance done on the roads out here when the Believers didn't want heavy machinery going past their farms. The religious nuts didn't believe in voting, but they had enough clout to discourage most voters from passing new property taxes.

He realized he was clenching the steering wheel and forced himself to relax. He had known it wouldn't be easy, living on Huginn. The wormhole connecting the two solar systems had made interstellar travel possible, but it hadn't made it cheap, and the cost alone guaranteed a world dominated by groups with deep pockets. He'd been ready to deal with Songheuser and their half-dozen competitors, all scrabbling to find a way to turn the forest moon into a cash cow. He should have expected organized religion to follow suit. Hell, he had. But he'd grown up in Mexico, where the Catholic Church still held onto some of its ancient power. He couldn't have been prepared for the presence of the Believers.

One part reformed Anabaptist and two parts New Age mystic, the Believers in the Word Made Flesh lay outside his Earthly experience. It wasn't until Peter landed on Huginn that he learned anything about the farming cult, and he wished he'd known what he was getting into before he arrived. Their quiet intractability was just as frustrating as the constant orders from Songheuser HQ. Both were more interested in their own plans than in studying the new world.

A figure stepped out onto the road, and Peter had to slam his foot down on the brake. "Jesus Christ!"

The dark-haired man in the road turned to stare at Peter. The Believer rubbed his bearded cheek absently, blinking like someone who had just come out of a dream. It took Peter a moment to recognize him without his flat straw hat.

Peter rolled down the window. "Matthias? Are you all right?"

"Pardon?"

Duncan had always said Matthias Williams was the best of the Believers, but right now he seemed even weirder than the rest of the cultists, and that was saying a lot.

"I'm sorry. I was just thinking about something on my way to check on the sheep." Williams said. "Phenomenology," he added, as if Pete had asked.

"You lost your hat." Peter frowned. The man, although close to Peter's age, reminded him a little too closely of his grandmother when she'd first developed Alzheimer's – the distracted expression, the weird comments. He hesitated. "Do you want me to drive you someplace? Maybe you should see a doctor."

"No, no, I'm fine." Williams smiled. "I'll just head home and write down this thought. Sorry to bother you."

He waved and stepped away from the UTV. Peter thought about pressing the man, but instead rolled up the window with a sense of relief. He didn't want to spend the next hour in Williams's company, sitting with him in the clinic while the usual throng of sick kids and injured loggers made their fuss. The Believer would certainly mouth some kind of pithy platitude about the mysterious ways of God, and Peter would want to strangle him, and at the end of the day, Peter would almost certainly come away with a cold.

He glanced in his rearview mirror as he pulled away. The Believer was still standing on the shoulder of the road, the lost expression back on his face. Peter squelched a feeling of unease and kept driving.

When the Believers arrived on Huginn, they brought an array of remarkably sophisticated biological tools with them, understanding as perhaps no other group before or since that humanity could not flourish on a world devoid of terrestrial fungal and bacterial allies. Humans are as dependent upon invertebrates, fungi, and bacteria as they are upon air and water.

– from "Huginn: A Fungal Future,"
Peter Bajowski, PhD, in NATURE

CHAPTER FOUR

Standish dropped to her knees and squinted into the darkness under her bed. "You just had to roll your ball under here, didn't you." She finally caught a glimpse of the yellow thing, which had managed to find the farthest, dustiest corner. "Stay back, Hattie." She grabbed the bottom corners of the bed. It was surprisingly easy to move, probably all lightweight plastic and cellulose fiber. Every centimeter of the planet was covered in wood, but the stuff was too damned valuable to justify using in mere employee housing.

The floor creaked a little as she grabbed for the ball, and she realized she stood on a trap door. "I see we've found the crawlspace, dear doggie." She tossed the ball over her shoulder and wiggled the latch. The crawlspace was probably only an access point for the pipes and floor joists, but curiosity still called.

She shoved the bed farther out from the wall and dropped to her knees beside the trapdoor. It opened easily.

It was a shallow crawlspace, maybe a meter deep. Peering into the opening, Standish could make out pipes silhouetted in the dim light coming from above and from the screened vents dotting the walls. Just beyond the square of light cast by the open trapdoor, a sturdy rectangle sat, the size and shape of a storage box.

Standish caught the handle on the lid with her fingertips and pulled it closer. It was the same dull green plastic as the ones in her office, and not particularly heavy. She pulled it up and then carried it into the middle of the room, near the couch.

The box sat there, dusty and sullen. She ought to call Peter Bajowski and let him know she'd found some of Chambers' stuff.

She picked up her hand unit and then put it down. The box had to have come from the office, which meant it wasn't Chambers' personal property. It was her responsibility. Standish carried it across the room to the coffee table. She took a beer out of the refrigerator and sat down cross-legged in front of the thing.

Hattie sniffed the box and sneezed. On Earth, the air in Standish's apartment had been triple filtered, keeping out pollens and molds and most viruses. The dog probably hadn't smelled dust since she'd been a puppy. But the box couldn't have been under the house too long – it was only a fine layer of dust. Standish put down her beer and removed the box's lid.

"A map?" She picked up a folded rectangle. She recognized the typeface and heavy paper stock; this was the same stuff the Songheuser survey crews used. She opened it and spread it across the bin. Green filled the entire sheet, suggesting a heavily forested area. She found the label on the top left corner: Sector 13.

She'd just marked this map down as missing this afternoon, and here it was, stashed under her house like treasure. She could understand Duncan leaving the map in his UTV or losing it in the field – from the gaps in the map files, she'd guessed that happened to him quite a bit – but hiding it under his house? She refolded the map and set it aside.

She picked up the next item, a thick file folder, legal-style, with long brass brads to keep everything in place. There was no label in the plastic tab on the side. After a gulp of her beer, she flipped through the right-hand stack. Bills of lading, she guessed. Carbon copies of invoices, creased and stained. She had thought carbon copies died out two hundred years ago.

Standish smoothed out one of the invoices and tried to read the smudged text. It looked like the shipper was a warehouse out of Earth. Scanning the prices running down the page, she found the shipping total and frowned. Zero. How the hell did someone ship this much crap all the way from Earth for free? Even email had a surcharge this far from home.

She flipped backward a few pages, looking for some sign of a credit or an overpayment, anything that would explain the reduced shipping fee. Nothing. Just free shipping on every page.

Standish put down the file. She couldn't see any connection between the file and the map of Sector 13, an unprepossessing rectangle of untouched forest. Everything else in the box looked like junk: a letter from someone who worked for the Port of Space City, full of statistics about the power of their wireless repeater. A note from Peter, written in a scrawl she could barely read. In the corner, the sketch of some kind of native life form stood out, the parts of the little plant (fungus?) carefully labeled in his illegible hand.

At the bottom of it all was a book. The thin volume looked ancient, the cover water-stained and bent. The dank stink of mildew rose off it. It was an entirely Earth-y smell, and Standish wondered if Peter's neuroses about contaminating Huginn with their Earth spores and bacteria was a little more spot-on than she'd originally given him credit for.

She opened the book cautiously. It felt like it could crumble in her hands.

"April 23rd," she read out loud. "Last month's Prayer Breakfast brought in the final thousand dollars we needed." She looked over at the dog, watching with her head laid on her paws. "Hattie, this is someone's diary," she explained. "And it's sure as hell not Duncan Chambers'."

She turned back to the front, but it had not been personalized. The handwriting was clear and simple, the printing of someone with either the drive to be read or a naturally forthright disposition. Given the "Prayer Breakfast" reference, it was probably the latter – maybe one of those first Believers of the Word Made Flesh colonists.

Standish thought about putting the book back in the box with the map and the other oddments, but something made her set it on the couch behind her. She put the lid on the box and then slid the strange thing under her bed. She'd take another look at it all later. At least she'd found one of the maps on her list of missing or misfiled papers.

She sipped at her beer. But why had Duncan taken the map of Sector 13? Of all the sections of Canaan Lake's surveyed lands, it had to be one of the most boring. Maybe she'd take one of the utility vehicles and check it out tomorrow. She ought to get a sense of which sections already had power and communications lines going through them. After all, it sounded like Songheuser's major priority for the area was getting everything ready for new development.

Which meant laying a whole lot of new cable – and since she was the only member of the communications department, she was going to be busier than a one-legged man in an ass-kicking contest. She drained her beer bottle and went to the refrigerator for another.

Huginn, Day 2

Yesterday, the shuttle let us down on the shore of Canaan Lake, where the beach is wide and smooth, made up of round, flat stones like slices of bread. They clack when you walk across them, and I can hear the youngest of us, ten year-old Elka Morris and her cousin Noah, out there playing even as I write this in the makeshift cabin we've set up as the kitchen.

The little ones play for now, but soon they will be working as hard as the rest of us. We'll break ground on the first field tomorrow. We can't afford to wait.

We spent all night taking stock of our supplies. It took hours. Each of the shipping containers the shuttle left on the shore stands taller than my head and deeper than my mother's house. We had to bring a great deal of Earthly things with us, because we need soil amendments and helpful bacteria to help our seeds grow in this strange ground. We don't know yet if our livestock, now mostly frozen embryos, will be able to eat any of the plants that grow here on Huginn. The company's survey teams noted a small handful of mushrooms and lichens that have promise as food for both men and beasts, but there's no way to know how commonly available these things will be in our particular region.

To our great dismay, this morning we discovered we are short several shipping containers. We have our seeds, supplies, and everything we need for running the cryogenics set-up, but half our winter food stores are missing. To make things worse, the temperature is far lower than projected. The cold and damp clings to me even beside this propane stove.

Matthias has put me in charge of medicines and what remains of our food stores. At least all the propane made it, so I can keep up with the demand for hot water. Several people are mildly ill with the effects of cryo, and Vonda Morris has been vomiting non-stop. Orrin and all the Morris clan are very worried about her. I do not think it is cryo poisoning, but Doc Sounds and I haven't ruled it out.

It's a good thing we have Bob Sounds with us, because we are nearly eighty kilometers from the nearest habitation, the corporate offices at the spaceport. There are plans to build a real town out there, but for now there is just a stretch of mud and four or five buildings made from freshly printed plasticboard. Our shuttle pilot pointed it out as we flew over.

Between the spaceport and our lake, there are just hills, each of them steeper than the last, with deep ravines cutting between them. The big trees, like massive horsetail weeds, grow on every last inch of hillside. I've never seen forests like this. Even on my trips to Seattle, where hundreds of acres have been converted to national park, trees do not grow so densely. We will have to fight the forest for every inch of land we need.

In the face of all that hard work, I am going to trust in God and my companions. Doc Sounds is not the only one of us with worldly experience. Mei Lin Perkins was an engineer before she came to the church. Several others, including Matthias, took classes from outside the faith once they knew they were coming to a new world. The forty-two of us, excluding the six littles under the age of sixteen, are a sturdy and handy lot.

Perhaps I would be more afraid if I wasn't so certain that this is what God intended for us. Without the hand of God to guide us, we humans would not have found the wormhole connecting our own solar system to this distant one. And it feels so much like Earth here that I can nearly believe I'm home. I suppose someday my children will run on this beach feeling as safe and comfortable as any child playing in the grass on the big church farms in Ohio.

This will be a challenge, no doubt, but we will overcome it, just as we have overcome all the challenges that stood between us and Huginn. I will add more water to tonight's soup, and soon, we will find a way to nourish our people with food provided by our new home.

Peter knelt at the base of a young horsetail tree, its skin still smooth and green and tender. At this stage it could be either species of the primitive plant – the moneymaking toothpick tree,

Yggdrasil Equisetum capralis, the Yggdrasil referring to the solar system the plant was a native of, or the forest giant, *Y. Equisetum forestis giganteum* – and he knew which one Songheuser would prefer. Capralis was easier to grow, easier to harvest, and easier to turn into strips of luxurious blond lumber.

Peter hoped this one would grow into the forest giant. Loggers found them difficult to cut; millworkers dreaded their arrival in the timber mills. But these big-armed trees provided the major framework of Huginn's ecosystem. Every landbound and flying creature on the planet depended on the horsetail tree for some aspect of its livelihood, but he would have loved them even if they didn't provide food and shelter for the moon's creatures. Their gravitas and rustling green fronds cast mystery over the entire world, and they called to him like no other life form.

He attached a weatherproof metal tag containing an RFID chip to the trunk. He'd come back and check on the tree in a year or two to see how it had developed. He could test its cells and use DNA to establish its species, but creating an opening in the tree's skin could cause it to absorb excess nitrogen out of the air and create an explosive gas pocket within the pressurized trunk. He didn't care much for logging, but he didn't want to see anyone's face blown off, either. There were a half-dozen accidents in the woods and at the mill every year, and people didn't always survive them.

He'd heard about the latest explosion, this one less than a hundred kilometers away in Jawbone Flats. People were already speculating that the accident stemmed from something more insidious than just a gas pocket explosion. Workers had died. The mill was still closed two days later. A normal gas pocket event caused a quick flash bang, maybe sent some shrapnel into a couple of workers. People died in the mills sometimes, but one at a time, the product of bad luck and bad timing – they took a shard of wood through the eye, or caught a broken saw blade in the side of the head just when they took off their hard hat to adjust the band. Stupid shit happened all the time. This thing in Jawbone Flats didn't feel like the usual stupidity.

Peter checked the map on his hand unit. GPS confirmed this stand of trees lay along the southwestern-most edge of Sector 13. Last week, he'd marked off the whole sector into smaller quadrants, but he still didn't feel he knew the area very well. This western side of the Canaan Lake survey area still held a lot of untouched land; much it had been zoned off for agricultural development until just a few months ago, when the Believers relented and signed over Sectors 13 and 14.

Duncan had been opposed to that sale. But that was just Duncan, always making new friends, giving advice, butting into things. Peter put away his hand unit. It was too damn easy to think about Duncan. He missed him just as much today as he did the day Dunc had gone missing.

Work. That's what he needed to focus on. He had trees to study, harvest impact reports to file, and an entire new tract of forest to map.

He set his course to follow the edge of the sector line. The sapling study required meticulous notetaking and sharp eyes. The forest canopy of dense tentacular horsetail limbs and bushy fronds of bitter-smelling needles cast a pall over the ground. While the canopy was dense and rich with still-unstudied life forms, the plants below fought for lifegiving sunshine, and a field biologist fought to see his own feet.

Peter hunkered down next to a patch of rock-eater lichen. He rarely saw the lichen's pink and yellow nets here in the deep forest. Horsetail trees grew in pockets of deeply digested rock fragments, soil created entirely by the hard work of lichens like these. This bunch suggested an outcropping of basalt, the stone so close to the surface that no horsetail tree could get purchase in the ground. He glanced up at the sky. A sliver of gray cloud cover peered back at him, and a raindrop landed in his eye.

He dried his face on the back of his gloved hand and began searching the edge of this little open area. Rain be damned, he felt good about this sector. He might find a whole stand of freshly sprouted saplings here.

Shifting to a kneeling position, he used his stylus to nudge aside strands of some unnamed greenish lichen so he could see the actual dirt below. He could concentrate more easily kneeling on a day like this. Ostensibly he was four percent lighter here on Huginn than back on Earth, but by the end of the wet season, his body felt like a waterlogged sponge.

On the far side of the lichen patch, a deep gouge in the ground revealed the work of a trudgee – the ground scooter. The sheep-sized creatures had thick, strong digging claws on their front end, perfect for excavation. One biologist, Dr CM Yant, had studied them and believed they survived on a diet of juvenile tree scooters and subterranean mycelium.

Peter remembered Yant's story more for its value as a warning than for the other biologist's results. Yant's grant had expired and she hadn't found a corporate sponsor for her work. Without money and a sponsor for her visa, she'd been forced off Huginn.

No one had studied the trudgee since. As far as Peter knew, Yant was right about what it ate, but he hadn't done much research on the topic. Songheuser didn't pay him to study animals.

Peter squinted at the green bits in the dirt, unsure if he was looking at uprooted saplings or something else. He took a handful of churned earth and brought it up to his nose. The tannic scent of fresh-fallen horsetail fronds had permeated the soil. With it, some kind of mineral tang caught his nose, as well as the meaty scent he associated with several species of fungi. The dirt smelled alive. He liked that. Good soil meant healthy trees and creatures.

He hesitated. No saplings meant there was no point rooting around in the dirt. But curiosity pressed him to keep looking.

The gouge the trudgee had dug looked shallow enough, only about ten centimeters deep, but it must have pierced a deeper pocket beneath the ground's surface. He could see a tree scooter-sized tunnel running beneath the opened earth, the top ripped off by the trudgee's digging. The original exit was camouflaged by an outcropping of an unfamiliar conk-like fungus. He got down on his belly and peered closer. Strands of white mycelium showed in the exposed tunnel walls, which clearly ran down into the tangled roots of the horsetail tree.

Peter pulled his I+ glasses from his field pack and shone a light into the exposed roots. It looked like several smaller tunnels opened off this tunnel's route before it passed into a clump of roots and then seemed to widen into a dark hole the size of his fist. Curious, he wormed his fingers through the mass of roots until he could slip his hand inside. Was it some kind of larder? A gathering area for foraging tree scooters to exchange scent information?

Something crawled onto his fingertip and Peter pulled free his hand. A small green creature scurried up over the back of his knuckles. He rotated his hand slowly, keeping the creature running in circles as it oriented itself toward the sky. "You're not a local, are you?"

The little caterpillar froze, its antennae quivering. It was definitely a terrestrial caterpillar. He knew the Believers kept Earth-born pollinators, but the creatures were heavily restricted. There was no good reason a caterpillar should be hiding underground in Sector 13. It couldn't eat any of the plants or fungi. By all rights, it ought to be dead.

He reached in his pocket for a specimen container and placed the caterpillar carefully inside. Perhaps it deserved a more careful study, no matter what Songheuser thought.

Before I came to Huginn, evil was no concern of mine. I knew that terrible things happened in the world, but I refused to ponder them. I knew God had set a course for all of us, and the suffering we experienced was a part of that course. If it seemed wrong, the wrongness came from only the smallness of my own human vision.

— from MEDITATIONS ON THE MEANING OF EVIL,
by MW Williams

CHAPTER FIVE

The UTV vibrated and jerked as Main Street devolved into an unpaved road. Standish shifted gears and set her teeth until the vehicle adjusted. On this setting, the old rig would suck the batteries dry in only a few hours – as the newest staff member, she'd gotten the shittiest truck. In that, at least, Canaan Lake had proven itself just like any of the other places she'd worked. She swerved to avoid a massive pothole, cursing more than usual. Hattie scrabbled not to slide off the bench seat.

But after spending the last two days stuck in the office, Standish figured she was just lucky to get away from the endless stream of friendly visitors. Out here, she was blessedly alone, just her and Hattie. She risked glancing at the farms crowding up against the shoulder of the road. Their fields rolled out in broad expanses of sunshine-sucking grass. With no trees, there was just too much open space for Standish's comfort. She wiped her palms, one at a time, on her pants.

The bright colors of the Believer farms were a welcome distraction. The crisp white paint made the many-colored crosses beside the windows and on the doors looked exceptionally vibrant. Beside fences and gates dotted with more of the colorful crosses, old-fashioned aluminum mailboxes gleamed like something out of a historical drama – the only way, Standish realized with a jolt, the outside world could send these folk communications. Meeting announcements, voters' guides, even the local news got screened through these ancient contraptions. For these people, her job didn't even exist.

Standish slowed to a stop for a girl to lead a brown cow across the rutted excuse for a road. The girl stopped to wave at her before breaking into a jog. The cow trudged behind, lost in its cud.

Standish shook her head. The smile and the wave were like any other eight or nine year-old kid's. Believers *looked* ordinary enough, no matter how different their lives really were.

Ahead, the road grew even narrower. Standish eased the cruiser to the farthest edge of the track and drew out her map. It looked like this road continued a few more kilometers, passing a couple of small homesteads before ending on the edge of Sector 12. There were logging roads that went farther, but she'd have to double back to find their entrances, and she'd have to cross private property lines in a few locations. She'd stick to this track and then try to follow Duncan's notes about walking trails.

She drove slower now, trying to get a sense of the place. Despite the distance from the mill, the occasional house appeared like an apparition in the trees. The forest crept closer to the road, blotting out more of the sky with every meter. Branches scraped along the roof and sides of the rig.

The road ended as if the overgrowth had grown tired of chasing the gray-graveled thing and simply swallowed it up. She stopped the UTV and wondered if she ought to leave the flashers on. There was no place to turn around, and anyone driving through the greenery would never see the cruiser in time to stop.

She gave a bark of laughter. Who the hell was going to rear-end her? She was at the end of civilization on the very border of the explored universe. She grabbed her gear and opened the door, still laughing. Hattie squeezed out behind her.

"Hello, lady."

Undergrowth rattled and snapped. Standish laid a hand on her tool belt. A pale figure scrambled under the lowest tree branch and out onto the road, all wild white-blond hair and stained khaki.

"Can I help you?" Standish snapped.

The figure pawed at the tangles of its hair, and she realized how small it was, how thin the arms were. The clothes hung on the little thing like cast-offs on a scarecrow. The hair parted to reveal a smudged and dirty face with a ridiculously pointed chin. "I'm Olive Whitley. You must be the new communications manager."

"Kate Standish." She put out her hand with some amusement. The kid was probably ten or eleven, but she had the gravitas of someone much older.

"I know your name, Miss Standish. It just escaped me for a moment." The girl tugged an elastic band off her wrist and bound back the explosion of hair. A few green bits stuck out of the top of the ponytail.

"Do you live around here?"

"My folks have a place just down the road. Actually, I wouldn't mind a ride. My shoes are wet from last night's rain, and I'd just as soon be done walking for the day. Blisters are the one thing that will send me out of the woods." She had already moved around the front of the UTV and opened the passenger side door. "Your dog looks nice. What's her name?"

Standish waved the dog back inside the vehicle. "Her name's Hattie." She slid into the driver's seat. She didn't really understand kids, but she knew she couldn't just leave this one out here in the woods alone, no matter how curious she was about Duncan's Sector 13 mysteries. "You like dogs?"

Olive looked at Hattie for a long moment, her dark eyes serious as she studied the animal. Her skin and hair were nearly white, making her eyes like holes in her thin face. Standish couldn't help wondering what the hell was wrong with her parents, letting her wander around in the woods with nothing to eat and wet shoes to wear.

"I've never seen a dog up close before. They're not much like sheep or cows, are they?"

"No, dogs are pretty different." Standish struggled to keep the laughter out of her voice.

"Can I touch her?"

"Yes, if you're gentle. Hattie loves to be petted." Standish smiled as Olive put out her hand and Hattie allowed the girl to stroke her white neck.

"She's not as fluffy as a sheep, that's for sure. But she's much softer than a cow or even Mr Matthias's horses. And he's very good about brushing his horses. They're by far the softest in Canaan Lake."

"Mr Matthias, huh?" Standish started the cruiser and backed a few careful yards before attempting a three-point turn that crunched brush under the cruiser's treads and made branches squeal on the roof. The motor pool was not going to be happy with her. "Do you know everyone in Canaan Lake?"

Olive leaned sideways in her seat until her nose touched Hattie's black one. "Her nose is wet."

"That means she's healthy."

She sat back in her seat and was quiet for about half a klick before she remembered Standish's question. "I know most folks. It's easy meeting people when you spend as much time traipsing as I do."

"'Traipsing'?" The UTV hit a pothole with a particularly nasty jolt.

"That's what Miss Sycamore, the school lady, calls it. It's got a nice sound, don't you think?"

So she did go to school. "Yes," Standish agreed. "A wonderful sound. Olive, where am I taking you?"

"My parents are in the next house. The one with the blue tarp on the roof, not the orange one. That's Mr Malik's." Olive pointed up ahead. "You can't really tell from here, but Mama's got a greenhouse. She buys horse shit from Mr Matthias and chicken shit from the Caldera farm. She's gonna grow oranges someday, she says. You ever have an orange, Miss Standish?"

"You can call me Kate. And yes, I've had oranges. We even had an orange tree in our greenhouse." The house with the blue tarp came into view. It was smaller than Standish's own house, and the walls looked weather-worn, slanting away from the road at an awkward angle. It didn't look like they'd bothered to build a foundation before they printed it, and the plastic had shifted and buckled in places. This wasn't company housing, that was for certain. Songheuser wouldn't let its employees live like this.

"My mama grew up with her own orange tree, too, Miss S– Kate. She's from Lompoc, California. She misses it, too." The cruiser hadn't even stopped, and the girl was already reaching for the door handle. "She'll be glad to hear I met you and that you're nice. She misses Duncan Chambers."

"You knew Duncan Chambers?"

But the girl had already jumped out of the cab and was racing toward the front door of the ugly little house. Standish stopped the engine and followed after her.

"Olive," she called. "Olive!"

The girl vanished inside. Standish paused on the bottom step of the porch for a moment, and then went up to the door, motioned for Hattie to sit on the top step, and knocked.

The door opened and smells of pot roast and fresh bread

wafted out. Standish stood rooted for a moment, caught in olfactory awe.

A face looked out at her, the high cheekbones and pointed chin strongly resembling Olive's. Her red hair looked natural. "Can I help you, ma'am?" Polite, but not friendly.

Standish came back to herself, keenly aware of the rehydrated oatmeal sitting in lumps at the bottom of her stomach. "I just dropped off Olive, and I wanted to make sure there was someone at home."

"I thought I heard Olive come through here." The woman's smile turned real. "Come on in." She put out her hand. "Melissa Whitley. You must be Ms Standish." She caught Standish's expression and chuckled. "The grapevine works fast around here."

Standish slipped inside. The house's shabby exterior belied the comfortable main room, where bookshelves and colorful quilts fought for wall space and a table filled with dried botanical specimens took the place of an entertainment system. A thick stack of drawings caught Standish's eye; the top piece was a detailed pencil sketch of a tree scooter.

"Olive's work," Melissa explained. "She's got an amazing eye."

"Pardon me for asking, but shouldn't she be in school? It's not some kind of holiday, is it?"

"Coffee?" Melissa didn't wait for the answer, but turned into the small kitchen and brought out a couple of mugs. "Olive goes to school when she wants to. She eats when she wants to, she sleeps when she wants to, and she does what she wants." She offered a mug to Standish, who took it and sipped reflexively. "Olive's not like other kids, Ms Standish. Her mind is exceptional."

"Don't you worry about her?"

"Of course I worry. But I might as well worry about whether the sun will come up tomorrow." She took a long drink of her coffee, studying Standish over the rim of her mug. "I could see the look in your eyes when I opened the door. You saw our house, you saw Olive, and you made up your own mind about us. Yes, my husband is a logger. I work night shift at the mill. But we're not trashy people."

Standish wished for Hattie at that moment. Everything was so much easier when she was beside Standish. "I didn't say you were. I'm just new here, remember? And Olive's not like any kid I've ever seen."

"She's not like any kid *anyone*'s ever seen."

Standish hesitated. She wasn't sure why she was checking up on the girl or trying to make nice with her mother. Maybe it was because she remembered herself at that age, giving the latest nanny the slip, escaping into the sewer system and the city parks. There had been whole weeks during winter and summer break that she'd gone from schoolmate's house to schoolmate's house, and only the cook's concerted unhappiness had brought her back into the familial fold. Olive wasn't so different from the kid Standish had been.

"Miss Kate! I didn't realize you'd come in. Mama, did you know Miss Kate had an orange tree growing up, just like you did? Isn't that some coincidence?"

Melissa looked from her pixie-faced daughter back at Standish. "It seems we have something in common, after all."

"It seems we have." Standish took another drink of her coffee and tried not to like the Whitleys too much.

At the intersection of First and Main, Peter stopped walking and picked some horsetail fronds out of his shirt collar. His boots were muddy, but that was normal for Canaan Lake.

Miguel Alvarez's face had stuck with him over the last night. He was on his way to talk to Deputy Wu and see if all the mess with the bones could be settled.

He took a right on Main Street, and then a left on Founders

Way. He could see the school sitting at the top of the hill, the tiny outpost of the library beside it. The sheriff's office sat drab and lonely on its side of the street, the only two-story building in town. They kept the drunk tank on the ground floor. Any dangerous prisoners were shipped out to Space City as soon as they were caught.

The stairs, running up the outside of the building, creaked under his weight. If it weren't for the gritty length of anti-slip tape laid on the edge of each step, he would have worried about falling off the flimsy thing. It said something about a town when its police station looked this makeshift.

He pushed open the door to the smell of overcooked coffee and steaming rain jackets. He didn't see Deputy Wu at the tidily crowded desk on the far side of the room.

"Pete Bajowski! What brings you to my office?"

Sheriff Vargas herself stepped out from behind her wide desk. The door frame had blocked his view of her. The smile on her face made her normally round cheeks look even more full.

"Sheriff Vargas, you know I prefer 'Peter.'"

She tapped her temple. "This memory of mine. I'll get it straight someday, Dr Bajowski. Sorry about that."

He forced a smile. "I just thought I'd follow up on those human remains I found the other day."

She waved him toward the stiff little chair in front of her desk and returned to her own seat. Everything about Maria Vargas sparkled with a certain earthy friendliness that read as genuine. Peter knew she'd spent five years in law enforcement back on Earth and then spent three more in special security at Songheuser's North American offices. He tried to keep that in mind whenever he dealt with her.

An ashtray, a cut glass relic from pre-space times, sat at her elbow full of paper-wrapped wads of chewed gum. She gave a little laugh. "Now, Peter, we don't know that thing was human. Could have just been some sheep bone dragged in from a field."

That wasn't the impression he'd gotten from Deputy Wu when he'd dropped off the thing. Peter reminded himself to keep his friendly expression glued in place. "You know, Miguel Alvarez approached me the other day. Said his little boy was dug up a few days ago. Frank hasn't recovered all the remains yet. Think maybe I brought in one of Luca's bones?"

The sheriff took a pack of gum out of her desk and put a stick in her mouth. "Could be, I suppose. Guess I'll know in a week or two, when the ME makes it out from Space City. Gum?"

He shook his head. The smell of cinnamon and sugar fought for dominance with the other scents in the room. "A week or two?"

"Identifying old bones is pretty low priority right now." She sighed. "It looks like two dozen people died over there in Jawbone Flats. Nagata Company's CEO is screaming at local law enforcement. Hell, I sent Deputy Wu over there to help out. We're short-handed enough out here without a man down – you better hope nobody needs any help with anything."

He cleared his throat. "How long do you think it'll take to track down the ..." He wasn't sure what the right word was. "Perpetrators?"

"Perpetrators. Oh, you make them sound like they're just ordinary criminals, maybe a bunch of kids playing a prank. This is going to take a while. These aren't just ordinary thugs. They had a mission. A plan. A cause."

She was chewing faster now, a swift hard chomp between each sentence, the gum moving from side to side in her mouth, a bright red ball. She brought the empty wrapper to her lips and caught it. "A terrorist ring," she summarized. "A bunch of goddamn ecoterrorists."

She took out another stick of gum and crumpled it into her mouth. He watched, riveted, as her white teeth gnashed.

He blinked hard. "Ecoterrorists? Like those Earth First nuts in the twentieth century?"

"Exactly. We're talking about people who are turning their backs on the companies that paid for their tickets to Huginn, people who don't give one shit about the lives of the hard-working folks trying to colonize this place. A bunch of good-for-nothing treehuggers trying to save the planet."

"Moon," he corrected.

She leaned forward in her chair. "Do you know something about these people, Mr Bajowski?"

"What? No!"

"Really? Because Yutani's security team got a proclamation from this group, and get this quote." She flipped open a file and removed a piece of paper. "'The wonders of Huginn are irreplaceable, like nothing else in all of human-occupied space – even company biologist Dr Peter Bajowski says so.'" She looked up at him. "You did write that, didn't you? That's not a false attribution?"

"I did write that, but don't be ridiculous – that's just tourist brochure stuff. I wrote that for Huginn Travel."

"Huginn Travel?"

"Yeah. Four years ago. I needed money to get set up here on Huginn, buy some furniture, that kind of thing, and they asked me to write a little something about the woods. Tourist stuff."

She reached for her hand unit, jotted a note with the stylus. She looked back up at him. He couldn't read the expression in her eyes. "How did you learn about this organization?"

"Duncan Chambers. He probably connected their cable or something. He knew everyone."

She leaned back in her seat. "Duncan Chambers."

"Right. Duncan Chambers."

She blew the tiniest of bubbles. The sharp crack of its popping made Peter jerk.

"You knew Duncan better than just about anybody around here, didn't you?"

"I guess so. We knew each other back on Earth, if that's what you mean."

"In the weeks before he disappeared, did he seem like himself?"

Peter wished she'd just spit out the gum. The sound of her chewing made his skin crawl. "You asked me that already. Back when he disappeared. I still don't understand."

"I mean, did he seem like he was using drugs or drinking or anything like that? It's a standard question."

"No. No, he was just like normal." Peter's shirt felt clammy. He wished he'd changed out of his field clothes.

She seemed lost in thought for a moment. She no longer looked at all friendly, and strangely enough, Peter found he preferred her like this.

"I'm going to tell you something that I put in my report but I didn't mention to anybody else besides Paul Wu. I wouldn't tell anyone, if I were you."

"Of course. What is it?"

She took the gum out of her mouth and studied it. "Duncan sent me a message the day he went missing. Said he was pulling out an old cable line and found bodies in the woods. Old bodies. Maybe something the dogs had dug up. He wanted to meet me after work to talk. He sounded freaked."

"And?"

"And then he disappeared." She put the gum back in her mouth. "Duncan knew the schematics for every communications, electrical, and wireless system in this town. And he knew everyone. He *liked* everyone. Don't you think dangerous people would want to use him?"

"You mean... like environmental activists," he said, very slowly.

"Ecoterrorists. Exactly. And then what if Duncan figured out what they were up to? Wouldn't they have tried to get rid of him?"

"Jesus."

"Yeah." She heaved a long breath, her soft cheeks puffing out. "I don't know. I liked Duncan. He was a good guy, a real community-minded fellow. I miss him. And maybe I'm just wound too tight with all this terrorist shit. Seeing connections that aren't there." She shook her head. "There's a lot of pressure coming down on me from Songheuser right now."

Peter got to his feet. "Hey, we're the ones who pay your salary. Let Songheuser's security guys do the worrying."

She closed the file folder with a snap. "I wish that were true. Most folks don't realize that the law gives Songheuser full access to all publicly managed forests – in exchange for providing forty-two percent of all local law enforcement and school budgets. And with the Believers talking people out of that last tax increase, it's more like Songheuser pays fifty-nine."

"Those assholes." Peter shook his head.

"Do you mean the company or the Believers?" Vargas picked up her hand unit. "Don't answer that. Thanks for coming in, Peter. Always good to see you."

He stepped outside into the dampness of early evening. After Vargas's office, the air felt chilly, cold enough to give him goose bumps. Or maybe it was just her words. What if Vargas was right? What the hell had Duncan gotten himself into? And had he dragged Peter into it without Peter even knowing?

Christ, he needed a beer.

Despite its role as an agricultural center, Canaan Lake has had a difficult relationship with dogs. Other communities on Huginn have had few if any incidents of dog violence and a negligible incidence of feral dog packs, but in its hundred-plus years of human settlement, Canaan Lake has reported more than thirty cases of wild dog attacks. In every case, the dog involved has escaped capture.

– from DARK SHORES: A HISTORY OF CANAAN LAKE,
by Remy Welser

CHAPTER SIX

Little ferny-looking plants grew out of the corners of the sign above the door, but the name still stood out legibly enough: Heinrich's Place. That was the name Niketa had sent to Standish's hand unit, but she still wasn't sure she wanted to go in. On the principle of "don't shit where you eat," Standish usually avoided partying with her coworkers. She reached down to rub Hattie's neck.

A hand clapped on her shoulder and she jumped. "Working late tonight, Standish?" Joe Holder grinned at her.

"Got a bit turned around on a maintenance call," she admitted. She'd lost plenty of time at the Whitley house.

"Well then, you've more than earned your beer. Let's get Belinda to start you an account, shall we?" He pushed open the door and half-shoved her inside. If she had to guess, she'd say he'd started drinking before he'd arrived.

Most of the faces at the bar looked familiar from the coffee welcome. Standish nodded at a waving woman and followed Joe to order, where a blond bartender scanned Standish's banking and employee information from her hand unit and got her set up with "auto-pay."

"Perks of a company town," the bartender, Belinda, said

with a wink. Standish had to agree.

A beer appeared, and a half-dozen people approached to pet Hattie; Standish felt a pleasant mellowness creeping over her. Brett the Hot Security Guard took a place at the bar beside her, giving off ripples of aftershave. He was deep in conversation with a knot of people who had moved along to stand beside him.

"Look," someone said – a big man she hadn't yet met, still wearing a security officer's uniform and looking a bit rumpled, "I'm not saying it's Nagata Company's fault that those treehuggers blew up their mill. I'm just saying it wouldn't happen at a Songheuser shop."

Joe Holder laughed the loudest at this.

Standish put her beer down. "Their mill blew up?"

Brett folded his arms across his chest. "Somebody boobytrapped their degasser. The saws started cutting and KABOOM!"

A middle-aged woman with red hair leaned in. "You don't know, do you? The horsetails – they get pockets of this gas, nitrogen something something. You've got to let the gas out before you cut them."

"Sounds like a giant pain in the ass."

"Welcome to Huginn!" the redhead laughed. "Ninety-nine percent annoying ninety-nine percent of the time!"

Standish reached for her beer and knocked back half of it. She recognized the value of cultivating a relationship with the office gossip, even if she didn't enjoy it. "You were at coffee yesterday morning."

"I helped with the pastries. Julia. From accounting." The woman squeezed in closer so she wouldn't have to shout. "You staying in company housing?"

"Yeah." Julia opened her mouth to ask, so Standish added: "Duncan Chambers' old place."

Julie made a face. "What a dump. I got out of company

housing as fast as I could. Renting a nice little place out past the cemetery."

Brett leaned in, his breath very beery. "Sure you've got plenty of room, but is dealing with the Fleshies really worth it? Can you even use your hand unit out there?"

"They don't care what I do inside my own house." Julia rolled her eyes. "Brett's been throwing me shit ever since I moved into the place. It's a bit of a pain, since the Believers won't let me park my cruiser out in front, but I don't mind leaving it up the street. No one's going to steal it."

"Hey, who's up for a pool tournament?" Brett bellowed. "I'm betting a week's beer money none of you asslumps can beat me!" He grinned down at Standish. "You don't want to miss this. Milton always cries when he gets his butt kicked."

The door swung open and Peter Bajowski paused on the threshold, his I+ glasses fogged over. Standish looked back at Brett. The others were pushing into the darker game room. "I'll just be a sec. Gotta feed the dog."

He shrugged, and Julia waved before they disappeared. Standish knocked back the last of her beer and hastily stood up. Bajowski was headed to the bar, one hand absently tucking his glasses in his shirt pocket. His heavy brown pants and jacket were spattered with mud. Standish moved over to join him.

He hopped up onto a bar stool. He was shorter than Standish by a few centimeters, and didn't seem to notice her arrival. Neither did Belinda. "Is there any of that vegetarian chili left?"

"You look like you've had a good day in the forest," Belinda replied. "You're so lucky you get to spend your work days hiking. Wish I could." She slid a dark beer across to him with a more-than-professional smile that the biologist missed – he was too busy reaching for a bowl of peanuts. "I still have chili, and I might even have some of that vegan cheese in the freezer," the bartender added.

"I'll take a bowl." He caught sight of Standish. "Oh. Hello."

"Hi. What are you drinking? It looks better than the stuff the rest of the Songheuser crew was swilling."

"He's got the new stout the Believers in Watsonville are putting out. Want to try it?" Belinda was already reaching for the tap.

"Yeah, that'd be great. And can I get a burger? With a patty on the side, rare, no salt, for Hattie?"

Belinda paused. "You're not supposed to have a dog in here."

"She's licensed and chipped."

"It's a health code thing. I'm sorry, but–"

"She's not going to get into the food or piss on the floor." Standish set her jaw. "Can't you just pretend she's not there?"

Peter frowned. "Hey, stop giving Belinda a hard time. It's the law. No animals unless they're service animals."

"This isn't about you, Bajowski."

Niketa slid between Standish and the scowling biologist. "Peter. Kate." She nodded at Belinda. "Can I get a mojito?"

"Sorry, we're out of limes." Belinda folded her arms across her chest. "Look, you like your dog, I get it. But the law is the law. No pets."

"A whiskey sour, then, Belinda," Niketa cut in. "Standish, didn't you explain that Hattie is an assistance animal? The paperwork's on file at the office."

Standish flattened her palm against the bar. She could feel Bajowski's and the bartender's expressions melting into pity as the words "assistance animal" sank in. Her first instinct was to throw Niketa across the room. "I guess I was just too hungry to think straight."

"Well, no one knows if you don't tell them." Niketa gave a tinkling laugh.

"A whiskey sour, right?" Belinda asked. She held out a glass. "Thanks!"

Belinda smiled kindly at Standish. "Your burger and your dog's patty will be right up." She hurried toward the kitchen.

Standish wasted a minute fussing over Hattie. Then she stood up and turned to Bajowski, who was focused on opening peanuts. "You and Duncan Chambers were good friends, weren't you?"

He grunted. Standish resisted rolling her eyes.

Belinda hurried by, slipping their plates across the counter as she passed. The speed of its arrival suggested heavy use of a microwave, and Standish expected the worst. Hattie bent her head to her meat and ate half of it in one messy bite. Standish folded a long stick of french fry onto her tongue, wondering how she was going to get Bajowski to talk. The potato dissolved in a pleasing cloud of starch and fat, better than anything she'd had in years.

"Yeah, he and I went way back," Bajowski said, finally. He stirred the cheese into his chili and she saw tired smudges under his eyes. "Why?"

"I found some stuff of his last night. A box in the crawlspace. I thought it was from work, but some of it looks personal."

He looked up from the chili. "I never looked there. What is it?" He still gripped his spoon, his wrist stiff, his shoulders and neck, too. He knew something about Chambers, she thought, something he hadn't told anyone else. Something that made him uncomfortable, especially around someone he didn't know.

"Hard to explain," she said. She bit into the burger and lost her train of thought in the hugeness of its flavor. This was what it was like to eat real food grown in real dirt, probably with no LEDs or hydroponics involved, and definitely no soy isolates or cultured yeast strains. Her heart swelled with gratefulness. If Songheuser hadn't helped her find Hattie, hadn't brought her on here at Huginn, she'd be sitting in some shitty dive on Ganymede or Luna, drinking filtered piss and eating something unidentifiable.

"You all right?"

"This is just really delicious," she admitted. "I'd forgotten what food could be like. God, I'm lucky Songheuser brought me here."

He turned his gaze back to his chili. "Yeah. Lucky. You and half the idiots in this town."

"What do you mean?"

"Nothing." He shoveled in a bite. "It's just that this is a beautiful place, and most folks are only here to pillage the trees for whatever they can make."

"That's a harsh way to put it."

"And accurate." He looked her up and down. "I wouldn't expect you to understand. You haven't been here long enough."

"Yeah, maybe you're right." She folded her arms across her chest. Was he going to treat her like she was stupid because she had an assistance dog? Was he sitting there thinking she was some dumb gimp or a nut who couldn't be bothered to understand his PhD-level thoughts? Jesus, she just wanted to sort out his friend's crap. "I thought you'd want to know about Duncan's stuff."

He shifted on his seat, putting his shoulder between the two of them. "I'll check it out sometime."

She grabbed her glass and her plate. Hattie had already finished. "Come on, Hattie. We know when we're not wanted."

She strode across the room without looking back. Peter Bajowski might have been Duncan Chambers' friend, but he was definitely a dick.

Huginn, Day 17
We've all been working so hard I haven't had a chance to even pick up a pen, let alone write in my diary. I was starting to feel lonely about it. I've always been a diary writer, even as a little girl, so going wordless runs against my nature.

I have to reckon most things about this place go against my nature, but like everyone, I am trying my hardest. We had some problems bringing the draft horses out of cryo, and with the cold and wet, they took some time to recover. The others have been clearing land by hand while I've tended the horses. The going is slow. Shane and Mei Lin were cutting a horsetail tree in the first field, and the bottom of one just blew out. Mei Lin's stuck in the hospital tent, a thousand splinters dug into her skin. Doc says she's lucky she didn't lose her eye. It was an example, I guess, that we're not on Earth, and not even the trees are like Earth trees.

We'll have to wait until the fields get planted before we bring any of the embryos out of cold storage. There's just enough hay and grain for the draft horses, not the ordinary livestock. Once the horses start working, they'll need to keep up their strength.

This morning, I caught Vonda Morris stealing from the horses' molasses bucket, and I slapped her across the face. She broke down and told me she's pregnant. We all knew the dangers of traveling in cryo during pregnancy, but she and Orrin couldn't stand the thought of staying behind. She's lucky she hasn't lost the baby yet.

I promised her I wouldn't say anything about it to anyone, not until she and Orrin are ready to tell the others. There's like enough chance the little thing won't make it to the halfway mark after all her body's been through. I know Vonda's scared for her baby.

And she's right to be scared. I'm scared, too. This world is no Eden. It's not even an Earth. I feel like it doesn't want us to be here, and that it fights us with all its strength.

I look for God's grace in every small goodness, as if a rare sight of the stars or a glimpse of an afternoon rainbow is a sign we'll be all right. I could really use a sign, no matter what it is.

•••

"What were you talking about back there with Bajowski?" Brett twisted the cube of blue chalk on the tip of his pool cue, the same gesture she'd seen in bars across the entire solar system. Even halfway across the galaxy, it was one of those neat little motions that suggested a certain pleasing competence of the fingers and wrists. Standish had lost count of the number of men she'd picked up over a game of pool.

She raised an eyebrow. "You noticed, huh?"

He leaned closer. His eyes were brown, and his aftershave smelled like artificial pine trees. "I'm just keeping an eye out for you. Since you're new."

She played along. "That's awful gentlemanly of you."

"I do try." His expression grew more serious. "I'd watch out for Bajowski, if I were you. He likes trees more than he likes his job, if you know what I mean. And he was always moping after Duncan, practically begging him to take him back, before he rebounded on poor Niketa. The guy's trouble."

"Bajowski was Duncan Chambers' *boy*friend?" That was news to her.

"Some people just can't let go of the past."

"Enough about Bajowski." She stepped closer to Brett and brushed her fingers across his collarbone. "Like you said, I *am* new here, and it is *very* dark outside. I don't know if I'll be able to find my way home by myself."

"I could probably help."

He was almost too predictable, but then again, she was looking for a lay, not a scintillating conversation. A security guard at the office made a good selection for her first conquest on Huginn – someone she wasn't necessarily going to see too much of, but easily accessible if he proved himself worth another outing. "Let's get out of here, then."

Brett racked his cue and followed behind her. The lights flickered and for a second the bar went completely dark. Fingers closed around hers.

"Just a power outage," Brett breathed in her ear.

A generator rumbled on, and half the bar's lights flickered back on, casting deep shadows around the room. The sound system stuttered and came back to life. Probably on batteries.

"I sure hope there are candles in my new place," Standish said.

"I'll help you look for them." Brett tugged her toward the door. Standish smirked when she caught Bajowski watching them.

Hattie bounded outside. They stood on the doorstep for a moment, the door swinging shut behind them, the sounds of music and laughter diminishing until the door thudded closed entirely, and the three of them stood in the silence of Huginn's night. The air smelled very clean. It had completely stopped raining for the first time since Standish had arrived.

"I'm going to have to go back to work for a second to make sure the night guy's got the backup generator going," Brett warned her. "But I'll walk you home first. You live in Duncan Chambers' old place, right?" He traced a circle on the inside of her wrist with his thumb.

Standish felt her skin prickle with anticipation. She may have been unconscious out there in outer space, but cryo or no cryo, her body knew a year was too long to go without sex. She pulled him close and pressed her mouth to his. The taste of beer and salt shifted from his palate to hers as his tongue moved behind her teeth. She pulled away with a pop of suction. "Yep."

"This way, then." He kissed her again, closed lipped, and the door pushed open behind them, thumping into Standish's back.

"Excuse you," she sniped.

Peter Bajowski turned sideways to squeeze past them. He didn't say a thing. To their right, a dog howled.

Brett took Standish's elbow and steered her onto the street. A few battery-powered lights showed in windows, but other than that the town was dark. "Let's pick up our pace."

"Are you really worried about a dog?" She glanced at Hattie, whose ears stood at attention.

He didn't answer. His legs were longer than hers, and now he was practically pulling her down the street. The fog had come up on the lake, and heavy paws of it crept along the beach and up the side streets. Visibility by her place would be negligible.

"Hey, you're not going to make it," Peter called after them. "Go back to the bar."

Hattie stopped walking and turned to face the other direction: up Main Street, toward Cemetery Hill. Standish shook off Brett's grip and caught Hattie's collar. "What's wrong, girl?"

Hattie growled.

"Get back inside!" Peter shouted.

A volley of barking cascaded down the hill toward them, a wild baying like nothing Standish had ever heard before. She stood frozen, stunned by the sound. Could dogs really make that kind of a noise?

Then Peter grabbed her arm and yanked her nearly off her feet. "Move it!"

Brett raced past them and threw open the door to Heinrich's. He held it wide. "Come on!"

Hattie leaped up the three shallow stairs, and Standish ran after her. Something snarled behind her and then they were inside, Brett slamming shut the door and bracing it with all his corded strength. Peter set his shoulder against the door, too. A horrible thud shook it and both men, and then claws scrabbled and scraped against the wood. Hattie dropped into a crouch, the thick ruff of hair across her shoulders bristling, her growl low and terrifyingly fierce.

All the sound had gone out of the bar. There was only Hattie growling and Brett's loud breathing and the squeal of claws against horsetail wood. Standish hoped like hell it was as strong as people claimed it was.

Then somewhere outside someone screamed, the deep hoarse cry of someone in real pain.

The pressure on the door stopped and the scratching went with it. Standish sagged. Thank God. Thank God it had gone.

"Shit." Peter thumped his fist against the door. "We've got to go back out there."

"Are you crazy?" Standish asked. "That dog nearly broke down the door."

"Yeah, and somebody's out there. You heard them."

"None of us know what to do," Brett said. "If we go back out there, we'll be just another mess for the cops to clean up."

Peter shook his head. "Sheriff Vargas is on her own – Deputy Wu went to Jawbone Flats. What if she's not at the station?"

"We can call her–" Brett began, but Peter kept shaking his head.

"You heard that scream." He pushed Brett aside and reached for the door handle. "We can't just let somebody die."

"I'll come," Standish blurted out. She knelt and stroked Hattie's neck. The dog's sturdy body trembled beneath her touch. "Stay, girl."

"You're not taking the dog?" Brett's voice was incredulous.

"She's an assistance dog. What's she going to do, calm them down?" She realized Peter had already gone outside and she squeezed out the door before Hattie could realize she was being left behind.

"Hang on," Brett called out, but she was already running to catch up with Peter.

Just ahead, Peter paused. The fog had already swallowed up Main Street.

"The sound came from the west," Standish said. "Not far."

Brett fell in step behind them. "I'm unarmed. What about you, Pete?"

"Do you hear that?" Peter hissed.

She paused. Brett's chin bumped into the back of her head. They all stood motionless, listening. The fog and night seemed to swallow every sound, as if Standish was suspended in space itself. Vertigo washed over her. Why had she left Hattie back in the bar?

Then she caught the bubbling, ragged sound that Peter had heard. "Somebody's hurt over there," she whispered.

Peter ran toward the sound, and she and Brett followed, slogging through the dark. Then the street lights winked back on, and searing white light blasted from the sign over the door of the next bar. "What's going on out there?" someone shouted.

They didn't need to answer. In the pitiless light, the body in the road looked not broken but shabby, the ordinary shape of a drunk passed out in the open. Only up close did the blood show. Peter dropped to his knees in the mud. "Hey, man, are you OK?"

A gurgle and wheeze instead of an answer. Something must have distracted the dogs or else they would have finished ripping the man's throat out – the left side of the man's face hung open, his white teeth showing between the pulp of blood and meat.

Standish's stomach turned over. Dogs had done this. Dogs that had once been pets and now gone wild. Dogs that could have been like Hattie, once.

"Oh, shit," Brett murmured. "Look at those fancy ass cowboy boots. That's Rob McKidder." He reached out for the man's hand. "You'll be OK, Rob," he said, in a louder voice. "You're going to be just fine."

The wheeze climbed in pitch and then there was a bubbling, a thick frothy bubbling, and Standish had to turn away before she vomited.

A siren sounded from the direction of the mill. But if it was an ambulance, Standish thought it might be too late.

The concepts that a solitary thinker delves into are the work of language, a higher level of language than mere communication. Is there morality, analysis, measurement, or logic without language? Do such things even exist outside of the language-using mind? Of course not. They are concepts built out of other concepts, not out of the stuff of the world. Language is the way we, alone of all the animals, create.
  – from THE COLLECTED WISDOM OF MW WILLIAMS

CHAPTER SEVEN

What a night. What a shitty night. Peter rested his forehead against a greasy cupboard door and waited for the coffee to finish perking. He could feel eyes on him as people passed by the kitchenette's doorway, but he kept his attention focused on the pot with its trickling stream of hot life.

He leaned back enough to slip a hand into the cupboard and grope for a mug. Had he slept at all last night? It seemed like every time he slipped into dreams, he saw the gaping hole where Rob McKidder's cheek used to be or he saw the dogs pouring down the hill. Pouring: that was the only word for the way they moved. They weren't a bunch of dogs running together; they were one mass of hunger and evil sweeping down over the town, like a flood or a tsunami or a wall of flame. He pressed the cool ceramic of the mug to his cheek. He'd never demonized the dogs before, not like the others in town, but now he understood it. Those things weren't *dogs*, not like his grandma's little fluffball with his crooked smile and long pink tongue, not even like Kate Standish's white shepherd.

Peter filled the mug at the sink and gulped back the water. Part of it, he knew, was that he'd never seen a dead person before. Not a real dead person. Old people in their padded coffins didn't count. Their bodies looked clean and fresh, the blood and pain wiped away and painted over, and the long span of their lives balanced out the loss. It was impossible to feel truly bad for someone in their nineties, laying there surrounded by tokens of the rich life they'd led. They'd gotten their full measure of breathing and loving and laughing, and it was only right that they went out and made room for the rest of the living.

But Rob McKidder had been Peter's age. Peter had seen him regularly at office functions, those interminable safety meetings Songheuser was always making them attend, and outside of his bad taste in boots, Rob seemed like a good enough guy. He talked a lot about his girl, a PR type working on Luna and hoping for a position with Nagata or Taaffe-Heinecken, maybe Songheuser if she got lucky. Only now she'd never come here. Who'd want to live on the planet that had killed her boyfriend?

The coffeemaker made a chug and gasp, indicating it had finished its work (horribly like the sounds that had come out of Rob McKidder last night), and Peter reached for the pot. His wrist trembled as he poured.

He caught movement in the corner of his eye and recognized the bottled red hair approaching – it was that insufferable gossip from accounting. He slid the coffee pot back onto the warmer and hurried out of the kitchenette, giving her a smile with tightly compressed lips. Let her think he was too emotionally scarred by the discovery of Rob McKidder's body to talk about the whole thing. Better to be thought delicate than have to listen to her probing questions disguised as concern. Or worse, be trapped inside the kitchen when Niketa arrived. They'd broken up five months ago, but that still didn't make it any less awkward to be in the same room as her.

Ignoring the elevators, he hurried upstairs to his office. Work. If he wanted to stop thinking about last night, work was the thing.

He crossed to the rain-streaked window on the far wall to check the terrariums on the sill. The oldest tank, full of broken rock and gravel, needed no attention. The opalescent spheres of Huginn's puffball just kept growing, slowly overwhelming the larger chunks of basalt while the rock-eater lichen spun out pink and yellow strands at its own quiet pace. He occasionally misted them, but so far was content to observe the process.

The tank beside it needed more care. He'd tried to replicate the forest floor in this one, a much more complicated task. The horsetail fronds he secured to the screened lid needed constant replacement as they shriveled in the office air, and he worried the falling needles would get moldy, suffocating the delicate pseudo-club mosses. The tiny plants had not evolved to cope with molds or mildews, but such organisms had been brought over on the skin and foods of the very first humans. The nasty invaders found Huginn much to their liking.

As did the caterpillar he'd found out in Sector 12, he discovered. As a rare sun break lit up the room, he could see the green chrysalis the creature had woven in the corner of the tank, a dark blob silhouetted in the light. Peter pressed his forehead against the glass, peering at the thing. The leathery pod gave away none of its secrets.

It was like Huginn that way, he thought. Duncan had lured him to the forested world with images of tree scooters and pink fungi, and Peter had discovered almost nothing of meaning beyond the growth habits of its pseudotrees. If only he was free to do real research instead of maximizing Songheuser's lumber production.

The hand unit on Peter's desk chirped. Peter sighed and flopped down in his desk chair. He reached for his coffee cup.

That ringtone he knew. It never meant good news.

"Mark!" He took a long drink. The background busy-ness of Central Office sounded over a flurry of typing. Mark Allen's face filled the screen, his shaved black head gleaming like it had been freshly polished. It probably had. Despite a PhD in forestry and a master's in botany, the man spent zero time in the field.

"Hey, Peter, how's your morning going?" Songheuser's head of forestry had always managed to convey that hearty cheer Peter associated with a certain breed of Norteamericanos who played softball after work and ran for office in their fifties. They used academics to rake in business connections and made money without even trying. In his youth, Peter had often played up his Oxford pedigree just to remind them he was too good to play their games. But out here, who gave a damn? Huginn was Huginn, and no degree changed the fact that Mark was in charge.

"Good." He didn't bother mentioning last night's dog attack. Mark didn't want to hear about stuff like that.

"Listen, buddy – you know we've just gotten access to Sector 14, right? Well, we'd really like to get some eyes on the ground. That Sector 12 survey can wait." Mark's brown eyes looked serious, but not too serious. If he ever ran for office, he'd be an instant win.

"Sector 14? Not Sector 13?" Peter found a survey map underneath his coffee cup and pulled it closer. Sectors 13 and 14 ran behind the big farming estates at the end of the lake. He couldn't see a single access road headed into 14.

"All in good time," Mark said. "Anyway, it's probably pretty similar stuff – mixture of capralis and forestis, lots of undergrowth, plenty of little critters for you check out. Aerial surveys aren't giving us what we need, but I know I can count on you."

Peter tapped the map. "14's got no major waterways.

You're not going to find hardly any capralis out there. I don't see why the company's making it a priority."

"We have our reasons." The man's smile spread, his teeth lighting up his face like Christmas tree lights. "Anyway, we're counting on you. You go out there, you document what you find, and you file regular reports. Easy stuff."

It wasn't any different from what Peter was doing in 12, but it meant trading an area with blended ecosystems for one with a monotonous stand of forest. It wouldn't do much for his research, that was for sure.

"One more thing, Peter." Mark threw it out like it was an aside. "What you find out there is for my eyes only. Just company policy on new land tracts. No big deal. Got it?"

Peter put down the map. "I got it."

"Great! Well, I'll be in touch."

The screen snapped off. Peter sat there, his skin prickling. Mark's eyes only.

Nothing he'd ever found had been classified. So what the hell did the company expect to find out there?

Standish sat at her desk, screwdriver in one hand, hand unit propped up in front of her. "Dewey, it was easily the weirdest moment of my life. I mean, even before I got Hattie, I liked dogs. But out there, I couldn't even move. I just stood there, staring at them."

Dewey's face moved in closer so that it filled the screen. Her gold eyeshadow was like sunshine, and right at that moment Standish wished it really were. Sunshine. Clean, bright, warm sunshine: that's what she needed after a night like the last. "But you're OK, right?"

"Yeah, Peter grabbed me just in time. I couldn't believe it when he wanted to go back out there. The man either has steel balls or he's nuts."

"Peter? You don't mean Peter Bajowski, do you?" Dewey

frowned. "The biologist? I've heard he's kind of weird."

"Sure he is." Standish put down the screwdriver, since there was no use pretending to work. "Here's the thing, Dew. Those dogs killed somebody. They ripped out his throat, right there in the fucking street. That could have been me. One minute later, and it *would* have been me."

"So you're lucky as hell."

"Yeah, I guess. It makes me wonder if I'm doing the right thing, coming here. I mean, I like it. I like my place, I like the food, and Hattie loves having all this space to run around. It's good for her. But a man got killed right in the street, and people–" she realized her voice was climbing, so she forced herself to take a breath "–people here at work are just like, 'That's why we don't like dogs.' That's fucked up, don't you think?"

"Well, don't hold Canaan Lake against the whole planet. If you keep your head down and work hard, you can always transfer to Space City." Dewey raised a finger with a sparkling nail. "Speaking of which, I was thinking maybe you could come into town sometime soon. Have lunch with me in a real restaurant with no wild animals waiting outside. Catch up."

Dewey's cheer sounded forced. Standish picked up the hand unit, as if she could pull her in closer and get a better sense of what was running through her brain. Dewey's eyes flicked away for a second, then cut back to the screen.

"Everything OK?"

"Yeah, I just… really want to see you. There's something I want to talk to you about." She looked worried for a second, and Standish squeezed the hand unit tighter. Her mind went to a thousand bad scenarios: cancer, a new boyfriend that didn't like knowing his girl used to be a boy, deportation, cutbacks at work. If it wasn't something that bad, Dewey would just say it flat-out.

She couldn't handle it if something happened to Dewey.

An icon on the bottom corner of the screen flashed green. "Shit. Got a work call." She paused, thinking fast. "I'll come out next weekend, OK? Unless you want to talk earlier. You can call me any time."

"OK. Next weekend sounds good."

"I love you," Standish reminded her.

"Love you, too." Her face moved closer for a second, then vanished into blank screen. Dewey could have been anywhere in the galaxy right then, back on Earth, on a spaceship, anyplace at all. Standish knew only about eighty kilometers separated her from her best friend, but right now, that distance seemed impossibly huge.

The green icon flashed again, and with a sigh, she took the call.

"Ah! Ms Standish. Thanks for getting here so quickly. It's almost impossible to get any work done without wireless." The woman beamed at Standish for an uncomfortably long moment and then put out her hand. "Winnie Gonzales. Chief Administrator for the Canaan Lake School District."

Standish raised a dirty palm. "I'm not sure you want to shake. I slipped in the parking lot." She looked around the small complex of arch-roofed buildings. It shared a strong resemblance with military and science outposts everywhere, from the cheap plastic of its Quonset hut-looking structures to the chainlink fence outlining the grounds. A few scrawny pine trees, imported from Earth, struggled to grow in the Huginn soil. "Canaan Lake has its own school district?"

Winnie chuckled nervously. "You're very amusing, Ms Standish. Now if you don't mind coming this way, you'll find the utilities area in the back of the upper school building." She eyed Hattie. "Your dog won't disturb anyone, will it? People are pretty worried about dogs after last night."

Standish pointed at the green vest she'd reluctantly brought out of storage and put on Hattie. People needed to know that Hattie was nothing like those wild dogs. Nothing.

"She's a trained assistance dog. You can trust her more than most humans."

"Well." Winnie laughed again. Her laugh was as thin as she was. The administrator urged Standish along the path running between the two largest buildings. Mud seeped between the plastic planks that someone had installed as a kind of boardwalk. Winnie's pumps skidded in the slick stuff, utterly the wrong shoes for anything but a carpeted office building.

She stopped at the lean-to at the back of the biggest building. "Here." She opened the padlock and threw open the door. Multi-legged creatures scurried away from the sun's light. "I'm sure you can make sense of this. If you could just let me know when you've finished, I'll come back and lock up."

"Where will you be?"

The woman paused, confused. "What?"

"Where will I find you when I'm done?"

"Oh." Winnie stopped and thought, perhaps poring through some kind of mental schedule. No doubt she kept busy, overseeing Canaan Lake's many educational facilities. "I suppose I'll be in my office. Building B." She pointed at the smallest of the structures, where a pot of scraggly primroses brightened the doorway. Standish had no doubt Winnie planted them herself.

Standish turned back to the array of cables and comm boxes. Whoever had installed the comm lines had not been the kind of wiring genius that Duncan Chambers had been. It might take her all day just to find the place where the main line entered the school grounds, and she'd probably need to dig to do so.

The shrill roar of children's voices made Standish glance

over her shoulder. The double doors on the side of the largest school building had opened, and a seeming flood of children spilled out. A woman and a slender, bearded man followed behind them. The man held a clear plastic case close to his chest. Some of the shorter kids leaped around him, obscuring the box's contents in their puppyish delight.

Standish stared at the man. His straw hat and black, simple clothes marked him as a Believer. What was he doing here at the public school? The Believers had their own school on the far end of the lake. The children milling about him seemed to know him well.

The group rounded the end of the building, and Standish, unsure of her motivations, followed after them. Hattie didn't need any encouragement to come along. She had grown up in a Believer community filled with children and seemed to miss their noise and chaos.

The group had paused at the edge of the school grounds, twenty or so children of a variety of ages, quieter now as they fell into a semi-circle around the two adults. The forest crowded up against the property line as if it were as eager as the children to see what was happening. Standish found a spot behind two of the taller children.

"It's almost time to open the box, so we need to be as quiet and still as we can. We want the butterflies to feel safe enough to come out." The Believer man put his hands on his knees, hunkering down so his eyes were closer to a child's level. "Now what do you think the butterflies are going to do when they get outside?"

Some kids called out, but most raised their hands, and the man pointed at one of these well-behaved children.

"They look for food!"

"That's right," he said, pitching his voice a little lower as a reminder they, too, needed to be quiet. "And where are they going to find their food?"

"On farms," somebody called out, and a mutter of agreement rolled around the group.

"Don't forget to raise your hand," the woman reminded them, her voice stern. She had the solid, soothing presence of a person who dealt with children on a routine basis.

"On farms," the man repeated. "That's right. Remember the flowers I brought in this morning? Well, those flowers are growing right now on my farm, and these butterflies are going to fly there as fast as they can so they can eat their lunch."

A hand shot up. The man looked at the boy with the raised hand and hesitated a moment. Standish eyed the boy. He was nine-ish, still young enough to be cute, but old enough to have learned to like being the center of attention.

The woman spoke. "Yes, Hallowell?"

"My dad says butterflies are alien creatures that don't belong on Huginn. He says they should only be allowed in labs. Why do you Fleshies keep them?"

"Hallowell, come here," the woman snapped. "You will apologize to Mr Williams right now."

Mr Williams raised a placating hand. "No, it's a valid point, even if rudely put. Butterflies are alien, Hallowell. But so are we. There are things we need to survive on this world, things that Huginn can't provide for us. Why, if it weren't for these butterflies, I wouldn't be able to grow hardly anything. And then what would we eat?"

He drew himself to his true height, and for the first time noticed Standish. His hazel eyes traveled from her face down to Hattie, and his smile tightened a bit. But he turned his attention back to the children. "Speaking of which, these butterflies are mighty hungry. Let's turn them loose."

The class fell silent as he knelt on the ground and removed the lid from the plastic case. The creatures within sat quietly a moment, feeling the air on their pale blue wings.

The breeze quickened and the first butterfly floated up on it, hardly needing to flap. And then the others lifted out of the box, shimmering, lovely. No one spoke. Perhaps no one breathed. Every child, even the adults, craned their heads back in wonder as the butterflies took to their new freedom.

Then someone shoved someone else, and the usual noise of childhood came over the clearing, and the teacher was waving, and the children were running away, someone crying, leaving Mr Williams and Standish alone at the edge of the oppressive forest.

Standish cleared her throat. "That was beautiful."

He nodded. "They are marvelous creatures, aren't they?"

Her duties and the open telecommunications shed called to her, but not as loudly as curiosity. "How did you find butterflies that could live on Huginn? Wasn't it difficult? I mean, bees don't seem to thrive here."

He did not look up from the box on the ground, now emptied of blue wonder and filled with only branches, old leaves, dirt. He shook it out. "Trial and error, I suppose. Believers were the first settlers in Canaan Lake. We've been here over a hundred years now, and we brought pollinators with us on our very first ship. This kind of butterfly is the most successful we've managed to breed."

"Oh?"

"The first generation did all right, and we've been encouraging them along ever since. No – not with some kind of genetic manipulation." He stopped Standish as if he had sensed the question rising up in her mind. "Just ordinary animal husbandry. We help along God's work, Miss Standish. We don't usurp it."

"How did you know my name?"

"It's a small town." He got to his feet. "If you don't think everyone in Canaan Lake knew there was a new communications manager at Songheuser headquarters, a woman with a *dog*, before you'd even unlocked your front door, you don't know small towns."

Perhaps he meant to put her off with such words. But there was something tremendously appealing about the man and his frankness. He was good looking, in an old-fashioned kind of way, and his hazel eyes were steady and intelligent.

On instinct, she stepped forward, holding out her hand. "Well, I don't know small towns, Mr Williams. I grew up in a city, and I've never lived anyplace smaller than a quarter of a million people. I'm in over my head here."

For a second, she wasn't sure if he would take her hand, but he put out his own and shook with a firm grip. His skin felt warm and dry, his calluses as pebbly as Hattie's paw pads. "Welcome to Canaan Lake, Miss Standish. It's good to actually meet you and this fabled animal."

He hunkered down to look at Hattie. "You're a beauty, aren't you?"

She flopped onto the ground and rolled over to expose her belly.

"She's trained to sit," Standish complained. "You've got some kind of way with dogs, Mr Williams." She found herself wanting to like him, just from Hattie's clear appreciation of the man.

"You can call me Matthias." He stood up. "There have been problems with dogs in Canaan Lake, you know."

"I saw it firsthand last night. A pack of wild dogs running right down Main Street."

"Not the first time, but the first in a long while. I heard Rob McKidder died."

Standish nodded. And then, maybe because Hattie had taken to him or perhaps because she knew the Believers of the Word Made Flesh knew animals better than any group of humans in the galaxy, she asked him what she'd been thinking all day, a question she didn't want to even consider, let alone ask someone else. "That won't happen to Hattie, will it Mist... Matthias? I mean, what makes the dogs go bad?"

He stared down at the white shepherd, his face serious but impossible to read. Hattie wriggled happily. "Keep her inside."

Standish opened her mouth and then closed it.

"Mr Matthias! Mr Matthias, did I miss the butterflies?"

A slender figure burst out of the trees, her blond hair white in the sunshine. Olive looked less like a wild creature today and more like some sort of forest fairy. Standish nearly expected wings to sprout from her shoulders.

Matthias smiled up at the girl. "Olive! It's good to see you, my young friend. I'm sorry to say that you did miss the butterflies." He stood up and Hattie rolled over to sit properly beside him. The green tuft of moss stuck to her ear ruined the pose a bit.

"Oh, Miss Kate and Hattie. I see you've met Mr Matthias." The girl put out her hand for the dog to smell. Greens and pinks stained her palm, and Hattie took her time snuffling over it. "Mr Matthias is my second-best friend. I helped him with the butterfly box. I know all the good places to pick leaves for the caterpillars."

"That's why I'm so surprised you missed their launch," Matthias replied. "School is important, you know."

"So is traipsing," Olive said. "I know more about the creatures and plants of Canaan Lake than anybody, except maybe Duncan Chambers, only he's gone." She shrugged. "Plus, I had to help Chameli with her colors. She pays me pretty well, and bills are due at the end of the month."

Standish's eyes met Matthias's. Standish liked the Whitleys – who wouldn't? – but she didn't like the sound of Olive worrying about bills. It wasn't any of her business, Standish reminded herself. But it wasn't Matthias Williams's business to worry about Olive either, and she could see the concern filling up his eyes.

He glanced at the sun. It sat low in the sky, and a phalanx of gray clouds moved toward it. The rain break hadn't even lasted a full day. "I'd guess the school day is nearly over. How about I walk you home, Olive? I wouldn't mind seeing your mama or some of your new artwork."

"I can drive you," Standish said. "That's a long way."

"No," he answered. "You have your work to finish, Miss Standish. But I do have some papers for you – some things Duncan Chambers left at my place, a project we were working on together. I hope you'll stop by in the next day or two. It's the farm closest to the junction of the Main Road and the gravel access road."

"Of course," she said, curiosity springing up inside her like a dog hearing the jingle of its leash. How did everyone know Duncan Chambers? He was the thread sewing everyone together in this town.

"Let's take my shortcut," Olive said. "Goodbye, Miss Kate! Goodbye, Hattie!"

She waved at the girl and called back: "Goodbye, Olive! Nice meeting you, Matthias."

He tipped his hat and slipped into the forest after the girl. The bracken rustled and settled behind them, and after a moment she couldn't see either of them, only the dense greenery of the woods.

PART II: HEPZIBAH'S BLUE

Evil grows in us the same way a crack grows in a ceramic mug. Our flaws stretch thin in the course of our lives and only our faith can keep our fragile selves entire. When things go wrong here, there is no Satan whispering evil into our ears, tempting us to misbehave. There is only our own uncertainty in our belief.

— from MEDITATIONS ON THE MEANING OF EVIL,
by MW Williams

CHAPTER EIGHT

The little moon had set, and it would be hours before the sun or Wodin nosed up in the sky. The lake lay evenly in its bed, not yet tugged eastward by Wodin's hungry grasp. The leader of the dog pack sat on the beach, breathing in the quiet town. A few blocks away, a clatter announced another dog knocking over a compost barrel. The leader ignored the noise. His nose had something to tell him.

There were new smells these days that he wanted to understand. Some came and went, bitter and bright smells, like the fear-stink of humans or the harsh burn of the bad-smelling bright-light place on the other side of town. But there were two pleasant scents he kept running into, and those smells had called him to the lake's rocky shore. The scents twined together, each one balancing the other like halves of a whole.

He touched his nose to the ground again, drawing in the perfume of fresh urine. Definitely a dog. A female.

But everything about her scent confused him. He could not make sense of what she had been eating or where she had been. She was alone, he knew that much. She had no pack to help her hunt or to watch her back.

He would have to change that.

•••

Peter locked the office door behind him. He liked HQ on Saturdays, the halls quiet, the lights dialed low. The terrariums didn't require daily maintenance, but he enjoyed monitoring them, and he liked the energy of the weekend office. The building felt imbued with a quiet purpose, as if the work inside slumbered, ready to flourish once the work week rolled around again.

The whole place reminded him of the chrysalis sitting on his windowsill, waiting, a vessel for change ready to unfold at the perfect moment. He'd done some reading on butterflies and moths, but he had to admit he was no closer to solving the mystery of the little caterpillar than he'd been the day he'd found it in the woods. It might be a simple anomaly, or it might represent a major adaptation, the kind of adaptation that allowed alien invaders to get a toehold in a new ecosystem. The thought troubled him. Molds and mildews were bad enough, but at least no higher-order life forms had found a niche here on Huginn. He hated the idea of his beautiful fungal world being chewed to bits by bugs and beasts that didn't belong here.

Peter paused on the landing, knowing where his thoughts were leading and not sure he wanted to accept their course. He'd thought more than once about using his free time to continue studying Sector 12. The company might not approve of the activity, but they wouldn't fire him for it. And there was nothing else to distract him from the work – his only friend on-planet was likely dead, and he hadn't had a lover since his disastrous attempt with Niketa. If he was going to be alone, he might as well be doing something to advance his career.

He ran back up to his office for his field pack and then hurried to the basement, past the operations office with Joe Holder's latest motivational poster spread across the door. He glanced out the glass door leading to the motor pool. The rain had let up a little, and he could see the pink of stray rock-eater lichen growing around the closest edge of the parking lot.

It looked like a sign. He'd been spinning his wheels since he got to Huginn, following orders, waiting for Duncan, waiting for direction. No longer.

Outside, the air smelled of the breeze coming off the lake, tangy and electrical. He drew it in deep. This was what being alive tasted like: wild, free, and purposeful.

Peter waved at the security guard sitting in the gate house at the far end of the parking lot and then looked around for his favorite rig. He'd never bothered buying his own UTV, hadn't even considered getting a moped. The town of Canaan Lake measured four kilometers from one city limit to the other, and Songheuser didn't mind if he used the company rigs for trips to Space City. Most of the other employees felt differently, of course. A ten-year loan from Nicolay Scott's car lot didn't seem to bother anyone else. Maybe they hadn't had to sell their abuela's farm to pay off her creditors. Maybe they hadn't married a woman who ran up credit card bills until they nearly lost their hard-earned condo. Peter preferred freedom these days, and he didn't mind using a borrowed UTV.

He *had* grown used to getting his favorite model whenever he felt like it, though. But the spot where he'd parked the newest UTV, the white one with the blue interior, stood vacant. He tapped his ID on the door handle of another rig and waited for authorization, wondering just who had beaten him to the lot. He tossed the field pack onto the bench seat – he preferred the bucket seats on the newer models – and slid inside. The vehicle started easily enough, but as he rolled toward the gate, he knew he'd gotten the one with the crap suspension. It would be a rough drive out to Sector 12.

"Hey, Lou," he called, sticking his head out the window

as he waited for the guard to raise the gate arm and let him out. The dreadlocked guard looked up from his hand unit, carefully tucked a stylus into his shirt pocket, and then got to his feet.

"Dr Bajowski. Nice morning, huh? I heard we might get a couple of sun breaks before the afternoon downpour."

"I sure hope so." Peter smiled. He liked Lou's relaxed take on his job. It was a pleasant relief from guys like Brett Takas, who guarded the office like it was the governor's mansion. "Hey, did you see who took the newest rig? The white one with the blue interior?"

Lou laughed. "Someone took your favorite, huh?"

Peter felt a twinge of embarrassment. "Something like that."

"Well, she couldn't have known. The new lady," Lou added in explanation.

"Kate Standish?"

"The one with the dog, yeah." Lou tapped a button and the gate arm lifted. "Too bad – she only beat you by about half an hour."

"Thanks, Lou," Peter called back as he rolled through the gate. "Good luck with the sun breaks!"

The cabin jolted as he hit the first pothole in the driveway. He bit back an urge to curse Kate Standish for getting up early. It wouldn't make his backside feel any better.

Huginn, Day 52

Today was a disaster. I write this sitting in the kitchen shack, with the utero tanks waiting in the cellar below. The weather remains far colder than the climate survey suggested. We're going to have to incubate some of the livestock now, instead of waiting for the fields to establish – we need the meat too badly. Rations are tight enough that the littles are beginning to look more like scarecrows than children.

We were desperate enough for protein that we went out
hunting leather birds. We'd thought about it for a long time
before we organized a hunting party – the leather birds are
so vicious-looking, no one wanted to go near them. Finally,
Orrin carved us bows and arrows and he and his dad taught
us to shoot.

Cheyenne Taylor and Maria Sounds had scouted out the
area and noticed a pattern to the creatures' flights around
the lake, suggesting a nesting site on the far side. It proved
a long walk, and we camped overnight at the northernmost
end. The forest here is not like the forests I've known on
Earth. There is a silence out here, a thick and heavy silence
unbroken by crickets or frogs or any voiced thing. I lay
wrapped in my blankets beneath our tarp and watched the
gray mist roll across the ground, swallowing up my friends
in their makeshift shelters. It was as if I was all alone in a
gray realm, a realm of nothing solid, a realm that watched
me and judged me and knew me alien. I didn't sleep until
the mist drifted away.

When sunrise came, the feeble rays did not drive away
the feeling of being watched. We saw no creatures, but I
felt as if the woods looked back at me, as if the horsetail
trees had eyes and not green fronds. The others took no
notice. I wished I could find some small reason to stay on
the lake shore, but instead we cut a trail into the depths
of the forest. There is no hint of humanity out here, not
even survey markers. Songheuser's surveys of the area
were done by satellite. I walked quietly, but every step
felt heavy, as if my footprints drilled into the very heart of
Huginn.

Matthias found the roost first, a rotten hole in the side of
a horsetail with ten or twelve candelabra branches. There
were at least twenty-five or thirty leather birds moving in
and out of the hole and gathered around it. I'd never seen

one so close before. Here in their tree, they showed no signs of fear.

The plan was for each of us to pick a critter and shoot it down. But the things made it too easy. They didn't even try to fly away. They just sat there shrieking, and a few came down out of the tree and sat on the ground beside the dead ones. Shane Vogel walked right up to one and stuck a knife in its side, and it didn't move a muscle to get away or protect itself. It just made one of their thin screechy noises and let him cut off its head. I picked up my one, but the others, they didn't stop there. They killed all the leather birds that came out of the tree and tied their feet together to carry back to camp. Not all of them were even dead. They cried and screeched for a long time as we walked, and the few that were left in the tree screeched and cried back at them. The sound made the hairs on my neck stand up.

Back at camp, we finally took a good look at our harvest. Leather birds are even uglier up close than hanging upside down by their talons: they've got no eyes, and their hides are all smooth greenish-brown. Their bellies open like a mouth lined with yellow hooks that rotate out as the slit flares open – if I had to, I'd guess they're used to grab prey. It's easy to imagine a big one flying into your face and grabbing onto your cheeks with those horrible hooks. Too easy. I'll probably have nightmares tonight.

Orrin used his ugly hunting knife to gut the first of the creatures. We brought out our kitchen knives and finished up a handful more to roast their gray meat over the fire. There was a chance it was poisonous, Cheyenne said, like the fungi and the ferns, but we were hungry enough to risk it.

The meat tasted like death.

I can't explain that flavor. It was just *wrong*. I put a piece in my mouth and I knew we had made a terrible mistake.

I couldn't make myself even swallow the stuff. Orrin forced down a bite and immediately threw up. Matthias tried a little and spent the rest of the day sick, laying on his side, moaning with pain. We gave him ipecac and hoped for the best. (His stomach is still sore today, but he seems to have recovered.)

We left the dead leather birds in a heap next to our camp fire. Twenty-five dead, and not a one of them worth eating. What a waste. What a horrible, horrible waste.

Standish shouldered her pack and doublechecked the reading on her hand unit. She hadn't done any wilderness trekking since her school days, but GPS would keep her from getting too lost.

All night, her meeting with Matthias Williams had replayed itself in her head. Brett had sent her an invitation to join him at Heinrich's, and she'd ignored it. Instead, she'd gone through the box she'd found beneath the house again, her mind running through thoughts of Matthias Williams and Duncan Chambers.

She'd gotten up first thing this morning and headed out to Matthias's place. She'd been excited when she stood at his front door, she had to admit. One part of it was the strange little mystery of Duncan Chambers and one part was something else, something that had everything to do with Matthias's kind voice and his patient way with kids and dogs. It was entirely ridiculous to feel so hot and bothered by a man who didn't even use electricity, but she had to admit he was somehow sexier than Brett the Hot Security Guard.

She'd been more than a little irritated when he wasn't home.

Now here she was, on her day off, trespassing on company property to figure out what happened to her dead boss. Sure, he'd only been her boss while she'd been in transit to Huginn, but she'd liked the guy in all their emails and interviews, and now the mystery he'd left for her prickled her conscious like a burr. Duncan Chambers had been investigating something out here in these woods. Maybe it was worth digging into.

A drop of rain found the seam between the top of her coat and bottom of her knit cap and trickled down her neck, jolting her attention back to the forest around her. She stomped her feet and stretched her calf muscles.

"Well, what do you think, Hattie? If you were Duncan Chambers, why would you have come out here?"

The dog turned her head to look at Standish, then turned her dark eyes back toward the forest, her ears pricked up.

"You hear something, girl?" Aside from a few small rustling sounds high up in the canopy, the woods were silent. This forest, Standish realized, was nothing like the forests she'd explored back on Earth. There were no birds to sing, no lizards or snakes to rustle in the undergrowth. It was utterly alien.

She put her hand unit in her pocket and made sure it was zipped tight. She didn't want to lose it out here.

She took a few slow steps away from the UTV. Peter Bajowski had claimed Chambers was an experienced woodsman who knew the area well. People took it as a given that the forest was dangerous, but she couldn't believe Chambers had gone into the woods of Sector 13 and simply vanished. Standish paused to adjust the straps of her pack. There was something obstinate inside her that didn't like it when things didn't add up. She couldn't overlook them or turn her back.

If there were any answers, they lay out there in Sector 13, and the only way to get there was to hike through these woods. She'd looked over the maps enough to get the lay of the land, and she didn't think she faced any rough country. She might have to ford a few streams, but it was nothing she couldn't handle.

She hiked briskly, moving between the horsetail trees and

the smaller plants whose names she didn't know. It didn't take long for the forest giants to close out the sky entirely. Some of the trees stood straight and tall, their long needles bursting from branches the size of her arms. Others stood like huge candelabras, their trunks ridged and bulging under the weight of limbs thicker than she was. She kept up the pace a good twenty minutes, her mind occupied by the task of finding a path between the trees and the thickets of ferny undergrowth. The forest smelled strange, layers she couldn't quite place. Something like ozone and old bones with the bitterness of a crushed aspirin tablet.

But the green and the dampness reminded her comfortingly of the Olympic National Forest. She kept expecting an elk or a raccoon to walk across her path. But instead she saw a new wonder, some kind of opalescent puffball growing on a fallen horsetail frond. It shimmered in the frond-filtered light.

Her feet slowed. There were sounds now, a soft scurrying coming from the bases of the trees and the occasional tiny chitter. She couldn't see the tree scooters, but she found herself looking hard for one.

She paused to bring out Hattie's collapsible water dish and gave them both a slug of water. It seemed like the forest opened up just ahead, beyond the next stand of human-sized purple-green ferns. With a frown, she slipped the dish into the pack and then slipped around the ferns. Her boots crunched on gravel.

"This is a road, Hattie." She risked a glance at the sky, now dense with gray clouds, and redirected her gaze to the gravel road. A UTV could drive this easily; there might even be enough room for a second to pass. A good-sized horsetail tree had fallen across it a few meters away, and she went to sit on its trunk. The tree was thick enough that her feet dangled as she took out her hand unit.

She checked the GPS. "We're in Sector 13 now, girl." She

knew the dog didn't understand a word she said, but she'd grown used to keeping her updated on the world. It felt rude not to, somehow. Standish expanded the image on her screen and frowned. "But this road isn't on the map."

She swung her legs over the trunk and jumped down on the far side. The road continued in a roughly southeasterly direction; if it didn't end or turn, it seemed like it could even connect to the main road. But there were several fallen trees blocking its length, making it impassable.

Storms happened all the time on Huginn, and when they hit, the thin soil and constant rains meant plenty of trees fell – hell, it looked like half the work orders that came into her office were caused by falling trees and broken branches. But a sudden notion made her check the tree's stump. If it had toppled in a storm, it would be uprooted or splintered at the base.

She followed the trunk into the ferns and stopped beside the flat stump top. Not fallen, then. Someone had cut this tree and left it laying across the road, and a tree this size had to be worth a lot of money.

So it was somehow worth more to someone as a road block.

She jumped onto the tree trunk and looked around her. The fallen trees were close enough together that their branches nearly obscured the gravel, and the other trees had enough overhanging branches to make a patchy tree canopy over the road. Anyone looking from the air would probably never even notice this road was there.

Was that why Duncan Chambers had been so interested in Sector 13? But how did it connect to the other papers she'd found in the crawlspace, like the shipping papers and the diary?

Standish remembered the map she'd tucked in her back pocket and pulled it out. It was just a printout of the same basic survey map she had on her hand unit, but Duncan had scribbled a few things on it in faded pencil. She found the first note: nitroscribble scribble. It meant nothing to her. Maybe it was just some kind of note about a cleaning product or something. She could check his desk about that later. But there, at the bottom, a penciled line – very faint – connecting the bottom of Sector 13 with the top of Sector 12. It was her road. This one.

Standish jammed the map back in her pocket. She had to find out where it went.

The leather bird is perhaps the most formidable of Huginn's fauna. Their strange – some would say unpleasant – appearance is analogous to some of Earth's most discomforting creatures, including bats, vultures, and pterodactyls. Perhaps that is why so little research has been done on their life cycle or even their eating habits. In fact, my studies suggest the relationship between the leather bird and the tree scooter goes far beyond the simple role of predator-prey.

– from "In Symbiosis: Tree Scooter and Leather
Bird Relationships in Mixed-Stand Forests,"
FORESTRY SYSTEMS JOURNAL, by Dr CM Yant

CHAPTER NINE

Standish and Hattie hurried forward, their feet crunching in the gravel. It seemed very loud after the quiet of the needle-covered forest floor. The trees on either side of the road grew even larger, and the density of their canopy leached the color out of the world. No vibrant lichen penetrated the shadows; besides the olive-green trunks of the candelabra trees, there was only the occasional ghostly outline of a Christ's fingers plant, its juicy protuberances like the bloated white glove of a dead Mickey Mouse. Something rustled in the canopy overhead, but Standish saw nothing.

Hattie stopped moving, her hackles rising. Standish unzipped her pocket and made sure the pepper spray was still inside, tucked beneath her hand unit. Duncan Chambers had come out here and vanished. Everyone had told her. But for the first time, she understood how something like that could happen.

She heard the rustling again, directly above her, a dry sound like a sheet of nylon scraping against a branch. Standish scanned the trees, her neck muscles so tight they ached.

The two leather birds stared back at her. No, not stared – those slits in their long faces were nothing like eyes. The moist edges widened and narrowed, widened and narrowed. The things were *sniffing* her.

She shifted around so she could keep her gaze fixed on them as she walked, backward now, but still headed in the right direction. According to the guidebooks, they had no interest in Earth creatures. She wasn't in any danger.

The leather birds kept their nose slits trained on her. Another settled on the branch behind the pair. It looked bigger than the others. At this distance, she thought they might be the size of a crow or maybe a chicken. Hopefully. She had no idea how large the creatures could get.

She forced herself to turn around and take a good look at the road ahead. It seemed to widen a little, or at least the sunlight looked a little brighter over there. She took a step forward. "Don't run, Hattie," she whispered.

They moved resolutely forward. The trees rustled above them.

Standish saw now that the road opened into a wide circular turnabout, a dead end save for a narrow trail leading into the forest, disappearing in the dark and the green. She walked steadily, her scalp prickling and creeping as if it could sense the creatures moving through the trees overhead. The clearing looked golden in the noon light. The drizzle had cleared up sometime while she'd been beneath the heavy tree cover.

The blow between her shoulder blades sent her sprawling on the ground. Hattie growled and barked, lunging at the creature on her back. Standish threw herself sideways, hearing something crunch as she drove her weight down into the gravel. A fierce pain lit up her shoulder and she jumped to her feet, slapping at her shoulders, swearing and shouting. With a hiss, the creature let go.

Standish raced for the narrow path leading into the woods. Fucking hell! "No interest in Earth creatures," her butt. She needed to hide from these creepy things.

A leather bird streaked across her path, but Hattie leaped at it, her teeth closing on air as the creature twisted around at the last second. Hattie yelped as it lashed out with the clawed tip of its wing, scoring a hit on her muzzle.

Standish punched at the thing but hit only tail. They were so fucking fast.

She reached the trail and skidded on leaf litter. "Hattie! Come on!"

The dog bowled past, shoving her off the path and into the trees. Standish followed her. A ferny frond slapped her in the face, and she stumbled. Hattie barked back at her as if urging her faster.

Then Hattie stopped in her tracks and Standish slammed into her, pitching forward and nearly braining herself on a low-hanging tree limb. She caught herself at the last minute on the slug-like limb of a Christ's finger. The thing pulped in her grip, the briny juices running down her hands and into her sleeves. The smell, both sharp and somehow mushroom-like, made her stomach heave.

Then she caught the other smell, the musk and sweetness of something long dead. Standish wiped her hands on her pants and glanced over her shoulder. The overgrowth hid them from the leather birds for a moment. Hattie made a perplexed little sound.

She took a cautious step toward the dog. "What did you find, girl?"

Hattie pawed at the heap resting against the base of the nearest tree. That red-and-blue plaid had never grown on Huginn.

"Holy fucking shit," Standish whispered.

The dead man said nothing. The meat had been stripped from his bones, leaving only a few yellowed scraps of skin clinging to his skull. Where the scalp remained, a few reddish curls still moved in the breeze. A glinting caught Standish's eye as some many-legged creature scurried between his teeth and vanished inside the hidden crannies of what had once been a face.

Then claws closed on her shoulder and a set of teeth drove into her ear.

Standish ripped the leather bird off and threw it against the nearest tree. Her feet moved with a mind of their own, stomping over the dead man's leg and careening into the forest, running hard. She crossed the trail again and leaped over a low-growing fern. There. Up ahead: a gigantic candelabra tree, the folds of its swollen trunk offering some kind of shelter. She slammed into the tree, looking for the deepest bulge to take cover behind.

Her fingers found a crack in the trunk, a narrow gap ending at about shoulder height. She peered inside. It was too dark to see anything, but she thought the opening widened inside, curving into one of the trunk bulges. She tossed off her pack and wriggled through. A shelf-like structure ran around the inside of the tree, some kind of growth ring, maybe. It made a low seat to hunker on. She couldn't really see outside – the folds of the tree nearly blocked off the slender opening. "Come on, Hattie. Get in here."

A thin, high pitched cry sounded someplace outside. The hairs on Standish's neck rose.

"Hurry!"

Hattie squeezed inside. There was no place for the big dog to go except Standish's lap. Standish grabbed her under the armpits and pulled her up. Hattie's claws scrabbled against Standish's legs, and then she was settled, her hindquarters filling Standish's lap and her hot breath filling Standish's nose. Outside, the cry sounded again, so high and thin it made Standish's ears ache.

How much time did she have before they found the

opening in the tree? And how hidden was she inside it? With Hattie like this, she couldn't fight them off.

The sound stopped. Standish held her breath. The things could be right outside, waiting for her to feel comfortable enough to come out of her sanctuary. She had no idea how smart they might be. Or how many there might be. One leather bird was small, but it was strong enough to knock her down.

Maybe they were what happened to that poor bastard out there.

Hattie wriggled a little, her claws digging through Standish's tough work jeans. They couldn't stay in here forever. She had to come up with a plan, a way to fight off the leather birds. She wished she had something more powerful in her pocket than just her stupid pepper spray.

She did have her hand unit. They were a long way from the receiving tower, but she might get a signal out here. She could call for help. Brett would come. And he had an air bolt gun.

She wriggled her hand toward her pocket. She had to twist herself slowly and quietly away from the wall to reach her side, and her elbow turned at an awkward angle. She could just feel the zipper pull. Her fingertips pinched closed on it at the same moment she realized the zipper pull should be on the other side of her pocket. She dropped it and patted the side of her coat, feeling the cold teeth of the zipper hanging open like the dead man's skull. Standish choked back a cry of rage.

She'd left the zipper undone. She'd checked for her pepper spray and then she'd left her fucking zipper *undone*. She wriggled her hand into her pocket, feeling around the inside desperately, but it was no good: the hand unit, the pepper spray, both were gone. She was trapped inside the tree with no way to call for help and nothing to fight off the creatures.

Something rustled outside the crack, and claws clacked on the trunk overhead. The leather birds had found her.

Huginn, Day 87
Vonda finally told everyone that she is expecting, so we women all got together to make her and Orrin a celebration quilt. It was strange, seeing all the familiar faces gone so pale and thin. We tried to have fun like we would have back on Earth, but it wasn't the same. Maria Sounds has a cough that won't go away, and Orrin's mama shakes too bad to do any of her fine stitching.

Matthias says not to worry. We replanted the communal field, and he says he's seen sprouts in it. I'd feel more relaxed if I could just sit down and be with him for a few minutes every day. But he is always busy with Orrin and Shane and Mr Perkins. They are hard-working men, always building, cutting wood, setting the boundaries of our new world.

I am terribly lonely, but I suppose I won't be for long: we're bringing the dogs out of cryo. It will be so good to have my Soolie to walk with! He is a good, good dog.

I'd be happier if it weren't for the reason. Last night I went out to the barn to give our first defrosted calf a bottle and found the poor thing on the ground, a leather bird perching on its body. I beat the leather bird off, but the calf was already unconscious from blood loss. The cut on the calf's neck looked as neatly sliced as a knife wound.

The leather birds never used to come around our fields, but ever since our hunt, they've been getting closer and closer. It's like they're punishing us for attacking them.

I can't help but be frightened of the things, but soon I'll have Soolie to help protect us.

•••

Peter picked up the black unit from where it lay in the gravel and turned it over in his hands. He'd seen Standish's UTV parked at the end of the road, and now he'd found what had to be her hand unit. He'd come to the far corner of Sector 12 because he'd hoped to find a few untouched stands of candelabra trees, and instead he'd run into a secret road and Standish's personal effects.

He'd have to go looking for her, of course. She was new to the forest; she could get hurt. The woods weren't safe for even an experienced woodsman like Dunc. Did she even know about red death puffballs or Judas grass? She could be dead right now.

Peter hurried down the road, hoping he'd find Standish on its relative safety. Not that he could understand what it was doing out here. The Believers had held Sectors 13 and 14 for the past hundred plus years, and they didn't need roads. They'd never developed the land – just held onto it in case their community expanded. He didn't know why they'd sold after all these years, but the deal had only gone through a few months before Duncan went missing.

And if the road was that new, he would have been the first to know. Engineering would have known better than to put in a road without getting a biological consult. The company wasn't going to bulldoze a single centimeter of dirt until they determined there was no value in the stuff. Any organism on the planet could be a gold mine in botanical pharmacology or some as-yet undiscovered applied technology. He had the company breathing down his neck for quarterly reports on that shit.

Just ahead, the road widened into a big graveled turnaround, probably created to park heavy equipment or even serve as a base of operations. He'd seen plenty of these set-ups on Huginn – a logging company would bulldoze a new road, send in a team of foresters, and then assess the area. Half the towns on the planet had started out like that clearing.

"Hattie!" a woman shrieked in the distance, and the fear in her voice cut through his thoughts like a chainsaw through a rotten trunk. *The dogs*, he thought, already reaching for the air horn on his belt as he broke into a run.

He hit the trail at the end of the road and sped up, following it on instinct. "Standish!"

She didn't answer. He had no idea where she was. He pushed himself faster, glad he hadn't given up running after all these years. "Standish!"

The rustling behind him spun him around. Just a leather bird. Had he passed her somehow? He spun around, skidded on a crushed opal puffball, and left the path.

There, a broken fern.

There, another smashed puffball.

He was on her trail. He could see the leather birds ahead now, landing on the branches of an exceptionally large horsetail tree. Its multiple trunks spread open in the largest candelabra he'd seen around Canaan Lake.

A leather bird made its warning sound, a low croaking deep in its chest that was nothing like the sounds they used to navigate. Peter took a step backward as he realized the creature faced him, threatened *him*. And then he realized how many, many leather birds there were on this tree. He had never seen so many in one place.

There was nothing birdlike about the ones moving up and down the tree trunk; they clung to it like badly designed dinosaurs, pulling themselves along with their clawed wingtips and spiky toes. Their spade-shaped heads looked too large for their bodies.

One moved lower, toward a crack in the base of the tree. It followed another creature that had already found the gap. The first leather bird rushed into the gap, and then a dog yipped.

Peter raised the air horn and squeezed the trigger.

Leather birds launched into the air, reeling, twisting, the aerial equivalent of staggering. One hit the neighboring tree and fell to the ground, stunned. Peter ran to the hollowed tree.

"Standish!"

Hattie squeezed out of the tree, a brown shape clamped in her mouth. Peter swiped at the thing. The dog whipped it out of his grasp.

"Thank God you're here." Standish crawled out backward, talking fast. "There were so many of them–"

"Hattie, give it to me," Peter ordered. He grabbed the limp tail of the leather bird.

Hattie growled.

"What the fuck?" Standish scrambled to her feet. "What's wrong with you, man?"

"They're poisonous." He tugged on the tail. "Shit, we've got to get it out of her mouth."

"Hattie, drop it." Standish frowned at the dog. "*Drop* it."

The dog looked at her for a moment. Peter crouched down, ready to grab the dog if he had to. But finally, Hattie placed the leather bird on the ground. It lay still.

"Do you have any water?"

Standish grabbed the pack lying beside the tree. A green slick of leather bird dung ran down one of the straps. She grabbed the water bottle from the front pocket. Hattie pawed at her mouth.

"We've got to rinse out her mouth," Peter ordered. He put his hand out to the dog, unsure of its response. Hattie had seemed like such a calm, friendly dog, but he didn't trust any dog that growled at him.

Standish fussed with the dog for a minute, and Peter watched them both closely. Something had taken a gouge out of Hattie's muzzle. Standish seemed better off. Fresh blood

showed on her ear and her neck was covered in scratches.
A little blood had smeared across her jacket collar. Standish
finished rinsing out Hattie's mouth and wiped off the dog's
lips and tongue with her sleeve. The dog sat through this
indignity calmly, happily, even. When Standish poured a little
of the water into a collapsible bowl, the dog licked her cheek
as if everything was normal.

He forced himself to take a deep breath. After what had
happened to Rob McKidder, he had to admit he was the last
person to think clearly on the matter of dogs. Hattie was well-
trained. For all he knew, part of her training involved food
and strangers. He'd seen the dog at a bad moment, that was
all. The growling meant nothing.

He sat down on the needle-littered ground. "I'm glad I
found you." He held out the hand unit. "You could have been
in real trouble without this."

She hugged the device to her chest. "I'm so glad you did."

"Maybe you should stay out of the woods until you've
been out with some experienced people. There are a lot of
things you need to know to live out here, and–"

She cut him off. "I found something." She got to her feet.
"You've got to see it."

"What?" She was already hurrying away, and he had to
stretch his legs to catch up with her. She was taller than him
by at least four centimeters. "What did you find?"

Instead of answering, she looked back at him. "Are we
safe? From the leather birds?"

"Yeah, we should be fine. They're super territorial."

"Territorial. Sure." Standish went silent, her eyes on the
ground, looking for tracks, and she realized she'd come off
the trail at yet another point, a place much closer to the
turnaround spot. She took another step and then stopped.
"There. Look."

He followed her pointing finger. For a second, he couldn't

make out anything beyond the clumps of pseudo-ferns and an oddball patch of rock-eater lichen.

Then he saw the yellow boots.

"Oh, sweet Jesus." He lurched forward. "Oh, Duncan, oh, sweet Jesus, Duncan." He dropped to his knees beside the body.

"It's him?" Standish hunkered down beside him, her hand on his shoulder.

He squeezed his eyes shut, wishing he could open them and not see the ugly yellow work boots. "He always wore that brand. Said they had better arch support." He opened his eyes unwillingly. "Oh, Duncan," he whispered.

He reached out and touched the red-and-blue plaid sleeve. "Was it the dogs or the puffballs that got you?" he whispered. "You always said you were safe out here. I agreed." He gave a dry bark that wasn't quite a laugh. "We were fucking idiots."

"Peter."

"No, we were. We came here because it was supposed to be this beautiful, magical wilderness, and it killed him, it killed Duncan. We're so fucking stupid!"

Standish shook him, hard. "Peter. Look!"

She pointed to Duncan's chest, where the last three centimeters of a silver rod stuck out of the worn plaid fabric.

"An air bolt." Peter shifted the body a little. The bolt didn't emerge from Duncan's back, but he could picture the line it must have made in Dunc's body. The bolt had penetrated just below the collar bone and traveled down and diagonally through the thoracic cavity. Its cruelly pointed tip had probably caught someplace in the contours of his vertebrae.

"An air bolt?"

He sat back on his heels, rubbing his hands on the crushed ferns beneath him. "It wasn't Huginn. Somebody killed him."

We all want to be unique. We cleave to the tiny things that define us as individuals. We rejoice in everything that marks us as beings different from all others, delighting in our free will. I believe that is what allows us to bring wrongdoing into the world.

— from MEDITATIONS ON THE MEANING OF EVIL,
by MW Williams

CHAPTER TEN

Huginn, Day 102

This week we built *our* house! As a work crew, we've gotten faster and faster at building barns and simple houses – after all, this is the third house we've built, and we've got lots of outbuildings – but I never get tired of stepping inside a new, fresh-smelling home. Being dry is a thing of beauty!

Of course Matthias barely got a minute to enjoy the new place. He carried me over the threshold like a real gentleman and we spent the night sitting next to our own fire, eating dinner by ourselves. It felt strangely quiet after taking communal meals for so long. We'll still be eating in the mess tent most nights, since we're still sharing food stores. I can't decide if that will be nice or sad. It was good to have my husband all to myself, no matter how brief.

Today I've stolen away for a few minutes to unpack my one crate of personal items. The crate looks smaller here on Huginn; it's half the size of the box of tack the Ohio Believers community sent along. (Not that I begrudge the space that box took up. I've been studying leatherwork and so has Vonda Morris, but neither of us has half the talent we need to match Earth-quality gear.)

Soolie is over the moon to smell everything that comes out of the box. How strange it must be to be a dog and wake up one morning someplace so different from where he fell asleep! For him, no time has passed since the morning I gave him two sleeping pills in a bit of minced beef. For me, it's been a little more than a year. Even with most of that spent in cryo, I know where the time went. For that, I suppose I'm lucky to be a human.

I have a few more minutes before I need to get back and prepare the midday meal. I think I will take Soolie into the woods and cut a horsetail sapling for some kind of shelf. Right now my house is four plain walls and a floor. There's no place to put treasures like my grandmother's clock or the book of recipes my mother put together for me.

Although to be honest, I'm not sure I want to look at that recipe book. We're down to lentils and rice in the stores, and if I even look at the names of some of Mother's dishes, I think I will cry.

Hattie squeezed her head and chest between the seats so she could put her paw on Standish's leg. Standish glanced at Peter to see if he minded the damp dog, but he sat slumped in the passenger seat, his cheek pressed against the window and his eyes hollowed out.

Standish started the rig and turned it around with care. Hattie wriggled until her front half rested on Standish's lap, and the rest of her squeezed into the floor space. The smell of dog and horsetail fronds filled the vehicle. Hattie rubbed her muzzle on Standish's damp and muddy knee, leaving behind streaks of saliva. She hadn't stopped drooling since she'd bitten that leather bird.

"Peter? Is Hattie going to be OK?" She glanced over at him. His head bounced against the glass as they hit a rough patch in the road, but he didn't seem to notice. "Peter?"

He didn't lift his head. "Yeah, I think. She didn't eat any of it, right?"

"Right."

"Yeah, she should be fine." He went silent again, and Standish drove on in silence.

They pulled up in front of the police station. Standish opened her door and jumped down. Peter didn't move.

"We have to go to the sheriff, Peter," she said. She thought of all the people who had used that same gentle voice with her: the nurses in the hospital trying to change the dressings on her face after the crawler accident, kindly bartenders at closing time; a half-dozen therapists and psychologists. Her memory brought up a sudden flash of Dewey, her hair fuchsia at that point, standing in the kitchen doorway, tears spilling off her fake eyelashes. She pushed the memories away and walked around the truck to throw open Peter's door. She wasn't a gentle person.

"Get out."

He blinked at her stupidly. His brain had hidden someplace beneath his grief, and ordinary words were not going to bring it up to the surface. All this time, he had hoped that Duncan was still alive. She saw that now. Before, he had seemed to mourn and move on, but he hadn't really. He hadn't let sadness touch the inside of him.

She shook his shoulder, hard.

"I am not going to let you just sit in the fucking car while I go talk to the sheriff. You are going to go in there with me and help Duncan." She grabbed his knees and spun him to face her. "You got it?"

"OK." He blinked again, but there was a little bit of intelligence in his face now. He slid to the ground and managed to stay upright.

It wasn't until they were standing inside a warm dry room that Standish realized how wet and filthy they really were. The woman behind the desk – a middle-aged woman with black hair pulled back in a neat French braid and her uniform neatly ironed – looked them from head to toe.

"You two need some coffee? Maybe a bowl of water for your dog, Ms Standish?" She got up and headed toward the coffee station in the corner without waiting for an answer.

"We found a body in the woods," Standish blurted.

The woman cocked her head. "Cream? Sugar?"

"A body," Standish repeated.

"It was Duncan," Peter said. He took a few steps toward the yellow plastic chair beside the desk and then sank into it. "We found Duncan. And he was murdered."

The woman pressed a mug into his hands. "Tell me everything, Peter."

"Sheriff, it…" He stopped, swallowing down a lump in his throat. "Standish, you tell her."

So this was Sheriff Vargas. Somehow Standish had pictured a woman with short hair and muscles bulging out of her sleeves, not this school principal-looking lady. She took a deep breath. "I was hiking with my dog," she began, because it was easier than admitting she'd gone out looking for Duncan Chambers' secrets. "We got chased by some leather birds, and then I fell over a dead body."

"And what were you doing out there, Peter?"

"Fieldwork. I found a new species, wanted to get some documentation on it." He turned the mug in his hands as if he wasn't quite sure what to do with it.

Vargas looked from one to the other. "You're sure it's Duncan?"

"Yes," Peter said. "I'd know his boots anywhere. His shirt. His–" He broke off and scrunched his face up tight. "I'd know him anywhere."

Sheriff Vargas reached for her hand unit. "Then you'd better take me to him."

•••

Huginn, Day 132

I sit here in the barn next to my pollinator project, stroking Soolie's white fur, letting the soft curls of it run over my fingers. He is abominably thin, but there's not much I can do about it. The livestock are on half-rations, and the dogs on half that. Cheyenne and John already lost their dog. It was so hungry that it tried eating a leather bird it caught out by the lake. It twitched and frothed at the mouth until John broke its neck.

The dog's body is hanging in the pantry. I know that meat is meat, and that we are all hungry enough to eat whatever we can find – but I am ashamed to admit I bowed out of cooking tonight.

It won't be long before we have to do something about Soolie. I gave him half of my breakfast, but watery oats are hardly food for a human, let alone a big dog like him. Maybe putting him down would be a kindness.

I know I should think about it that way instead of thinking of it as losing him. But I can't help wanting the company of my dog. I am so lonely. I hardly see Matthias. He is always working, and I am always alone, whether I am in the kitchen cooking or in the barn, hatching out bees and butterflies as if we remain on the schedule we drew up back on Earth. If we were, then by now we would be feasting on turnip greens and seeing the first heads of oats forming out in the fields. We hadn't counted on the cold that never seems to leave. Our seeds rot in the ground and the sprouts that survive grow thin and spindly. Even with our imported microbes and carefully nurtured compost piles, this place is inimical to plant life.

And other life, too, I think. I've found cuts on the horses' legs, small gashes that weep blood as if the flesh is too weak to hold it in. People whisper about what causes it, but I know it is the leather birds, punishing us for that despicable hunting trip. Only Soolie's presence keeps the things away. I've seen him knock one out of the air and rip its wings off, even though he drooled for hours after touching that poison flesh.

I need Soolie. I have to find a way to keep him strong and healthy.

I looked up for a moment just now. There were sounds outside, some kind of clanking. I could see Vonda Morris, her face all hollows and her arms like twigs. She didn't know I watched her as she scooped handfuls of dry dog food into her mouth.

Her eyes are big and round and sad, like Soolie's eyes. The eyes of a poor dumb animal, far from home.

Standish pulled into the narrow driveway in front of Duncan's plastic house. Her house now, Peter remembered. It was only a few blocks from his own place, but it still rankled. Anyone else would have given him a lift. He reached for the door handle.

"You're staying with me tonight," Standish announced. She was out of the UTV before he could answer, opening the door for him. "You shouldn't be alone."

He followed her toward the house, too surprised to answer. Where had the rude bitch from the spaceport gone? She held the door to the house and he staggered inside as if his legs and back had aged fifteen years in the afternoon. Maybe they had. The sight of Duncan's yellow boots had rearranged something inside of him. His innards ran the wrong way, stifling his breath and his heartbeat.

She pressed a cold bottle into his hand and steered him toward the couch. It ought to hurt, seeing Duncan's sagging sofa, but the part of Peter that made feelings had been blocked behind some other misplaced body part. His appendix, perhaps. He remembered the scar on Duncan's side from an appendectomy in the field, Antarctica or the Galapagos.

Had it hurt? Could it have possibly hurt as much as finding Duncan's body with an air bolt jutting out of its chest and mushrooms growing out of his eyes?

He lifted the bottle and found it was already empty. He put it down by his feet. Peter thought of asking for another, but Standish was out of sight, clattering in the kitchen behind him. Only Hattie remained, her white ears turned toward him, her dark eyes serious.

"I came to Huginn because of him," Peter found himself saying to the dog. She gazed back at him attentively. "I had a great job in Hawaii. I had a wife. A crappy marriage, but a hot wife." He laughed, as he had taught himself to do every time he told this speech. "I left it all because Duncan tricked me into coming here."

Standish appeared in the corner of his eye, hooked the toe of her boot on the leg of the coffee table, and pulled it closer to the couch. "Tricked you into coming here?"

She put down a tray of snackish-looking things, peanuts and apple slices, some waxy-looking brown cubes that might have been fudge.

"Halvah," she explained. "Don't worry, it's vegan."

He reached for a piece. It melted on his tongue the way his marriage had melted under his yearning to go to Huginn.

"He showed me things." Belatedly, he noticed the beers beside the tray and he leaned forward to grab one. "A tree scooter."

"That's all it took? A tree scooter?"

"It was what I'd been waiting for my entire life," Peter explained. The beer cap twisted off with a pleasing hiss of carbonation. "Creatures and plants that nobody had ever seen. A world of fungi and lycopods, just waiting for an expert like me."

"You and Duncan were a thing, right?" She shoved a slice of apple into her mouth.

"Forever ago. When I was in grad school," he clarified. "Duncan was a guide in Belize while I was doing field work down there. We made it work a long time. A long time for Duncan, I mean. He needed adventure. He couldn't be tied down to one place or one man. I knew it when I went in. After we broke up, I met Meg, and Duncan and I stayed in touch as friends. Good friends, but just friends."

"So he didn't break your heart."

His second beer was nearly empty. He reached for a handful of peanuts to keep from draining the bottle. He didn't want to be drunk in front of this woman he didn't know. He sat up a little straighter. "Of course not. Like I said, I knew Duncan was just a temporary bit of fun."

She rummaged in the pack on the floor and pulled out a ball of pink yarn and a plastic hook. He remembered his *grandmother* crocheting. It seemed like a weird pastime for a woman like Standish.

She hooked a bit of yarn. "I get that. I like a bit of fun myself."

"Like Brett Takas?" He smirked. He'd dozed off waiting for the police to meet them in Sector 12 and woke to see Standish flirting with Takas, who was wearing a shiny temporary deputy's star. Vargas had been directing two EMTs into the woods with a stretcher. Peter had closed his eyes then, pretending to sleep so no one would talk to him, the warm weight of Hattie's head on his knee helping him sink beyond pretense.

"Well, he is fun," she laughed.

Now he put down his beer and turned so he could face her, studying the broad shape of her mouth and the pleasing way her jaw ran into two square corners. "I can be fun."

He leaned toward her and cupped his palm around the curve of her long neck. Her olive skin was warm against his beer-cooled hand. Then he pulled her to him and kissed her.

Her lips parted against his and for a second he tasted malt on her tongue, and it was the hottest, sweetest, sexiest thing he had ever tasted.

She pushed him away. "I'm not going to have sex with you," she said, laughing a little.

His face burned. "Shit." He tried to get up, but the dog was in the way, and Standish pulled him back down by his shirt tail.

"Don't be an idiot." She laughed again and then got it under control. "It's not like you even want to fuck me. You're still in love with Duncan, for Christ's sake."

"You're crazy."

"I'm crazy? I didn't leave my marriage to follow my ex-boyfriend to another planetary system." She put a fresh beer bottle in his hand. "Look, I get it. It is easier to drink and screw than it is to feel."

And just like that, all his feelings snapped back in place, his heart central in his chest and wishing it was an appendix again. "You get it? You *get* what it's like to see your best friend, your fucking soulmate, dead in the woods? Nobody fucking gets that!"

Hattie put her paw up on his knee. Her wet tongue slapped at his cheek, mopping up tears he hadn't noticed.

Standish got up. "If you think you're the first person to have life shit on you, you're in for a surprise, Petey."

"Screw you."

"You wish." She picked up a beer bottle and put it down. "Look, I didn't lose my boyfriend, but I nearly died out there on Goddard Station when my crawler derailed. I hung upside down with my face pressed against this tiny little window, listening to my air slowly leak into space, just waiting for someone to save me. Waiting for hours with nothing but this vast, sucking darkness punctuated by stars.

"I couldn't function for three years. My whole career was

built around space stations, and I couldn't even *think* about space without losing my shit. The only thing that helped was distraction. Drinking. Fucking. Picking fights with the bartenders that tried to eighty-six me.

"I lost my job. I got deported to Earth. If I hadn't taken Songheuser's aptitude tests and scored so high, I'd be a welfare case doing yet another stint in rehab. Hell, I'd probably be dead by now."

She picked up the beer and turned it in her hands, her eyes focused tightly on the label. Silence settled over the beer and peanuts and he couldn't bring himself to break it. Standish sat down on the floor beside Hattie, massaging the area around the dog's ears.

"I had half my face ground off that day. Worker's comp rebuilt my cheekbone and gave me physical therapy so I could talk again, but it didn't help with the anxiety that hit me whenever I saw the sky." She paused. "That's my story, man. I don't tell it to just anyone."

He took a long pull of his beer. "Thanks," he finally managed.

"You've saved my life twice," she said. "I think I'd like to have you as a friend."

"A friend." He rolled his eyes and then felt like a dick for it. At least she couldn't see his face.

"Hey, I have high standards for friends. I've got about one other in the whole galaxy. So count yourself lucky."

He took the olive branch. "I'll count myself lucky if, *as your friend*, I can teach you a thing or two about surviving out here. I'm tired of saving your ass."

"Whatever you say, Pete." She stuck out her tongue.

He rolled his eyes. "Peter. Never Pete. And definitely not 'Petey.'"

She reached for another beer. "Aren't your parents from Mexico? How did you get a name like 'Peter Bajowski'?"

"Hey, the US isn't the only place with immigrants, you know. I had a Polish great-great-grandfather." He gave a little shrug. "Kids in school gave me a lot of shit for it once my parents brought me back from Mexico."

"They lived in the States? So why were you down south?"

"My folks were both working two or three jobs to pay off their student loans, so my grandma took care of me when I was little. Leaving her was hard."

She picked up her yarn and flipped the half-finished pink blanket across his lap. "Yeah, I bet."

"I still miss her." He pulled the soft blanket up to his shoulder. It was extremely soft. He couldn't help yawning. Standish murmured something that might have been a question, but Peter missed it. His eyelids were already slipping shut.

The more I think on the metaphysics of the universe, the more certain I am that we, like everything else which exists, are but manifestations of God. We are not flawed, for we exist, and all that is, is God, flawless and complete.

I imagine it is as if we are an exhalation of God's breath, vibrating to the tenor of His endless existence. We are all but words in His infinite song.

And evil? Perhaps evil appears in the moments of silence between the words.

– from MEDITATIONS ON THE MEANING OF EVIL,
by MW Williams

CHAPTER ELEVEN

The next morning Standish drove Peter back to Sector 12 and waved awkwardly as he got into his rig and drove away down the road. It was one thing to proclaim they were friends and another thing entirely to wake up and find him snoring on her couch. She hadn't had a slumber party since she was twelve and discovered half the girls were there because their parents wanted to score points with her dad. She stopped trying to make friends then, and she was sadly out of practice.

Her one lasting friendship was a result of the other's persistence, not any skill or effort of Standish's. Louisa Dewey had refused to be ignored or forgotten.

Standish checked her hand unit. There was plenty of signal right here, as good as at her house, even, and she had Dewey's avatar up on screen in an instant. She wondered what ridiculous ringtone Dewey's hand unit was set to these days.

The screen went dark as the connection formed and then Louisa Dewey's face took shape, her eyes heavy and her head still shrouded in plastic from her weekend moisturizing treatment. "Standish?" She blinked a few times. "What the hell are you doing up so early on a weekend?"

"Having adventures. Did I wake you?"

"Yes." She paused. "What do you mean, 'adventures'? I hope this is a reference to some new conquest."

"I should have been out with my latest conquest, but instead I tried to get myself eaten by the local fauna. And uncovered a dead body." Standish quickly explained the previous day's events, downplaying her terrifying experience inside the hollow horsetail tree.

Dewey listened in silence, her lips pressed tight. As the story came to an end, she looked troubled. "So Duncan Chambers was murdered?"

"It would seem so. Hey, Dewey, did you ever meet Duncan?"

"Just once. It was a few months after I first came to Huginn. He stopped by Space City to pick up a special order, and a bunch of us had lunch together. He seemed like a good guy. Very funny, very cheerful."

"Was there anything strange about him?"

"You mean murder-inducing? I don't think so. But I got the impression he was kind of nosy. Asked a lot of questions, wanted to really understand what everybody was working on. I figured it was just part of his Mr Personable thing, but I guess some people could take it the wrong way." Dewey yawned. "So we still on for next weekend? You must be hankering for some civilization after your troubles yesterday."

"We are!" Standish grinned. When she and Dewey had been assigned as roommates back in trade school – before she'd ever even heard of Goddard Station or the Yggdrasil system – the two had immediately gotten a reputation for their powers to turn an ordinary weekend into an epic event. Their shared love of tequila and table dancing had brought them together, and a tendril of friendship had connected their hearts while Standish wasn't looking.

"That's good." Dewey's lips went thin again. "I'm glad you made it to Huginn, but I wish you were here in Space City. Canaan Lake sounds dangerous."

"I was never in any real danger," Standish lied. "Besides, Hattie protected me. She yanked that leather bird off my back, and I swear she nearly ripped its wings off. So I hope you're laying in a supply of treats for my protector." Her steadfast companion, curled in the passenger seat, made a little snore.

"Since Hattie's the reason I got you to come to this system, I already put a steak in the freezer. Give her a hug for me."

"Sure thing."

"Well, I've got a lunch date, and I need to glamorize. You be careful out there, Kitty Cat."

"I will, Louisa. You know me."

"Not comforting, girl." She made a showy air kiss. "Love you. Bye."

"Love you, too."

The screen went dark. Standish sat for a moment, still smiling, thinking about Dewey. Dewey had never once asked her for anything, not even money for a beer when she'd been between jobs. Standish's apartment back on Earth had been full of presents Louisa had sent her from across the galaxy, and she had no doubt there was some trinket wrapped up for her arrival in Space City next week. And more steak for Hattie, too.

She reached out to rub the dog's ears. "Did you hear that? Dewey already got you a steak. I bet she'll even find you some nice ground beef now that you're a hero dog."

Standish frowned. Swiss shepherds might be hero material, but given Hattie's upbringing, she ought not to be. Therapy dogs were trained to subdue their aggressive and protective instincts, which might cause real trouble in public situations. "And what about your docility chip, girl? I didn't think you could bite anything bigger than a piece of kibble."

Hattie let out another snore, less the stuff of heroics and more comedic fare. Standish started up the UTV and turned it around. Hattie hadn't seemed any different since they'd arrived on Huginn. She slept more deeply when she napped, perhaps, but that was probably attributable to less ambient noise and more exercise. She acted just as well-behaved around people in town.

Standish drove slowly, giving Peter plenty of time to reach HQ and sign in his rig. She hoped he wouldn't wait for her. They could be friends, but she didn't need to hang out with him all the time. She needed time to think about things.

Hattie, Huginn – there were just so many pieces that wouldn't come together in her mind. What had Duncan Chambers been doing out there? What did the papers in his box, like the bills of lading, mean? What had happened to the woman writing the diary? And what about the road, the hidden road in Sector 13 with Duncan's dead body at the end?

An idea struck her. Hadn't everyone told her Canaan Lake was a small, small town? The kind of place where everyone knew everyone else's business? Peter might not have known anything about the hidden road, and neither had Sheriff Vargas or any of the townies, but someone who lived at this end of Canaan Lake had certainly seen something. Especially if that someone liked to traipse through the woods.

Peter waved at the security guard – not Lou, but a muscular chuckle-head who was probably a crony of Brett Takas – and pulled into the parking lot. Just a day ago, he'd checked the UTV out of the motor pool, and in that time his world had turned upside down. Standish had been right. As little as he wanted to admit it, she'd nailed it when she said he'd been waiting for Duncan to show up. He'd known Dunc fifteen years, *fifteen* years, and there had never been a scrape the man hadn't been able to get out of. Laying fiberoptic cable on Mars, he'd gone off the map for a week and come back with a story of building his own air filters out of tape and spare parts. Hiking in the Alaskan protected wilderness, he'd fallen in a crevasse and broken two legs and an arm and been rescued by pair of climbers visiting from Peru. As long as Peter had known Duncan, he'd moved in and out of the elliptic of Peter's life like an erratic comet with stories in its tail, its unpredictability its only constant.

So it hadn't been so crazy, imagining that in a year or two Duncan might call and explain that he was on Jupiter or terraforming Ganymede or building the first wilderness preserve in outer space. Duncan came and went. He was a force of nature, not a mere man. And Peter had loved him for it.

Shit. Standish was right. He wasn't over Duncan.

A rapping on the window beside him made Peter jump.

The man outside chuckled. Peter restarted the UTV and rolled down the window. "Good morning, Joe."

Joe Holder leaned in through the window. Up close, Peter could see just how thin his blond hair had gotten on top. "You OK, Bajowski? You've been sitting in there for five minutes. I thought I'd better check in on you."

"I'm fine, Joe. Just got some bad news yesterday, that's all. Got a lot on my mind."

"I heard about Dunc. That's too bad." He made a tut-tutting sound with his tongue. "It's hard to believe a guy like Duncan would think suicide was an option."

"What the hell are you talking about?"

Joe took a step back. "That's the talk down at Heinrich's. Sheriff Vargas is investigating it as a possible suicide."

"He was shot in the chest with an air bolt. It's not the most believable way to kill yourself. Plus, you know as well as I do that Duncan didn't carry a bolt gun. He was opposed to hurting the local animals."

"Guess you didn't hear. Brett Takas filed a report two days before Duncan went missing – an air bolt gun was stolen out of the security team's ordnance locker."

Peter stared at him. Joe was a big man, probably a good ten centimeters taller than Peter, his broad face the same American potato-shape that had filled state legislatures across the Rust and Bible belts. It read as truthful, but Peter had somehow never liked him much. "Did they ever get it back?"

Joe shook his head. "Hell of a thing."

Under Joe's benevolent gaze, Peter rolled up the window and shut off the engine. Peter had to open the door carefully so as not to push it into Joe's pot belly.

"You going to be all right, son?"

"Sure," Peter said, and felt his teeth squeezing together. He forced his jaw to relax. "See you tomorrow, Joe."

"All right, Pete. And if you need anything, you let me know. Any friend of Duncan's is a friend of mine."

Peter couldn't bring himself to respond. Sheriff Vargas couldn't really believe Duncan killed himself; the idea was insane. It seemed like somebody didn't want there to be a murder investigation, and he had a bad feeling it was somebody at Songheuser.

He walked toward the security gate and hopped over it. It was a violation of company safety and security policy, and it felt good.

Standish pulled into the Whitleys' driveway. It was the last house on the road leading into Sector 12. If anyone had noticed construction vehicles and unusual traffic headed into the woods, it would be Olive Whitley.

Not her parents. With both of them working, they weren't home enough to notice anything unusual. But Olive was uncannily observant, and school hours didn't mean much to her.

Standish turned off the engine and studied Olive's house. No utility vehicle sat under the makeshift carport, but a trickle of smoke rose from the chimney. Standish stepped out into the sifting drizzle and climbed the stairs to the porch. The hinges on the screen door protested as she pulled it open.

The plastic magnified the sound of her knuckles like a town gossip spreading bad news. There was no window in the front door, not like her own, and she noticed the screen door was a late addition, pieced together out of strips of horsetail. The woodwork itself looked neat and trim.

The door opened. "Miss Kate!"

"Hi, Olive. Would it be all right if I asked you a few questions?"

"I was just going out. You can give me a drive into town." Olive hoisted a heavy pack over her bony shoulder and smiled. Then, without waiting for a response, she headed down to the UTV and squeezed into the passenger seat with Hattie.

Standish shook her head. She liked the little waif, but she had a feeling Olive didn't hear the word "no" very often.

She started the engine. "So where am I going?"

"Back toward town. We'll pass Mr Matthias's farm, then make a right on Dreger Road, and a left on Chameli's driveway. It's a long one, and you'll feel like you're getting lost. New people always do. But she's got a good view of the town, and on a clear day, you can see the lake."

Standish tried to make sense of the directions. Without Olive's warning, she would have missed Dreger Road entirely. "Road" was not a word she would have used to describe the two narrow ruts cutting through someone's field. Olive pointed out the graveled drive headed up the flanks of the hill, and Standish found herself jolting along another rough track. The trees looked skinnier than those out in Sector 12 or 13, their fronds a younger, brighter green. This section of woods must have been logged and then allowed to grow again, the forest reclaiming the land for itself.

Standish turned the conversation back to the task at hand. "Olive, do you know all the roads around here?"

"Sure. It's my job to know the lay of the land."

"What do you know about a gravel drive in the woods at the edge of Sectors 12 and 13? It starts a little ways away from the place where I first met you."

Olive pointed out the window. "Did you see that? Biggest purple tree scooter I ever saw."

"No, I missed it." She glanced across the seat at the girl. Olive stared intently out the window. "Olive, please tell me about that road. I know you know about it."

"It's just a road," Olive said. "Ain't nothing to tell. And that's Chameli's house, right there. Watch out for her UTV."

Standish stopped the rig behind a battered and ancient UTV with pink ribbons tied onto its antennas. "Olive, you do know something."

Olive shook her head, hard. "I'm not telling you nothing about that road."

"Why not?"

The girl bent over to pick up her backpack. "Because Duncan told me not to, that's why."

Then she threw open the door and jumped out of the rig. "Chameli! Chameli! You've got to meet my new friend!" Hattie jumped down and looked back at Standish for permission to follow the girl.

Standish sighed and turned off the engine. Duncan Chambers had once again stumped her. She followed Olive and Hattie across the uneven yard.

The house Olive headed toward had seen better days. Its printed plastic was losing a war with the elements. Yellow strands of lichen had rooted in the ridges and gaps of the plastic blocks, and now instead of looking like a corporate bunker, the house resembled a retreat for some kind of nature spirit. A porch built of green-skinned horsetail wood only contributed to the image, especially with concrete planters of colorful rock-eater lichens like flowerpots framing the door.

Olive pounded on the front door, giving Standish time to look around. The house sat in a little clearing, the slender trees on the west side carefully managed to minimize shade on the small patch of garden. A gap between the trees let her look down at the town below, most of the buildings hidden by the tree cover. The waters of the lake glinted gray, a ribbon of tarnished silver between the black flanks of the hills and the broad green plain of the town.

"Chameli!" Olive hollered again. Standish turned around at the sound of a set of hinges creaking.

"Is that my Olive girl? Come in, sweetie." The swarthy woman at the door stepped forward to clasp the girl in her arms. She drew herself up when she saw Standish. "And who is this?"

"This is my friend, Miss Kate."

Standish put out a hand. "Kate Standish."

Chameli shook. Her grip was strong, her palm large, warm, and soft. She was a tall woman, taller than Standish, and a sturdy plumpness softened out the blunt bones beneath her skin. If she had been thin, it would have been hard to imagine a child, even a child as unusual as Olive, wanting to hug her.

"Kate Standish," she repeated. "I see." The large woman stepped backward, holding the door open with her broad shoulder. "Rain's going to pick up any minute."

Just to lend credence to her pronouncement, thunder crashed in the distance. Standish hurried inside.

Inside the tiny mud room, Olive pointedly removed her shoes and set them beside the inner door. Standish hesitated. "Should I leave my dog out here?"

Chameli eyed the creature. "Depends. She a good dog or

a bad one?"

"Hattie is the best dog," Olive said. "She'll behave."

The girl disappeared into the house proper, calling behind her for the dog. Standish shook her head and began tugging off her boots.

Inside, Chameli's home had the same layout as Standish's own house. Smells assaulted Standish's nose: toasted cinnamon and spices overlay a strange sharp smell, like singed horsetail. Her nose crinkled. There was one more scent she knew, and it took her straight back to her mother's art studio.

"Turpentine?"

Chameli smiled. The marionette lines that framed her mouth were astonishingly deep. "Expensive, but I'm old-fashioned. I prefer oil paints to acrylic."

"You're an artist?"

"Mostly a craftsperson," Chameli corrected. "Once in while, when I have an idea worth splurging on, I make art. The rest of the time I work on bits and bobs for craft fairs." She nodded at a desk covered in wire and bright snippets of plastic.

Standish picked up what appeared to be an earring in progress, a brilliant yellow sun grinning too broadly at the world. Her mother had been a sucker for such things, the cheap trinkets vendors seemed to sell in every tourist town they'd ever visited. "Kitschy."

Chameli took it from her. "Kitsch sells."

"Chameli, did you bake any cookies? I'm sure Miss Kate missed lunch. Me, too."

"I'll get them." Chameli strode across the room to the corner kitchenette. A cooling rack sat on top of the half-sized refrigerator, and Chameli swept half a dozen cookies off the rack onto a plate. She did not look like the kind of woman who baked cookies or called children sweetheart. She didn't look like she made trashy earrings with folksy motifs, either.

Standish had worked with women like Chameli, women with sharp eyes and strong muscles, women who worked hard until their bodies couldn't take hard any more. Standish had left the Earth to become a woman like Chameli, the kind of woman who was so different from her own fragile mother that nothing of her mother's world could ever affect her: not society, not money, not even art.

And yet. The smell of turpentine.

Standish looked around the shabby house, ignoring Olive's exclamations about cookies and the domestic sounds of mugs striking the plastic tabletop. Chameli's painting studio was tucked into the space between the sagging couch and the coat rack, half-hidden by rain gear. The craft table was the focal point of the house, the obvious, clamorous call to attention. Anyone, even Chameli, could overlook this small shelf built out of unpeeled horsetail, a palette and a jar of brushes sitting on one end, a canvas tacked up at the other. Standish crossed to it.

A horsetail tree leaned out of one corner of the canvas, a sharp diagonal that smothered the rest of the scene. The piece was unfinished, but had been sketched in with a sure hand. Chameli made no attempt to differentiate between one penciled dog and the next, but in their headlong thrust across the fabric, their sense of purpose rang true. One dog pulled ahead of the others, its front paws stretching beyond the frame of the image. The leader of the pack.

Chameli stepped in front of the picture. "It's not finished."

"I know. It's still amazing."

Chameli's lips tightened. "We'll see." She turned away. "How are those cookies?"

Olive took a cookie from the plate and obligingly bit into it. Standish went to the sunken couch and took a seat next to her, waiting for the girl's verdict. She chewed slowly, with a steady thoughtfulness.

"They're good," Olive declared. "Did you add vanilla? They don't taste like your usual."

"Observant little thing, aren't you? Yes, I got vanilla from a new shop in the city." Chameli poured something hot and dark into her mug from the kettle. She filled Standish's without asking. "I'm guessing this isn't just a social call, Olive."

Olive sat the rest of the cookie down on the edge of the plate. "I brought you something special, Missus Chameli."

"Just Chameli, and you know it. Must be something special if you're breaking out the honorifics. You find a mother lode of rock-eater out there?"

"I've got rock-eater, sure, but that's not special." Olive picked her backpack up off the floor and zipped open the front pocket. "No, this I found out in Shade's Hollow. Never saw anything like it before in my life."

She took out a plastic box, the kind dry goods from Earth came in. She used two hands, as if whatever lay inside was precious and fragile.

Chameli took it. The lid opened with a snap. "Oh, my."

"It was a butterfly graveyard," Olive explained. "They'd been there a while, so they were all hollowed out inside, empty as eggshells. But the wings were unspoiled. Can you imagine that?" Her eyes shone. "There in the hollow, a whole sheet of blue, like a rainbow lost its stripe and the poor thing curled up to wait for the other colors to come back and find it."

Chameli lifted a slice of cool blue out of the box. To Standish, it was like watching her pick up a splinter of sky – not Huginn's endlessly gray sky, but Earth's, the kind of blue that showed above wild places and rough rivers on the clearest, warmest days. She reached reflexively for Hattie's collar.

Chameli put the sky back inside the dry goods box. "I can pay your usual fee today, but I'm going to have to owe you the balance. I can't afford this on my pension."

"It's OK. I know you're good for it." Olive picked up the cookie and slipped it into her pack. "The wings are just the same color as Saint Hepzibah's robe."

"Saint Hepzibah?" Standish took a sip of spicy chai.

Olive pushed the cookie plate closer to Standish. "She's not a real saint, you know."

"I don't know," Chameli said. "Maybe no church has ever recognized her, but people around here believe she's the real thing. She's the woman you see on all the graves," Chameli explained. She made her way into the kitchenette and added back at Standish: "She was one of the first colonists, I guess. Helped the Believers protect their animals from the dogs."

"When I die, I want a Hepzibah on my grave. I don't want to get dug up and eaten."

"Oh, hush, child." Chameli returned with a stack of credit chits. "Here's a third of what I owe you."

"Thanks." Olive turned to Standish. "Could you drop me off in town? I need to pick up some powdered milk for dinner."

"I'm going that way."

The girl was already headed for the mud room. Standish couldn't decide if her confidence was endearing or annoying, but she supposed it was a good survival trait.

"She's not like anyone, is she?" Chameli shook her head. "She lives in her own world."

"She lives in Huginn. More than anyone else, I think. She belongs here." Standish got up from the couch and gave the room one last looking over. All the colors and simple forms reminded her powerfully of home – not her one-bedroom plastic house here by the lake, but the big house in Sacramento that her mother had filled with antiques and tchotchkes.

"Can I buy those earrings?"

"They're not done. And you don't even have your ears pierced."

"They're for a friend." She wasn't even sure it was a lie. Maybe she'd take them home and decide she'd better give them to Dewey.

"They're not done," Chameli repeated. "But here." She lifted down a small box and riffled through it for a second. "This seems better for you."

She held out a necklace, very simple, just a hammered square of tin strung on a leather cord. The figure painted on the tin had golden hair and a blue mantle, her face soft and round and smiling. A few butterflies hovered above her head like a halo. "Your own Saint Hepzibah."

Standish took it and held it in her palm to study for a few long seconds. Saint Hepzibah looked back at her, her eyes warm and understanding. Her robe reminded Standish of the sky, and yet she felt no urge to reach for Hattie. It seemed a good sign. "Can't hurt," she said.

Colonialism demands maximum resource extraction at any cost, human, environmental, or societal. Where there is an other to project the consequences upon, then the colonialist can reap benefit unscathed by extraction and production. Finding a planet outside the terrestrial solar system was the greatest boon to the colonial mindset since Columbus's discovery of Hispaniola.

— Olive Whitley, A New Common Sense (pamphlet)

CHAPTER TWELVE

Huginn, Day 168

She can't be even seven months along, but Vonda's water has broken, and I'm alone with her waiting for Doc Sounds, and I don't know if he'll even come. He shut himself in his house after Maria died last week, and he hasn't come out even for meals.

Oh, God, I don't know if I can do this.

I've helped with lots of babies before, but nothing about this pregnancy is normal.

Oh, God, the blood –

– Later –

Doc Sounds came, little help as he was, save for sewing up Vonda's belly, and my stitches would have been finer than his. Now he comforts Orrin while Vonda sleeps. I asked Orrin for a name – something to put on the tombstone, at least – but he couldn't bring himself to speak, let alone name that ill-made scrap of flesh.

I believe it was a mercy of God that it never drew breath and that Vonda never saw what passed for its face. No mother should have to see that, even if it was her bad choice that ruined her baby in the first place. She should have never gotten pregnant when she knew she was going into cryo.

Sometimes I wonder why God gives us free will when we make such terrible decisions.

I've bundled the little corpse in the quilt we made for it, and now I am just waiting for Matthias to return from digging its grave next to Maria Sounds.

The cemetery has grown every day this week.

Standish awoke gasping from dreams of open sky to find Hattie prodding her face with a cold nose. It was like the fingers of some icy angel pulling her from terror. Standish fumbled to stroke the dog's soft ears, the thick ruff of hair around her neck. After a long minute, she sat up and shivered. She'd sweated through her nightshirt and the damp had worked into her bones. The square of tin at her throat was the only warm bit of her.

From experience, she knew there was no point staying in bed. The dream would only come back.

So she took a hot shower and then bundled into work clothes and her only sweater. She should buy more clothes. She hadn't done anything to settle into her new life or new home; Canaan Lake had folded her so tightly in its octopus arms of wild dogs and trouble, she hadn't been able to think beyond the strangeness.

She reached for Hattie's lead. She should have known Saturday's misadventures would trigger a response. She reminded herself that while she felt like shit right now, she and Hattie still had her anxiety under control. She'd been fine yesterday, hadn't she? Even Peter's snoring hadn't bothered her.

She would see him today at work, she supposed. Would it be awkward? Would he want to get beers? She opened the door and led Hattie outside.

The air felt soft on her skin, the rain gentle as butterflies' wings. The softly sculling shapes of the clouds overhead made the world seem friendly despite the monstrous dogs and vicious leather birds.

She slowed her pace a little. Was she safe here on the lakeshore? She hadn't even brought her hand unit. Anything could happen out here and her only protection was a dog who ought not be able to bite.

"Fuck, I'm an idiot."

She heard something then, as if in response to her voice: a low rumbling that shook the sky. She craned back her head in time to see the low streak of light made by a shuttle hurrying overhead, its vapor trail reflecting back the lights of town in a creamy orange scribble across the clouds.

It was easy to forget she was on a world connected to the rest of the galaxy. Canaan Lake was all woods and wilderness, but there was more to Huginn than just Canaan Lake. There were other towns consuming and producing, importing and exporting, transforming the raw materials of a planet into useful goods. The spaceport connected them all, sending out material and bringing in money and people. It was the beating heart of humanity.

She thought then of the bills of lading she'd found in Duncan's secret box. All those trips on and off world, and not one with a shipping fee. She wanted another look at those.

She urged Hattie back toward the house, breaking into a jog as they went. The sky in the east showed a very faint hint of pale gray at the horizon, a promise of sunrise. Darkness still reigned supreme, clinging in thick masses around the edges of things. She nearly ran into the cart sitting in front of her house.

"Ma'am? I saw your lights," a young voice said from her porch.

She edged past the horse and saw the boy she'd met by the lake her first day on Huginn. The produce boy. "You're up awfully early."

"My dad's seeing to the milking," he explained. "And this is the best time to catch people working the third shift at the mill." He rapped his toe tip against the crate sitting on her door mat. "Your first produce box. I hope you like the radishes. I grew them."

Standish tried to remember the last time she'd eaten a radish. She couldn't imagine her parents serving such a humble vegetable. "I look forward to them."

He moved toward his cart and stopped before he passed her. "Your dog's on a leash today."

"It seemed like a good idea," she said. "After that wild dog attack."

He looked away from the dog then and she thought he blinked hard and fast. "My dog ran off. He was a good dog, but he still ran off."

"I'm so sorry."

He nodded and then got into the little wagon. "You take good care of your dog, Miss. Watch out for her."

She took the vegetable box inside and fit it into her barren refrigerator. The poor boy. She couldn't imagine what she'd do without Hattie.

And then, before she could forget it again, she opened Duncan's box and dug out the folder full of shipping invoices. She checked the signatures. They were all Songheuser ships, and they had all been received by the same person: M Williams.

M Williams.

Duncan had noticed that Matthias Williams had some kind of credit with Songheuser's shipping arm. Had he gone to Matthias? Was that what had happened? She couldn't imagine a Believer owning an air bolt gun, but the man was smart enough to use that for his advantage. She checked her hand unit. She had three hours until she'd be expected at HQ, and if she was lucky, Matthias would be up already, tending his orchard.

Peter squeezed through the door of the Mill Cafe and between two old men blocking the way. He was pretty sure the entire first shift and half the loggers in town had come in for breakfast this morning. He found a clean spot at the counter and ordered his breakfast. A new waitress shot him a smile and then bent over to grab a fresh caddy of silverware. He watched with admiration.

"Mind if I sit here?"

He pulled his coffee cup closer, wrestling his eyes away from the waitress's hemline to make a hospitable expression at the older woman beside him. "Help yourself."

"Thanks." She took a seat and the cute waitress filled both their mugs. The old gal had to be a regular. He thought he recognized her from someplace, maybe a potluck or a community meeting. She had the sturdy build of a woman who'd spent her younger years working hard.

"Your usual, Chameli?" the waitress asked.

Peter recognized the name, for sure. Chameli Paulus had led the group that had argued against letting the Believers sell their land in Sectors 13 and 14 to Songheuser. Her statements had crossed his desk, and even though her lack of training was obvious, he'd admired her commitment to local natural history.

He put out his hand. "I'm Peter Bajowski. I remember your notes about Sector 14. You've done a lot of data collecting out there."

"I know who you are, Dr Bajowski. Part of the reason I sat here." She took a drink of her coffee. "Thanks for remembering me."

The waitress appeared with Peter's breakfast and he took a moment fiddling with his food before answering. "Sounds like you've got a question for me." He forked beans and potato into a tortilla and took a bite large enough to give Chameli a chance to pour out her heart. She was probably looking for support fighting the next phase of development out on the edge sectors – he knew these political old ladies. They never gave up.

She surprised him by pulling out a plastic box with a snap-on lid. "I source a lot of pigments from the woods," she began, and stopped, misreading the confusion on his face: "Oh, don't worry. I'm damn careful how I get the stuff. I'm not out crushing rock-eater in the field or stripping whole trees of their lichen. I know how to tread lightly in the woods."

He took another bite instead of answering. He was more interested in what she was doing with the pigments; he didn't know a thing about the woman besides the fact she irritated the hell out of the company.

"So one of my dealers brought me this yesterday." She pushed the box toward him. "I'd say it was Hepzibah's blue, but there's something different about these. Maybe a subspecies?"

Not political wrangling at all, but actual biology. And a question worth investigating. He dried his hands on his napkin and opened the box. "Wow."

There had to be at least a hundred dead butterflies in the box, or at least the wings of a hundred dead butterflies. He reached into his shirt pocket and took out the tweezers he carried with him as a matter of course. With care, he lifted out a wing and held it up to the light. The blue scales shimmered softly, their powdery color a good match for the sky over his parents' house in Monterey, the kind of blue that made you want to throw off your shoes and jump into the sea for a quick swim. "Magnificent."

"Do you see the gold?" Chameli pointed to the border of tiny gold dots running along the edge of the wing. "That's not normal for a Hep blue. I've been using their wings in my work since I started making jewelry, and I've never seen that."

An artist. It explained the pigments. Peter looked away from the wings to see her eyes, gray and serious, fixed on his face. "Do you mind if I take one of these back to the office? I'd like to examine it more closely."

She nodded. "Sure. I've got plenty. And I'm more curious about something new than I am worried about making a batch of paint."

He found a plastic bag in his pocket and bagged a specimen, making a quick note of who he'd gotten it from. "Any idea where your source found these?"

"She'll never tell. Trade secret."

"Drat." He took another bite, thinking it over. It seemed Earth insects were adapting to this world with new kinds of caterpillars finding a place to live in the forest and new kinds of butterflies winging through the skies. All of these changes happening, and not even a graduate student keeping track of them. Biologically speaking, these were the most exciting events in the whole galaxy – and the only observations being made were those he squeezed into his days off.

Chameli began work on a bowl of Cream of Wheat. He watched her for a moment, thinking. Someone like her – someone who spent time outside and paid attention to the world around them – could be very useful. She was at least another pair of boots on the ground.

He had another thought. Not only was she a citizen scientist, but she'd been on Huginn a lot longer than he had.

"Hey, you've been here a while, haven't you?"

She washed down a bite with a swig of coffee. "It'll be twenty years in three months."

"Have you ever heard of leather birds attacking anyone?"

"Leather birds?" She shook her head. "They'll bother your cow herd if it gets too close to one of their nesting trees, but all told, they don't have much interest in anything terrestrial."

"That's what I thought. The leather birds–"

"Leather birds?" The man speaking had the kind of voice that could carry over a chainsaw's roar. "What do you two know about goddamn leather birds?"

The whole room had stopped talking. The coffee maker made a soft gurgle and went silent.

Peter turned around slowly. He didn't know the man behind him, but he'd seen dozens of his kind since coming to Huginn. The beefy build, the weatherbeaten skin, the waterproof coveralls, all spoke of life out in the elements, wrestling nature for a living. Men like that had PhDs from the school of hard knocks, and they looked down on anyone who couldn't out-muscle or out-shout them.

"We're just shooting the breeze, man. Don't let us bother you." Peter swung to face his breakfast, hoping the man would move on.

A hand descended on his shoulder and spun him back around. "Oh, you ain't bothering me. I just want to make sure you're not letting some treehugger preach to you about them things. They're a menace, that's what they are."

Peter pushed the man's hand off his shoulder. "I'm a company biologist. I don't need a report on leather birds from a logger." He didn't mean to make the words come out so full of attitude.

"Oh, I see. You're the smart one here."

"Yes, I am." Peter had been on this side of the conversation his entire adult life. From condo developers to timber fallers, they all hated to be told they weren't the smartest men in the room, as threatened by Peter's degrees as if the diplomas might physically crush their dicks. "You see, a leather bird's physiognomy is built out of an entirely different sequence of amino acids than ours is. They get no nutrition from our flesh. Plus, they're about the size of a hawk. Big for a bird, but no real threat to a man of your size."

"You talk big, but you don't know the woods."

"I've spent the last four years in these woods, and I'm not riding around in a saw-mech. I actually look at the creatures on this planet while you're playing masters of the universe."

It was too much and he knew it even before the man's fist shot out. He had a second to be glad he'd left his I+ glasses in his satchel before his head smashed backward and he slammed into the edge of the counter. Ceramic shattered. His face hurt.

"Stop it." Chameli shoved the big man aside with ease. "Just stop it." She kept her hands up, ready for the man to make another move. "You all right, Dr Bajowksi?"

Peter wiped blood off his top lip. "Yeah."

"Then get the hell out of here before you cause any more trouble. Some of us have breakfast to finish."

He didn't need encouragement. He found his satchel tucked beneath the counter and headed out the door. The bell jingled as it swung shut behind him. He guessed he'd just go to work early. There was coffee there, after all.

At the end of the parking strip, Sheriff Vargas rolled down the window of her UTV and stuck her head out. "You eighty-six'd again, Peter?"

"Just thrown out."

"You'd best remember there are only so many places to eat around here," she called out, laughing.

Peter gave her a wave. She was right, but some days it felt smaller than others.

The UTV's lights lit up two circles like owl's eyes on the horsetail gate in front of Matthias Williams's house. Standish turned off the rig and waited for her eyes to adjust. The sun had come up during her drive, but Wodin's shadow lay heavily over the moon, smudging everything gray.

The farmstead had several outbuildings, but Standish found Matthias at the whetstone in front of his barn, a wide and alarming array of honed blades around him: shovels, loppers, hoes, and scissory-looking things she couldn't identify. He stopped pumping the foot pedal of the grinder as she approached, but did not get up from his three-legged stool. Once again, the silence of his place unnerved her.

For the first time, she wondered just what she was doing out here. Sheriff Vargas had Duncan Chambers' body. This was her case to solve. She had training and skills and a gun, whereas Standish had only curiosity and a canister of pepper spray in her pocket. She'd be in real trouble if she'd just stumbled onto Duncan's murderer.

It was possible, she supposed. If the shipping invoices Duncan had found were clues to some kind of Believer-Songheuser conspiracy, it was just possible Matthias had been forced to kill the man.

Hattie went to Matthias's side and began sniffing his boots. Matthias rubbed the dog's ears, smiling at her.

Possible, Standish reminded herself. Just really unlikely.

"Something I can do for you, Miss Kate?"

"You were friends with Duncan Chambers, weren't you?"

He reached for a hoe. "Most of Canaan Lake was friends with Duncan. He liked people." He took a file out of his pocket. "Too bad you didn't get a chance to meet him."

He began filing at some imperfection in the hoe's blade. Standish studied him. She was strong, although she still needed to recoup muscle after her time in cryo, and she was tall. On a good day, she thought she could overpower him, especially if she fought dirty. But Matthias had all the advantage here, and if he had killed Duncan, he'd have no qualms sticking that file through her throat.

She knew she should be nervous, but she somehow wasn't. "I live in Duncan's house," she began.

Matthias looked up. "You do? Was any of Duncan's gear left behind or did Peter clear it all out?" His hazel gray eyes were clear and curious, his posture relaxed.

"He left some stuff. Food and whatnot. And some papers that I found."

"Papers?"

"I'm not sure they're Duncan's."

Matthias put down the hoe and file and stood up. "Let me get you a cup of tea," he said. "I don't mean to be inhospitable."

Hattie pawed at his leg.

"Hattie," Standish snapped. "Come here."

"She's taken a liking to me." He patted the dog and then pushed her paw off his leg. He began walking toward the house.

"She's trained not to put her foot up. Come here," she ordered again.

Hattie trudged to her side. She'd never seen the dog act like this.

"If you don't mind, I'd rather she stayed on the porch," Matthias said. "I'll bring her out some water, if you'd like."

Standish kept a good hold on Hattie's collar. She could hear Matthias's footsteps inside, a squeak of metal and a sudden whoosh of water. She made the sign for Hattie to sit and then narrowed her eyes at the dog. "You stay." She couldn't understand why Hattie was acting like this.

Matthias placed a clay bowl full of water down beside the dog and then pushed the door open for Standish. "Ladies first."

"I'm not much of a lady."

"Manners are what separate us from beasts." He waved at the open doorway.

The early morning sunlight, still weak from Wodin's heavy

shadow, did little to light up the room. Standish paused in the doorway, unsure where to go to keep an eye on Matthias, and realizing as she thought it that she'd left her back exposed to a man she half-heartedly suspected of murder. She was shit at this detective thing.

Matthias hurried past her to light the oil lamp on the table, and color spilled out everywhere.

She had never seen a room so full of color.

Every flat surface had been painted with some kind of pattern or creature: parrots and blue birds and cardinals winged across butter-yellow cabinet fronts, where green turtles replaced the handles. Pink and purple baskets filled with dried herbs and produce hung from the high ceiling. Even the wooden floor had green vines and fantastical flowers entwined around its edges. She turned in a slow circle, taking it all in.

"The paint's not very tough," he admitted. "I have to touch it up. That's why I didn't want Hattie to come in here. Claws, you know." He slipped off his boots and went to the corner cupboard. "There's tea," he said. "Cold, that's how I take it."

The back side of the cupboard was cunningly made of pierced tin, and a little breeze wafted out of it as he took out a jar of yellowish liquid and a pie. She hadn't thought much about life without refrigeration. It suddenly seemed like a fantastic luxury.

He put the jar and the pie on the little kitchen table, its surface still plain wood, although its legs were the same green as the painted vines they rested on. She took a seat and sternly reminded herself that just because the man liked to paint cute animals didn't mean he wasn't a killer.

"So you painted all this?"

He brought down plates and cups. "Gives me something to do at night. And it reminds me of my wife."

"Your wife?"

"She loved animals." He cut a slice of the dark brown pie and slid it on a plate. He pushed it across the table. "Shoofly. Belle Sounds made it."

She found herself leaning in, curious. "Who's Belle Sounds?"

"Just one of our people. Came over about a year ago from the Ohio farms and married one of our natives. Her husband's been a good friend over the years." He sat down across from her and smiled. "I think she's worried I can't cook for myself."

"And is she right?"

He had dimples. She hadn't noticed that, but they flashed at her now. "Depends how you define cooking."

She laughed. "I'm about the same." Taking a bite of the pie, she found it sticky-sweet and tremendously rich. She couldn't believe this man had killed Duncan, or that any of his people had, either. "Matthias, tell me why you don't pay shipping on Songheuser ships."

"*Those* papers. I thought that might be what you meant."

"Those papers. Yeah."

He picked up his fork, put it down. "The Believers of Canaan Lake had some trouble when they first came here. It was Songheuser's fault, so they made a very generous settlement with us in exchange for dropping any kind of lawsuit. As long as our people maintain farms in Canaan Lake, we're entitled to use Songheuser's ships for free shipping to and from the planet."

"The first colonists got here over a hundred years ago."

"Well, we are mostly self-sufficient, and our products are mostly used locally. But when we first arrived? Yes, it was a very generous settlement."

"What the hell did Songheuser do?" Even as she said it, she remembered the diary. The woman who'd written it had been one of those first settlers, she was sure of it. She itched to go home and read the thing.

"I don't know all the details," he said. "As you pointed out, it was a long time ago. But as far as I can tell, the company failed to ship all the colonists' supplies. The first crops failed, and more than half the settlers died in their first year at Canaan Lake. It was a devastating blow to the community."

"That's horrible." Standish frowned. "But why was Duncan interested in your shipping papers? And how did he get them?"

"I gave them to him. He said he was looking into something about the amount of traffic at the spaceport. I just assumed he was trying to gather enough data to persuade Songheuser to expand their communications department. Duncan thought we needed better coverage out here – all over the planet, really."

"You sound like you think that's funny."

"I don't need to send video mail or whatever you call it. I'm content with my lot."

Standish took another bite of the pie to cover a laugh.

He put down his fork. "Why are you smiling?"

"Because email is pretty much the whole reason I'm on this planet, and you don't even believe in it." She took another bite of the sticky pie and then remembered. "You said you had some papers to show me."

"Yes." He got up and opened a bin filled with potatoes. He brought out a big yellow envelope tucked in the back. "Duncan wanted to update the survey maps. He didn't think they were current."

"Was he right?"

Matthias nodded. "He'd found at least one road that wasn't on the maps. A service road, out in Sector 13."

"I've seen it. That's where we found Duncan's body this weekend."

"We. You mean you and Peter Bajowski." Matthias sat down at the seat beside her. He held the envelope tightly enough to crumple the edges.

The shoofly pie in her stomach turned over. She owed Peter her life, twice over, but she knew the face Matthias was making. "Is there something wrong with Bajowski?"

He hesitated. "I don't have any proof."

She waited. He was close enough she could smell him, a clean smell like cut grass and earth.

"Duncan was working on a project toward the end," he said, slowly, as if he was still working it out in his head. "He said it had something to do with this group of Songheuser biologists he'd been drinking with at the Night Light. He was really worried about the project, but he didn't want to talk about it until he'd done some more digging."

The Night Light. It was the closest bar to her house, but it wasn't a favorite with the office crowd. Anybody who wanted to drink without making a lot of gossip at work would know that.

"And Bajowski's a biologist," she mused.

"I don't trust him. He doesn't like Believers or farming, and he's made that clear at plenty of community meetings. Plus," he hesitated again. "Plus, Duncan told me he thought Peter was jealous he had a new boyfriend. He said he knew Peter was still in love with him."

Standish pushed away her pie. She knew it, too. And jealousy was a powerful motive for murder.

There was just one thing: she couldn't believe Peter could kill anyone.

For humans, language is the way we create. Engineering is an application of math, the language of measurement and quantification. Music? Yes, a language, with different dialects created in different ancient Earth communities and regions and times. Paintings speak in shapes and colors that are dependent on human visual systems and deeply embedded notions of symbology. These different kinds of languages give us the power to manipulate our own world, but each limits those manipulations to the forms of the tool itself.

Languages in all their infinite variety are rooted in our bodies and our societies, and those roots are like strictures. We are defined by them as we define with them; we are strangled by them as we close our fingers around their throats.

– from THE COLLECTED WISDOM OF MW WILLIAMS

CHAPTER THIRTEEN

Huginn, Day 174

The baby. No one can stop talking about the baby. Vonda still lays in bed, Orrin doesn't leave their house; only Doc and I saw the little thing, but somehow everyone knows what happened. In prayer meeting, everyone's eyes were on me. I tried to ignore them and think on God, on what He would want me to learn from all of this.

Everything I learned on Earth is a jumble in my head. Perhaps it is because I am so hungry.

In the garden I planted behind the house, only the potatoes have sprung up. If potatoes can look wild, these ones do. It will be a long time until harvest, and I already fear the roots I'll dig. Will they be *potatoes*, round and harmless and wholesome, or pale grub-like things, their fat and loathsome bodies full of poison and stained with mold? I'd believe anything of this world now. Oh, that poor broken child!

Elder Perkins blames cryo. It is an unnatural thing, a kind of death, he says, and all that entered that death must be corrupted and deformed. Is he right? Can he be? Everything we've brought with us has passed through the sere darkness of space. All of us and all our creatures rested in the cold sleep of cryo for eleven long months before we reached this world.

I do not know if we brought death with us or if it was already waiting for us in this cold, wet place, and I do not know if our decision to come to Huginn was guided by God's grace or our own untrustworthy will.

I am praying for a sign that we are right with God.

Standish's brain was full as she headed to Heinrich's on Friday after work. It had been a long week, a week she'd spent avoiding Peter Bajowski and wondering if Sheriff Vargas was making any better headway on Duncan's case than she was.

She stopped and stared. Just past the Mill Cafe, Main Street had been blocked off for a few blocks, the street itself filled with booths and tables. It looked like the kind of arts festival her mother would have been irresistibly attracted to.

"Hi, Miss Kate!" Olive Whitley called over her shoulder as she darted by.

Standish tried to catch her elbow but missed by a mile. The girl was headed toward the table where Chameli was setting up a display of jewelry.

"Oh, it's Last Friday!" Niketa cooed as she caught up with Standish. "You should check it out."

"Last Friday?"

"It's this farmer's market-slash-art show thing they started last year. Artists come from all over for it." Niketa urged her into the crowd, nudging her toward a vendor selling necklaces carved from polished links of horsetail wood.

Standish shook her head and left Niketa behind. She just

wanted a beer and a burger, not noise and a crowd.

Then a stand caught her eye and she stopped. She'd never seen yarn so soft-looking, or colors so vibrant. The pink and yellow looked just like rock-eater lichen.

"Soft, isn't it?" A woman suddenly appeared behind the table, hoisting a basket filled with more varieties of yarn. Her bonnet and old-fashioned dress marked her as a Believer.

Standish pulled back her hand. "Sorry."

"Don't be," the Believer woman said. "That how I persuade people to buy my yarn. The softness is irresistible."

"That's for sure."

She stepped out from behind the table. Beneath the blue bonnet, her hair was a striking corn yellow. She could have been an entertainer with that hair and figure. "Are you a fellow craftsperson?"

"I crochet," Standish admitted.

"And you have a dog," the woman added in a surprised tone.

"She's very well-behaved."

"I see." The woman put out her hand. "I'm Vonda. You must be Kate Standish. I've heard a great deal about you."

There was something offputting about the woman, a chilliness that came through despite her friendly demeanor.

"It's a small town," Standish said. She reached for a skein of fluffy purple. "Can I pay with a funds transfer, or..."

"Funds transfer is fine," Vonda said, watching Standish enter the details on her hand unit. "I've got more of that dye lot if you run out," she said. "Stop by the Morris farm any time. Sector 3."

Vonda Morris. The name was familiar, but Standish couldn't place it. She hadn't met that many Believers since she'd arrived in Canaan Lake, either.

"Thanks." Standish gave her a wave and tucked the yarn under her arm. She was glad she'd found the stand, but she wasn't so sure she wanted to spend more time with Vonda Morris.

She hurried toward the bar, which was still quiet enough that Belinda was reading a book. Standish waved at the bartender. She reached for a bookmark.

"Whatcha reading?"

Belinda made an embarrassed face. "Nothing." Standish caught a glimpse of the spine – *The Monkey Wrench Gang* – before Belinda thrust it behind the beer taps.

Maybe in a town like Canaan Lake, reading environmentalist fiction was something to be embarrassed about. Standish wouldn't give her shit about it, though. She settled onto a stool. "Cool fingernails."

Belinda studied her hand. "They just turned green the other day. Do you think that's a medical thing?"

Standish blinked at her. "They *turned* green?"

"Weird, right? Anyway, you want a stout?"

"Please. And I'll take my usual."

"I saw you coming. Hattie's no-salt patty should be up in a second."

"Hey, Belinda," someone called out from behind Standish, and Standish winced a little.

She turned around to smile up at the speaker. "Brett. Long time no see."

"What gives, Kate? I thought you liked me."

She'd somehow managed to avoid him, too, this week. They'd played pool on Wednesday, but she'd given him the slip. This thing with Duncan was more interesting than sex. Not to mention Brett was an honorary deputy for Vargas. She couldn't exactly admit she was working on the case with her new Believer comrade when Brett was a legit operator.

"I do like you, Brett. I just… Finding that body kind of cooled me down." She paused, measuring the odds before playing the disability card. "It really stirred up my anxiety."

"Do you need a doctor? HR can recommend a shrink in Space City."

"Actually, I'm headed there tomorrow." It wasn't a lie, either. She'd added a check-in with the psychiatrist to her visit with Dewey, since she wanted to keep on Niketa's good side. It would be a waste of time, but she'd signed the contract with Songheuser, and staying on Huginn meant staying employed.

"You'll miss Rob McKidder's memorial service, then."

"That's too bad. Maybe we can get together Monday?"

"Next week's going to be hell for me. Got a company veep coming into town and all us security boys will be working double shifts." He plopped down on the barstool and waved at Belinda.

A company VIP. Standish hoped she had a lot of off-site work orders next week. Then another thought occurred to her. "That'll cut into your work with Sheriff Vargas, won't it?"

"Oh, I haven't done anything since we hauled Dunc's bones out of the woods. We're still waiting for forensics to get around to the autopsy. Plus, Sheriff's thinking it was just an accident or maybe a suicide. I mean, who'd kill Duncan Chambers? Everybody liked him."

"An accident? How could somebody *accidentally* shoot themselves in the chest?"

"Hey, those air bolt guns need a lot of maintenance. He could have been trying to adjust the chamber, and *pow*! Bump the trigger. I've seen weirder things, sweetheart. And Duncan did *not* know his way around firearms." Brett's hand settled on her thigh, heavy and hot as a fresh-grilled steak. Standish stood up.

"I've got to make an early start tomorrow," she said. "I'll see you when I get back."

She walked away before he could get any ideas to go to bed early with her. She didn't believe Brett's accident theory for even a second, not when Chambers was snooping into the town's secrets. If Brett was right, and Sheriff Vargas wasn't going to investigate this as a murder, then she and Peter were the only people in Canaan Lake trying to figure out who killed Duncan Chambers.

The silk tie lay heavy in Peter's hands. He laid it on the back of his neck and slid his fingers slowly down its serpentine length, smoothing the gray fibers against his skin. The last time he'd worn a tie was at Duncan's memorial service. They'd sat in stiff-backed chairs with a blown-up photo of Duncan smirking down at them, the air filled with the stink of hothouse flowers brought in from Space City. Duncan would have preferred a few swags of horsetail fronds and a pot of Christ's fingers, but Songheuser had hosted the service.

He made a half-Windsor and slid it into place, doublechecking the knot in the mirror. The tips of his shirt collar stuck down on either side of the silvery knot like bared teeth – canine teeth. Not really the thing to wear to the funeral of a man ripped apart by wild dogs, but tradition was tradition. If Duncan's memory had to be profaned with the waste of Earth-flavored imports he never would have approved, then it seemed only reasonable poor Rob would get buried surrounded by men in toothed collars. We celebrate your death with our death grip on tradition. He realized his mind was wandering, and he headed out of the bathroom.

It had been over a week since he'd found Rob lying in the street, and he hadn't stopped dreaming of it yet. There were circles like trenches under his eyes, and he'd started dozing off at his desk while he was labeling specimens. Just one night, that night he spent on Standish's sofa, had offered him any kind of decent sleep. If he could sit at the bar all evening, letting the stupid wash of conversation and the beer foam soften all the edges away, he might have been able to sleep, but he couldn't stand all the eyes at Heinrich's.

"It's a small town, man," he reminded himself. "A damn small town."

He slipped on his dress shoes and found his keys on the shelf by the door. His hand unit sat beside them. Most mornings he checked his email first thing, but not today. He wasn't going to get sidetracked with memos from the higher-ups. Today was just about Rob McKidder.

Outside, a weak sunlight trickled over the street. A man and woman left their house, dressed in black and clearly headed to the same place he was. McKidder hadn't been a churchgoer, but the Catholic church had become sort of a community center for the town, and Father Donovan had a nice, non-liturgical ceremony ready for these occasions.

Peter was glad there wouldn't be a real mass. He could remember going to church with his abuela, the air bristling with incense, the wonderful rustling of people's best clothes moving from pew to kneeler, but the act of recalling it made him uncomfortable. His parents, agnostics both, hadn't discouraged him from going to church, but once he'd left Mexico the magic had seeped out of the whole thing. He could still remember the pain that had crept across his grandmother's face when he told her the transubstantiation was the stupidest fiction of all time.

He regretted doing that to her, but damn it, he was a scientist. Religion had meant something to him before he could use reason and education to sort through the mysteries of the world. Of course he had outgrown it.

The tinny recording of the church bell began, and Peter hurried up the street. The church sat across from the police department, and he had to dodge the puddles and ruts so as not to ruin his dress shoes.

Once inside, Peter dropped into a pew and looked around himself. Most of the town had gathered in the plastic-smelling church. Lou from security sat a few rows ahead, crying so hard his shoulders shook. A huge bundle of white roses sat on top of the blessedly closed casket, and he saw Niketa setting up one of those ugly floral swags beside it. He sank down in a pew, but he could feel the eyes on him from every direction. He had found McKidder's body, after all.

The service began. Father Donovan delivered a few comforting beatitudes. Joe Holder spoke – it sounded like he and Rob had a long history working together, going back to some ratty station off Ganymede – and then Niketa said a few words about McKidder's family. HR planned to send both Rob's girlfriend and his aging parents a card and a gift basket. Niketa reminded them all of the gathering in the meeting hall on the west side of the building, and asked everyone to chip in a credit or two for the refreshments, generously provided by the Woodworkers Auxiliary.

Peter found himself caught up in the flow of mourners. He'd meant to head straight home, but now he was beside the refreshment table, where the scent of scorched coffee presided over plates of store-bought cookies. He took an oatmeal-raisin and a cup of the too-thick black stuff, unsure what to do next. He couldn't escape without drawing attention to himself.

An older woman squeezed past him to get a cup of coffee, talking back over her shoulder to a friend. "The dogs never *killed* anybody before. They were always a menace, but this–"

Her friend tromped on Peter's foot as she hurried to catch up. "Things are going to hell around here," she declared and took a handful of chocolate chip cookies. "Dogs, ecoterrorists, Duncan committing suicide–"

A group of children ran through, nearly knocking Peter down. He took a few steps away from the refreshment table, looking for someplace safe to hole up. Instead, he found himself closer to the main knot of people.

Joe Holder's voice boomed out over the group. "I talked to

Deputy Wu yesterday. Sounds like they've caught at least one of those eco-assholes."

People shifted so they wouldn't miss any gossip. A knot of men had gathered around Joe, most of them security and operations types from the mill and the company office. Peter saw one logger he knew.

"I hope he gets the death penalty," Brett Takas said. "Twenty-five people died in that explosion."

"What are you doing to make sure it doesn't happen here?" Peter didn't know the woman, but her voice sounded shrill.

"We've doubled guards on every shift," Brett reassured her. "And we're keeping close tabs on anyone known to sympathize with environmentalists."

Joe's eyes caught Peter's just then, and Peter felt the hairs rise up on his neck. He couldn't help but remember his conversation with Sheriff Vargas about the flyer the ecoterrorists had quoted – the flyer he'd written.

He stuffed a cookie in his mouth and hoped like hell nobody remembered the fight he'd gotten into at the Mill Cafe. Because if word got out he spent his free time defending leather birds, he would certainly end up on the short list of environmentalists in town, and he had a feeling that was enough to put him in jail around here.

Dr Holt looked up from her hand unit. Presumably she was looking at Standish's file, although she might as well have been doing her tax return for the expression on her face. "And ever since the accident you've suffered from acute anxiety, despite neural stim for post-traumatic stress?"

"My other therapist said it was residual agoraphobia. I'm almost perfectly fine unless I get a good look at the sky," Standish explained. "The stars are my biggest trigger."

"Mmm-hmmn." The psychiatrist made a note with her stylus. "It says here that you were deported to Earth after starting a fight in a bar that caused close to twenty thousand dollars in damage. You broke your nose and sent a man to the hospital with a crushed larynx. Space station legal and psychological council blamed alcohol abuse caused by your untreated anxiety disorder."

"But it hasn't bothered me at all since I got Hattie. Like, not at all."

Dr Holt pushed back from her desk. The highlights in her copper hair probably cost her as much every month as Standish had spent on rent back on Earth. Being a shrink on Huginn must be pretty lucrative. "I'm glad you've had such success with animal therapy, Ms Standish, but I'm in agreement with your employer. Your anxiety is a significant issue, and eight months is not enough time to be certain it will completely control the problem."

"It's been almost two years if you count the time in cryo," Standish joked.

Dr Holt raised an immaculate eyebrow. "Are you funnier when you're not this uncomfortable?"

"I'm not… uncomfortable." Standish caught herself rolling up the edge of her T-shirt and forced her hands to lay flat in her lap. "I'm using humor as a tool to help us connect."

"That's odd. Most of your relationships with your previous doctors were distant, to say the least." A smile twitched at the corner of Dr Holt's lips, giving her a mischievous expression. "I think Dr Warner mentioned an incident involving a bottle of water and his head?"

"He deserved to have his head soaked," Standish snapped. "He was a dick."

"I went to graduate school with Dr Warner. I'd say that's an accurate description of him."

Standish could only stare at her.

Dr Holt unfolded from her seat, her posture as refined as a ballerina's. But Standish had to admit there was more to the woman than class and fancy diplomas. She almost liked her.

"I'd like to get you scheduled for some regular sessions, but I know things are a little hectic in Canaan Lake right now. When things settle down, please set something up. I've sent a couple of prescriptions to your hand unit – one for a low-level anti-anxiety and depression med, and another for panic attacks. I want to keep this condition under control."

"Like I said, Hattie's got this. Since we started working together, it's like I don't even *have* anxiety. She's really my better half."

Dr Holt shook her head. "And like *I* said, I'm glad you've had such good luck with animal therapy." She reached for the button that opened the office door. "But what would you do if something happened to Hattie?"

Standish left the office, Holt's words replaying in her head. She stopped in front of the elevator and stroked Hattie's ears. "I'm not going to let anything happen to you, girl."

The dog wagged her tail.

Standish brought up GPS on her hand unit. A red dot flashed on the corner of the map, indicating the nearest pharmacy. Standish turned off the notification and found the route to Dewey's apartment.

She drove through the blocks of bland office buildings at the fringe of Space City and headed toward the skytowers in the downtown. The buildings got larger and larger closer to the city center. No cheap plastic printing here: this was grade-A construction with overtones of pre-First Depression USA. These were multinational conglomerations, and they weren't about to let anyone forget it.

She turned onto Monroe Street and headed into a comfortable neighborhood filled with four- and five-story apartment buildings. Most had made some attempt to obscure their simple construction. Balconies and courtyards added texture to every building, and a few boasted art deco facades that echoed the ornate skytowers where their inhabitants likely worked. Standish found the guest lot for one particularly charming building and then made her way through the covered courtyard. A man and woman sat on a bench beside the small fountain, oblivious to her presence. Their little dog jumped up, though, and barked at Hattie. The building's door swung open and Dewey came out in a pink raincoat.

"I was just about to go pick up some liquor," she said. "I thought you wouldn't be here for another hour."

"I got an early start." Standish squeezed her tightly. Then she pushed Dewey out to arm's length. "The new implants look *good*. Work that nice had to cost a bundle."

Dewey pulled out of her grip, clearly uncomfortable. "I work a lot of extra hours. Anyway." She waved around her with a bright smile. "What do you think of the place? Classier than anyplace I've ever lived."

"Remind me not to have you over to my house," Standish grumbled as she followed Dewey into the pink-tiled lobby.

Dewey drew back the bronze grate of the elevator. "Heroes first."

Standish led Hattie on board. "Do you have anything for an early lunch? We're starving."

Dewey laughed. "Some things never change. Yes, I was prepared for your rapacious appetite. Good cheese – *cheese*, can you believe it? – bread, sliced meats, that steak for Hattie. I've got some wine, too, nothing too good, but what do you expect on a planet this cold?"

They got off on the third floor and Standish watched her friend closely as Dewey led them down a hallway apparently papered with gold chevrons. A closer inspection revealed the walls had been printed with the design, all the class and charm just floating on the surface. Like Dewey's good mood.

"So what's bothering you?" she asked as the door closed

behind them. The sweet vanilla of Dewey's favorite perfume hung over the apartment.

"Lunch first?" Dewey didn't meet her eyes as she went to the fridge.

"How about you talk while you get lunch? I don't want to wait."

Dewey disappeared into the refrigerator for a moment and appeared with a bottle of white. "I might need a drink. You might need a drink."

"I might need a drink?" Standish took the bottle out of Dewey's hand. "Dewey, what the hell is going on?"

"Look, I've been hearing things about Canaan Lake. I know you found Duncan Chambers' body, and I know what that must have meant to you."

"It meant I found a dead body." Standish took a long drink of her wine. "There's no reason to worry about me."

"I'm the only person in this system who knows they ought to worry about you." Dewey sat down on the couch and patted the seat beside her. "Ostensibly, my job is part of Huginn's government. Huginn is recognized as a territory of the North American Trade Federation. It has none of the rights or responsibilities of any state in the NATF. The way the laws are written, Huginn is just like a space station: the property of the corporations that built her."

"I've worked on space stations. I know all this."

"Well, let me remind you who built the infrastructure of Huginn. Eighty percent of the first survey work was done by Songheuser Corporation. Fifty-five percent of the initial spaceport was built by Songheuser. Thirty-five percent of all the roads on this world: built by Songheuser."

"So Songheuser's a big deal. What does this have to do with me?"

Dewey put her wineglass down on the coffee table. "Songheuser is a dangerous company." She took a deep breath.

"I was going through some old logs, trying to sort out some details about orders for the station on Muninn. There were parts that kept failing, circuits that should have had a longer lifespan. I thought maybe a manufacturer was screwing us. It led me to a contractor named Lohmax-Keysound.

"The more I learned about them, the worse it got. I discovered Goddard Station contracted out the station's construction and operations management to Lohmax-Keysound. Several major installations overseen by the company have had critical failures based on the sourcing of inferior parts. About three years ago, a class-action lawsuit against them triggered an investigation by the NATF Trade Board. The suit created a fund for those stricken in several accidents caused by the company's *knowing* use of recalled parts in their exterior maintenance tracks."

Standish licked her lips, which were suddenly dry. "Once again, what does that have to do with me?"

Her voice sounded smaller than she'd expected it.

"The NATF determined that the accident on Goddard Station – *your* accident, Kate – was caused by Lohmax-Keysound's negligence. If you hadn't been moving around – if you'd received and signed the papers – you would have received three-quarters of a million dollars."

Dewey took Standish's hand. "I kept digging. Lohmax-Keysound is a shell company for a subsidiary of Songheuser Corporation. Do you really think it was a coincidence that Songheuser reached out to you when they did? That their headhunters *just happened* to seek out communications tech workers at the same time lawyers were looking for you? When did you go to Ohio for your training with Hattie?"

Standish pulled her hand free. "You're saying I got my job, I got Hattie, just so Songheuser could save three-quarters of a million bucks?"

Dewey took a deep breath. "I'm saying that last year

Songheuser took over the contract to manage Goddard Station. They could do it because outside of a very tricky paper trail, there's nothing to connect them to Lohmax-Keysound, and they'd like to keep it like that."

"Fuck."

"Yeah."

Standish couldn't stay still any longer. She jumped to her feet. "Jesus Christ, Dewey, that's just what's happening at Canaan Lake, and I know it. Duncan had these papers, maps and stuff. He knew about the secret road out there in Sector 13. He knew something about the company!"

"Stop it."

Standish pushed on, pacing. "That's it. Songheuser is covering up something. God, maybe they even killed Duncan. That would make some kind of sick sense."

"Standish, shut up!"

Staring at her friend, Standish dropped onto the couch.

"You can't talk like that. At most, you can try to get your money from that suit, but you can*not* talk about Songheuser like that. You'll have your visa rescinded and find yourself on a cargo hauler back to Earth before you can even find your attorney's phone number."

"How do you know?"

"Because I've seen it happen." Dewey took a long drink of her wine and then gave Standish a weak smile. "I can get you a job in my department, I know it. So just hold tight. Don't go stirring things up yet, Kitty Cat. I don't want to lose you again."

Standish took a deep breath and looked out the window. From this angle, the skytowers blocked out the sky, their pointed tops and sharp spires directed at the sun. Those companies were giants who strode between worlds, who owned whole cities and spun the futures of entire planets in their wake. An ember of hatred flickered to life in her chest.

"Please, Kate."

"OK, Dewey. I'll mind my own business. Besides, the sheriff thinks Duncan was probably a suicide anyway."

Dewey gave her a hard look.

Standish forced a wide smile. "Hey, I brought you a present!" She reached in her pack for the soft scarf she'd made last night from Believer yarn and watched Dewey's face soften into happiness.

But Standish barely heard her coos of delight. She was thinking. Would Dewey have made such a fuss if she wasn't sure Songheuser had something to do with Duncan's death? Standish had a feeling there was more to her friend's story than she'd shared.

*What does a dog know? Can it know its creator? Can it
know it is a creature spun out of love and logos, or does it
only know sensation, instinct, immediacy? Do dogs think?*

*It is impossible to take that last question seriously. One
has only to watch animals for the briefest moment to see that
they feel and have intentions just as we do. The difference is
only that they do not name things.*

– from THE COLLECTED WISDOM OF MW WILLIAMS

CHAPTER FOURTEEN

Huginn, Day 179

Alex Perkins destroyed the cryo tanks this morning.

I'd been waiting for something bad to happen ever since
I saw Vonda's baby, but when I walked in and saw the mess
in the root cellar, I fell on my knees and cried.

I had gone into the kitchen early to start a tray of bread.
Bread's a nice word for what I make out of ground pinto
beans and sawdust, but it's something to dunk in the
flavored water I'll call soup, and it's nice to get up before
anyone else and start the ovens. It's really something, being
warm and dry. You don't appreciate it until you're outside
in the rain all the time. I turned on the ovens and I headed
to the food stores to get another bag of beans. It's cold down
there, colder than my mama's root cellar, and the blue lights
of the cryo tanks are all the light we've got.

But this morning, the root cellar was dark, and the stink
of death lay over the room, like the slaughterhouse before it
gets washed out. I had to go find a lantern to see just what
happened, but of course I already knew. Hadn't Perkins told
us all that he blames cryo for what's happening to us?

Every last cryo tank had been smashed open. The

embryos made a pinkish-gray pulp on the dirt floor, and cryo liquid pooled around the legs of the shelves. I began to shake with anger.

All those lives, put out like a candle.

What a waste. An unimaginable, horrible waste. Even if we couldn't have raised those creatures to adulthood, we could have incubated them into something edible. To waste those lives when every morsel of food is a treasure and a terror all at once? Waste them, when I'm so hungry that my hair comes out of my head in handfuls?

I warned Matthias, but he refused to see that people were unhappy. Matthias might have been able to convince everyone to come here, but he can no longer make them want to stay. The anger inside me burns brighter and brighter, and I'm not sure who I'm angrier with: Matthias or Alex Perkins.

At least Matthias isn't gloating over his mistakes. Perkins *boasted* about what he had done. Bragged right to our faces.

Matthias and some others are taking Alex to the spaceport tomorrow – to leave him there for good, shunned from the community. I don't know yet if Mei Lin will go with him. Matthias is taking the last of our money to buy supplies. It's an eighty kilometer hike through territory nobody knows and every last inch of it forest and mountains. If he makes it back alive, it will be by the blessing of God.

We could use one of those.

Standish turned reluctantly away from the lake and headed toward the path to the office. She'd spent the drive back from Space City turning over the events of the last few weeks, coupling and uncoupling ideas without getting the engine of her thoughts under control. She had seen a man killed by wild dogs. She had found the dead body of the man who had hired her, the man who should have been her boss. She couldn't believe people in town were still more worried about the sabotage at the Nagata mill than either of these deaths.

She paused beside a shoulder-high fern frond. The mill was the heart of the town. Without the mill, there would be no Canaan Lake, no matter how many Believer farms there were. The town was as much a monument to Songheuser Corporation as its art deco skytower in Space City.

The rain sifted between the fronds of the small trees to mist her face. She closed her eyes and drew in a deep draft of the soft, moist air. Even here, just meters away from her office, the air smelled wild and free. To her left, Hattie's collar jingled. The dog was probably sniffing the base of the ferns and reveling in the smells.

Standish opened her eyes. It wasn't just the fresh air and the comforting gray sky. It wasn't just the beauty of the lichens and the horsetails. She felt more alive on Huginn. There was space enough for her and Hattie to do what they wanted, when they wanted. There was soil and sky instead of sidewalk and manmade structures. Standish hadn't been anyplace as *real* as Huginn since her family stopped taking camping trips, and she'd nearly forgotten how much she craved that authenticity.

"I don't want to get deported," she said aloud.

She set her shoulders. That was what mattered: staying on Huginn. She would take Dewey's warning and stay away from the mystery of Duncan's death. She would ignore the hidden road in Sector 13. She would get to work and do as she was told, because there was no way she was going back to Earth.

She broke into a jog and ran the rest of the way to the office. She was eager enough to get to work she nearly forgot to get her morning cup of coffee. She ran up the stairs at twice her usual speed, pulled out a mug, and filled it as quickly as she could.

"Hi, Kate. We missed you at the memorial service."

"Oh, Julia. Hi. I had a doctor's appointment in Space City. I'm sorry."

"Of course, you didn't really know Rob," Julia said in a mournful tone. Then her face brightened. "Did you hear the news? An operations honcho is coming down from HQ. I guess the company wants to make sure our mill is better prepared in case those ecoterrorists decide to target us."

"I thought I heard something. Do you know when he's getting here?"

Julia squeezed past her to plug in the tea kettle. "Oh, it's a woman. And she's not expected until Thursday or Friday. I bet Brett's going to be super busy this week." She raised an eyebrow.

Standish ignored the obvious dig for information about her sex life. "Is it just the one VIP, or are there others coming, too? I heard that last time the company sent bigshots, it was a whole team of biologists who spent their free time living it up with Duncan and Peter at the Night Light."

Julia scoffed. "Not Peter. He got eighty-six'd from the Night Light two years ago. He, like, punched the owner in the face when he realized they were trying to run some kind of ground scooter fighting ring."

Standish put down her coffee. "Eighty-six'd?"

"Yep. That guy is kind of crazy." Julia tore open a packet of tea. "I can't believe Niketa ever went out with him."

"Well, love is blind, right?" Standish picked up her mug again. "I guess I should head down to my office."

"Oh, yeah. Work." Julia paused. "You know, now that I think about it, I remember those guys. Only one of them was a biologist. He was a real nobody, not even from Space City. A specialist in horsetail cultivation – kind of cute, if you like them nerdy. The rest were operations types. And it wasn't Peter hanging out with them and Duncan. It was Rob

McKidder. I remember, because I swear all those guys were like Rob clones." She sighed. "Rob was so much fun."

"Sounds like you'll really miss him," Standish said.

Julia blinked hard. "Oh gosh, I need a hug."

She threw her arms around Standish, sloshing the coffee in her mug. Standish tried not to grimace. The woman's shoulders shook.

"There, there," Standish murmured. She couldn't help replaying Julia's gossip in her mind.

So there was a connection between the two dead men: the project Duncan had been worried about before he died. Matthias had thought Peter was a part of it, but Songheuser had clearly left him out of the loop.

Peter. She had to tell him about this.

But if she told Peter, she'd be drawn back into the mystery despite Dewey's warning.

She patted Julia on the shoulder, immobilized by her own indecision as much as the accountant's tight embrace.

Peter was just slipping into his field jacket when his hand unit buzzed on his desk. He thought about it ignoring it, but kicked his desk chair out of the way to reach the stupid thing. It was Mark Allen.

"Hey, Mark."

"Peter! Nice to hear you, buddy. Life treating you well?" Mark leaned in, smiling broadly. There were pouches under his eyes and patches of grayish dry skin around the corners of his mouth. Even his shirt looked wrong, the collar unstarched.

The heartiness seemed excessive even for Mark. "Fine," Peter answered cautiously. "What can I do for you? I was just about to head into the field."

"Glad I caught you, then. That's why I'm calling. The company has a new project they'd like you to add to your work in Sector 14, and I'd like you to get started right away."

Peter reached for the chair behind him and slid into it. He reached for his stylus. "OK."

"I'm going to need you to do some small-scale field tests with a new compound I'm sending over on Friday with Victoria Wallace. You know, the operations veep. The compound's designed to be used on horsetails – a pre-treatment to prepare them for cutting."

Peter made an educated guess. "A degassing agent."

"Yep. The Holy Grail of Huginn lumber production: something to improve safety in the woods and hopefully even eliminate the degassing process in the mills. After what happened in Jawbone Flats, I think we're all looking for some better solutions."

"So if the compound's not coming until Friday, what do you want me to start on?"

"I want you to set up the field study sites. I'll send over the specs in a minute, but basically, I need at least a dozen – twenty would be best – discretely sized test plots containing a variety of flora. Everything we've seen in the lab says this stuff is safe enough to bathe in, but I'm not going to hose down the forest in anything that kills rock-eaters and tree scooters. I want this done right." Mark paused. "I *trust* you to run this right, Peter. Some of our people want to rush this through. The mill safety issue alone has the execs champing at the bit."

Peter had a feeling Mark wasn't telling him the whole story – the man looked like squeezed shit. But he knew better than to pry. "You know me, Mark. The science always comes first."

"That's why I picked you." Mark's phony smile dissipated. "Keep me posted, right? On everything." He glanced over his shoulder. "Everything," he added.

"Gotcha."

The call disconnected. Peter sat back in his chair. He had a bad feeling about all of it: the compound, the pressure the company was heaping on Mark, his own role in the whole situation. If the company was going to roll over on anybody, it would be Peter. He was a low man on the totem pole, a field biologist with a reputation for environmentalism. This could all go south in an instant.

Someone knocked on his office door. Peter jumped. For a second, he didn't answer, but the pounding sounded again.

"It's not locked," he called out.

The door swung open. For a second no one entered, and then a very slight girl stepped inside. She closed the door behind her. Peter had never met Olive Whitley, but he had heard enough from Standish and other folks in town to recognize her.

"What brings you to my office, Miss Whitley?"

She looked around the room a moment. Her eyes lit on the terrariums and she hurried toward them. "I like your collection."

"Thanks."

"I kept a terrarium in my room, but my mom made me get rid of it. Everything got moldy so fast, she said it wasn't good for my lungs."

"They're a lot of work," he agreed.

She stooped to see inside the tank with the chrysalis. "You're interested in butterflies, too."

"Is that why you're here? To talk about butterflies?"

"Yes." She turned to face him. Her eyes moved over his face, examining it with the same care and intensity Peter might have brought to a study of a new type of fern. "Chameli gave you the blue ones I found."

"I still have them." He tapped the plastic box on his desk. "They're a great deal like the blues the Believers brought to Huginn, but there are some interesting adaptations. The coloring is the most obvious difference, of course."

"The gold sparkles."

"Yes." He paused. "Do you have any idea what kind of caterpillar they come from?"

She shook her head. "I don't see many caterpillars. They're usually just on the Believer farms. Even for insects, a hundred years is barely enough time to start adapting to this alien an environment."

He laughed. "You sound like a fellow biologist."

"I've been studying." Olive moved to his side, still looking at him carefully. She reached out and put her hand on his arm. "I wasn't sure about you."

"Why not?"

"I had to see for myself, even though Chameli said you were the best person to look into the butterflies." She smiled. "You're a lot like me, I think."

Peter scooted down in his seat so he could meet her eyes. They were darker than his, even, and difficult to read. "What do you mean?"

"I bring Chameli samples of anything I find in the woods that she'd think was beautiful. But you? I could bring you anything, and you'd want it."

He sat back in his chair. He'd been given a compliment, he knew, and probably the best one she could give. "Then we are alike." A thought struck him. "Olive, have you ever seen a caterpillar living in a tree scooter nest?"

Her eyes widened. "You have?"

He nodded his head toward the tank with the chrysalis. "That one did. I don't know why the scooters brought it into their nest, but I think it means something. If I could find more, it might be important."

"It might mean the world is changing," she said, her voice nearly a whisper. "That the differences we brought from Earth are fading away. I think… Huginn is in us, Mr Bajowski. It's hard to explain, but I think it's changing us in ways we never could have imagined." She hurried toward the door.

"Where are you going?"

She turned to look at him. "I'm going to find you more of those caterpillars. Don't worry, Mr Bajowski. I won't let you down."

Goose flesh prickled on Peter's arms. Her words were very nearly what Mark had asked of Peter. He raised a hand to wave at her, but she was already gone.

Muninn's pallid light slid across the surface of the lake, casting the crests of the waves white and the troughs a secretive black. A light rain clung to Standish's exposed skin, and she worked her hands deeper into her pockets, glancing from the lake to the dog. Hattie sniffed at a stick that had washed up on the beach.

The waves lapped softly on the stony shore, but Standish could hear the music of one of the bars just as clearly. It was payday.

She picked up the stick and tossed it for Hattie. The dog gave a puppyish leap and raced after it. There was no one else to see such undignified behavior. The rain kept most people away from the beach, and there was rarely anyone out fishing or boating or just enjoying the waters. Human instinct had brought the settlers to build their little town beside the lake, but the coldness of the waters kept most people turned landward. Standish wondered if she could buy a kayak in Space City. It would be nice to paddle toward the far side of the lake and see things from a new perspective.

A few people actually lived over there. One of the engineers at the mill was working on his dream home, hauling loads of lumber and supplies on a barge he'd built himself. On the weekends, his friends went back and forth with gear and crates of liquor. He'd been working on the house for three years. Given the amount of liquor crossing the lake, it would probably take him at least another three to finish.

Standish threw the stick for Hattie again, this time away from the lake. Muninn was setting. She'd better get to bed soon, or she'd be worthless at work tomorrow. Outside the house, Hattie made sad eyes at her, so Standish let her carry the stick inside. Hattie settled down in front of the sofa to gnaw it as Standish pulled off her boots and slipped into her pajamas.

For a moment, Standish lay in bed, her eyes fixed on the ceiling, certain she would never sleep. She couldn't help thinking about the connection between Rob McKidder and Duncan Chambers. It meant something, and she knew it, even if she didn't want to. She began a tedious breath-counting exercise to distract herself from the situation. Eventually her eyes crept shut.

A whine pulled her out of sleep. The dream hung heavily on her, the same dream she'd had before, the dream of running through a landscape composed of scents and perfumes, the wind ruffling the sensitive hairs on her shaggy white limbs.

She sat up in a rush, pawing at the blanket with hands that felt misshapen and hairy. Who was she? Where was she? Parts of her had gone missing, leaving her body half-unmade. She gasped for air, anxiety rushing to fill in the empty spaces.

Hattie's whimper jolted her into normalcy.

"Hattie? What's wrong?" The room was dark, the light of Muninn entirely gone.

Hattie's nails screeched on the plastic of the front door.

Standish got out of bed. "Hattie?"

The dog whined again. Standish turned on the lamp beside the couch. Hattie did not turn away from the door; if anything, she clawed at it harder and faster. Her whine crept up in pitch.

Standish's mouth had gone dry. "What's out there?" she whispered. She took a few unwilling steps to the dog's side. She pressed her ear to the door.

She heard nothing, just the clack and scrape of the dog's nails. Standish straddled the dog and gripped her paws with her left hand. Hattie squirmed, but Standish held her tight. Standish listened.

A tiny sound came from the other side of the door, the sound of air snuffed up into wet nostrils. Standish pushed the blinds aside a few centimeters and pressed her cheek to the door, squinting into the darkness. The plastic felt horribly flimsy.

The faint light of the street lamp on the corner barely made it to this end of the block. She could just make out the neighbor's UTV, a sleeping elephant in front of their house. A shadow moved beside it and then disappeared into the darkness beyond.

Something thumped against the door.

Standish took a step backward. Hattie whimpered and yanked her paws free of Standish's grip. She jumped up on her hind legs and began to bark, her voice huge in the small space.

"Hattie! Hush!"

As if in response, a deeper bark came from the other side of the door. Hattie threw back her head and howled.

Standish covered her ears and backed away from the dog, nearly falling over the back of the couch when she hit it. She slid to the floor, keeping her ears covered and her eyes fixed on the door. Had it shook in its hinges when that thing out there hit it? Would it hold? She realized how weak and exposed she was and jumped to her feet.

A voice raised in a howl outside, and then another and another. The sound clawed upward in pitch as if it could rip its way into heaven.

And then it stopped.

Standish stood frozen. Nothing. No sounds. No thumping against the door. She wished like hell she had one of those air bolt guns. She waited. And waited.

Then Hattie turned away from the door and pushed her head into Standish's hand.

"Good girl, Hattie. Good girl." She could feel the dog tremble.

During the early twenty-first century, agricultural production was threatened by the near-disappearance of bees, one of the most important terrestrial pollinator species. Habitat destruction, neonicotinoid insecticides, and the mismanagement of commercial hives were all blamed. But all of these were symptoms of a much larger disease: agriculture and landscape management based on industrial strategies.

Living things cannot be treated like cogs in a machine.

— "WE ARE ALL GREEN," GreenOne

pamphlet, anonymous

CHAPTER FIFTEEN

Huginn, Day 186

The house is so very, very empty. Matthias and the others haven't come back yet, and those of us waiting drift like boats without anchors. We gather together for meals and huddle close around the tables. The soup I make now is as thin and salty as my tears.

Cheyenne, weak as she is, helps me tend the big communal field after our other duties have been attended to. Half the fields have been abandoned for lack of hands to work them. We buried Mrs Morris this morning, Orrin's ever-smiling mother. One of the Vogels painted the cross for her grave in all the colors of the rainbow. If she looks down on us from Heaven – if she's not too busy playing with little Elka and singing with Pappy – Mrs Morris would be happy to see it.

Vonda came to the funeral. It was the first time I saw her outside since the baby died. She looks strangely well after all that rest, better than she had looked even before the baby. The way she looks makes me want to check the food stores and count the livestock.

She invited me to come sit with her after the funeral, but I couldn't bring myself to do it. I'd rather sit in the silence of my own house.

It is abysmally empty there. I know Matthias is doing his duty, and that is a comfort to me, but I cry for Soolie night and day. Oh dear Lord, why did I have to wake him to this nightmare? Matthias said I should break his neck, but I couldn't. I begged Doc Sounds to do it, but out in the woods, where I couldn't see or hear. Doc took him way, way out, but when he went to bring the axe down on Soolie's head, Soolie ran away from him, and Doc couldn't catch him.

I couldn't put Soolie down mercifully, and now he will starve out there or die of poison. Because I am a coward.

There is no truer animal in all creation than a dog. A dog's heart beats so steadfastly you could set the clock of the universe to it. If he can, I know Soolie will try to come back to me. No matter how sick, no matter how hungry, he will follow his heart home.

But one thing has come out of this suffering. As I've prayed alone, I've realized I must not blame God or Matthias or our church for any of this. Our plans were made in good faith. It was Songheuser Corporation that left our rations, Songheuser that allowed Vonda to get inside that cryo tube even though she was pregnant, Songheuser that starved my Soolie for their own sick profits.

I pray that God will punish the Songheuser Corporation for its wrongs.

"Hey, Belinda." Peter dropped onto the last stool at the bar, rubbing at bits of lichen that had crept under his collar. He'd managed to set up one of the test sites today, a nice patch of mixed small plants and Christ's fingers. He had some other sites in mind, but the diversity in this one site would really please Mark. It felt good to be sitting down after hiking and stooping and squatting all day.

The guy on the seat beside Peter picked up his beer and headed toward the back room.

Belinda turned to face Peter. "Surprised to see you in here. It's been a while." She picked up a pint glass. "Beer?"

"That'd be great. Any chili tonight?" He was too hungry to imagine heading home to cook.

She hesitated just a moment. "Just burgers tonight. The cook took a trip to Space City. Sorry to let you down."

Peter watched her pour his draft. Her mouth was set tight, her shoulders, too. "What's going on, Belinda?"

She slid the ale across the bar. "Nothing. Just a busy night tonight. Some guys from the mill having some kind of meeting in the back room, drinking faster than I can switch out kegs." She gave the back corner a significant look. "You're probably better off eating at home."

Peter leaned back on his stool, trying to see into the other room. The neon beer signs did little to illuminate the space, and the pool table was uncharacteristically empty. He could hear plenty of voices, though. The establishment was packed, folks squeezed in at the bar and crowded around every table. He saw Julia from accounting and Niketa ensconced at a booth in the corner; for a second Julia's eyes caught his, and then they whipped away. The only open seat in the joint was the stool beside Peter.

"I've been coming here for four years," he reminded her. "I drove you to Space City when you had to get stitches after that big bar fight. You can't bullshit me."

She dropped a bowl of peanuts in front of him. "Keep your voice down."

He lowered his voice. "What's going on?"

She wiped at the counter, her voice practically a whisper. "That guy they caught at Jawbone Flats? He's been talking. He said he knew Duncan."

"Everybody knew Duncan."

"They were… together. *Together* together. And this guy, he wasn't just some random mill hand or a logger with a grudge. He worked for Songheuser in engineering. He still owed the company half his shuttle ticket, lived in company housing, helped organize the office holiday party. And all the time, he was planning to destroy the mill."

"What does that have to do with me?"

"Everyone knew you were still hung up on Duncan. Niketa told the whole town."

"So now people think I killed Duncan because I was jealous?"

Someone waved her over for drinks and she hurried to pour pints. Peter cracked open a peanut, the salt rasping at his worn fingertips. He wasn't sure what was worse, the sheriff saying Duncan killed himself or the town gossips saying he'd done it. *Someone* had killed Duncan. Someone needed to be brought to justice.

"I'm surprised you'd show your face in here, Pete."

Peter squeezed the peanut shell tight in his fist. Then he turned around, his face schooled into pleasantness. "Joe. How's it going tonight?"

Joe wasn't alone. A group of mill workers stood behind him, most of them unfamiliar to Peter. He saw Paul Wu, out of his deputy's uniform, standing at the back of the group, looking anywhere but Peter's face.

"Paul. I didn't realize you'd made it back from Jawbone Flats. Glad you wrapped things up out there."

Paul didn't answer. Joe took a step closer to Peter. "Paul's been telling us a lot about the case. Like the fact that bastard wasn't working alone. Creep hasn't spilled any names, but it's just a matter of time."

"I've never been to Jawbone Flats," Peter said, feeling the peanut shell crackling in his palm. "So don't go getting any ideas."

"Maybe you haven't done anything yet, but that doesn't mean you're not planning something."

Peter slid off his stool. "I'm too hungry to listen to this shit." He squeezed his way past Joe and the closest of his thugs, trying not to hurry, to keep his breathing easy, his eyes fixed on the front door. Then the toe of a boot struck his shin and he went sprawling, hitting the ground hard.

Joe's knees popped and crackled as he hunkered down beside him. "Ever think this town ain't the right place for you? Not a lot of other fag boys these days. And if you think we're going to let you fuck with our mill the way your limp-wristed buddy did in Jawbone Flats, you've got another think coming."

Peter didn't say a word. He got to his feet and finished walking to the front door. He wanted to kick it open, but instead he pushed it quietly and stepped outside into the rain. The droplets soaked his hair and ran down his face in rivulets.

He kept walking. His feet knew the way even if he'd left his brain behind him back on that bar stool. The mud sucked at his shoes but he didn't slow down. There was one place he could go in this town, one person who had claimed to be his friend, and by God he could use a friend right now. The porch light was off, but a warm glow showed between the slats of the window blinds.

The rain had saturated his clothes and now the cold seeped into his flesh. His energy was gone, burned off in his struggle to keep his anger under control. He had to rest his forehead against the door as he knocked at it. "Standish." He knocked harder.

He couldn't hear anything, not even the dog's nails on the plastic floor. "Standish!"

The light flicked off.

Then he noticed the scooter parked at the end of the block. It was Brett Takas's.

There was no point knocking any longer.

•••

After another tense workday spent gossiping about the threat of ecoterrorism, a crowd of people blocked the doorway at Heinrich's. This went beyond the usual mad rush of Songheuser day shifters struggling out of their raingear; half the town had to be cleaning off their boots and looking for an open seat. Standish peered through the horde and managed to catch sight of Lou and Brett at a booth. Hattie made a pained sound as someone's heel stomped on her foot.

They finally made it to the bar, Standish stroking Hattie and feeling bad. She just couldn't sleep at her place alone, and the thought of walking there in the dark made her skin crawl. It was easier to just eat at the bar and let Brett keep her company at night.

"Busy night!" Julia squeezed in next to Standish. "I think they're short-handed."

"Yeah, I don't see Belinda anywhere. I thought she worked weeknights."

Julia shrugged. "I saw her on my way here. It looked like she was hiking on that trail behind the motor pool. Leather bird watching, maybe."

"Leather bird watching?" Standish raised an eyebrow. "In the dark?"

"How should I know? I get the impression she's into that kind of hippy crap. I've seen her behind the office two or three times with a spotting scope, looking like some amateur biologist or something. That Chameli Patel is into that stuff, too."

The bartender shouted something at Julia and she ordered a cocktail and burger. She was immediately distracted by the man beside her, who complimented her drink choice. Standish tapped her on the shoulder.

"Like what?" Standish shouted.

Julia waved her off. The bartender caught Standish's eye, and she placed her order. She tried to catch Julia's attention again, but she was too entwined with the man beside her, studying his hand unit like it contained the answer to the universe.

Now, hours later, the conversation replayed itself in Standish's head. Ever since last week's incident with the dogs at her door, she'd found herself waking in the early hours of the morning, her brain suddenly activated. One night she found herself worrying over every detail of the night they'd discovered Rob McKidder's body. Last night she had merely mulled over her conversation with Dewey in Space City. Tonight, it was apparently Julia and Belinda's turn to haunt her brain. Why the hell was Belinda hanging out behind the Songheuser office building? If she was some kind of nature nut, she'd surely know there were better places to watch leather birds.

Grumpy, Standish slipped out of bed. Hattie sat up from her place beside the door, but Brett didn't move a muscle. Standish reached for her clothes, tossed on the chair in the corner. Her belt jingled and she froze. Brett had been working double shifts all week. It wouldn't be fair to wake him.

He rolled over but kept sleeping. Standish crept into the main room and eased the door shut behind her. She hurried to the kitchen, stepping into her underwear and pants as she went. Ever since the night Peter had stood on her porch, knocking like he was planning to break down her door, she'd been crashing at Brett's house. She was careful to let him think it was all just happenstance, the two of them sucked together by coincidence and bedroom heat – she didn't want him to do something stupid like offer her a drawer in his bureau. But she was glad he'd been amenable to some nighttime companionship.

Peter trying to suck her back into their investigation. Dogs trying to break down her door. She couldn't handle her place right now.

Brett's kitchen was neat and stylish, like the rest of his little house, and her to-go box from Heinrich's was the only thing in his fridge that didn't look like health food. She thought of the produce wilting in her own fridge and felt a pang of guilt. Maybe she'd bring it over here and get Brett to cook for her. She snagged the remains of the club sandwich and then headed out the front door.

"Your breakfast is at work," she reminded Hattie. "We'll be there soon."

The dog's expression was disapproving. Hattie didn't like Brett's place, where she was exiled to the floor and she had to take her bathroom breaks in the muddy side yard instead of along the beach.

"This is all temporary," Standish reminded her. "Just till I can order a stronger front door." She ruffled the dog's ears and then led her toward the comforting blandness of the office, where two security guards circled on every shift and cameras watched benignly over the exits.

"Morning, Kate." Joe Holder's voice came from the shadows at the top of the stairs.

"You're up early, Joe." It was barely six a.m.; Wodin still sat on the horizon like a big gray blimp. "And you know I prefer 'Standish.'"

He chuckled. "You spacers. Stiff as the military." He gave a little grunt and she saw him stand up, rubbing at his lower back. A toolbox sat on the top stair beside him. "This door's been sticking."

"Don't you have people to do that for you, boss?"

"Sometimes, a man has to do for himself. I thought of a few last-minute fixes to get the place ship-shape for Victoria."

"Victoria?"

"Chief of Operations Victoria Wallace." His grin spread. "*My* boss. We worked together back on Ganymede, oh, ten years ago. She's the one that brought me here."

"I forgot we had a VIP coming in today." She reached for the door handle. "Seems like a pretty big deal."

"The biggest thing we've had here in Canaan Lake since they put in the sawmill."

The door closed behind her, but she still heard his self-satisfied chuckle. She had never met anyone so easily pleased by their own wit. She was glad Holder's work kept him out of his office most of the time. If she had to listen to that laugh on the other side of the wall all day, she'd go bugnuts.

Standish checked the coffee pot – just sludge from the night guards – and popped her sandwich in the microwave while she filled a pitcher of water to take to her office. The kitchenette was still quiet, the hall leading to the main floor offices dark. She started another pot of coffee, took the sandwich and the water downstairs, and filled Hattie's water dish right away. The bag of kibble sat on top of the second desk, the one that should have been Standish's. The debris of Duncan's former existence held the bag upright.

Once again, the sight of all that mess needled Standish. She might not care if her desk was dinged up or that her couch was covered in dog hair, but she liked to know where all her shit was. A stack of old work requests slid off onto the floor as she lifted the kibble.

"Damn it," she growled. She gave Hattie an extra measure of duck-flavored mystery meats and dropped the bag on the floor. "Fucking Duncan."

She plopped onto the floor next to the dog food bag. "Fucking Duncan," she repeated, pleased with the near rhyme. She picked up the work orders, which belonged in the filing cabinet on the other side of the room. She'd never worked at a station that kept paper backups, but power outages were common enough here to necessitate the antiquated system.

This bunch looked nearly old enough to be shredded – most of them were three or four years old, their paper yellowed and faintly greasy, the same cheap shit the rest of the universe used. Horsetail wood made paper too fine for ordinary mortals.

She put aside the oldest papers, which she really could shred, and noticed a brighter white poking out from the midst of the others. This page couldn't be more than a few months old, but a bit of sticky resin, the kind of goo that came out of broken Christ's fingers, had welded it to the page above. She pulled carefully.

It looked like an ordinary work order, although some of the text was obscured by the fibers left behind from the other piece of paper. She found the date – February 1st, just four months ago. Rob McKidder's flourish of a signature nearly jumped off the bottom of the page. Most people didn't sign their name clearly enough to read, but he certainly had, and just the letters of his name made her skin feel prickly. A dead man had signed this, had sent it to another dead man. They had lived and worked and then one day they had simply stopped being, and now all that remained of them were bits of paper and their markers in the cemetery.

She smoothed the work order and looked at it more closely. It felt like a sort of memorial, studying what he had ordered for the company. This wasn't his last request, but it was probably the last one that had passed through her office.

"Fiberoptic line, fiberoptic transceiver, three portable generators," – the next chunk was obscured with sticky stuff – *"seven closed-circuit radios, and whatever sundries necessary."* She looked up from the paper. "Necessary for what, Hattie? This is the kind of crap you'd need for a new field station."

There was a note at the bottom, smeared graphite in Duncan's spiky handwriting. *"Clear out by April 15th, all except conduit (12 - 13)."*

The dates were Huginn dates, not the official company calendar, which counted days by fixed Earth hours; twenty-six day months made things convenient, if inaccurate, for old-fashioned types. At any rate, she could probably just recycle this note.

But Standish held on to the work order, not looking at it, just thinking, letting her fingers play over the paper. 12 and 13. She remembered the clearing in Sector 13, big enough for a field station, and a road good enough to serve it.

Clear out by April 15th.

Why would someone build a field station and just tear it down? She folded the paper and stuck it in her shirt pocket. Her hand rested on it for moment, the crinkled paper hidden beneath the fabric, just as it had been hidden in the mess left on Duncan's desk.

A knock at the door made her start. She clambered to her feet as the door swung open.

"Standish, you've got to meet Victoria." Niketa beamed at her. "Joe and I insist."

People were piling in, filling the space with chatter. Some were Canaan Lake folks she recognized, but others must have come from Space City, and Niketa hurried to introduce them in a barrage of names that flowed over Standish without collecting in her brain. Joe Holder's chuckle moved down the hallway and he squeezed inside, a blond woman at his heels.

"Kate Standish is our new communications manager, Victoria. She's been a terrific addition to the team."

Standish realized she was still sitting and scrambled to her feet. "Ms Wallace. It's an honor to have you here."

The woman stepped around Holder. She was older than she'd looked at a distance; the blond tones in her hair artfully subdued the strands of silver. Every last inch of her was coiffed and polished, but she'd made no effort to erase the lines around her eyes and mouth. In her blue pantsuit, she looked more military than society, and Standish knew that was just the impression Victoria Wallace wished to cast.

"You've been in communications a long time, haven't you, Standish? I've heard good things from the folks at Goddard and Pescano stations."

Standish had almost forgotten she'd worked on Pescano. Most of the things that had happened to her after Goddard and before Earth had passed in a haze of tequila.

Standish found herself shaking Wallace's hand. If Holder was Standish's boss and this woman was his, then ultimately Wallace was the one signing Standish's paycheck. She hoped like hell her hand didn't have kibble crumbs all over it.

"Let me show you the motor pool," Holder said, and the herd squeezed back out the door, their voices rumbling in the low-ceilinged hallway.

Niketa cleared her throat. "Standish, I'd like to talk to you about something."

They were alone.

"Sure, shoot."

Niketa eased the door shut. "I'm sure you understand that the safety of COO Wallace is our number one concern right now."

Standish nodded.

"I know you spend a lot of time off campus. The whole community sends you work orders."

"Well, we are the only communications provider out here."

Tension came off Niketa in waves. Standish cleared her throat and tried to look attentive.

"I like your sense of humor, Standish. I also like you. I know you've been through a lot in the past five years, and that the company has really stepped up to help you through it."

Standish thought of Dewey's warning and felt her own tension level shoot up. "I've been lucky like that."

"I'm just asking you to keep an eye on things out there. If you hear anything – if you see anything out of the ordinary–"

"I got it. If I see something, say something. The whole

planet's worried about ecoterrorists."

"Moon," Niketa corrected. "Huginn's not a planet."

The pedantry stiffened Standish's back. "Right."

Niketa reached for the door knob and paused, turning back to meet Standish's eyes. "And Standish, if you could pay special attention to Peter Bajowski, that would be a great help."

She closed the door behind her.

Standish stood in place for a moment. Her ribs felt tight. It was hard to breathe. It was one thing when the town gossip started talking about Peter, but when the company wanted her to play the spy? And they had an axe to grind for Peter? For a second she thought about sticking her head out the door and telling Niketa to go to hell, but she'd have to breathe to do that.

Hattie nudged her in the leg, and Standish dropped to her knees. Hattie pushed her face close to Standish's, sniffing at her nose and mouth, her big dark eyes concerned. "Shit, shit, shit," Standish whispered.

There was right and there was wrong and there was self-preservation, and she didn't know how to make them all come together. It was like one of those build-it-yourself kits, the little ones that had first taught her about electronics and wiring – they had all the parts, but sometimes, no matter how closely she read the directions, she couldn't figure out how to put them together. She could stand up to Songheuser and lose everything, or she could just let them keep steamrolling over good people like the fuckers they were.

She drew in deep breaths of doggish air until she could stand up again. She didn't know what to do. She didn't know who to trust. But she did know that there was a box in her house that Duncan Chambers had tried to hide, and it was full of secrets Songheuser didn't want told.

No species evolves in a vacuum. All living organisms develop in relationship with the beings around them, and those relationships are often complex. Rarely do two species have merely symbiotic or parasitic interactions, or serve simply as predator or prey.

— ECOLOGY: AN INTRODUCTORY TEXT, Dr Peter Bajowsk

CHAPTER SIXTEEN

Peter got an early start on Saturday, heading out to Sector 12 with his breakfast in his pocket and mug of coffee wedged between the window and the dash. It went without saying that security and ops had all the good UTVs. He hoped like hell he didn't spill coffee all over his lap and cook his nuts off. This week had been bad enough without personal injury.

Once he passed the last of the houses, he unwrapped a granola bar and bit off half. This whole week, he'd felt as if every eye in town had been fixed on him, waiting for him to make some kind of mistake or just crack under the pressure. His only comfort was the fact that Sheriff Vargas hadn't sent for him yet. Local gossip might have him pegged as a terrorist and a murderer, but there didn't seem to be any kind of proof connecting him to the crimes.

He should have never dated Niketa Shawl. He'd fit in just fine here before he'd taken up with that woman; he was just another company guy, the sort of unmemorable figure that was welcomed on the softball team but forgotten for Happy Hour invites. Stuffy, stodgy, uninteresting Peter Bajowski. He couldn't imagine why a classy chick like Niketa had ever gotten interested in him in the first place, let alone freaked out about commitment and forced him to dump her in the ugliest manner possible.

The road came to an end and he parked the UTV. He finished the coffee. Of course he had a hunch what Niketa had seen in him: his degree from Oxford. Once people learned about it, they made plenty of assumptions about the size of his bank account and the gilt on his family tree. Nobody looked at an Oxford diploma and thought of a working class family with Guatemalan coffee farmers and Polish immigrants as their roots, even though Peter's last name ought to give away half of that. Niketa had wanted those old-Earth connections, all the polish and class she'd never gotten bouncing from Luna to Ganymede to Huginn.

His boots shushed over fallen horsetail fronds, and his thoughts about Earth and gossip began to fade into the back of his mind, then vanish altogether. None of it mattered when he was out here. He wasn't in the field to test Songheuser's compound – he'd gotten that taken care of yesterday afternoon, applying the stuff to two test sites.

No, this was his own project, because he realized that nothing else really mattered besides his research. Learning how this forest worked. Nailing down what connected all these wild and weird species. Back on Earth, even as a child he'd had a solid grasp of the water and nitrogen cycles, but in a hundred years no one had studied what made the nutrients go round here on Huginn. The leather birds ate the tree scooters. The tree scooters ate the lichens and horsetail fronds. Or at least that's what everyone assumed. Peter had never seen a tree scooter nibbling on a horsetail. In fact, he'd never seen one eat. He ought to start more terrariums and study the creatures more closely. But which species to select and what to put in their tank were difficult details.

The ground began to slope upward, the bedrock showing through the thin soil in some places. The tendril of a stream followed the folds of the stone, although in places the Christ's fingers and rain palms obscured the waterway entirely. Even here, where it rained for over forty-three of the year's forty-eight weeks, water drew life to itself.

Up ahead a huge candelabra tree had toppled over, and Peter hurried forward, excited.

He scrambled over a limb the thickness of his waist, noting the healthy canopy, the still-green pseudo ferns clinging to its branches and the smaller orchid-like plants clinging to the seams where branches met with the trunk. The life forms hidden in this tree hadn't had a chance to wither from their fall from the clouds; they couldn't have landed on the relatively dry ground more than a day ago. There was still a chance he'd find tree scooter nests in the root bole.

Where the tree had once spread itself into the thin clay soil, it was as if a great hand had scooped out the earth. He hopped down into the hollow, aware of the pungent smell of broken roots and crushed vegetation.

Fuzzy pink tree scooters scurried up the walls of the pit, pausing occasionally to grab hunks of the white strands of mycelium in the exposed soil. He picked up one of the little creatures. This was a medium-sized scooter, about the size of a mouse, with a pair of glossy black eyes and a many-segmented body covered with spiky fur. Its stomach was only lightly fuzzed. It twitched one of its slender, delicate antennae.

At least one entomologist had theorized that the tree scooters lived in a hive-like society with the kind of rigid caste system seen in ants and bees. The same species showed morphological differences that supported such a notion – the kinds of scooters seen away from their nest usually had short, thick antennae and densely furred bodies. This one must perform some sort of duty inside the nest.

It wriggled in his grip and he set it carefully on a rock. It rubbed its forelegs over its head and flanks as if to wash away the feeling of his fingers and then hurried on its way.

Excited, he followed the line of scooters to a fist-sized opening in the wall. Several of the delicate-feelered scooters zipped out the opening. They paused when they felt the carbon dioxide of his breath upon their bodies and then moved quickly away.

A larger scooter emerged, moving more slowly as it used its foreleg to hold something green on its back. Peter leaned in closer and realized there was a small, motionless caterpillar tucked into the tufts of the scooter's fur. He was almost certain it was the same variety as the one in his office. The pattern of spots on its side was familiar; the soft, moist body identical. For a moment, Peter thought the caterpillar might be dead, a meal to be moved to the new nest. But then he saw the legs twitch a little, digging their little hooked feet deeper into the tree scooter's fur.

It wasn't being carried. It was *riding* the tree scooter with the scooter's help.

Another scooter came out of the hole, similarly burdened with a caterpillar, and then another. Another burdened scooter emerged more slowly, trudging along until it came to a broken bit of root. Then the scooter stopped and held still. To Peter, who could rarely resist anthropomorphizing animals despite his training, it looked totally wiped out.

He held his breath as the smaller tree scooter approached the tired-looking one. Here was his chance to observe tree scooter societal behavior. He trained his hand unit's camera on the pair.

The new arrival pressed its first two pairs of legs against the body of the green caterpillar, its legs flickering up and down the insect's sides. Peter zoomed in with his camera.

A green bubble, tiny, no larger than a pin head, began to extrude from the caterpillar's back end. The little scooter whisked the bubble away and carried it to the tired scooter's mouth. For a second, nothing happened. Then a black threadlike tongue shot out of the larger scooter's mouth. The bubble vanished into its mouth. Then both tree scooters hurried on their way, the larger moving with noticeably more energy.

Peter sat back on his heels, awed. This kind of behavior happened all the time on Earth. Ants kept aphids for just this purpose, and if he remembered right, there were even some species of butterfly that kept a similar arrangement with ants. But these weren't ants.

And more importantly, this wasn't Earth.

Somehow, a symbiotic relationship had developed between two species from entirely different solar systems, creatures that until now he had assumed didn't share enough biological similarities to serve even as prey and predator. He was seeing something entirely new, something that no human had witnessed in the whole galaxy. He was seeing the possibility of Earth creatures and Huginn creatures finding a way to live together in something like harmony.

He reached in his field bag for a plastic specimen box. He had to find out what these caterpillars turned into. If he was lucky – really lucky – he might have found Olive's butterflies.

Standish rapped on the Whitleys' door, noticing more of the details than the last time she'd stopped by. A little wreath hung on the battered plastic door, a bunch of twisted grasses with dried lichens and flowers woven into it. She wondered if it was Olive's work. The door swung open.

"Kate." Melissa Whitley looked relieved. "So glad you made it out so quickly. Today's the day I send videos to my parents. They're so hungry for news about Olive."

"That's grandparents for you."

"They love her, but they don't really understand her. I think the videos help." Melissa hesitated. "Olive isn't like other kids they know."

"She's awfully mature for her age."

"Yes, that's part of it. The other part is… I don't know. Sometimes I think Olive is more connected to the trees and the ferns out there than she is to people. Sometimes I catch her talking to them."

Standish shifted uncomfortably. "I think it's normal for kids her age to identify with plants and animals."

She didn't want Melissa Whitley to think of Olive as a weirdo. The kid was strange enough, she needed her mom to have her back, to see her as a *kid*, even if the rest of the world told her she was some kind of nature spirit. Hell, Standish herself sometimes thought Olive seemed more like an elf than a normal kid. But that didn't mean her mom should.

"Maybe that's it. I just can't help thinking I shouldn't have read her all those fairy stories when she was little. When we first moved here, she missed her grandparents, she was afraid of all the trees and the rain. I had this book of Swedish fairy tales, and I'd just read them to her over and over, because they made her happy." Melissa paused. "But after a few months, it was like she started turning into something from the stories. She got so pale and so focused on plants and animals. She wanted to be outside all the time, wandering wherever she wants.

"Sometimes I look at her and I think being here on Huginn has made her more like a little *vätte* than a little girl."

"A *vätte*?"

"A forest spirit."

"Look, moving is hard for kids. She liked the stories, that's all. And she got excited about living here. It's not some magical transformation. She's a kid."

"You don't get it. When I say Olive changed, I don't just mean that her behavior changed. She *physically* changed to look like the illustrations in her books. Olive had blonde hair and blue eyes before we moved here. She had freckles. Now look at her."

Standish opened her mouth and closed it. Olive did look... odd. Her white hair and near-black eyes were strange for anyone. But what Melissa was talking about was impossible. Standish had a rational thought. "Hair color can change in response to minerals in the water and eyes are sometimes affected by the quality of light. And cryo – well, that's got to have some kind of effect on a kid's body."

Melissa gave a weak laugh. "That's true. Maybe I'm reading more into this than I ought to. Maybe she would have turned out like this even if we'd stayed home."

It was past time to change the subject. "Where's home?"

"Ganymede. My folks went out there for the mines, but wound up in the greenhouses. You want a coffee?"

Standish couldn't imagine thinking of Ganymede's domes as home. There was no atmosphere there to block out the stars. And given the misty look in Melissa's eye she got from talking about the place, Standish had a feeling she wanted to continue that line of the conversation. "No thanks – I want to wrap this up so I can take the rest of the day off."

"Oh, gosh, I'm so sorry. I would have waited to report it until–"

Standish cut her off. "It's no problem, Melissa. I was looking for some overtime, and I'd rather help out your family than catch up on my filing."

"Are you sure?"

Olive's mother looked so concerned Standish had to laugh. "Yes, really. How long has the cable been out?"

"Since late evening, I guess. When I came back from work, Judd had left me a note. He already checked the box and the line running along the side of the house and didn't see anything."

"Well, I'll check it again, just to be sure. But it's probably something farther down the line." On Earth or even one of the stations, rats were the biggest culprits in cable outages. But most of the problems she'd seen on Huginn came from lines eroded by lichen or from plain human stupidity, like the time the mill's groundskeeper cut the south office block's cable bundle with his weed eater. The idiot was lucky he hadn't electrocuted himself.

Melissa led Standish and Hattie around the side of the house. This was the last property on the cable line running down this street; since no one else had called in for service, the problem had to be located fairly close by. Standish slid on her thick work gloves and smiled at her guide. "It'll probably take me a few minutes to check the line. I'll keep you posted."

Standish followed the cable from its entrance point in the house and then down to the ground, where it ran into a sturdy black plastic pipe. On Earth, most home lines ran to the roof and then out to a utility pole. Here on Huginn, half-assery prevailed. If she had a dollar for every wire conduit some construction worker had just dropped on the dirt, she'd have given herself a hefty raise already. If she didn't find the problem at the juncture with the street's main cable line, then she'd have to pull the wires out of the conduit and deep clean the whole thing. Not her favorite activity, but at least she wouldn't be doing it in some dirty alley or air duct. Even in the rain, Canaan Lake was the prettiest place she'd ever worked.

"Stay put, Hattie." The conduit ran down a slope of fist-sized rocks, most covered in rock-eater lichen and shrouded in button ferns, before dropping into the ditch beside the road.

An engine growled, and Standish waited for a log truck to roar past, its bed loaded with slender horsetail trees from Sector 11. It was second-growth timber, the land heavily managed by Songheuser, and according to the gossip she'd heard at Heinrich's, some of the most productive land on Huginn. She jumped into the ditch, where a knee-high metal column announced the underground cable line junction. It stood cockeyed, one side bashed in. The wires lay on the ground, their ends ripped through.

"What the hell?" She knelt beside the column. It was sturdy metal, not plastic, and it must have taken a serious hit to smash it so badly. She'd need to bring a new one from HQ; she didn't keep one in the rig. She'd never seen one demolished before.

She could hear the grumble of another log truck's engine working to get up the grade from the intersection with the Sector 11 logging road, but kept her attention focused on the problem at hand. She could make a temporary fix with wire clips, but she'd need to fix the box eventually. At least Melissa Whitley would be able to send her parents those pictures of Olive tonight.

A horn blasted, and Standish looked up to see a battered UTV crawling toward her, a log truck practically eating its back end. The truck's horn sounded again. The UTV eased to the shoulder of the road, and the log truck whipped around it. They were always in a hurry to get to the mill, Standish mused, and grinned to see the driver hastily straighten out the rig before it entered the next turn.

Then Hattie let out a volley of terrified barking as the back end of the log truck slid sideways. Gravel sprayed into Standish's face. Even as she threw herself backward, she knew there wasn't enough room in the ditch to save her.

The sharp smell of fresh cut horsetail overpowered everything else as the truck's bed slid over the edge of the road.

And then silence.

"Jesus! Standish, are you OK?"

Hattie barked louder. Standish sat up. Her face stung, and

the side of her head hurt – she must have hit it on something, maybe the cable box. The log truck rounded the next corner and disappeared, its driver blithely unaware that he'd nearly come off the road.

"That asshole nearly killed you." Peter offered her his hands and pulled her up. "You've got some cuts. I have a first aid kit in the rig."

"I guess I know how this cable box got smashed." Standish rubbed her hip, which hurt too. "I'll have to move it away from this corner."

"You're hurt, you're bleeding, and you're worried about the cable box?" Peter shook his head. His rig sat half-on, half-off the road, the driver side door still open. He climbed in, closed the door, and came out the passenger's side with the red first aid box. "Let me see your face."

"It's seen worse."

He soaked a gauze pad with something acrid and began swiping at her cheek. "I don't think anything's embedded in your skin, but Jesus! That's damn close to your eye." He swiped again, his touch gentle.

She looked over his shoulder. The seat of his UTV was covered in plastic boxes, most of them filled with plants, dirt, and even a few pink tree scooters. "Don't you have the day off?"

"I could ask you the same." He pulled the wrapper off a bandage. "I'm doing a little research for Olive. She's found these weird butterflies and asked me to check them out."

"You know Olive?"

Hattie jumped into the ditch and licked Standish's hand. She began sniffing around Peter's crotch, and he pushed her nose away. "Too friendly, dog. Too friendly." He leaned in to stick the bandage on Standish's cheek, smiling a little. "Yeah, she came to the office. Cool kid."

Damn, he was nice. Half the town might be trying to

persuade her to cut him off, but she had never met someone so easy to like. She pressed down on the edges of the bandage and wondered how to tell him she was sorry she'd been avoiding him without sounding like an asshole.

Because she was suddenly desperately sorry. People were spreading rumors about him, that he was an ecoterrorist, that he murdered Duncan in a jealous fit, that he was a troublemaker with a chip on his shoulder. She knew he was none of those things, and yet she'd done nothing to clear his name.

She would have never treated Dewey like this.

Standish took a deep breath. If Dewey was right about Songheuser, then Standish was about to risk her job and her place on Huginn to help Peter Bajowski.

"Well," he said, his voice suddenly awkward. She knew from the sudden stiffness of his face that he was thinking of the night he'd come knocking on her door. "We should get out of this ditch before another log truck comes around."

She nodded. And then added, quickly, before she could talk herself out of it: "You know Matthias Williams, right?"

"The Believer guy?"

"I'll just be another minute with this cable box. Go to his place and I'll meet you there."

Peter leaned back against the side of his rig. "Why?"

"Because he wants to figure out who killed Duncan, and if we all work together, we might solve this case."

A log truck rumbled by, rocking the UTV. The specimen boxes shifted on their seat, and Peter caught one as it toppled. Standish leaned closer to see it. A pink tree scooter huddled on a clutch of moss, a soft green caterpillar tucked in beside it.

"They're friends," he explained.

She smiled at him. "Like us."

He got in the rig. "I'll see you at Matthias's. Don't take too long."

•••

Huginn, Day 195

It's been two weeks with no sign of the men, and today I slaughtered the very last cow. Its eyelids were pale pink with anemia, and it had cuts all over its legs. Vonda said she saw leather birds hounding it at night, but some wicked, suspicious part of me wonders if one of us has been at them. The cuts look so straight, so smooth. Like they were made with a knife.

I bashed it over the head with a sledge hammer and Mei Lin cut its throat and we knew we should save all the blood for sausage, but we could not help but press our mouths to the cut and let the hot stuff run down into our bellies. But it felt so strange to have a full stomach after all this time. It didn't feel good or bad, only *strange*, as if my body had forgotten what to do with real food. Then we were both so tired we had to drop down in the mud and just rest.

The leather birds got closer and closer and the rain soaked through all my clothes, but I couldn't get up. I'm so tired of working and being hungry and scared and alone. I'm so tired.

No one sleeps at night. Something moves out there in the dark, something howls. It's the dogs, of course. All the dogs we killed so that we could live.

Peter parked his UTV in front of the horsetail-wood gate, and sat there wondering what he was getting into. He had never really talked to Matthias Williams before, had avoided the Believers of Canaan Lake as much as possible. He supposed their hypocritical stance on technology rubbed him the wrong way. They'd been happy to use science and technology to expand their agricultural empire to the far side of the galaxy, but now they just pranced around on their horses, undermining the town's work to rejoin the twenty-third century.

Their rules looked pretty self-serving from where he stood.

A small cart, pulled by a glossy black horse, stopped beside him. A vaguely Asian woman in Believer dress tilted her head so she could see into the driver's side window. "Are you here to help with the curing shed, too, good sir?"

He struggled for an answer. "I'm meeting a friend here? We're supposed to… help Matthias with… something."

She laughed. "Sounds like you got yourself roped into a work party. Come on out of that UTV and ride in with me. It's easier to show up with someone else, isn't it?" She opened the gate and led the horse through, then got back in, waiting for him with a kind smile.

Peter got out of the vehicle and climbed up into the cart. "I'm Peter Bajowski. It is nice to meet such a friendly face."

"Mei Lin Vogel. It's nice to meet you, Dr Bajowski. I've heard you're Canaan Lake's resident expert on botany."

Her voice, educated and friendly, clashed with his ideas of Believer women. He'd expected them to be housebound, meek little creatures, sewing every moment they weren't chasing their passel of children. But this woman seemed worldly enough.

He glanced over at her and saw humor flicker in her eyes as if she knew what he was thinking about and laughing at him for it.

She stopped the cart in front of Matthias's barn. A painting in primary colors looked down on them, a bold red circle nearly filled with a yellow sun and an assortment of multicolored birds, flowers and butterflies. "That hex needs repainting," she murmured. "I'll ask Shane about it."

"That… hex?"

"Oh," she waved a deprecating hand, "just one of those folk customs we've grown attached to. The Vogel family brought their old Pennsylvania traditions of painting lucky charms on outbuildings. It's no offense to God, we figure, since it's not as if we believe they're some kind of magic. The Good Book warns us that 'Thou shall not suffer a witch to live,' but it does encourage celebrating the traditions of the forefathers."

"Mei Lin." Matthias Williams appeared in the gap between the barn and the house, a hammer tucked into his belt. "I see you've brought a friend."

She hopped down, laughing that chiming laugh. Standing up, she was smaller than Peter had realized, barely taller than his shoulder. "A friend of *yours*, Matthias. He said he came to help."

"I didn't know you knew today was a work day. In fact, I didn't know you cared much for our people, Dr Bajowksi." He folded his arms across his chest.

"He's with me," a voice called out, and Standish hurried forward.

The contrast between Standish and Mei Lin Vogel could not have been more pronounced. Standish was nearly as tall as Matthias Williams. Her work clothes, waterproofed canvas with dozens of pockets and zippers in shades of black and gray, looked as if they had been manufactured with the latest technology, and her hair, the same black as Mei Lin's, stood up in rumpled prickles. Everything about her looked sharp and tough, even a little masculine. Hattie's sturdy white shape made a neat complement to the woman.

"Mei Lin, have you met Kate Standish?" Matthias came forward to steer the two together. Standish shook Mei Lin's hand and managed to look friendly enough.

Peter wondered just how Standish had gotten to know Williams, but he knew better than to ask, especially not in front of Mei Lin, who was eyeing Standish suspiciously. Peter felt like giving Standish his own suspicious expression.

"Is Shane still here?" Mei Lin asked. "If you don't need my help building, I thought I'd set up lunch inside."

Two other men appeared behind Matthias, one tall and skinny, one with a build more like Peter's. "We've finished," the shorter one said. "You need not strain your back today, good wife." He stepped forward to put a hand on Mei Lin's shoulder.

The other man came forward. His face had a long, predatory quality that made Peter uncomfortable. "I'm Orrin Morris. You're a friend of Duncan Chambers, aren't you, Dr Bajowski? I remember you speaking at his service."

"Yes," Peter agreed. "There were so many people that day, I'm sorry if I can't remember meeting you."

"I don't imagine you would." Orrin's lips tightened. "I also remember that you were an advocate for the property tax increase on the ballot last year."

Mei Lin stepped forward. "Orrin, I brought that roast chicken you like so much. Would you like to help me set up lunch?"

"That's all right, Mei Lin," Matthias said quickly. "I told Miss Standish I'd be lunching with her and Dr Bajowski. I had forgotten about the shed raising when I invited them over."

"Oh." For the first time, Mei Lin's face lost its veneer of pleasantry. "I suppose Orrin and Shane can return to our home for the meal. I simply assumed you'd stick to tradition."

"Tradition has never been Matthias's strong point," Orrin said, his voice cold. Peter wondered if they'd stumbled into an old argument. He couldn't read the stockier man's face at all. The three Believers all fixed their eyes on Matthias.

"Go on," Matthias said. "We'll talk later."

"Shane, you should patch up Matthias's hex," Mei Lin said. "It's looking shabby."

"We can't have that, can we?" Orrin said. "Wouldn't want the dogs getting in with the horses."

"The dogs?"

"The hex is for the dogs," the shorter man said, his voice so deep it was nearly a growl. "They don't like it or the symbol of our Lord."

"No, they don't," Matthias snapped. "Now go," he ordered. "We'll talk another day."

"Yes, another day," Orrin agreed. "Mei Lin, Shane. I'll get my horse and follow you."

The other Believers hurried away, leaving Standish and Peter alone with Matthias. "Let's go inside," he said. He wasn't commanding them the way he'd ordered the Believers; he sounded tired but reasonable.

The colors of Matthias's kitchen surprised and dazzled Peter. The plain white exterior of Matthias's house and barn had not prepared him for the blues and yellows and the many, many animal figures. It was like walking into one of the Believers' hex images, and he found himself turning in a slow circle, trying to take it all in.

"Tea?" Matthias asked. He didn't sound any happier.

"I'm fine," Peter said, at the same moment Standish said "Please."

Matthias poured her a glass and carried a dish of water out to Hattie. He returned and leaned up against the counter. "So what is this about, Standish?"

"Peter didn't kill Duncan," she announced. "I know he didn't."

"How do you know?" he asked.

"Because I know," she said. She pushed the cup of cool tea a few centimeters across the table. "I know in my gut it has something to do with Songheuser."

"What?" Peter asked. "You… what?"

"Duncan knew the company was up to something. He was worried about some kind of secret project that Songheuser was hiding from *you*, Peter. They brought in another biologist."

"That doesn't prove anything," Matthias pointed out.

"They hid the road in the woods," she countered. "And don't forget – that's not the only thing they've covered up." She gave Matthias a hard look.

"What?" Peter leaned forward. "What do you know, Matthias?"

"The company made a mistake when the first colonists arrived on Huginn," Matthias said. "More than half the colonists died of starvation because their supplies weren't delivered. The company made the Canaan Lake colonists a big settlement – free shipping for perpetuity – if we'd keep quiet about it."

Peter shook his head. "Why'd the settlers take it? If people died, wouldn't they want to see the company punished?"

"Because we – I mean, the original settlers – needed material from Earth. They needed all new stock of embryos and enough food to get them through another year. But the cost of shipping before the discovery of uranium on Muninn? Was astronomical. It tripled the cost of any item. To survive, the settlers had to make that deal."

"And Songheuser got off looking like a bunch of good guys."

"The first settlers thought they had no other choice. They signed the papers and they kept their promise."

"Except not today," Peter said. "You're breaking your word by telling us."

Matthias gave a little laugh. "Who's going to believe the two of you? I live out here on a farm, and even I've heard the gossip. Standish is so unhinged she depends on her dog to keep her under control. And you're an environmentalist with an overactive sex drive."

"Fuck you," Standish said, but there was no fire in it.

"Maybe you're right," Peter said. He could see the terrible clarity of Matthias's logic. He'd seen just what people thought of him this week, and it was ugly. "But your people's secret has nothing to do with Duncan and his murder. Why do you care who killed him?"

"Because he saw us as more than just our religion,"

Matthias said. "He saw us as part of his community, and he tried to help us when no one else would."

"Sectors 13 and 14," Standish blurted. "Duncan tried to keep you from selling to Songheuser."

Matthias nodded. "But it was part of their price," he said.

"What price?" she asked.

He hesitated.

Standish reached for his arm. "What price?" she repeated.

"The price for making sure that property tax failed," he explained. He turned sad eyes to Peter. "It would have crippled us. You don't know how hard it is to make money on a farm."

Peter didn't know what to say. Songheuser making secret deals with the Believers. Songheuser fixing elections. Everything he thought they'd left behind on Earth was being written again here on Huginn.

Standish balled her fists. "Fucking Songheuser. You know they were the reason my accident happened? The one that nearly killed me and triggered my agoraphobia?" She shook out her hands, her cheeks flushed. "They're the reason all those Believers died. They're the reason Duncan's dead. We have got to stand up to them. We've got to make them pay for what they've done!"

"We've got to prove all that," Peter reminded her. "It's still a pretty big stretch to say Songheuser caused Duncan's murder."

"Well, we'll prove it! We'll find some more clues and solve this case."

Matthias raised an eyebrow. "I think our first step is to make sure our friend here doesn't get brought in for the crime."

He smiled at Peter, and Peter smiled back.

PART III: AN OATH OF DOGS

Who wrote the Good Book? God steered the hands of many men to write its passages. I once thought His guidance would override any error or bias implicit in the writer, but I have come to see that we humans can pollute any kind of wisdom.
       – from MEDITATIONS ON THE MEANING OF EVIL,
       by MW Williams

CHAPTER SEVENTEEN

Muninn sat heavy in the corner of the sky, but the dogs did not need light for this work. They knew all they needed to know of digging and dirt and the rich smell of the things humans hid beneath the earth, and their muscles had trained themselves to the task. The pack leader's mouth filled with slaver. Even through twenty centimeters of damp clay, his exquisitely tuned nostrils picked up the scent of rancid flesh.

Claws hit wood and one of the dogs made a frustrated growl in the back of its throat. This was the hardest part.

All around them, the eyes of the blonde saint fixed themselves on the dogs, and the crosses leaned in closer. The dogs were careful not to brush into any of these things. The big brown boxer lookalike still bore a scar on its flank from coming up against a cross. The image stood out black and hairless, like a grill mark on meat. The dogs remembered the smell of the brown dog's flesh burning, the bitter nasty stink of it. They remembered and they learned from it.

Wood crunched and splintered. Nothing could withstand the will of the pack, not for long. Their strength was terrible.

They dragged the body from the grave. The shroud proved tougher than the usual fabric, some sort of artificial stuff the dogs associated with the people who came from outside, the people who were not of the lake or its mysteries. It tasted bad and cut their tongues. They tugged and ripped and clawed at it until the body came free, its burial finery still neat. The bag of entrails slipped out of the bottom of the shroud and hit the ground with a squelch. The stench of rot gases filled the air.

The others fell upon the broken bag and the pack leader let them feast. This they could have. This he could allow.

The part of him that sat in the back of his mind, the part of him that was not instinctive or sensate but rather some slippery *other* that the dog mostly ignored, prodded at his dog mind. There was another reason for this trip to the graveyard. They had not waited for the faithful to leave off their vigils beside the grave, to grow tired of their nightly rounds of the cemetery, to abandon this body to the ground, simply to devour it as they usually would.

He barked and the others stopped. Gore and mud streaked their muzzles. Their eyes glinted in the faint light of the moon. The pack leader sank his teeth into the stiff leather of the dead man's boots and tugged. The cords of the dog's neck stuck out. The man was slender and hollowed, but it was no easy task to pull him across the broken ground and through the maze of crosses and saints. The others hurried to help.

He was their leader. They had to help him.

They dragged the man down the slopes of Mount Hepzibah, loose bits of him sloughing away as his body jolted over stones and button ferns and along the pavement. The *other* part of the pack leader's mind urged him to take the body farther and farther, beyond the point where the dogs had brought down the man nearly a moon cycle before, past the places of food smells, all the way to the quiet building that faced the bad air place.

The body looked flattened and battered as it lay on the steps of the quiet building. The dogs backed away from it.

There was something bad about the dead man. They had forgotten it while he had been under the ground, growing fragrant and tender, but now they remembered. There had been an evil smell about him, a smell that called to them like the scent of fresh meat or the sound of the leader's howl, and so they had followed the bad man into the town and cut him down like anything else that threatened their pack.

The leader rubbed his muzzle on the ground and then trotted away from the bad man and the bad air place. His tail bobbed above his back like a happy flag. They had done good work.

They ran into the woods where the branches shrouded them from the light of Muninn and the wind and mist scoured the smells from them. They ran until the *other* parts of their minds went silent and they were only dogs and the trees were only trees and the creatures flying above were only birds.

Huginn, Day 197
He's back. My Matthias has returned to me.

The group never made it to the spaceport. They climbed the mountain at the north end of the lake and began the trip west, but found the way cut off by a steep ravine. They followed it north for kilometer after kilometer, looking for a way to cross. Its banks, Matthias told me, were as steep as the walls of a house, the surface naked rock in most places. The ravine finally began to narrow, and they found a spot where a big candelabra tree had fallen and made a kind of bridge. No one liked the look of it, but it was the best path they'd found yet, and Craig Thomas and Alex Perkins went out to cross it. Perkins went first. Something about those long dark days in the woods had broken him down, and he was eager to get to the spaceport, eager to get away from us and this place.

Perkins had always been afraid of heights, Matthias explained. He wanted to go first so he could get the crossing over with. When the tree snapped in the middle of the ravine, he fell in perfect silence. Matthias saw his face. The man was so scared, he told me, his eyes were welded open and his mouth fixed in an "o" of pure fear. He couldn't have screamed. He was frozen in terror.

The screaming started for real about a second after Perkins dropped. The tree hadn't broken clean; no, it split into threads and pieces, and Craig Thomas's leg went down between two long shards of wood as the back half of the tree slid down the bank and caught on the rocks. He would have fallen to his death if he hadn't gotten caught in that tree, but it wasn't any kind of favor. The men roped up the broken trunk so it wouldn't finish its plunge, and they fought to drag Craig up to solid ground.

None of them had eaten in a day and a half, when the last of my sawdust bread ran out, and where they found the strength to lift both Craig and that big tree, only God knows. I imagine He granted it to them. But as the tree swung up, its roots smashed down, clubbing Bill Ferguson over the head. He dropped hard and cold as stone, and Matthias thought he might be dead. Craig was screaming, Bill was knocked out, and Perkins was gone.

They turned back. What else could they do? They still had another forty or more kilometers of rough country between them and the spaceport, and two of their men were hurt too badly to walk on their own. Plus, they were out of food.

I held Matthias in my arms as he told me all this. His shoulders shook as he cried. The proud man who brought us here is gone, and only this thin, sorry creature has been left behind. I know he thinks that we will all die and that it is all his fault.

Cheyenne Taylor can't get out of bed any longer. If I can bring myself to leave Matthias's side, I will go to her and see if I can tend her, but I know there's not much I can do.

What she needs is food and rest and hope, and I can give her none of these things. So I will sit here with my sleeping, broken man and listen to the rustling wings of the leather birds outside our cabin window. I do not know if it is a worse sound than the distant howling of the dogs.

Peter's first thought upon awakening was of the specimen boxes he'd dropped off at the office. Today he would build two terrariums, one with only tree scooters and one with a mix of scooters and caterpillars. He should really set aside a few of the caterpillars to study on their own, but he wanted to focus on their interactions with the tree scooters. He had no guarantee any of the creatures would live outside of their natural environment. But he would make as many observations as he could and learn as much as possible.

Terrarium construction filled his head as he walked down Main Street, eager to get to his office.

"Don't go any farther," someone called, and he recognized Lou by his dreadlocks and his blue security jacket. Not by his voice, which had gone high and tight and shaky.

"Lou? Everything all right?" He took a few steps forward.

"Oh man, you shouldn't see this."

But it was too late. The pile of black rags on the front steps had already caught Peter's eye. It could have been garbage, but he knew it wasn't; his stomach turned over and he found himself taking another, unwilling, step forward. He couldn't look away from the body's cowboy boots.

"Is that Rob McKidder?"

Lou gave a kind of stifled sob. Peter remembered how much the man had cried at the funeral. "Lou, you shouldn't look at that." Peter turned him away from the bloated, tattered thing, but couldn't resist glancing back at the battered corpse.

It was bad enough the dogs had killed Rob in the first place, but to dig him up and *display* him like this – Jesus.

Standish walked up the street toward him and gave a wave. "Hey, Peter. What's going on?"

"Standish, don't–"

But of course she had already passed him by, curiosity drawing her to trouble like a cat to a bowl of poisoned tuna. She spun around, nearly knocking Peter down, her hand clamped over her mouth.

Peter hadn't noticed the smell before, but now the stink wafted toward him, heavy and rank. He put his arm around her shoulder. "Come on, let's get away from that. The police wouldn't want us to get too close."

In the background, Lou's hand unit buzzed and Peter heard the muffled tones of a conversation. He thought he recognized Deputy Wu's voice, but he wasn't sure.

"Did the dogs do that?" Standish pulled Hattie closer to her. He was glad to see the dog was on a lead today.

"Probably." He put his sleeve over his nose to draw a deep breath. "It's what they do. Dig up the dead and eat them."

"He wasn't eaten, though."

"I know. Let's go to the Mill Cafe and have a cup of coffee until all this is taken care of."

They walked toward the restaurant. The first-shift rush would start in a few minutes.

Standish stopped beside the front door. "Why Rob? Why kill him? Why dig him up again? Why not eat him?"

He waited for the door to open and a woman in coveralls to pass them by. "They're just dogs, Standish. Does it matter why they do things?"

"Are they really just dogs?" she asked, and he urged her to the nearest booth. He could see Rob's figure stretched out like some mummified Christ figure, the sun winking on the silver tips of his boots, and found he couldn't answer her question.

•••

Muninn and Wodin still lay behind the horizon, and in the dark it seemed as if the horsetails had pulled themselves closer to town. The trees' shadows wrapped the streets in secrets. Anything could be hiding in those patches of blackness: a dog, a murderer, a flock of leather birds. Standish felt for her pepper spray and hurried toward Main Street. She wished she'd just waited for Peter to finish up with his terrariums before she headed to the bar.

But every time she turned back to her filing or desk tidying, Rob McKidder's body appeared in her mind's eye as if the image had been glued onto the backs of her eyelids and now flashed itself every time she blinked. Blink: teeth marks in the shiny black leather of his boots, one of the silver medallions at the ankle half-ripped away. Blink: the moist patches on the side of the cheek where the skin had worn off, revealing the yellow pearls of fat beneath. Blink: the smart little mustache above lips shriveling away from black stitches, the mouth never to speak again.

What she wanted the most was to talk to Dewey. Now that she was committed to getting Songheuser by the balls, she needed every last piece of dirt she could get on those bastards – even whatever Dewey was hiding. But Dewey wasn't returning her calls. Maybe Standish could have stayed at the office if she'd had Dewey's light-hearted banter to distract her from the creepy shit happening in this town. As it was, she'd had to go to the bar.

She picked up her pace and was nearly running when she hit the front door. Hattie gave a yip as the door slammed shut on the fluff of her tail.

"Oh God, Hattie, I'm sorry." Standish freed the dog's plumed tail. "Are you all right?" Tears welled up in her eyes. The tail looked fine, no hair loss or anything, and she was nearly goddamn crying. This town was getting to her.

"You need a drink, Standish?"

It was Belinda's day off. She couldn't remember the name

of the little man behind the bar, but he obviously knew hers. She nodded. "Tequila?"

"It's Ganymede rotgut, but we got it." He measured out a double and reached for a jar. "Lime powder with that?"

"Neat." She picked up the glass and waited for the liquor's perfume to hit her. She'd never been able to resist tequila. Just the smell of it made her mouth water.

She closed her eyes and tossed it back. For a second, she was twenty-eight again, bad-mouthing the miners at a bar on a space station whose name she couldn't remember. The tequila tasted like sex pressed up against a dumpster, like a nose bleed running down the back of her throat, like the dust lining an air duct separated from the black of space by only a few centimeters of hull. She hadn't had tequila since she'd arrived on Huginn.

"Another?" the bartender asked.

The warm sense of Hattie sitting next to her leg stopped her. "Maybe later."

She turned to face the room. The bar was half-full tonight, but she recognized most of the faces. The loggers and mill workers were staying away, but the office crowd was drinking. They had known Rob McKidder, worked with him closely. Just thinking about him getting torn up out of the ground had made them need the company of others.

"We should have patrolled the cemetery another week," someone said.

"He'd been in a fridge for a week and thoroughly pickled," his buddy countered. "We couldn't have known."

"There was already a cross on his grave," a woman added. "I thought that kept them safe."

Standish passed the little knot of speakers and caught a glimpse of Brett's broad shoulders beside the pool table. That was what she needed. Not more tequila, but a warm body and a soft bed to while away the rest of the night.

"Brett!" she called out.

He turned around, and the look on his face stopped her in her tracks. "What's wrong?"

"You had breakfast with Peter Bajowski this morning? What the hell is wrong with you?"

"What?" She took a step backward, confused and startled.

"Everybody saw you at the Mill Cafe. Sitting there as cozy as a couple of tree scooters under a fern. You want the mill to blow up?"

Standish drove her finger into his chest, no longer confused but pissed. "What the hell are you talking about?"

"Bajowski worked for those ecoterrorists at Jawbone Flats."

"Oh, come on. There was just one guy. One bomber. There isn't some vast conspiracy to destroy lumber production on Huginn. There's just one nutjob with a grudge."

He shook his head. "You're stupid if you think that's the case. All those peace, love, and beautiful vista types on Earth are sending their biggest troublemakers here to turn Huginn into one big national park, just like on Earth – and Bajowski's one of them. It's a matter of time before he shows his stripes."

"You're insane! Bajowski is a paperpushing nerd who wouldn't know how to build a bomb if he wanted to. Which he wouldn't, because all he cares about are stupid little mushrooms and caterpillars and shit. He's harmless."

"That's what he wants you to think."

"Bajowski is my friend and I trust him. And you're an idiot, Brett." She marched out of the bar.

It had gotten darker while she'd been inside. She pulled the pepper spray from her pocket and picked up her pace. Hattie pressed herself against Standish's leg, but even with her comforting presence, the street lights seemed half as bright as usual. Standish broke into a run, her boots slipping in the mud. She couldn't make it home quickly enough.

She slammed the door behind her and flipped the deadbolt, leaning against the door as she caught her breath. The printed door felt flimsy, the deadbolt more symbolic than a deterrent to anything that wanted inside.

The dogs were out there, and they knew where she and Hattie lived. A canister of pepper spray wouldn't do much against a whole pack of them.

She shoved the couch in front of the door. It wasn't much of a barricade, but it was better than nothing.

A flash of metal on the floor caught her eye, and she stooped to pick up the square of tin that had somehow gotten kicked under the couch. The necklace Chameli had given her. The blue-gowned saint looked at her with quiet, resigned eyes. The Believers put figurines of her in the cemetery, Standish remembered. She slipped the leather lace over her head. The metal was cool against her skin for a moment and then unnoticeable.

Standish sank onto her bed and pulled her knees to her chest, her eyes fixed on the barricaded door. Her hand crept into her pocket for her unit. It took her a second to dial.

"Standish? I thought you were going to the bar." Peter's avatar filled the screen, but she could easily picture him making his puzzled face.

"It didn't go so great. You want to cook some food together? I've got a box of produce in my fridge."

"Sure. I'll be done here in half an hour or so. You have any beer?"

She reassured him on the state of her supplies and hung up, marginally comforted. Knowing Peter, a half an hour probably meant something closer to forty-five minutes. She kicked off her boots and reached for the diary on the nightstand. If she had to kill time, she could at least learn more about the history of Huginn. She opened to the first page and tried again: "Last month's Prayer Breakfast brought in the final thousand dollars we needed to finish paying our passage on the *Roebuck*."

The metamorphic nature of Huginn seems more pronounced in Canaan Lake, affecting people in even the first wave of settlement. Primary sources from that time are rare, but the notebooks of MW Williams contain this suggestive quote:

I pushed my people, my caterpillars, hard. They believed in my vision for them, treading along blindly, chewing their rations and hoping that the skies of Huginn would someday be welcoming to their wings. But we proud caterpillars did not become butterflies, flying in the light of the wholesome sun. We metamorphosed into moths. Dark creatures. We came to this moon and became things of the moon.

What did Williams mean? Was this a metaphor or was he actually implying those early settlers experienced a physical metamorphosis? It's impossible to be sure. What we do know is that more than two dozen people died that first winter.

– from DARK SHORES: A HISTORY OF CANAAN LAKE,
by Remy Welser

CHAPTER EIGHTEEN

The steps to the office had been rigorously cleaned; Victoria Wallace, if she was still around, wouldn't have to be offended by the damp marks Rob McKidder's body had left behind.

Peter took a sideways step. Had the body been right there? Or more to the left? He couldn't stand the thought of walking where it had sprawled.

"Dr Bajowski, I'd like a word with you."

Sheriff Vargas's voice was pleasant as ever, but Peter felt ice creep down his back. He turned around, slowly. She wore her big-brimmed hat and a completely unnecessary pair of mirrored sunglasses. Deputy Paul Wu stood behind her, looking uncomfortable.

"Sure. You want to come into my office?"

"That'd be lovely."

The pair followed him inside. He wished he'd come to work early today. A woman from engineering stopped on the staircase and stared at him for a long moment before scurrying up to the third floor. He paused on the second floor landing, half to let her get upstairs ahead of him and half to play for time. "You need a cup of coffee or anything?"

He hoped those bastards in accounting heard him. He sounded as collected as a museum catalog.

"No, I'm fine. You, Paul?"

Deputy Wu mumbled something unintelligible. Peter assumed it was a negative and took them up to his office. As Peter unlocked the door, a couple of millwrights passed the little group, eyeing them curiously as they headed toward the skybridge that connected the office building to the mill. By lunchtime, the whole town would know Vargas had been up here.

He offered the sheriff and Paul seats on the two plastic chairs he usually used as gear drying racks and then perched on the edge of his desk. "What can I do for you?"

Sheriff Vargas crossed her ankle over her knee and put her hat on her lap, looking as comfortable as she would have been on a bespoke sofa. He had to admire that level of class.

"We understand you were one of the first on the scene yesterday."

"Rob McKidder's body?"

She nodded.

Surprise flitted on cool wings through Peter's chest. He thought this would have something to do with Duncan. "Yeah. I got here just as Lou was calling it in. Hell of a thing."

"Can you describe the state of the body?" Deputy Wu got out a little notepad.

Peter thought carefully about the morning and then described the stairs, the body, Lou and Standish's position. The sheriff asked him to repeat a few key details, like the teeth marks in the boots. Remembering the state of the corpse made Peter glad he'd skipped breakfast.

The sheriff pushed her shades back on top of her head. With her heavy curls pulled back, she looked a good five years younger. Her eyes were sad. "The dogs have been getting worse and worse," she admitted. "I'm thinking about organizing a hunting party, although no one seems to have any idea where they hole up during the day. I've put in a request with the governor's office for the funds to bring in some trackers. Nobody local's got the skills for this."

She stood up, and Paul stiffly unfolded himself from the too-small chair. Peter knew this was his chance.

"Sheriff? Can I ask you something about Duncan Chambers' murder?"

She raised an eyebrow.

"Why did you never bring me in for questioning?"

She raised her other eyebrow. "Your whereabouts have always checked out in your favor. Belinda told us you were at Heinrich's the whole night Duncan went missing. You kept bugging her about staying off her feet."

"She had that cut on her foot," Peter said slowly, trying to remember that night.

"Well, Belinda's word is a good enough alibi for me. Plus, it's always looked like a suicide. That note we found in his office was pretty clear that he felt bad about working for Songheuser all these years. I figure his new boyfriend tried to turn him into one of those ecoterrorists and it broke him. Duncan couldn't have ever hurt anybody."

She turned to the door and Peter leapt to his feet. "A note? You never mentioned a note."

"It was private information, kept sealed for the case. Now that I've declared him a suicide, I figure it's safe enough to mention."

He tried one last time. "But if it was a suicide, wouldn't the gun have been right there?"

"The dogs, Peter." He opened his mouth to protest the stupidity of the claim, but she raised a hand to cut him off. "They mess with everything here in Canaan Lake. Right?"

"I don't see why dogs would–"

"These dogs don't act like ordinary dogs. Sometimes they do things we just can't explain."

There was an odd note to her voice, and her expression seemed pained. As if she believed the words coming out of her mouth as little as he did.

She settled her sunglasses and hat back into place and gave him a nod. Then they were gone.

Peter went back to his desk and sat down, his stomach twisting. He reached for the breakfast bar in his pocket and then dropped it on his desk. His stomach didn't hurt because he needed breakfast. The sheriff wasn't the only one telling tall tales about Duncan's case.

He turned on his hand unit and brought up his record from the motor pool. He didn't take many trips to Space City, and the mileage would jump out at him. He scrolled back to April and brought up his calendar in the corner. There was the night Duncan disappeared. There was the trip to Space City, a week before. He doublechecked the calendar and the mileage log.

He put down the hand unit, his gut gone hollow.

Belinda's story – Peter's alibi for the night of Duncan's death – was phony.

Peter had almost certainly spent part of the night at Heinrich's because nine nights out of ten he went there for dinner and a beer, but a week after treatment, Belinda's cut should have been well on its way to being healed, and even if it wasn't, he didn't know her well enough to exchange more than a few pleasantries. So why had Belinda lied to Sheriff Vargas?

He tapped the breakfast bar, turning the question over and

over. It made no sense. Neither did the note the sheriff had found on Duncan's desk, or her lie about the dogs taking the air bolt gun.

He needed to talk to Standish.

She'd spent the morning answering work orders, and to be honest, she was glad to be out of the office. Everyone in the building was either morbidly focused on the discovery of Rob McKidder's body or still blathering about Victoria Wallace, and she wanted to put both of them out of her mind. Victoria Wallace made her think too much about her parents. When she'd been young, her house had been filled with women like Victoria Wallace, perfect women who used their faces and wits with equal success. If her mother had gotten her way, Standish would have turned out just like her.

Standish wiped a smear of mud off her hand onto her pants and laughed out loud. She certainly hadn't turned out the way her parents planned.

She pulled up to the motor pool just as Peter was coming out. He stood beside the back door and waited for her to park.

"Turning that machine in? I'd rather have that one than the crap heap I'm going to get stuck with."

"You baby," she said with a grin. "It's good for you to drive something with no suspension. Strengthens your back muscles, going over all those potholes."

He put his hand on her shoulder, steering her away from the building. "Got a second?"

"Yeah, I was thinking about heading to my place and fixing some lunch. You can come."

"Great." He didn't say a word until they were well past the guard shack and alone on the path leading back down to the lake, Standish's favorite shortcut home. She let Hattie off her leash. The dog bounded into the trees, sniffing the ground intently.

"Sheriff Vargas stopped by this morning."

"Is that good?" She studied his face. He looked worried.

"She told me why she'd never had me down as a suspect in Duncan's murder. Belinda said I spent the whole night at the bar, trying to keep her off an injured foot."

Standish raised an eyebrow. "That's sort of specific and weird."

"Yeah, well, I did give Belinda a lift into Space City when she needed stitches in her foot one night. But it was more than a week before the night Duncan went missing. I can't think of any kind of reason she'd tell a story like that."

"Maybe her memory's shit."

"Belinda?" He shook his head. "Six people can order different drinks and she never mixes up a one. She might be just a bartender, but she's a sharp cookie. And weirder than that, Sheriff Vargas said my whereabouts had always checked out. Which meant she checked the logs for the travel pool. So why did she believe Belinda's story?"

"But you're off the suspects list. No matter what that says about Belinda, that's good news for you."

They came around the last turn in the path, the lake stretching out like a silver sheet. Standish stopped, remembering something Julia had said one night. "Actually, that's not the first weird Belinda story I've heard. I just remembered hearing that people have seen her lurking on this trail."

"This trail? It only goes from the beach to the office."

"Right? Julia said Belinda was carrying a spotting scope, like a bird watcher." He made a confused face. "Maybe she'd see a few canopy snakes, but they're usually so well camouflaged you can't see them unless you're climbing trees. And I know Belinda's interested in nature, but that still seems far-fetched."

"We should definitely keep an eye on her," Standish said.

Hattie raced back from the edge of the water, eager for a petting. Standish worked her fingers into the dog's thick fur and realized, for the first time since landing, that it wasn't damp. "Hey, it's not raining."

"It's nearly the dry season," Peter reminded her. "We get more and more rain breaks until *poof!* We get three solid weeks of sunshine."

He picked up a stick of driftwood and tossed it for Hattie, completely oblivious to Standish's discomfort. She took a deep breath. The dry season. She could handle the days, she supposed. It was the stars she'd have to watch out for. Maybe she should have filled that prescription, after all.

Hattie trotted up to her, tongue lolling, and Standish shook off the tendrils of anxiety. She had Hattie. She'd be fine.

"Come on, Peter, I'll make you a sandwich."

They went up to her house and she let them in, wondering just what to put on a vegan sandwich. She hoped he liked lettuce.

"I don't know what comes next," he admitted. "The sheriff still claims Duncan killed himself and that dogs took the air bolt gun. I tried to press her on it, but she just cut me off. I think she's hiding something."

Standish found some hummus and added that to the sandwich. Vargas had never seemed too eager to investigate. It was almost as if she had a reason to want to sweep Duncan's death under the rug.

Maybe she did. Didn't Songheuser underwrite the sheriff's department? Didn't they pay for just about everything in Canaan Lake?

Standish dropped the spoon back into the hummus. "Shit."

"Something wrong?"

"I'm fine. But I'm pissed. Think about it: Sheriff Vargas doesn't *want* to find Duncan's killer," she explained. "She's covering for someone with deep pockets."

He took the hummus from her. "You really think so?"

"It makes as much sense as anything. There are just so many loose pieces." She nodded her head toward the diary resting beside the coffee pot. "Things here in Huginn go wrong somehow. I've been reading about the first colonists – they were literally starving to death trying to get a foothold here."

"I can't imagine that their problems have any connection to Duncan's murder."

Standish shrugged. The colonists and Duncan both had problems with Songheuser. The company's evil was like a strand of yarn sticking out of a crocheted sweater. If she could just work that end free, she could pull out the whole thing.

She knew the diary mattered somehow. She had only read a few pages, but she could tell there was something bigger going on than just an unexpectedly cold wet season. And the Believers themselves held another mystery. The names, for one. She didn't think they were just tradition or a coincidence. How many Mei Lins could there be in a hundred years of Believer colonization? And how many Shanes and how many Orrins?

But if she told Peter, he would look for a logical reason behind the repetitions, and she wasn't ready for logic just yet. For now, she would read, and observe, and figure out how the past was going to help her catch Songheuser.

Huginn, Day 198

We found Craig Thomas on the beach this morning, the skin ripped from his limbs and his insides strewn across the sand.

Doc stooped to examine the body and just sat down on the rocks, crying hard. I helped him up.

I couldn't hold back tears, either. I tried to make myself look at Craig, but it was nearly impossible. It wasn't just the raw meaty hollow of his ruined torso – all of him looked *wrong*, the flesh stripped from his arms so that the bones showed clean and white in half a dozen places. Leather birds didn't do that. They didn't even have teeth.

I thought of Soolie and my stomach went tight.

Doc spoke to himself, his voice low and cold and emotionless, and it took me a little while to realize that his words meant Craig had died sometime in the night from his head injury.

Something had done this to him after his body had gone stiff and cold.

"But what did it, Doc?" I had asked. "What could have stripped the meat off his bones?"

"It must have been an animal," he said, and I wasn't sure if he believed it.

If it had been an animal, then it had been Soolie. And if it hadn't been Soolie... well, that was worse.

"Pete!"

Joe Holder's voice boomed down the hall. Peter turned slowly, pinning a smile on his face.

"What can I do for you, Joe?"

Joe came out of his office, grinning hugely. Not for the first time, Peter thought the man's teeth looked too big for his face. The elegant figure of Victoria Wallace appeared in the doorway of the office, leaning casually against the frame.

"Glad I caught you before you headed out in the field. I have some good news."

"Oh?"

"You're always complaining about the roads, right? Well, we had a town council meeting last night. You must have overlooked the notice on your hand unit. You used to come to every meeting!"

"I've been a little behind."

"You missed a great meeting," Joe pushed on. "Right, Victoria?"

The sleek blonde head gave a nod.

"We've approved a new property tax measure for road work and city improvements. After what happened to that little Alvarez boy – no one wants to see that happen again. The vote will be coming up next month."

A few weeks ago, Peter would have danced to hear such news, but after his meeting with Matthias his perspective had shifted. "A new property tax? Are you sure that's such a good idea? The last one failed pretty spectacularly."

"It was actually fairly close," Victoria Wallace interjected.

Peter turned his gaze on her. "You keep up with Canaan Lake politics?"

She smiled. "It was discussed at the meeting. It's a fascinating town you have here. I'm glad I'm learning more about the communities outside Space City. After all, these small towns are vital to Songheuser's lumber production."

"Thought you'd be a bit more excited, Pete. This is good news for all of us."

Peter raised his hands as if to shake off a misunderstanding. "Oh, I'm excited. I just don't want to get my hopes up. Last time the measure seemed like a certain win. I'd hate to see this one come to the same bad end."

Joe chuckled. "I have every confidence that this time, property taxes will be going up."

He was still laughing as Peter stepped out into the motor pool. The sound made Peter's neck hairs prickle.

He'd forgotten that Joe sat on the town council. In fact, mill department heads made up the majority of the positions; Heinrich Chu was the only business owner on the council Peter could think of. It hadn't seemed important in the past. Now it represented Songheuser's death grip on the community.

What did Songheuser want with another property tax measure? They'd shot down the last one as part of their deal with the Believers. And the farming community would be just as badly hurt by this measure as the last one. The Believers were not going to be happy when they learned about this.

Peter turned onto the logging road that zigzagged through Sectors 11 and 10. He was driving behind some of the biggest of the Believer farms, headed for the deep forest of Sector 14. The road petered out in a square turnaround just big enough for a truck and a loader.

He parked the rig and got out. Forest surrounded him, but he could still hear the deep bellows of someone's cows. Peter headed for the trail he'd cut through the underbrush. He hadn't thought about the farms when he'd set up the test sites. Sector 14 was steep, undeveloped country, not much good for anything but timber, but he knew it held the headwaters of two or three big streams. Those streams were the primary water source for the Believer households in the flat land below.

He hurried toward the first test site, thinking hard. This wasn't just some boring test, another boost for the company's bottom line. This was big science. What the company did up here could have real effects on the entire town.

On Friday afternoon, he'd dosed horsetail trees in two of his meticulously cataloged test sites, and now he was ready to collect the first batch of data. It would be weeks before he could be sure of an effect on the horsetail trees, but the smaller creatures would surely be responding to the degassing compound by now.

He felt increasingly nervous as he made his way toward the first site.

The wrongness hit him like a punch to the nose. The smell alone would have warned him that something had gone terribly wrong. He broke into a run, crashing through the button ferns and slipping on exposed stones. He came to a halt in a patch of Christ's fingers along the edge of the carefully marked plot.

"Shit," he whispered.

The horsetail tree stood tall, its top green and still perfectly erect. But the undergrowth, a rich variety of button ferns and lichens, was dead. Every last inch had succumbed to some sort of gray, powdery mildew that was like nothing he'd seen before on this world. The stink of it hung over the whole area. Peter reached for the mask he kept in his field pack. He had to see more closely.

He brought out his hand unit and began taking pictures. Mark Allen had to see this.

Mark had said this stuff was safe enough to bathe in, and Peter trusted Mark. But maybe Songheuser's chemical people couldn't have predicted this. They worked in clean rooms where mildew never had a chance to spread. This chemical might be perfectly harmless in a laboratory, but in a real forest with real humans carrying their own microbiota, things were obviously different.

A tiny sound stopped him, and he knelt down beside the slimy remains of a stand of rock-eater lichen. A tree scooter scrabbled between the shriveled, blackened bits of lichen. Peter leaned closer. The scooter skidded on a patch of damp slime and came to a stop on the rock. Its antennae trembled uncontrollably. Between the segments of its furry pink body, he could see dark threads of the same mildew that had killed the plants. The scooter fell on its side, its legs flailing in agony. Then it curled tight, shook itself all over, and went still.

Everything in this four-hundred-meter square was dying.

Peter jumped to his feet and began to run. He had to see the second test site.

My own choices undid me and ruined my people. I have struggled to understand what happened here in Canaan Lake, but I do know that when things grew terrible here, we acted as dogs.

Oh, my poor, sweet people: We acted as dogs, and we became as dogs.

– from Meditations on the Meaning of Evil,
by MW Williams

CHAPTER NINETEEN

Standish looked from the house on the corner to the paper in her hand. The descriptions on these Sector 10 easements were frustratingly uninformative, lacking names or detailed platting notations. She'd been sure this farm was the one mentioned in the document, but there was no cable box here beside the road.

Defeated, she got back in her UTV. Her duties rarely took her onto Believer property, and now she was glad of it. Even in their legal documents, the neo-Mennonites operated differently from the rest of the world. None of the farmers owned their own land – it was all held by a larger community group, the property managed by church elders. The Believers she'd spoken to either refused to answer her questions or pretended they weren't worldly enough to understand what she was asking.

She'd have to ask Matthias for help. He may have been a Believer, but he certainly didn't act like the rest of them. He had an old-fashioned quality about him, but at least he lived in the same reality she did.

A young woman opened the gate beside the road and led a brown cow out of it, the rest of the small herd stringing along behind them. Standish tapped the steering wheel impatiently.

"Rush hour in Canaan Lake, Hattie," she grumbled. The dog stretched out on the seat and rested her head on her paws.

The girl caught sight of Standish and her eyes widened. She dropped a half curtsey. "Sorry, good woman!"

"No problem," Standish called back.

She scanned the field as she waited for the cows. A sturdy white farmhouse and barn sat on the field's flanks, their doors and shutters emblazoned with the brightly painted crosses and floral designs so typical of the Believers here in Canaan Lake. She liked the colors, actually. It brought a cheer to the farms that was missing in the town's muddy streets.

The last cow strolled by, and Standish started up the engine. She reached Matthias's house shortly. Hattie had settled into a deep sleep on the short drive, so Standish left her in the vehicle while she approached the front gate.

"Ho, Standish," Matthias called. He pulled the last envelope from his antiquated mailbox. "I wasn't expecting you."

"I've got a couple of cable junction boxes I need to find, and I thought you might be able to tell me more about them. The property easements are useless."

He flipped through his mail as they walked. "I'd be happy to take a look at them," he said absently. Then he stopped in his tracks.

"Something wrong?"

"Shane!" Matthias bellowed. "Get down here and see this."

Standish hadn't noticed the battered-looking ladder leaning against the side of the barn, or Shane Vogel working at the top of it. He must be updating the hex image on the barn as Mei Lin had suggested.

The stocky man made his way down to the ground, a small paintbrush tucked behind his ear. "What is it?"

Matthias held out a piece of paper, and the men stood in silence as Shane read it. Standish studied the hex. Another colorful floral design, lots of reds and yellows. She liked it, although it seemed subtly different than the art at the other farms she'd seen.

"They're trying to get rid of us, Matthias. Their first attempt failed, so now they try again, with higher costs. It's Songheuser, and you know it."

"It's not Songheuser. We have a deal."

"You and your deals," Shane spat. "Look what it's done for us."

"I'll take care of this. Songheuser–"

"Songheuser's not the only answer. The rest of us have been talking. Maybe Vonda and Orrin are right. Maybe it's time for a change in leadership."

Matthias's face twisted and went red. He opened his mouth and closed it again. Then he spun on his heel and marched toward his house.

"What's wrong?"

Shane narrowed his eyes at her. "What do you care?"

"I care because I'm Matthias's friend." She folded her arms over her chest. She thought she'd imagined the unfriendliness she'd felt the last time she'd seen Shane Vogel, but today it came off him in waves.

"You're an outsider, and you're trying to influence Matthias. I don't trust you or your friend Peter Bajowski. He's always been against us."

"I'm not–"

But Shane was already walking away. He grabbed the sides of the ladder and hurried up it, his feet thudding on the wooden treads with the weight of his anger.

There was a horrible crunch, and Standish spun around to see Shane flail at the air, the shards of a broken rung clattering to the ground. The ladder wobbled and then canted sharply.

For an instant, he hung in the air, the ladder balanced on one leg.

But only for an instant. Then he was falling.

"Shane!" Standish screamed, running toward him.

The man lay flat on his back, the ladder crumpled beneath him. Broken wood and yellow paint had gone everywhere.

"Are you all right?" She dropped to her knees beside him.

His eyes were open, and he blinked at her. She reached for his hand. "Can you talk?"

His mouth flapped like a fish's and no sound came out. She felt something warm and wet against her knee and saw blood pooling around her.

"Matthias! Help!"

So much blood. But she couldn't see a wound. She undid the buttons of his black coat with shaking fingers. The linen shirt beneath showed a spreading red stain on his side.

She ripped open the shirt. "Oh my God," she whispered.

Now she could see the tip of wooden rung sticking out of his belly, the wooden rung that had pierced him in the back and gone all the way through his torso.

"We've got to get you to Space City, quick."

"No." Matthias's voice sounded behind her. "We don't believe in that. If God has destined Shane to die, then this is his time."

She stared at him. "How can you say that? So calm, like you don't give a shit? This is your friend! He's going to die if we don't get him to a doctor!"

"If it's my time to die, I'll die." Shane gave a dry laugh. "Right, Matthias?"

She turned back to the injured man. He'd gone pale, nearly gray, and as he gasped for air, the bloody wooden spike trembled. A rivulet of blood ran down his side, diverted sideways by a lumpy scar on the other side of his belly. The purple keloid tissue looked just like a cross.

A cross. It was like their stupid religion was laughing at her. How could they believe so devoutly that they would refuse medicine they needed? How could they live like this?

Matthias squeezed her shoulder. "Standish. Please go get Mei Lin. Shane doesn't have much time."

Standish got to her feet. The wet stain of Shane's blood, cold now, made the knees of her pants cling to her flesh. She lurched away from the two Believers, her heart sick with what she'd just seen. The waste of it. Shane, throwing his life away – for what? Some ancient rule the rest of humanity had given up centuries ago.

She glanced over her shoulder at them. Matthias had taken her place beside Shane, holding his hand. She could see the hex Shane had been painting, the yellow splatters of spilled paint. The flowers looked funereal now.

Flowers. There were only flowers on Matthias's barn. She got into the UTV and reached dully for the ignition. That was the difference between the art on his house and barn and the other Believers': no crosses, despite how much he believed in them.

Peter's keys slipped out of his fingers with a jangle. Christ, his hands were sweaty. But how could they not be? How could he be anything but terrified after seeing those ruined, mildewed patches in his forest? Mike Allen's degassing compound was a chemical threat on a par with DDT or Agent Orange.

They couldn't use this on a large scale. Even if there was a way to eradicate the mildew spores that were endemic to human development, if they put this on the forest they risked environmental devastation. Sector 14 was part of their own watershed, and if that stuff got in the water supply – he couldn't even let himself think about it. This new degassing compound had the power to turn the entire moon into an uninhabitable stretch of rock.

He'd nearly uploaded the pictures right there in the woods before reason hit him. He couldn't trust email with this.

Someone had blown up the mill at Jawbone Flats just because they hated logging – what would they do if they learned Songheuser was testing a toxic chemical that could kill the whole forest? Peter wanted environmental protections as much as any environmentalist, but not at the expense of human lives. He knew people who worked in the mill. For every company toady like Joe Holder, there was a Lou or a Niketa, decent folk just trying to get by.

No, he had to go to Space City and show Mark his data in person. He fumbled the key into his office door.

A clattering spun him around. A woman stood at the end of the skybridge, her pink raincoat dripping on the carpet.

"Belinda? What are you doing up here?"

She hastily picked up the purse she'd dropped. "I'm here to see you."

"In the skybridge?"

"I got turned around, that's all." She hurried toward him, gripping his elbow. She smelled powerfully of ferns. "I've got to talk to you, Peter."

"Now isn't really a good time–"

But she was already squeezing between him and the doorframe, pressing her way inside his office. He followed with a sigh.

"This is your office, huh?" She went straight to the window terrariums. "I love these things you've built. The creatures and plants are so beautiful."

He reached for the I+ glasses on his desk. "I'm only here a minute; I've got to head out. Maybe we can talk later."

She turned to face him. "This is important, Peter. What I've got to say could change your life."

"You've already changed my life. I had a visit from Sheriff Vargas. I know what you told her about the night Duncan died."

"I just told her the truth."

"It wasn't the truth, and you know it. You hurt your foot the week *before* Duncan went missing. I wasn't at the bar taking care of you that night."

She took a step closer. Her red-blond hair had strings of moss in it. "Peter, I admire you so much. You're not just another brainy biologist. You've got guts. You were the only person who tried to stop that trudgee fight ring, the only one in the whole town who gave a damn about those little creatures. When I heard about that, I knew I had to find a way to get you on my team."

He took a step backward. The look on her face, the gleam in her eyes – the zeal came off her in palpable waves. "What are you saying?"

"Didn't you ever wonder why I came here? I mean, no one comes here just to be a bartender." She gave a little laugh and stretched out her hands to him. "The group that sent me knows that people need wilderness. Without it, they go crazy. Just look at all those sad sacks back there on Earth."

"I have to leave, Belinda," he said. "I have to go to Space City." He put his I+ glasses in his pocket and backed toward the door. "If you don't leave with me, I'll have to call security."

"There's more to it than just *nature*, Peter. When you believe in it, Huginn can make you something entirely new. Something more than just human." She took another step closer. "Become one of us. With your brains and your connections, you could help us do so much."

"I don't want hear any more. Just go."

"Don't you feel Huginn reaching out to you? Can't you hear its voice at night, begging you to help it? I do, Peter. And I think you do, too." The words burst from her like a stream escaping its dam, and she broke off, half-gasping for breath. She swallowed and reached out to him again. The palms of her hand were a deep green, like the skin of a horsetail tree. "Once you let yourself believe, you become a part of Huginn.

I know you love this world and that you want to save it. So join us!"

He sidestepped her. "You sound crazy."

"I know you have what it takes. I'm giving you a chance, and if you don't take it, you'll regret it."

"A chance to do what? Blow up sawmills? No thanks." He opened the door and held it wide. "Get out of here."

"You're making a huge mistake. Remember that I gave you a chance."

She went out the door and he closed it behind her, sagging against the frame. He ought to call Sheriff Vargas and warn her Belinda was nuts.

And she'd left her purse on the windowsill beside his terrariums. He thought about going through it, but he didn't have time. He'd drop it off at the police station later.

He glanced at his watch. He could still make it to Space City before the office closed. Belinda was trouble, but this degassing compound was a far bigger problem. He'd find Standish and let her know about Belinda's breed of eco-psychosis when he got back from the city. Together, they'd figure out what to do.

He opened the door, checked the halls for the redheaded bartender, and then ran back downstairs as fast as he could. He hoped like hell Mark Allen could still stop Songheuser.

Huginn, Day 198
It gets worse.

We wrapped up the remains of the body and hid it in the root cellar, and then Doc and I went looking for Matthias. He had to know what had happened to it.

We checked every field. We checked our house and the barn. No Matthias.

Neither one of us wanted to go to the Morrises, not after that night with the baby, but if Matthias was anywhere, he'd

be with Orrin or Shane. So we went to Orrin's house in a
kind of dread.

No one answered, even though smoke rose from the
chimney.

"What if Vonda's sick again?" I asked Doc. She'd looked
so well the last time I saw her, but I'd buried too many of
my friends not to be worried for her.

He pushed open the door.

The smell of cooking made my stomach howl with
hunger. If you've never gone hungry, maybe you don't
know what happens to the body when it smells food – real
food, not sawdust skimped together with water and glue –
for the first time in weeks. My mouth filled with saliva. My
stomach wrenched itself into a knot of painful need.

Had they been stealing from our stores? How could they
have food when no one else did?

A pot of stew simmered on the embers of Vonda's stove,
but there was no sign of Vonda or Orrin. Doc rushed to the
stove while I stood at the edge of the room, held back as if
by some invisible fence. There was something wrong with
Vonda's kitchen. A strange smell came from that pot, a smell
I didn't like.

I took a tentative step toward her counter. There were her
knives, brought all the way from Earth in their knife block,
just like mine, but beside them, Orrin's big hunting knife lay
in its scabbard. A thumbprint showed on the soft leather,
made from something dry and brown.

Old blood, I was certain of it.

I suddenly saw the cow Mei Lin and I had slaughtered, its
eyes pink-rimmed from anemia. We all blamed the leather
birds for the wounds on our livestock, but the cuts had
always bothered me – they'd been so neat and artificial, the
kind of cut a sharp knife might make.

This old stain was the kind of stain that might have been

made by someone slicing open a vein in a calf's leg to collect its blood for his sick wife.

I felt a sudden certainty. Orrin Morris: that's what had happened to the cows, and that was why Vonda was so much healthier than everyone else. They had stolen from the entire community for their selfish gain.

"They're *dogs*," I whispered. "Thrice damned greedy dogs!" (Writing this, I can't believe how close I was to the truth – and how far away.)

I turned to see Doc blowing on a ladleful of clear broth. He took a long drink of the stuff.

"What does it taste like? I think they've been bleeding the livestock."

He spat a hunk of gristle into his palm. "That's not blood. We haven't butchered any of the sheep or goats – so where'd it come from?"

I couldn't help seeing Craig Thomas's mutilated body with the flesh carved off the bones.

Ms LUPO: *You don't argue that you set charges with the intent to destroy Songheuser's timber processing facility. But how did you convince the others to go along with you?*

Ms BAYER: *As a group, we all agreed that the government of Huginn is a shill for the corporations, and those companies are run by people utterly unlike those of us living on the moon. Look at the way we in GreenOne have changed. Are we even the same species as the people on Earth?*

Ms LUPO: *Let me get this straight. You believe that certain people living on Huginn have become physiologically different from humans living on Earth?*

Ms BAYER: *Lady, I turned green and started growing moss for hair. Is that normal where you come from? Huginn does things to you when you start to believe.*

– from the oral transcript of
THE PEOPLE VS BELINDA BAYER

CHAPTER TWENTY

Standish put down the diary, troubled by the writer's words. Poor Hepzibah. She had loved her husband and her life. She'd loved her dog. And she'd lost all of it because Songheuser had failed to send the right boxes to the right place. There was something else about the diary that bothered Standish, but she couldn't put her finger on it. She didn't want to read any more tonight, that was for sure.

Standish reached for her hand unit and reread the terse message she'd gotten from Peter. She couldn't understand why he'd go to Space City this afternoon, but after seeing him racing away from the forest she had to imagine there was something serious going on. She sighed. She wished he'd stayed in Canaan Lake. After what happened to Shane Vogel today, she didn't want to be alone.

Hattie looked up from the foot of the couch, her eyes

pleading for fun. Standish got up and peered outside. The clouds had returned after sunset, she realized. The sky was sealed up tight, the stars put safely away.

"Let's go for a walk, girl." She snapped on the dog's lead and took her outside. An idea struck Standish, and she headed away from the lake, toward the knoll at the end of town.

Mount Hepzibah: the hill looked prouder and taller now that she knew who it was named for. Standish and the dog passed by the lights of the bars and the diner and then through the little residential area at the end of town. The cemetery hill climbed steeply from the last of the back yards, its bulk announcing the city limits.

Standish knew enough of the town these days to take Cemetery Drive through the last of the houses, bigger, nicer models than the quickie-prints where she lived. She'd heard Joe Holder lived on Cemetery Drive; he must make a lot more money than she did. She unlatched the wrought-iron gate and slipped inside the cemetery.

Large concrete containers filled with azaleas and other terrestrial plants greeted her inside. The smell of fresh-clipped grass still hung in the air. She could have been back on Earth instead of halfway across the galaxy.

The cemetery's design encouraged the feeling. She'd visited a historical cemetery in Oregon that looked just like this one, the headstones sitting on grassy terraces that wrapped around the curved side of the hill. Some terraces had cement sidewalks and shallow stairs to connect them to the tier above and below; some didn't, and the paths were just wide strips of grass. In some places, the sidewalks just ended in the middle of the terrace, as if the builders had stopped for lunch and forgotten to come back.

She climbed to the first tier of headstones and admired the brightly painted crosses at the foot of almost every grave. There seemed to be far too many for a town of Canaan Lake's size, but she supposed the bulk of them belonged to Believers.

If it was their time to die, they died.

She stooped and stroked Hattie, wishing dogs appreciated hugs. Then she drew herself together. She'd come here for a reason.

She pulled out her hand unit and shone its light on the nearest headstone. The names in Hepzibah's diary had always bothered her. How many Matthias Williams could live in one town, even in a span of a hundred-plus years?

She had to wipe away fallen horsetail fronds before she could make out the text:

"Modesto Chavez, Day 4, Leap Week, 2199," she read out loud, and then shook her head at the convolutions of the Huginn calendar, a blatant attempt to make day-to-day life feel more like what the settlers had left behind. Maybe some day they would rename their months and their days to make them something wholly, uniquely of this world.

"Come on, Hattie. Most Believers are Anglo, I've noticed. Let's keep going." Standish looked around, wondering which way to go.

One huge headstone marked off the center point of the cemetery, she realized. Whoever had been buried there must have been important. The stone stood nearly her own height, surrounded by dozens of smaller crosses and several statues of the little blue saint. Her fingers went to her throat and touched the tin of the necklace Chameli gave her.

"Watch your step," a voice growled.

"Excuse me," she gasped.

A figure unfolded from the ground to her right, a wizened old man with tufts of white hair. He rubbed at the small of his back. "You on graveyard patrol tonight?"

"No, I was just taking a walk."

He fixed his gaze on Hattie. "You going to let her dig?"

"Oh, no! No, Hattie is a good dog. She doesn't dig." Her

heartbeat was slowing now, but she still felt nervous of the strange man.

He spat over his shoulder. "I was just checking the infill on Rob McKidder's plot. I don't think the dogs have been back since they dug him up." He sighed. She realized the man must be Caretaker Frank. Peter had pointed him out on her first day in Canaan Lake, but she hadn't seen the man since. "Was going to fill in that hole in the Believer side, but it was a long day."

"Hole? In the Believer side?"

He waved a hand to the far side of the cemetery, where the number of crosses and figurines redoubled. "Been there a while, but I keep forgetting about it. The Believers never complain." He stooped to pick up a rake. "I'm going down to the Night Light. You want to come?"

"No," she said. "Thank you. I'm not drinking today."

"Suit yourself. Just remember to close the gate behind you." He set off and she watched him a moment before turning back to the great headstone. God, she hoped her job never made her as weird as that.

She made her way down the path and paused in front of the big stone at the center of the cemetery. "Hepzibah Williams." Someone had left flowers on the grave, gladiolas, still fresh.

On the tier above Hepzibah's grave, a dark hole stood out from the smooth grass. The hole looked a few weeks old, the sides sunk in and a few small grass shoots coming up in places. She got close enough to read the name on the stone and felt goose bumps rise on her arms.

Orrin Morris.

She scrambled up to look more closely at the hole and the graves around it. Fred Eames, April 3, 2212. Alice Campbell, September 19, 2260. Mei Lin Vogel, December 20, 2243. She picked up her pace, nearly running along the row. The dates got older the closer she got to Hepzibah's stone: Robert

Sounds, February 15, 2158. Cheyenne Ferguson, June 13, 2156. Shane Vogel, March 19, 2157.

It didn't make sense. Maybe that was Shane's grandfather, but Mei Lin *Vogel*? What were the odds of two Mei Lins marrying into the Vogel family in the past twenty-five years?

Standish tripped as she darted down to the next row and fell on the grass. She pushed herself to her knees using a headstone.

"Matthias Williams," she gasped. She brushed a clump of lichen away from the lettering. The stone was nearly sixty years old. She stumbled to the next one. "Matthias Williams," she read again.

And then someone tapped her on the shoulder.

She whirled around, a scream in her throat, and the scream froze because it was him, Matthias, his face serious. "Wh–" she began and had to try again, "What are you doing here?"

"We're burying Shane tonight," he said. "I came early to put flowers on my wife's grave."

She remembered the gladiolas beside the tall headstone and felt her mouth go dry.

"You shouldn't be here," he warned her. "Not tonight."

"Why are there two Matthias Williams buried right here?"

He straightened up. "Actually, there are four," he said. "And five Orrin Morrises and six Shane Vogels. Three Robert Sounds. Three Mei Lin Vogels."

"Why?"

"That's what Duncan asked." He studied her face closely. "Where did he hide the diary? I went through his whole house and I never found it."

"It was in the crawlspace," she admitted. Her heart was pounding so hard her chest hurt. "Did you kill Duncan?"

"No." He sounded infinitely sad. "But I didn't save him, either."

She looked from him to the stones around her. Only the

one had flowers in front of it. Only Hepzibah's. "What are you?" she whispered.

"We acted as dogs," he said, and it sounded like something he'd told himself a thousand times. "We acted as dogs, and we became as dogs. And God won't let us forget it."

Standish dug her fingernails into the palm of her hands, suddenly more angry than afraid. "What the hell does that mean?"

"It means you need to get out of the cemetery, Kate. It's not safe tonight."

And then a bright yellow light flared in the sky and an explosion rocked the ground under their feet.

The road back to Canaan Lake had never seemed so dark before. Peter slowed the UTV to a crawl, the headlights pitched to their lowest setting. The road's twists and turns were covered in a dense, eerie fog that seemed to creep inside the UTV and Peter's very skull. His brain felt thick and damp, his heart miserable. His presentation to Mark had done nothing.

How a man like that could be powerless, Peter couldn't understand. The office itself reeked of importance. Sitting in the uncomfortable chair facing his desk's vast acreage, Peter could look out the window and catch a glimpse of the governor's mansion, an unsubtle reminder of the power Songheuser wielded over Huginn as the first and wealthiest of the extractions corporations.

The first sign something was wrong, Peter realized now, was that Mark's secretary hadn't been eager to let Peter beyond the bland waiting room. The young man had kept Peter waiting nearly an hour, and when he'd finally gotten inside the office, sunset had filled the big window, spilling pinks and oranges across the desk and staining Mark's face. Despite the special effects, he looked grayer than ever. The bags under his eyes had grown since his last conversation with Peter.

"You knew the compound was dangerous, didn't you? That's why you wanted *me* to test it and not some company lackey."

"Peter, what are you doing here?" Mark tried to stand up and fell back into his seat again. While his office still looked like something out of *The Great Gatsby*, all early-twentieth-century money and power, Peter saw that Mark's pinched face no longer belonged. Peter had always thought of his boss as an unflappable society boy aimed effortlessly at success, but at this moment, he saw that Mark was just another academic outmatched by the sharks of the business world. Men like Peter and Mark didn't belong on the same courts as company execs. They didn't have the bloodlust for it.

"They said they changed the formula. They said it wouldn't cause any more problems."

"Any *more* problems? It's caused problems before?"

"That's classified information." Mark waved Peter toward a chair. "Did you bring the results from your first tests?"

"Right here." Peter tossed a memory chit down on his desk. "That chemical might work in a lab, but in a real-life setting, it's a killer. It could wipe out the entire ecosystem if we keep using it. And I'm not sure what kinds of effects it will have on Earth biologicals. What if it got in the water supply?"

Mark slipped the chit into his top drawer. "I see." His voice quavered.

"You see? No, you don't see! You've got to stop this, Mark! You've got to stop this before it gets out of hand."

Mark spun his chair around to face the smoldering pinks of sunset. There was a dry rash like some kind of lichen spreading across the back of his bald head. "I don't know if I can."

"You're the head of forestry for the whole company. They

have to listen to you!"

Mark's head dropped. "Victoria Wallace doesn't listen to anything. The only thing that matters to people like her is the bottom line."

"Even humans can't handle the level of toxic mold spores I saw in those test sites. If they use this, people will die!"

Mark turned around. "What makes you think Songheuser cares?"

"They have to care about the horsetails. If we wipe them out, where will Songheuser's money come from?"

"I've got two other company foresters saying the compound causes no problems when used in uninhabited areas. If the compound really works, what do you think will matter more to Songheuser: protecting a few towns or getting bigger, cheaper harvests out of the unexplored middle of the continent?"

"But the workers–"

"There are always more workers, Peter." Mark looked ready to cry. "If anybody is going to help your town, it's got to be somebody outside of the company. Somebody with connections to the government. Someone who might actually care."

Peter had no idea who that person could be. But Standish's friend Dewey might.

Standish stumbled back from Matthias. The brilliant yellow in the sky behind him had collapsed on itself, turning to a truculent orange glare.

"The mill," she said. "They've blown up the mill!"

She broke into a run, the repeating tombstones and Matthias's weird words forgotten. Two dozen people had died in the Jawbone Flats attack, and they'd only lost the degassing facility. The explosion here looked big enough to destroy the entire mill. She had to help.

She passed a knot of Believers at the cemetery gate. A blonde woman who might have been Vonda Morris called after her, but Standish only ran faster. Her boots pounded on the concrete of the sidewalks – sidewalks, they didn't have those at her end of town – and Hattie's claws clicked behind her. Lights turned on in a house just ahead, and a familiar figure stepped onto the front porch.

"Joe!" she shouted. "Can you give me a ride?"

He threw open the passenger door of his UTV and hurried around to the driver's side. She and Hattie squeezed inside. Joe fired up the rig, his face pale, his lips tight. She had never seen him without a smile before.

Sirens came on, impossibly loud, and Standish realized she had no idea where they came from or that Canaan Lake had any kind of emergency response. Was there a firehouse? She hadn't done any work orders for one.

"The volunteer fire department." It was like Joe was reading her mind. "I hope they get there before we do."

A big yellow rig pulled out in front of them, its lights flashing and its eight wheels spraying mud. Joe raised his hand unit. "Unit 1, this is Joe. I'm behind the VFD's pump truck. I need stats from our fire suppressant system."

Someone cleared their throat. "We can't tell, sir." A crash overpowered the voice.

"Repeat, Francesco." The hand unit gave a little crackle. "I said 'repeat'!"

They swung to the right as the pump truck made its wide turn into the mill's yard. Joe slid the UTV to a stop in front of the office's front steps. He turned to Standish. "Get down to the security office. If they've got any spare backpack fire rigs, you sign one out and go wherever they send you. And leave that damn dog behind."

She jumped out of the UTV, one hand gripping Hattie's collar tight. The stink of molten plastic already burned her eyes and nose. This was no place for a dog.

Across the street, something popped and boomed, and a chunk of metal streaked past them to smash through the window beside the front door. Hattie yelped in fear. Standish hoisted the dog into her arms. Glass crunched under her boots as she marched to the staircase with the dog in an awkward grip.

"Please don't run away, please don't run away, please don't run away."

She didn't realize she was whispering it like a mantra until they hit the basement level and her own wheezing voice sounded over the sirens and the explosions. Here it was practically peaceful.

Standish dropped the dog and held her between her knees while she unlocked her office door. Her hands were shaking. Her whole body was shaking. It sounded like the end of the fucking world out there and she was going to go back out in it. She urged Hattie inside the office and dragged the dog bed under her desk. The office seemed safe enough, but Standish knew it was an illusory safety. If that skybridge went up, the whole building would be in danger.

"I'll be back." She pushed the dog down into the bed and hugged her tight. "I'm not going to let anything happen to you, Hattie. I promise. Because I can't live without you. You know that, right?"

The dog pushed her nose into Standish's face, licking nervously.

"I'll be back. Now stay!"

Standish opened the office door as narrowly as possible and squeezed out quickly, not certain the dog would follow a command in a situation like this. She was tremendously scared, and Standish couldn't blame her. Standish didn't lock the door behind her. If the building caught fire, she'd need every second to get Hattie out.

The hallway was no longer empty. People ran in both directions, most of them sturdy men she recognized as Brett's friends and coworkers. She ran behind one and they both crowded into the security office. Someone was shouting at their hand unit.

"Fall back, Francesco!" She recognized the voice as Brett's, wound high-pitched with nerves. "Man, get out of there!"

An explosion sounded, its shock waves rattling the building even in the basement. She grabbed the door frame. "Jesus fucking Christ."

"We need all hands at the chip pile," Brett shouted. "Grab a backpack and get moving."

She squeezed past the man in front of her and seized Brett's elbow. "How do you use one of these things?"

He hesitated. The radio gave a burst of static and then went painfully silent.

"They're big fire extinguishers," he explained. "Point the hose at the base of the flames and keep moving. Your goal is to guide any survivors away from the building while the real fire crew handles the problem."

"OK." She reached for a pack. It weighed nearly as much as Hattie did, and she had to work to get it slung onto her back. She took a few awkward steps forward.

"Fuck." Brett spun her around. "You'll need this." He held out an air mask. "The fire suppression system is pumping out aragonite and there's not going to be much oxygen left. Be careful, Standish."

She felt a wave of gratitude for the man. "Thanks."

Then she hurried after the others, hoping like hell they knew where they were going. She'd never spent much time at the mill, and now she regretted it. As they zigged and zagged through the busy yard, she dropped her mask over her face. She might be able to breathe better, but she still couldn't see shit. She could barely make out the back of the woman in front of her. There would be nothing worse than getting lost in this inferno. Her air could only last so long.

Someone waved her toward a building with flames shooting out the upper stories. The whole place was shrouded in black smoke, but a red glow saturated the smoke and cast the area in a hellish light. The person ahead of her threw open the building's door and propped it wide. Shrieks and screams tumbled out.

People were dying in there.

Standish and her crew pressed inside. Someone slapped the side of her pack and a white LED came on, trained forward. The white light pierced the smoke for a few feet and then vanished in the gloom.

"Help!"

They surged forward, one hand on the left-hand wall, one on the shoulder of the person ahead. The person in front of her paused to gesticulate wildly and Standish realized they intended to split the group in half, one moving forward, one headed to the left. She went to the left, her stomach climbing in her throat. Overhead, steel and plastic shrieked and groaned. The whole building could go up any second, and they hadn't found anyone yet.

She hit a heavy door and touched it with the back of her hand. Still cool. The door knob turned, but it wouldn't open.

She put her shoulder into it. Something heavy blocked the door, and as she shoved someone screamed. The door flew open, and Standish stumbled forward into someone crying and shrieking and gasping with pain. The air was still clear here, and Standish could see a staircase leading upward.

The staircase was filled with people. Some lay on the treads, some barely clung to the railing, and she realized the air was clear because the smoke and oxygen was being sucked up into the upper layers, and there was nothing for these people to breathe, and she had only her own air to offer them.

Something boomed overhead and flames shot out the second story landing. Someone leaped over the railing and smashed down in front of Standish, fire clinging to every inch of their body. She thumbed on her fire extinguisher, blasting at the flames. Bits of white fluff floated up on hot air currents.

"Come on!" someone shouted.

The person on the floor didn't move. Standish had put out the flames, but the cooked thing there was beyond helping.

The crowd in the stairwell surged forward. Standish tried to squeeze out of the way and keep the door open for them, but someone shoved her and she went down. A boot dug into her calf. Someone kicked her in the head so hard stars shot up in her eyes.

A hand seized her elbow. "Get up," a voice shouted in her ear. "Get up!"

They yanked her to her feet. The air in the corridor was filling with smoke, but Standish still recognized the blond hair and fierce blue eyes of Victoria Wallace. Another figure crashed into her, and Standish caught the two before they fell. The second person swayed and nearly collapsed.

"I got you," Victoria said, her voice rough. "Help me with her," she ordered Standish.

They slung the other woman's arms over their shoulders and followed the others toward the exit. The white lights of the rescue crew guided them forward, and Standish knew that without them she and Victoria would have lost their way as they staggered through the smoke. The injured woman's blood seeped through Standish's jacket like spilled tea.

And then they were outside, all the way to the edge of the mill yard, where people were laying the dead and the injured on the muddy street. Standish and Victoria lowered their victim to the ground.

Despite the soot covering her face and the blood soaking her coveralls, Standish recognized the woman. How could she forget Melissa Whitley's pointed chin, so much like Olive's?

Standish dropped to her knees to hold the woman's hand. "Please be all right," she whispered. "Please."

"She'll bleed to death if we don't do something." Victoria stripped off her jacket and the blouse beneath it and held them out to Standish.

Standish pressed the fabric to Melissa's side, racking her brains for past first aid training. None of what she'd learned mattered out here, nearly an hour from the nearest hospital. Melissa could die before help came from Space City.

"Keep applying pressure," Victoria ordered. "I'll get more supplies from security. Don't let her die."

Victoria headed toward the office, her white bra and pale skin gleaming as Muninn slid out from behind the cloud of smoke, lighting up the street. Standish trembled and turned her eyes back to Melissa's face. She could feel the stars above, pitiless and cruel as they circled behind the second moon.

Muninn, she remembered, was one of the Norse pantheon, one of blind Wodin's companions. He would fly out over the battlefields, searching for the slain. Tonight there was plenty for him to see.

In the hills, a dog howled.

What is understanding, after all, but that which makes sense of the connections and underpinnings of the world and all our experiences?

Understanding is primarily a thing of words.

– from THE COLLECTED WISDOM OF MW WILLIAMS

CHAPTER TWENTY-ONE

Peter slowed for the final hairpin of Cemetery Curve and caught flashing lights in his rearview mirror. He crept to the side of the road and watched as three ambulances shot past him. His hands on the steering wheel went instantly clammy. *One* ambulance was unusual for Canaan Lake. Most people just reached for the super glue and drove themselves to the hospital in Space City if something went bad. He'd met plenty of loggers who'd driven in one-handed, their finger or hand or arm packed in a plastic bag filled with ice.

He wiped his hands on his pants and reached for his hand unit. There had to be news if the ambulances were already arriving from Space City.

The social media networks were buzzing with rumors, but SC News One was flashing a video update. Peter hesitated. A fire truck shot past the rig, rocking the UTV on its axles. He didn't really want to know, but he had to.

He clicked the video.

A moment of static, and then a low-resolution image filled his screen – probably footage shot on a hand unit and then run through software to strip away identifiers. Three figures stood in silhouette against a white background, their faces and bodies shrouded in green fabric like the ghosts of horrible trees. Their voices had the metallic bark of a voice changer, and at first he could barely make out what they were saying.

"GreenOne is proud to claim the firebombing of the Canaan Lake sawmill. It's only right that Songheuser Corporation should experience the kind of devastation that the forests of Huginn experience every day. This world is under attack by the commercial enterprises that control the puppet government of Huginn!"

It was impossible to tell which figure was speaking or if someone was narrating over the image. One of the figures held up a hunk of white, rubbery stuff that looked all-too like the plastic explosives in old-time action movies.

"If the corporate schemers do not clean up their act, we will be forced to take action on another mill. The people of Jawbone Flats and Canaan Lake have already paid the price for their participation in the destruction of our world's ecology. Now other towns must wake up. Shut down your death machines before we do it for you!"

He turned off his hand unit and sat in silence for a moment, trembling. He wiped his nose. Canaan Lake was still six kilometers down the road, and he could already smell smoke.

Belinda was a part of this. She'd found him and threatened him, and he still hadn't taken her seriously. And why? Because she was a bartender? Because he'd spent the last year and a half flirting with her, paying more attention to her backside than what she said? He could have stopped this before anyone got hurt.

Peter pulled onto the highway, the UTV's tires screeching a little. Belinda rented a little house from a Believer family just outside of the city limits. It had always seemed a strange location for a woman who commuted via bicycle, but now it made a certain kind of sense. She loved nature, after all, and apartment living didn't offer much privacy for a terrorist.

He turned onto the muddy drive leading to the farm and parked the rig in the grass. Belinda's cottage – it must have been some kind of shed once, but she'd added some decorative touches – sat closer to the highway than the rest of the property. Her bike wasn't leaning inside its shelter.

That was a bad sign.

He tested the front door. It wasn't locked. Peter looked around. A group of sheep huddled against the fence, watching him idly. He still felt as if there were eyes on him as he opened the door.

The smell of flowers and oranges filled the little cottage. Peter stopped in the doorway and looked around himself, getting oriented. Whatever else Belinda had been, she was clearly the kind of person who kept their house neat and good-smelling. He could see his reflection on the polished horsetail planks of the floor.

"Belinda?"

He cleared his throat. "Belinda?" he tried again, louder.

Outside, a sheep made an irritable sound. The house stayed silent. Peter did not relax.

There was only one room to the place, although a low counter marked off the kitchen area. A battery-powered hotplate sat on the counter with a small cooler beside it. He flipped open the cooler's lid. A handful of radishes sat submerged in a puddle of melted ice, a bottle of beer beside them. The beer felt warm when he touched it.

He turned to examine the sleeping area. The bed, a lightweight futon, was folded into its couch shape, and the end table beside it held a stack of books – *The Monkey Wrench Gang*, by Edward Abbey, Kafka's *The Metamorphosis*, some hippy-dippy novel by Starhawk – and an empty water glass. Belinda didn't seem to own much.

A man's voice hollered outside, and Peter tensed. He peered around the ruffled curtain on the door and was relieved to see a Believer walking up to the front gate. The man must be coming to visit the owner of the farm.

Peter turned back to his investigation. There was nothing in the room to connect Belinda to the ecoterrorist cell, unless a bowl full of potpourri on a floating shelf counted as terrorist material. He picked up her hairbrush from the kitchen counter. A few strands of red-blonde hair and a thread of moss were caught between the bristles, but other than that, even the brush looked clean.

With a frown, he turned back to the floating shelf. There was something tucked behind the potpourri bowl, a brochure he'd assumed she'd tacked up to add a little personality to the room. A stunning photo of a rock-eater lichen field filled most of the page, a backlit group of horsetail trees adding depth to the image. The picture, now that he actually looked at it, was familiar.

He leaned closer. Oh, yes, he knew that quote only too well: "The wonders of Huginn are irreplaceable. The moon offers a wilderness of colors to soothe the soul." This was *his* brochure, the one he'd written for that wretched travel agency that had landed him on the ecoterrorists' radar. It wasn't proof that Belinda was a member of GreenOne – not real, physical proof – but it was connection enough to show Sheriff Vargas.

He hurried outside and came to an awkward stop. The man he'd seen through the window stood beside Peter's UTV, talking intensely with another bearded man. He hadn't heard them at all.

"Can I help you, good man?" The taller of the pair looked at him with an impatient expression. His voice was polite enough, but Peter could tell he would be glad to see him go.

"Just dropping something off for Belinda."

Peter passed them as quickly as he could, but he couldn't help but hear the whispered exchange:

"Matthias says he has a plan. We should trust in him. Besides, it's our way!"

"But Vogel is right. The last time we let Matthias make a deal for us, we lost a sixth of our property. Where is our future if we give it all to Songheuser?" The shorter man waved a yellow pamphlet, clearly furious about it. It looked like the cheap paper the town used to print the bulletins they sent to the Believers.

The taller snatched it from his hands and gripped it as if to rip it in two. Peter could see the word "tax" written across the top.

"Excuse me," Peter said. "Would you mind if I looked at that?"

The tall man thrust it at him. "Keep it. I'm tired of reading it."

"Thanks." Peter got into the UTV before the other one could say anything and pulled out onto the highway. He couldn't help glancing at the bulletin, catching words here and there.

He pulled over and reread a section, his face twisting in disbelief.

He had to show this to Standish. The new property tax was even more vicious than they'd thought.

The Mill Cafe had set up an outdoor buffet breakfast for the rescue workers, and Standish was happy to sink into a chair with a cup of coffee and a stack of flapjacks. Black goo kept dribbling out of her nose, and every inch of her felt bruised or scorched. Even the coffee tasted smoky.

Julia from accounting appeared at her elbow. "Wet wipe?"

Standish looked at her hands. Her palms had a silver sheen and there was a black rime all around her nails. "Much appreciated."

Julia began polishing Standish's nearest hand. "I can't believe how brave you were. People were talking about how you and Victoria Wallace saved all those people. It's amazing."

Standish forked a chunk of pancake into her face so she wouldn't have to answer. If brave meant "nearly pissing yourself," then sure, she'd been brave.

Julia got out a third wipe. "And did you hear about the big announcement? Everyone's talking about it."

"I've been a little busy."

Julia dropped the wet wipe. "Oh my gosh, you've got to see it." Julia brought out her hand unit. "I've already watched it twice. I can't believe how terrific Victoria looks after all she went through last night." She tapped the screen and held it in front of Standish's face.

On the screen, a clean and polished Victoria Wallace stood behind a lectern draped in Songheuser's colors, an NATF flag filling the wall behind her. A pair of I+ glasses clamped on the tip of her nose toned down her general sexiness.

"We will not be bullied by these eco-insurgents," Wallace began. "Songheuser Corporation isn't going anywhere. In fact, I'm proud to announce a new partnership with the townspeople of Canaan Lake that will strengthen the community and improve business practices."

Wallace paused for effect. Standish reached for the hand unit, but Julia maneuvered it out of reach, clearly worried about Standish's grimy condition. "The city council is right now moving to authorize a special session vote on a property tax measure that will invest more than four million Huginn dollars into local law enforcement and infrastructure over the next five years. The townspeople's investment will keep our mill safe and bring in necessary development as Songheuser moves to expand our operations here in Canaan Lake."

Wallace leaned closer to the microphone. "That's right. Songheuser is planning not just to rebuild this mill, but to double its size and bring another four hundred workers to this community. Because we believe in Canaan Lake and its people!"

Julia sighed. "Wasn't that stirring? 'Because we believe in Canaan Lake'? And can you imagine this place with another four hundred workers? We could actually attract our own hairdresser. Maybe even another restaurant. It's going to change the face of the town!"

"It's... pretty exciting. Yep." Standish got to her feet. "You know, I totally forgot about Hattie," she fibbed. "She probably needs a walk. I'd better go to her."

"But you haven't finished your pancakes."

"Hattie comes first," Standish said, hoping her smile passed for real. Victoria Wallace's big announcement stank worse than the stench of scorched plastic coming off the mill. Songheuser may have taken a hit when the ecoterrorists detonated that bomb, but the company had come back swinging – and looking more sympathetic than ever.

She hurried up to her office to get Hattie. What good did GreenOne think it was doing? Songheuser had insurance, and what insurance didn't cover, the government of Huginn would certainly kick in. This attack wouldn't cost the company a penny.

The only people who'd be paying were the people of Canaan Lake.

She followed Hattie down the trail to the lake, her blood boiling. Good people had gotten hurt today. Like Melissa Whitley, who was just trying to make a home for her family and doing the best she could.

"Standish!"

She turned. "Peter!" She surprised herself by grabbing him in a tight hug. "I'm glad you're back from the city."

"I'm glad you're all right! Why are you so filthy? Don't tell me you were at work during the fire?"

She explained the night's activities, enjoying his astonishment as she described her heroism. When she was done, his face turned serious.

"Look at this," he said, holding out the bulletin. He caught her up with his trip to Belinda's cottage, then pointed out a clause in small print on the second page of the pamphlet. "This section talks about what zones will be affected by the property tax. It specifically says that industrial, mining, and timber areas are exempt from this special session tax."

"So Songheuser's property won't be taxed."

"Yeah." His finger stabbed the back page. "And look who sponsored the thing."

"Joe Holder! I should have known. He's the head of operations. If anyone's looking out for Songheuser's bottom line around here, it's him."

"Joe knows everything about the mill and about this town. He goes to every city council meeting, and he's been here for six years. If there's anyone who knows anything about what Duncan was digging into – about what he was doing before he died – it's Joe." Peter began pacing excitedly. "Can you spy on him?" he asked. "Set up a camera in his office or something?"

"Well, he's my boss, so I've got a good excuse to get in there. I could probably find a way into his house and snoop around there, too."

He was already nodding. "Yes. Yes. Absolutely. Standish, we have to get to the bottom of this. Whatever Songheuser's up to – the secret road, the maps Duncan was hiding, this new property tax – I think it's all connected."

"Me too," Standish said, and felt a cold rage kindle in her chest. "And we're going to prove it."

The office's front door was blocked off by debris and operations staff, so Peter hurried down the side courtyard, pleased by his meeting with Standish. They were finally making headway on Duncan's case. If Joe Holder knew anything, they'd get it sorted out.

As for Peter, he was going to make things right with Sheriff Vargas. He just needed to grab Belinda's purse out of his office. They'd have GreenOne behind bars in no time.

He rounded the corner to the motor pool, noticing the sheriff's deputy in tense conversation with the security guard standing in front of the guard shack. The last time he'd seen Paul Wu, he'd been skulking around the edges of Joe Holder's circle of toadies and looking embarrassed about it. Peter hoped the bug up Wu's ass had crawled out.

The deputy turned to face him. "Peter Bajowski."

"Paul. You helping with the bombing investigation?"

"Dr Bajowski, I'm going to have to ask you to step away from the utility vehicle."

Peter took a step backward. "What?"

"Not a step closer to the building! And get your hands up!"

Wu's service revolver was pointed at Peter's chest. Not an air bolt gun, but a genuine firearm. Peter raised his hands slowly.

"I'm not the one you should be arresting, Paul. I've got information–"

"Get away from the entrance!"

Paul seized his wrist and twisted it up behind his back. His shoulder gave a scream of protest, the joint creaking under the strain. Paul's knee pushed into the back of Peter's leg, driving him to the ground. He gave Peter's back a sharp nudge so he fell into the fragile greenery of the flower bed beside the office's door. The deputy's weight flattened Peter's back as the deputy wrenched Peter's free hand behind him. The tiny silhouettes of pseudo-club moss stood outlined in Peter's vision.

"Peter Bajowski, you are under arrest for the bombing of the Canaan Lake sawmill. Whatever you say can and will be used against you in a court of law." Paul's voice rolled over Peter's head in monotone waves.

"I wasn't even here!"

"We found the transmitters in your office, courtesy of an anonymous tip." Paul jerked Peter to his feet. "I'm taking you in."

The government says we should be grateful to corporations like Songheuser, who have built what infrastructure exists on Huginn. But in truth, the corporations are like interstellar parasites, stripping the world to send the profits back to Earth. They invest the bare minimum in their employees and this world, and they refuse to clean up the devastation they leave in their wake.

This is colonialism in its most naked, greediest form.

– Olive Whitley, A NEW COMMON SENSE (pamphlet)

CHAPTER TWENTY-TWO

Standish slammed the door of her UTV. Just moments ago she'd been happily cutting the connection on Joe Holder's cable box, looking forward to finally figuring out what Duncan had been up to. Then she'd checked her hand unit and seen the news. How could Vargas arrest Peter, of all people, for bombing the mill?

She squeezed past a line of UTVs with the logos of at least three different law enforcement offices emblazoned on their sides and caught up with a woman carrying a box of breakfast pastries up the police department's stairs. Standish trudged up behind her, her back and legs protesting about her all-nighter. She'd pictured herself bursting into the station and demanding to see Peter, but now she wasn't sure she had the energy to do much bursting.

The pastry bearer opened the door, spilling out a cacophony.

The Canaan Lake sheriff's department was not built with the intention of holding more than six or seven people, and there had to be at least twice as many crowded in there right now. Hattie would have hated all the chaos if she hadn't stayed in the UTV: Joe Holder was shouting at the sheriff; Victoria Wallace sat in a desk chair, watching him with her lips set tight. Several members of the volunteer fire department huddled around the coffee pot, looking hungrily at the box of pastries in the hands of the young woman Standish had followed up the stairs. The girl smiled winsomely as she leaned down to place the pastries beside the coffee pot, and a small cross painted in many colors swung out of her shirt.

Standish's gaze followed the pendulum swing of it. A Believer cross, like those covering the cemetery and sticking out of flowerbeds around town. People might not share the Believers' religion, but their beliefs still ran through Canaan Lake, as strong a thread as Songheuser's paychecks.

"All right, all right," Sheriff Vargas said, her voice cutting through Joe's without losing its calm authority. She squeezed between a young man and woman in brown uniforms, probably help from another nearby town, and stopped in front of Standish with a pleasant smile. "How can I help you, Ms Standish? I hear you were a big help out there last night."

"Uh… thanks." Every eye in the room had fixed itself on her. Her new popularity was going to be short-lived. "I'm here to see Peter, if that's OK."

"Sorry. No one in or out today. But get yourself a pastry, Standish. You look like you're about to fall down."

"No thanks. I just came to check on Peter."

"I insist." Vargas steered Standish toward the corner table with the coffee pot and the box of donuts. "I've got my doubts about this arrest but for right now I think Peter might be safer in here than outside," she confided in a low voice. "The security footage from the mill and the office building just finished downloading. It ought to reveal who planted those explosives and how a set of transmitters wound up in Peter's office."

Standish frowned. "Why are you telling me this?"

Sheriff Vargas poured two cups of coffee, her eyes flicking around the room as she did so. "I worked a long time to get here. Private security, mostly. I know a lot about swimming with sharks." She passed Standish a cup. "That doesn't mean I like them."

Standish sipped her coffee, wondering just what the hell the sheriff meant.

"You hear about the property tax the city council proposed?"

"Yeah." Standish reached for a bear claw.

"Thirty percent of the funds it will raise are for new roads and infrastructure. Fifty-five percent is earmarked for law enforcement. Songheuser might be happy they can move more lumber, but not nearly as happy as I'll be with a budget that doesn't come out of their pocket."

"Feeling a little under their thumb?" Standish murmured.

A volunteer squeezed by to grab a donut. Vargas took a drink of her coffee and raised an eyebrow. Things began to come together in Standish's head – Vargas's treatment of Duncan's disappearance, the phony declaration that he'd committed suicide, Standish's own suspicions about Duncan's investigations into the company's doings in Sector 13. Songheuser might own the sheriff's department right now, but that didn't mean Vargas liked it.

"Thank you for the donut," Standish said in a conversational tone. "How can I help Peter?" she added in a whisper.

The sheriff moved away from the table and around the corner. The coziness of the office's main room disappeared in this corridor; a draft came from the grate of the freight elevator, and the overhead light flickered. She stopped in front of a doorway giving off the piney scent of disinfectant. "Here's the bathroom," the sheriff said loudly.

"Peter told me about Belinda when I booked him," Vargas continued, softer. "If she's part of this GreenOne business and she lied to me about Peter's alibi, then there will be a lot of pressure to reopen the Duncan Chambers case. Plenty of people have it out for Peter, and they want to see him in jail – for any crime."

"Who?"

"It doesn't matter. What does matter is finding the murder weapon. Without it, all I've got is a cockamamie suicide note that won't hold up to any real forensic testing and a lovesick ex-boyfriend with plenty of motive. I have a hunch that air bolt gun is still in the woods someplace. Maybe you can take a metal detector and spend a few hours out there. You probably won't find it, but you'd have a better chance than I did with a group of Songheuser-approved volunteer deputies."

Standish caught Vargas's forearm. She could feel hard bands of muscle beneath the stiff fabric of her uniform. "Are you really saying Songheuser covered up Duncan's murder?" If so, she was the second person with Huginn government connections to hint at it. Damn, Standish needed to get hold of Dewey!

"I'm *saying* I don't believe Peter Bajowski had any part in it. He's an honest man, honest to a fault. And he's too soft-hearted to even eat a cheeseburger."

Standish gave a dry laugh. "That's true." She glanced over her shoulder. Sheriff Vargas would have to return to her desk soon. The chaos had gotten louder in there. "Do you really believe that property tax is going to change things here in Canaan Lake?"

"Oh, if it passes, things are definitely going to be different." Vargas smiled, revealing large, white teeth. "You ever see a dancing bear, Standish?" The smile grew. "Do you know what happens when it gets off its chain?"

It wasn't a smile, Standish realized. It was the bear inside Vargas preparing to rip into her captors' flesh.

"Oh hell, now what?"

Joe Holder's booming voice brought them all to the front windows. At the end of the block, horses and wagons filled Main Street.

"Looks like you've got yourself a Fleshie problem, Sheriff," he added.

"It looks like every Believer in town's down there. What are they up to?"

"I see my father's buggy," the pastry woman said. "It looks like he's turning onto this street. Maybe he's headed to the post office."

Sheriff Vargas opened the door and they all followed. Standish eyed the gathering mass of Believers. She needed to get past them if she was going to get back to her place to grab her outdoor gear.

"They *are* headed for the post office," Sheriff Vargas said. "But they're just standing in front, waiting for something."

"What's in the post office?" Standish asked. She hadn't had a reason to go inside.

"They handle permits and registrations as well as the mail," the sheriff said. She pulled the brim of her hat lower and headed toward the gathering. Standish stayed close. They joined the Believers standing in front of the plain shoebox of the post office. There had to be fifty or more neo-Mennonites lining School Street, with the majority knotted around the post office.

"What's going on, Mr Eames?" the sheriff asked the nearest farmer.

He barely glanced at her. "Believer business."

"If you're blocking the street, it's my business. Now what's the matter?"

A group of Believers on foot turned the corner from Main Street, and the mass of Believers went silent. In their black wool homespun, they could have been a flock of ravens waiting at a deathbed.

Standish studied the walkers. The Believers around them seemed to pull away from the group, unwilling to even brush their sleeves. She recognized a few faces: Vonda and Orrin

Morris, Mei Lin Vogel.

The crowd shifted, and she saw a figure standing alone in front of the post office. Matthias watched the group come toward him and did not step aside as they neared. The group paused.

"Don't do it," Matthias said. "You know it's not our way."

A man stepped past Vonda Morris, a short man with light brown hair. "We'll do what we need to do to protect ourselves, Matthias. That's our way now."

Standish took an unwilling step forward. "Shane?"

The sheriff frowned at her. "Yeah, that's Shane Vogel. And it looks like he's in charge."

Shane pushed past Matthias, and a dozen or so Believers followed him inside. Matthias watched them go, his face twisted in misery.

"They're registering to vote," Vargas said, her voice astonished. "They're registering to goddamn vote!"

Matthias jammed his hands in his pockets and walked away. In a moment, he was gone. Standish turned away. She climbed into her UTV and sat in silence for a moment, stroking Hattie's head and thinking hard. The Believers – or at least some of them – had turned on Matthias and all their old ways.

And Shane Vogel was not only alive, but well enough to walk.

That, out of all of it, made the least sense.

Standish's hand unit flashed a message alert at her. She felt a second's disappointment when it wasn't Dewey, and then surprise: Olive Whitley? She steered with her elbow as she tapped the alert.

Please come. Home alone.

Standish felt a surge of frustration. Peter needed her – she had to get to Sector 13 while there was still daylight. But she couldn't turn her back on Olive after what had happened to the kid's mother. She started up the UTV and crept between the buggies down to Main Street.

She turned into the Whitley's driveway and wondered if she ought to put Hattie on her lead. The front door of the house burst open before she made up her mind.

"Miss Kate!" Olive charged out of the house and threw open the UTV door. Her wiry arms squeezed tightly around Standish's neck.

"Hi, Olive." Standish gave the girl a hesitant pat.

The girl buried her face in Standish's shoulder, her whole body quaking. "You saved my mom."

"I was just helping the firefighters."

"Can you come in? Please?" She took a step backward, dragging Standish out of the rig. "Please?"

There was no denying that kind of sweet neediness. Standish followed her inside, Hattie at her side.

"So you're all alone in here?" Standish felt glad she hadn't ignored the kid's message. There was one light turned on in the place, a bare LED bulb over the kitchen sink which only managed to illuminate a heap of dirty dishes. Clothes and blankets had been strewn across the main room as if a bomb had gone off.

One had, of course. Standish felt sick and pried her hand out of Olive's too-tight grip.

"Have you had breakfast?"

"Breakfast?"

Standish picked up a pink sweater, the kind of garment a man would grab and then reconsider when packing his wife's suitcase for the hospital, and folded it into a square. "Did you even get dinner?"

"Dad was making spaghetti when the mill called," Olive said, her voice very small. "I forgot about it."

Standish put the pink sweater on the couch and made her way into the kitchen, searching for a light switch. With more light, she could see a pot filled with a black and brown mess that might have once been noodles. She opened a cupboard and was glad to find cereal. "Let's get you something to eat."

She poured cereal and real cow's milk, and put the girl down in front of it at the table. If there were words for these times, Standish didn't know them.

Olive stirred her cereal, watching the circles she made in the bowl. "Dad called from the hospital. He sounded like a robot. He says Mom has a perforated bowel, three cracked ribs, and a ruptured spleen. She has to have a long surgery and she'll be in the hospital for a couple of days."

"I was there when the EMTs looked her over. She inhaled a lot of smoke, too. The surgery will be easy, but it's hard to fix lungs when they get full of shit."

"It's going to cost a lot of money."

"Well, it happened at work, so Songheuser's insurance will cover it."

"Yeah, but Mom won't be able to work for a long time after that." Olive took a bite of cereal and swallowed it without chewing. "Mom's job covers a lot of our bills, like the UTV loans and the credit card."

Standish opened her mouth and closed it. It wasn't like she had a spare couple of grand to help out. Standish wanted to find Belinda and her crop of GreenOne freaks and punch their faces in.

She picked up the pot of scorched noodles and scraped at the mess, using plenty of muscle.

"I think I can take care of it," Olive said. "Chameli gave me a lot of money for the blue butterflies, and I know where I can get more."

"Yeah?" Standish dumped the black stuff into the garbage and began scrubbing like she could scrub away the whole night, the whole explosion at the mill.

"I found them in the woods behind Jeff Eames's farm,"

Olive explained. "I think they live in the hills. I'm going back tomorrow to look for them."

"Well, that'd be a nice way to help your family. As long as you're careful out there and you make sure Mr Eames doesn't mind you being on his property."

Olive drained the milk from her bowl. "It ain't his anymore. Songheuser owns it, and I don't think they care much about butterflies."

Standish rinsed out the pot and put it in the dish drainer. She remembered what Peter had said about the dead zone his tests had created and the company's insistence on pursuing the degassing compound. "No, they probably don't."

Olive laid her head down on the table. "Miss Kate, I wish my mom were here."

Standish hesitated a second and then squeezed the girl's shoulder. "Me too, Olive."

Peter sat on the cold floor of his cell. Posie Eames had brought him a late lunch of pasta and vegetables, and now the scent of stale garlic lay over the cramped space. On the other side of the wire mesh, another cell sat empty. The sheriff's department didn't usually arrest more than one person except when Songheuser's paychecks came on a Friday.

The freight elevator grunted and whirred, and Peter came to his feet. It was probably just Posie coming back for his empty tray, but he wanted to meet her with dignity. He wiped his hands on his pants. He could hear hushed voices, but the speakers weren't in eyeshot yet.

"Peter Bajowski."

He took a step forward, surprised to hear an unfamiliar woman's voice. It took him a minute to recognize Victoria Wallace.

"COO Wallace. Nice of you to stop by."

"I wanted to lay eyes on the man who thought he could

bring Songheuser to its knees."

"It's not me. I don't have any problems with Songheuser, and even if I did, I could never hurt anybody. Especially not innocent millworkers."

"Pretty words, Bajowski, but I know better." She pulled out a pair of I+ glasses and slipped them on. "Video 321, projection."

A light flashed on the glasses' temple, and an image appeared on the wall beside Peter. He recognized the paneling before he recognized the back of his head. It was footage from Mark Allen's office, and he could hear his own voice, furious and desperate as he begged Mark to stop the chemical tests.

"You look pretty angry with the company to me." The image switched off, and Wallace moved closer to the door of his cell, close enough that she could smell her perfume, some sparkling floral stuff that seemed too pretty for a shark like her.

"I hope you like Earth," she said with a smile. "Because even if you get out of this cage, I'll have your visa stripped before you can check your email."

Peter gripped the mesh of the door to steady himself. Anything he said would be a waste of breath.

"Goodbye, Bajowski. I hope you feel like a hero."

Then she left him, alone and trembling. He squeezed his eyes shut and rested his forehead against the door. Even here in the basement, he could hear the rain coming down outside.

Huginn, Day 199

I've been hiding in the pollinator shed. I don't know what time it is, although there's a little gray light coming in through the window, enough to see this page. I don't want to write any more, but I have to. I'm coughing up blood now, and someone needs to know what happened.

I wrote the last entry here after Doc Sounds and I came

back from the Morris's house. The town felt empty. No one was working out in the fields; no one answered our knocks on their doors. I took my diary and my Bible into this shed while Doc continued our search.

When he threw open the door to the shed, I knew something else was wrong.

"Craig's gone."

He could barely say the words. His eyes wouldn't focus on me and his legs wobbled underneath him. He looked sick, like he was about to pass out.

It took me a minute to understand what he meant: that someone had taken Craig's body from the root cellar where we'd stored it. I had to take Doc by the elbow and march him back to the kitchen and make him a cup of tea before I could get any sense out of him. He couldn't find anyone. Craig's dead body was missing. We were alone here.

I couldn't believe it. Wouldn't believe it. And the more he kept repeating it, the more I couldn't stand it.

Finally, I had to see for myself. I stumbled out of the kitchen and down the muddy track to our house. The rain soaked my skirts and through my bonnet. I fell once, twice. My legs could hardly hold me any longer. Matthias wouldn't leave me. He would be at home, ready to take me wherever the others had gone.

And sure enough, there was smoke coming out of our chimney.

I fell through the door and Matthias was right there with his hand under my elbow. The cabin felt so warm. He set me beside the fire and put a blanket around my shoulders. There was a smell in the room that I couldn't quite place, but it made my stomach buck and clench.

"My sweet love," he whispered. "You are the thinnest of all of us. I promised God I would take care of you as my own flesh, that I would protect you and keep you well. How

I have failed you. I brought you to this place and now you are dying."

"I'm fine," I said, or maybe just tried to say. My run had taken all the strength out of me. I couldn't remember the last time I'd eaten.

He knelt before me with a steaming bowl. "Please drink," he said. "It's just broth, you can drink it."

The broth was a clear, light beige. A scrap of bay leaf floated on the surface. It could have been tea. It could have been anything.

"It's leather bird," he said. "Vonda found a way to cook it safely."

"Vonda?" My head spun. Was that what we'd found on her stove? Leather bird soup?

He pushed the spoon close to my face. It smelled wonderful.

I remembered the way the leather birds' bellies opened up into that sharp-edged slit, the yellow lining of their orifice as unwholesome as death. I turned my face away.

"Please," he begged. "It sounds bad, but it's the only way we're going to make it through this winter. I can't live if you die, Hepzibah. I'm not *me* without you."

The smell made me cry out. Nothing had smelled this good, not since the last of the lentils ran out or the final bit of oatmeal vanished. Even the dogs we'd butchered hadn't smelled this delicious.

He leaned in, his eyes huge and terrified. "Please eat it. Don't think about it, just eat it."

And then I knew. I knew it wasn't leather bird.

I got up. My mind had gone completely clear and hollow; I could see the words of scripture as if they were printed in front of my eyes and repeated themselves over and over in the bowl of my mind: "Him that dieth of Jeroboam in the city shall the dogs eat."

"Eat it!" he screamed.

I pushed him as hard as I could and launched myself out the door. Just a moment ago, I could barely walk, but now I was running. I had to run someplace, anyplace away from Matthias and Orrin and Vonda and the things they had done. Leather birds swooped over my head and tree scooters chirped at me, and as I ran I swore I could understand their voices, that I knew what the creatures of this place wanted, and it was for us to go, to leave them to their place and let them live as they had always lived. I tripped over a fallen horsetail limb and hit the ground hard. Something crushed under my hand and I smelled the sour stink of red death puffballs.

I crawled a few feet farther, choking on the cloud of spores, and then my strength gave out and I collapsed on the damp ground.

I woke in darkness, coughing. My arms ached and my ribs hurt where I'd fallen on them. I was going to die if I lay here. I had to find shelter and something to eat.

I remembered my pollinators. There was a little sugar left in the bottom of their food stores; I'd hidden it from everyone to give my bees a chance at survival. Now I needed it. The others would try to force me to join them in their sin, but I would not. I would go to the pollinator shed and come up with a plan.

I sat up and realized where I was: the cemetery. I'd tripped on the cross we'd planted on Cheyenne Ferguson's grave and collapsed in the soft dirt.

But the whole cemetery was soft dirt. Every smooth-packed grave had been churned up and left untamped, the crosses flung willy-nilly. Someone had dug up the graveyard, like the dogs of Jeroboam, looking for the dead.

My lungs burned as I forced myself to my feet. My soul reviled this place, these people, the ones who had been my friends. I wanted to run into the forest, toward Space City, but I remembered Matthias's journey and made myself turn back toward town. There was still hope in the pollinator shed.

But as I walked, the sounds of the night changed. I heard voices off in the distance. I heard crashing and crunching in the brush. And then I heard the sound of a dog crying in pain.

The crashing grew louder and a pack of dogs streaked past me, dogs of all sizes, brown dogs and white dogs and black dogs and dogs of disparate parts and breeds. I had never seen so many dogs, and they were all chasing one brilliantly white creature.

"Soolie!" I shouted, and the dogs stopped to stare at me. We hadn't brought this many dogs to Canaan Lake. There was something strange and terrible about them, as if they were only the shells of dogs and what hid inside them was something monstrous.

Their growls filled my ears as I moved toward my dog.

He stood on shaking legs, his hide streaked in gore and his shape pitifully thin. His eyes were dull as he looked at me, and I knelt beside him to stroke his neck. I could not keep looking in those eyes. They were full of pain and suffering that would not be there if I had not given into my own weakness and fear and simply killed him.

Then he collapsed. The dogs fell in on his body and I broke into a run. For a moment, I thought they would drag me down and rip me apart as they were ripping apart my Soolie, but they let me go. I ran out of the forest and into the pollinator shed and I latched the door behind me and hid under a shelf.

I could hear screams outside. I dared not move all night.

Dear Lord, I described Soolie's eyes, but I didn't tell you about the other dogs. Their eyes were human, Lord. And one pair was Matthias's hazel.

Our mental landscape is tilled by words and all our ideas are grown from their seeds. Words are the shape of our world.
— from The Collected Wisdom of MW Williams

CHAPTER TWENTY-THREE

Standish slowed her UTV to a crawl as it entered the makeshift track Sheriff Vargas's team had cut into the forest. She glanced overhead. There were probably two or three hours of daylight left. She hoped that was enough to find the bolt gun.

The sound of her tires changed from the crunching of underbrush to the crackle of gravel. She'd reached the secret road, the road that somehow connected everything: Duncan, his murder, Peter's trouble. Whatever was going on in Canaan Lake, this road lay at the root of it.

Vargas's team had cleared the trees and the driving was easy. When the road came to its end she sat in the rig a minute, her mind spinning. Sectors 13 and 14 had belonged to the Believers until their big sale to Songheuser, which had gone through just before she arrived in Canaan Lake. But the road and the clearing, the paperwork for the communications equipment, all of that was months older.

Which meant Songheuser had been out here illegally. Whatever they'd been doing, they'd wanted it done where no one would see them and where no one could connect them to the damage. Then they'd covered it up.

She opened the door and got out. The air smelled clean

here, the bitter smell of horsetail fronds and ferns refreshing after a day of smoke and soot. Hattie jumped down beside her. The dog looked nervous, as if recalling her previous encounter with the native fauna. Standish shouldered the pack with the air horn and the pepper spray. She hadn't been able to find a metal detector, but at least she had something to protect herself with.

Standish gave her gear one last check. Everything seemed accounted for. She made sure her hand unit was tightly buckled onto her arm where she could reach it, and she tapped the screen. The signal was strangely strong here, but Dewey still hadn't responded to any of her messages or calls. She set the unit to vibrate. She had no idea if loud sounds would frighten away the leather birds or call them to her, and she wasn't about to take any risks.

Looking around the clearing, she saw the trampled gap in the brush – a clear signpost pointing to the spot where they'd found Duncan's body and where the volunteer search team had concentrated their efforts. She'd start to the north of that, at the farthest end of the clearing. Her boots shushed through the pseudo-club moss.

The ferns and Christ's fingers were so thick here she had to search around for a stick and smash them out of her way, beating a path into the woods. Something rattled in the bracken to her right, and she caught a glimpse of a lavender-hued trudgee disappearing into the base of a horsetail tree.

Rain began pattering on the branches overhead, but very little moisture penetrated the thick canopy. This must have been what the forest had been like when Hepzibah and her fellow Believers had arrived at Canaan Lake. No roads, no clearings, no houses: just horsetails and undergrowth.

Standish paused, remembering the diary with a pang. The settlers hadn't realized how close they'd been to the dry season, had they? Poor Hepzibah, hiding in her pollinator shed, utterly hopeless in the cold and rain, hallucinating that the people she knew were turning into wild dogs. If she had only lasted a few weeks longer, perhaps she would have found a way to make it. She was the exact opposite of Standish, one dreading the rain and one dreading the dry.

Standish stooped to pet Hattie. "It won't be so bad with you around," she said, and Hattie lolled her tongue as if she appreciated the sentiment.

Standish pushed on, jabbing at the ground with her stick. Duncan's killer wouldn't have taken the air bolt gun too far into the woods. No one would want to wade around in this mess for long for fear of getting lost. That was if the killer had left the bolt gun in this sector. They could have just as easily thrown it in the lake. Why was she wasting her time out here when the gun was probably sitting at the bottom of the lake, buried in weed?

Hattie gave an inquisitive bark, and Standish turned her head.

"What did you find, girl?" Standish ducked under a tall fern frond and stopped, surprised to see an open expanse about the size of her front room with a wireless transmitting tower sitting in the middle of it. It stood about thirty meters tall, its frame untouched by moss or lichen.

She stepped forward, a Christ's finger popping underfoot, and put out her hand to touch the tower. "Carbon fiber. And new."

She craned back her head, her eyes following the structure into the sky. Rain silted over her face without the thick canopy to block it, although the taller trees around the clearing's perimeter nearly closed over the tower's top.

It wasn't a complicated structure, and the individual pieces would have been fairly lightweight. Someone could have set up a small printer and made the pieces right here in the woods. It wouldn't have taken any special tools, and the whole thing could have been done using only the equipment Songheuser already kept on hand.

This was the reason Duncan had made notes about the conduit in Sector 13. If he could have brought in an underground line to connect this tower to the Canaan Lake transmission station, it would have simplified the entire network and more than doubled the service area. But according to Songheuser's records, this tower didn't exist.

Like the road behind her, this had been a temporary installation that Songheuser had wanted to remain a secret.

Standish took a second look at the tower. She understood why it was there – with the gas pockets in the trees, you couldn't mount a transmitting platform on a horsetail, no matter how much cheaper it would be – but she didn't understand how it had stayed a secret. Anyone flying over this sector or looking at a satellite photo would have seen it.

"Oh, fuck me," she whispered.

Someone had seen it, of course. Someone who routinely checked Huginn's satellite feeds to make certain the planet's communications networks were in good working order. Someone who had records for every transmitting station in the world.

Of course Dewey had known. That was why she was so suspicious of Songheuser. But something had made her keep quiet about it. Standish tried to imagine what they'd held over her friend. She wasn't the kind of woman to sell out easily.

Then it hit her: the boob job. Those C-cup tatas Dewey was so proud of after a lifetime of push-up bras and padding hadn't come cheap. Standish had assumed Dewey's government job and careful saving had provided the means to make up for starting hormones so late in her teens, but wasn't Sheriff Vargas proof that the Huginn government wasn't exactly rolling in cash? *Songheuser* had subsidized Dewey's dream in exchange for her silence.

She hoped it was worth the price. She still couldn't see any reason to turn a communications tower into a secret.

Behind Standish, Hattie growled, and the low rumble sent the hairs up on Standish's neck.

"What is it?" Standish brought up her stick like a baseball bat, turning in a half circle. She scanned the trees, looking for leather birds.

Hattie gave an angry bark.

The ferns rustled, and a brown dog appeared on the track Standish had just made. Its big head was low and wide, somehow snakelike on its long neck, and a string of slaver ran from its curled lip.

"Fuck."

Standish took a step backward, but there was no place to go. The transmission tower cut her off.

Another dog appeared in the corner of her eye, its shaggy gray shape low to the ground. They were stalking her just as they had stalked Rob McKidder down Main Street. She took an uneasy step up onto the bottom crossbar of the tower. Could they climb a metal ladder? God, she hoped not. Hattie couldn't.

Could she climb? Could she climb a slick ladder high enough to get out of the dogs' reach, all the while carrying Hattie? The dog had to weigh forty kilos, if not more.

"Come on, Hattie." She dropped to the ground and reached for the dog's collar. It was like tugging a tree out of the ground.

Hattie growled again and the brown dog took a step forward. Now Standish could see it better. Its short coat was marred with scars and wounds, a circle of raw pink flesh standing out on one side of its chest, a raised purple scar on the other – the purple scar oddly like a cross.

She'd seen a scar just like it on Shane Vogel's ribs.

We acted as dogs, so we became as dogs.

What if Hepzibah hadn't been hallucinating when she wrote about the dogs with human eyes? Standish's mouth felt like dust. "Hattie, come!"

She yanked hard on the collar, lifting the dog's front legs. Standish stretched her other arm to get a grip around Hattie's ribs, but she was too slow. The brown dog surged forward, snarling, its teeth slashing at Standish's face. She stumbled backward and smashed into the transmission tower, loosing Hattie.

Hattie rushed forward, slamming into the other dog, growling, biting, snarling. The baying and yipping of dogs was too loud for Standish to even think. A gray shape rushed at her and she kicked at it. A dog yelped, and Standish scrambled up onto the transmission tower.

"Hattie!" she shrieked.

The gray dog sank its teeth into Standish's boot and yanked hard. Standish kicked free and climbed to the next crossbar. Her hand slipped and for a second she hung from one fist, but then her feet found purchase and she caught herself. The gray dog leaped, its claws raking Standish's pants. She climbed higher, her heart pounding.

Hattie gave a screech of pain. Then she ripped herself free of the brown dog, her white fur spattered red all over, and tore off through the trees.

"Hattie," Standish sobbed.

The pack raced after Hattie, save for the gray dog and a shaggy black Labrador-looking beast that began to circle around the base of the tower. Standish climbed up another rung. The wind was stronger up here. The lanky metal structure swayed a little, the carbon-mesh vibrating like a tuning fork. Standish clamped her arms around the nearest strut and pressed her face to the mesh, squeezing shut her eyes. If the rain picked up, it would be even harder to hold on.

She opened her eyes and found herself level with most of

the trees. She'd climbed higher than she thought. The forest stretched out around her, a great green swathe of trees, a green so dark it was nearly black. If she fell, she would vanish into that blackness, as impossible to find as Duncan Chambers and the air bolt gun that had killed him.

A patch of gray to the south caught her attention. It was a large rectangle, probably the size of the whole mill yard, and she thought that if she had kept running the day the leather birds had been chasing her, she probably would have run straight into it. The trees there looked like skeletons, their fronds dried and fallen. The distinct shape of a UTV sat in the middle of it, a blanket of dead fronds laying over its cab and hood. She thought she saw two dark shapes inside, but if that rig had moved in the last six months, it had been only at the hands of the wind.

Her tower rocked a little harder and Standish cried out. She hooked her leg around the strut and clung tighter. Now that she had seen the zone of dead gray, she couldn't look away.

This was what Songheuser had been hiding when they'd closed their road and torn out their work station. This was their secret.

To the west, a dog howled, long and loud, and the dogs at the base of the tower took up the call. Standish pressed herself tighter to the strut as the rain fell over her in cold rivulets. She couldn't tell her tears from the rain.

Hattie was gone. Half of her *self* was gone.

The dogs howled again, and she thought she had never heard a lonelier sound or felt so alone.

The early morning sunshine made the broken glass sparkle on HQ's steps as Peter walked with Sheriff Vargas toward the front door. One of the windows had been boarded over, and smoke stained the Songheuser logo. They paused in front of the doors and turned back to look at the scorched and battered mill on the other side of the street.

It was impossible to take in the full extent of the disaster with one look. Parts of the exterior fence had been torn down to let the fire trucks get access to different parts of the mill yard, and heaps of rubble sat beside the road where work crews had cleared it out of the emergency vehicles' way. Most of the mill's buildings were intact, but the whole place had a disfigured, unhappy look about it. Peter had never seen the mill yard empty before. It looked lonely without anyone moving around in it.

"This turned out to be a pretty crappy frame-job. Once the security tapes were reviewed – and Songheuser wouldn't listen to my team's opinion; the tapes were analyzed by four different law enforcement agencies – it was pretty obvious you were innocent. I can't hold you for a crime you didn't commit," Vargas said. "But are you sure I shouldn't keep you another day for your own safety?"

"I'll be safe enough here." He gave her an attempt at a smile. "Don't take this the wrong way, but your jail cells aren't really that comfortable. Plus, I like a little privacy when I pee."

"The town is wound tight. I saw Belinda set those charges on the security cameras, but that doesn't mean anyone else is ready to believe she's a part of this. You stay low. Don't leave the office."

"I shouldn't need to." Peter looked over his shoulder at the wreckage. "I can't believe Belinda was willing to do this."

"No one's going to believe it." Vargas sighed. "Her frame-job might not have held up, but it bought her enough time to get away, and people won't want to give you up as a suspect. You *sure* you don't want an armed guard? I could put Paul Wu on it. He likes you more than you think."

"No, I'll be fine." He hoped he wasn't lying to the both of them.

"Then I'll leave you here. Remember – keep a low profile until we get some of these people behind bars. Belinda couldn't have done this alone."

"Sheriff?"

"What is it?"

Peter hesitated. "Why are you helping me? What's in it for you?"

She shook her head. "Jesus, Pete, why do you have make it personal?"

"Because I get the feeling it is?"

She sighed. "I signed up for this job to protect people like you. Good people, who go to work and do their jobs and go to city council meetings and try to make their communities decent places. My job is to *keep* this town a decent place." She tucked her thumbs in her gun belt and stood a little taller. "A lot of people have been telling me how to do my job lately, and I'm getting sick of it."

"So you're 'sticking it to the Man'? That's what this is about?"

She rolled her eyes. "Don't ruin my counterculture insurgence by being a terrorist or some stupid shit. Get in that office and keep your nose clean, Pete, and I'll keep looking after you."

The sheriff turned on her heel and headed back down to her rig. Peter watched her for a second and turned to face the office. It looked more battered than it had with Vargas beside him.

He stepped inside. The empty office building held the same atmosphere he'd felt when he'd gone to close up his grandmother's house after she moved into assisted living. The walls were still there, but the life had gone out of the place. The smell of smoke clung to everything.

His office had been neatly locked up after the police search, and that comforted him a little. Even after he'd been cleared, he'd worried he'd be coming back to a pink slip, his stuff boxed up on the curb just to show him his politics were that unwelcome. But his terrariums were all intact and his gear was still stowed where it ought to be. He began misting his plants and studying his specimens. The club moss in his flora-only tank soaked up the water, fluffing visibly. He had to throw out one of the transplanted ferns, which had failed to take root and then succumbed to some kind of powder mildew.

But the flora in the terrarium with the caterpillars and scooters seemed to have survived their uprooting and settled into their new home. The tree scooters looked happy, too, or at least busy, the scooters moving in and out of their burrow and digging energetically around the base of the tiny horsetail seedling in the corner. Peter put down the mister and knelt beside the windowsill, impressed by all the activity.

A scooter burst out of the burrow hole, paused to rub its antennae with prickly forearms, and scooted toward the horsetail seedling, its legs a blur beneath its pink segmented body. As much as he'd like to retain an objective perspective on the little thing, he had to admit it was awfully cute. It buried its face in the fluffy humus at the base of the seedling and came up with a mouthful of stringy white mycelium.

Peter reached for the tweezers he kept on a tray beside the terrariums. He'd seen that mycelium before, and now he was kicking himself for overlooking the stuff. He plucked a clump of mycelium-rich humus. He didn't need a microscope to know this came from a terrestrial organism, not a Huginn native.

The lichen- and fungus-like organisms of Huginn were only *like* terrestrial lichens and fungi. These organisms were roughly commensurate to the things he'd known on Earth, but their differences were substantial – despite the easy analogies his Earthling brain wanted to make. Sure, Y-fungus (some pre-settlement biologist's lazy naming strategy for the genera) made mycelial chains that spread through organic material, dissolving them in an almost identical fashion to Earth's mushroom species. But like most things on Huginn, the mycelium of Y-fungus came in fantastical colors and constructions. Webs of needlelike structures forming regular polyhedrons were typical structures for a Huginn native. White strings? That was an Earth strategy.

He put the mycelium in a dish for further examination and turned his attention back to the scooters happily mining the stuff and hauling it to their burrow. He couldn't imagine they were eating it. Outside of the honeydew he'd seen the scooters harvesting from the caterpillars, he hadn't seen any organisms successfully feed on anything from the other solar system.

So what were they doing with it?

He slid aside the cardboard that obscured the back corner of the terrarium, exposing the tunnels of the creature's home. The scooters hurried to and from the largest chamber, a room about the size of his doubled fists, where the caterpillars had taken up residence. Little heaps of mycelium and dirt surrounded the four caterpillars, who had clearly grown in the past few days. They slurped up strands of mycelium like customers at a ramen shop.

Peter replaced the cardboard. The caterpillars had clearly found a perfect foodstuff in the mycelium, and he'd seen the tree scooters milking the caterpillars for their honeydew. Their symbiotic relationship was obvious.

But what kind of mycelium was it? And was it helping or hurting Huginn's forests? Some mushrooms killed trees. Others poisoned the creatures around them. This mycelium could be a dangerous import.

He frowned at the other tank, the terrarium with only rock-eater lichen and a sampling of club mosses. There was a difference between this tank and the one with the tree scooters, but he couldn't put his finger on it. After all his years in the field, he knew the sensation currently prickling him – a feeling something like walking with a rock in his shoe. He was missing something and it was nagging at him in a powerfully annoying way.

He caught movement out of the corner of his eye and forgot the irritation of the other problem. The cocoon in his third tank had finally hatched. The butterfly sat on top of the hollowed structure, slowly flexing its blue wings. Light danced across their golden freckles.

Peter jumped to his feet and grabbed the box Chameli had given him. He opened it carefully, despite the tremor of excitement in his hands, and used a pair of tweezers to lift one of the specimens from the box. He held it out and compared the two creatures. The wing shape, the color, the golden specks: he had found it. He had found Olive's butterflies.

The real question, though, was whether or not the symbiotic caterpillars were the same as the first one he'd captured. If they were the same, that meant he'd identified the two major life stages of a terrestrial life form that had somehow managed to not just adapt to an extraterrestrial environment, but also establish a symbiotic relationship with an alien life form. But unless he sequenced their DNA – not likely for now – then he'd have to wait for these new caterpillars to go through metamorphosis before he knew for certain he'd found the same species. Which meant waiting and watching.

The feeling of the rock in the shoe returned, and he pushed it away. Peter went to his desk to check for messages from Mark. As he sat down, he felt his shirt catch on his desk drawer. It was a cheap desk with rough corners, and he was always careful to push the drawers completely closed. He only had so many shirts.

Frowning, he pulled open the drawer and felt ice go down his spine. All his notes about the degassing compound were missing.

God's plans are quieter than you'd expect. He could shout the truth, bellow it like thunder, put it on a sign and give it armed deputies so as to make sure it was protected and followed. But God is no bully eager to show off his strength. His power is all around us, if we only have the ears to listen to its gentle melody.

Sometimes I hear only the silences between His words, and at those times I weep to think how weak my hearing is.

– from The Collected Wisdom of MW Williams

CHAPTER TWENTY-FOUR

Standish lay on her bed with a pillow hugged tight to her stomach. A sliver of sunlight had appeared on the floor in front of the door, warning her that Wodin had passed out of the sky and that there were gaps in the clouds. Thinking about the sky made it hard to breathe.

Dr Holt had been right. Standish had been so smug back in her office, blowing off her prescriptions. But something *had* happened to Hattie, and now Standish was trapped alone in her bedroom, too tense to get off the goddamn bed. A tiny sound like a mosquito's buzz filled the room, and Standish realized it came from her, a strangled whine squeezed unwillingly from her anxious throat.

The soft rapping on the front door was barely audible over the irritating noise.

"Standish?"

The door knob rattled and the door swung open. She'd been too fucked up to even lock the door behind her when she came home. She still wasn't sure how she'd made it out of the woods, let alone driven home. It had been raining. Maybe that had helped.

"Kate?" The figure in the doorway was backlit by the

searingly bright sunshine. He closed the door and gloom restored itself to the room.

She forced herself to sit up and wiped her cheeks with the back of her hand. "Matthias?"

He came to the bed and perched on the edge. "I was so worried." His hands fumbled across the bedspread until they found hers. "I saw Hattie with the dog pack. I thought–"

"She ran away. Well, they drove her away, but still. She ran away just like all the other dogs." She blinked hard, even though he couldn't see her. She couldn't stand the thought of anyone seeing her crying.

"She's not like them," he reassured her. "Hattie's a good dog."

She scooted closer to him. "They're not... ordinary dogs, are they?"

He put his arm around her shoulder. "No."

His shoulder was warm and solid, and he smelled like rain and strong soap. He seemed entirely normal, not like someone who might have lived for more than a hundred years and probably turned into a dog at night. And yet it all added up. Hepzibah's diary? Olive Whitley's strange transformation from a regular kid into a girl who was practically a forest spirit? The dreams she herself had where Hattie had truly become her other half, just as she'd secretly believed?

Normal didn't seem to apply here on Huginn. There was a magic in belief here that didn't exist on other worlds.

"I'm just glad you're all right. I thought – well, I don't want to think about what I thought." His hand found her head and stroked it, just as she would have stroked Hattie's.

That was too much. Her confusion boiled into something like rage. Standish sat up and snapped on the light. He winced, his hazel eyes blinking hard.

"I want to know everything. What are the dogs? Who are you? And why isn't Shane Vogel dead?"

"He was."

"I know he was, I was fucking *there*!" Anger simmered in her chest, pushing away the last threads of her anxiety. She'd used anger to fight it before, anger and sex and booze. Now she had something worth being angry about. "You're not going to lie to me."

"I couldn't if I wanted to." He stretched out his hand and she pushed it away. "When I saw Hattie running with the dogs, I knew I couldn't lie to you anymore."

"Who are you?" she repeated. "Were you really married to Hepzibah Williams?"

"Yes." His Adam's apple bobbed. "I remember her like I don't remember much else. I really loved her. I know that."

She jumped to her feet. "You don't 'remember much'? What, is a hundred years of life on this moon too much for you?"

He stood, his palms out. "You have to understand. Until recently, I didn't understand it myself. I could remember certain things, things like getting here, trying to start our farm, watching Hepzibah die. But it was all a muddle. And I didn't know about the dogs. I wasn't sure, not until..." He winced a little. "Not until the night before last."

"What happened that night?"

"When I woke up in the cemetery after you left, I was me, only–"

"A dog."

"Part of me was used to it. Part of me knew what to do when they started digging up Shane's grave. I was one of the pack, one of them. But then he came out, and he drove me off. I was alone for first time in a hundred years. All the pieces started coming together." He sat back down on the bed, his eyes blind to her. "We deserved to be punished for as long as it took."

"Punished for what?"

"For what we did! We acted as dogs, and we *became* as dogs."

The words made her shiver. She sat down on the bed and held his eyes with hers. "What do you mean?"

"You saw them at the post office, Shane and Vonda and all of them. They didn't want me to be their leader any more. I'm all alone."

"You're not alone. You have me and Peter," she snapped. "Now tell me what this is all about."

"I started remembering things differently after Duncan disappeared. We were out there in the woods and there was this smell. A *wrong* smell. And when I smelled it, I started to remember. I would be working in my fields or falling asleep, and I'd remember what it was like to be a dog. And when I was a dog, sometimes I'd remember what it was like to be a man."

"And that never happened before?"

"Maybe. But it never mattered, so I let it go. Until I learned it could matter."

"What the hell does that mean?"

"Do you know Bob Sounds?"

She shook her head impatiently.

"About six months ago, he… changed. He started avoiding me and Orrin. Then one day, I saw that he had a big white streak in his hair. We've lived here a hundred years and none of us have aged a day. He hadn't, not until then."

Standish shook her head. "Well, what made *him* change?"

He clasped his hands in front of him. "A group of Believers from the south coast moved up here, and Betty was with them. When he met Betty… well, he found a new reason to be a man."

She opened her mouth and closed it again.

He looked up at her, his face pained. "I loved Hepzibah. I know I loved her. But somehow when we came here, I forgot how to care about anyone. And then one day I realized I had lost a friend because I was too lost in my own world to notice he was in trouble. I'm not going to let what happened to Duncan happen to anyone else I care about."

On the coffee table in the middle of the room, Standish's hand unit buzzed.

"Matthias, I–"

The hand unit buzzed again.

He glanced at the coffee table. "You should get that."

"Yeah." She got to her feet and stomped to the table. "Shit. It's Joe Holder. He needs me to fix his cable." She made a face. "I cut his cable so I could sneak into his house and spy on him. To help solve Duncan's case."

He stood. "Then you've got to go."

She looked at the door. Sunlight filled the entire square of the front window. "I can't go out there, not without Hattie. I can't do it."

"We have to find out what happened to Duncan. It matters to all of us, even if I'm not sure why. Even the dogs want to know what happened to him. That smell out there, they can't resist it. And it has something to do with Duncan." Matthias took her hand. "So you've got to go. You can do this, Kate."

"I don't know how. I'm scared."

"Sometimes we have to do the things that scare us. They might still terrify us when we get done, but at least we know we're really alive."

She gave him a weak smile and reached for her toolbox.

Peter headed to the lake shore. He wasn't stupid enough to take Main Street back to the office, not when the whole town wanted him in a jail cell. When he'd made a food run to his house in the cover of Wodin's shadow, he had just turned up his hood and kept his head down, hoping like hell no one would recognize him if he kept moving. Now that it was time to get back to work, people were moving about, milling around in the street looking for something to fill the hours while the mill was closed. There was a strange undercurrent of tension in the town, as if everyone was holding their breath, waiting.

The gray waters of the lake were a welcome respite from it. He wished he could stay here all day, watching the wind stir the water and the trees. But hiding from this problem would only make it worse. He had to let Mark know about the missing notes. He'd checked his house, just in case he'd taken them home without thinking, but they were really and truly gone.

He paused and drew in a deep draft of cool, mineral-scented air, letting it clear his mind for a moment. This was what he had to fight for.

The tree scooters might have brought him to Huginn, but just living on the moon had come to mean everything to him. The crispness of Huginn kept him on his toes, the newness always challenging him to learn more, to work harder. He had never lived anyplace that had made him feel so alive.

He hadn't blown up the sawmill, would never do something so horrible – but he had to admit he understood why people had. There had to be a better way to live here than just pillaging and terrorizing the land. Humans were guests here, and they needed to act like it.

"That's him." The man's voice came from behind him, sending the skin between Peter's shoulder blades crawling. He looked backward and saw three big men making their way down to the beach path. A hard-faced woman followed, a wrench in her hand.

He picked up his pace, looking around for some avenue of escape. He'd passed Standish's street a minute ago, and now he was in the forest proper, the thick undergrowth that had filled in the original settlers' plots. The path would bend in about a hundred meters and make the shortcut to Songheuser's back door, but right now it was tightly hemmed in by Judas grass and bracken. If he was going to get out of here, he needed to move fast.

Risking one more glance over his shoulder, he saw the others had quickened their step, and his heart gave a jolt. He'd hoped they were just out to scare him, but the way they walked, the intensity of their expressions, suggested something worse. He saw a dreadlocked man fall in behind the woman with the wrench and felt a pang of recognition. Even Lou the Security Guard had judged him guilty.

"Get him," the woman snarled, and the men broke into a run.

Peter ran. Their boots were impossibly loud on the dirt path. Their breathing sounded in his ears, the panting of wild animals, and he wondered if Rob McKidder had heard that sound the night he'd died. Peter dodged an outstretched tree branch and ran faster. He could see the white roof of the office up ahead, just a hundred meters away.

Something slammed into his back and he went down. His face skidded across a rock and then he was on the ground, the air driven out of him by the massive weight of the man who'd tackled him.

Fingers curled in his hair and lifted his head.

"You're not getting away with this," the woman said. She had the spidery build of a spacer. "You think you can just walk around this town like we don't know what you did?"

"My brother's dead because of you!" The man holding Peter's hair slammed his face down in the dirt.

"I ain't going back to Ganymede," someone else said, and a boot drove into Peter's hip with an explosion of pain.

"Lou! What the hell are you doing?"

Peter's head was dropped.

"We're… Nothing, Brett. We're not doing anything."

"Get the fuck out of here!"

The weight shifted off his back and then feet pounded back toward the lake. Peter lay still, breathing. Thank God that kick had missed.

A pair of boots appeared in front of Peter's face. "Do you need help?"

Peter pushed himself to his knees and waited for his lungs to recover from their smashing. His whole face throbbed, and his eye felt like it wanted to swell shut.

"You look like shit." Brett sounded conversational as he hoisted Peter to his feet. "Let's get you some ice for that face."

"Thanks," Peter said. He touched his lower lip and found it swollen, too. "You're really something, Brett."

"I'm just doing my job," Brett said. "You're on Songheuser property, which means the company is liable for you." He gave Peter a hard look. "You might not have set that bomb, Bajowski, but you encouraged those ecofreaks, and people know it. You might think about heading back to Earth for your own safety."

Peter followed Brett into the security office and took the ice pack the man offered. There was a picture on the desk behind Brett – a photo of Brett and Rob McKidder with Joe Holder behind them. Joe's arm was slung around Rob's shoulder, and he was smiling like a man who'd won some kind of major prize. They each held a leather bird by its ankles, and Rob had an air bolt gun swinging jauntily in his free hand.

"You must be a hell of a shot," Peter said. "Those things move fast."

"Well, mine was roosting, but Joe – he shot one down that was on the wing. The man's a legendary shot. He and Rob used to go out all the time hunting leather birds. They know the forest like the backs of their hands." Brett frowned. "You're going to need another ice pack."

He stooped to riffle through the first aid drawer, but Peter couldn't take his eyes off the photo. Rob McKidder and Joe Holder. His mind was spinning.

Joe met her at his front door with circles under his eyes and a coffee stain down the front of his shirt. He caught Standish glancing at it and looked down. "Shit," he said, in lieu of "hello." "I've got to change before Victoria sees me like this."

"Did you even get a chance to sleep last night? You look worn out." Standish followed him into the pleasant foyer, feeling some of the tension fall out of her as she escaped from the sky. She jammed her ballcap – no Hattie, but it helped block her view upward – into her back pocket and looked around herself. Prints of vaguely familiar paintings hung on the wall in gold-colored frames, and a faux marble-topped bureau sat beside the doorway with a scented candle poised beside a row of key hooks. The place was a far cry from her two-room plastic shack.

"No time for sleep. Between talking to the cops and trying to organize repairs, there isn't time for anything." He trudged into the kitchen and reached for a stainless steel pot. "Coffee?"

The kitchen had cheerful yellow curtains with chickens on them, and a ceramic rooster stood next to the sink. Standish had never stopped to think if Joe lived alone or had a wife or what. It was hard to imagine him outside of work. "Yes, please."

"Now I've got to deal with this crap." He dumped powdered creamer into his mug and stirred hard enough to slosh coffee onto the counter. "My wife can't be home alone all day without a sure way to get a hold of me. You know how the signal is around this town – can't depend on it for shit." Standish's expression must have expressed her confusion. "My wife's an invalid," he explained. "Posie Eames sits with her most mornings, but she's alone in the afternoon. She can mind for herself, mostly, but she gets lonely. And what if something happened? If the power went out or her chair tipped over?"

"Joe?" a voice called out from the next room. "Joe, who are you talking to?"

"Just the cable girl, Eileen!" He put down the coffee. "I better check on her. The cable line's in here, anyway."

Standish followed him into the comfortable living room. A blond woman smiled at Standish half-heartedly as Joe knelt down beside her wheelchair. Her neck trembled as he leaned in to kiss her cheek.

Standish turned away, more than a little embarrassed to see her boss so exposed. He looked so tender and kind as he adjusted the blanket on his wife's lap. There was no sign of his forced laugh, the one that echoed through the halls at work. Standish hunkered down beside the entertainment center and ran her fingers around the cable jack. "Any other jacks in the place? If there's a short in one, it can mess with the others."

"There's one in the bedroom, second door down the hall." He began talking about snacks with Eileen, whose voice quavered softly.

Standish slipped into the hallway. She'd hoped Joe would have just sent her with a spare key or left the front door unlocked like most of her work requests. Having him here made it nearly impossible to search his house for clues. She stood in the bedroom doorway and shook her head. The pinkness of the place was overwhelming.

"Eileen's favorite color is pink," he explained from behind her.

"I thought it might be yours," she joked. She wanted to go through the drawers and look under the bed, but with his eyes on her she had to go straight to the smaller entertainment center on the wall and pretend to inspect the jack.

"It's cryo sickness," he blurted. "From the trip here. Less than half a percent of travelers get it. Knocked me on my ass when it happened to Eileen. We woke up, and she couldn't move. They treated the paralysis, but she'll never get full control of her muscles again. The nerves are wrecked."

She sat down on the floor. He looked like he might cry. "Jesus."

"Hell of a thing." He took a breath, steadying visibly. "I don't know what I'd have done if it wasn't for Victoria's help. She got us the best doctors. Songheuser took care of everything. If it weren't for her, Eileen would be in a hospital bed in Space City with machines breathing and eating for her."

"Sounds like you owe her a lot."

"Yep." He joined her beside the entertainment center. "I'd do anything for Victoria Wallace. She's a great woman."

"I can see that." Standish got to her feet. "I'm going to guess your problem is with the cable juncture outside your house. Probably got hit by a rock or something. These old cable boxes go out all the time."

"All right. I'll see you out." He patted her shoulder with his heavy paw. "You're all right, Standish. Especially without that dog around."

"You don't like dogs?"

"Not anymore. I keep catching glimpses of them in the trees. Like they're watching me."

Her fingers closed on the front door, and she looked back over her shoulder. "What do you mean?"

"You know how some people smell good to mosquitoes? They're always getting bit when nobody else does? Well, I'd swear there was something about me that smelled good to those dogs. I thought Rob was crazy when he told me they were sniffing after him, but I think he was right. I started keeping my hunting bolt gun in my rig all the time, just to be safe."

"I guess you're irresistible."

Joe gave her a strange look. "I guess," he said.

She went to the cable box and waited for Joe to close the front door before she reconnected the cable, all the time thinking about Matthias and the smell the dogs couldn't resist.

Huginn, day 199

I

what is that sound?

Language contains and expands our human understanding of the world. We create it and are created by it. What we say and what we believe become, in very real ways, ourselves.
– from THE COLLECTED WISDOM OF MW WILLIAMS

CHAPTER TWENTY-FIVE

The sky roared and the walls of the shed rattled. The caterpillars in their boxes scattered in a blind panic, crawling over and under each other and twisting in the leaves she gave them for feed. Then the roar resolved into the grumble of engines and Hepzibah recognized the sounds of a shuttle. She put down her diary and got to her feet. It took all her strength, and she had to stop and lean against the wall, gasping. Something felt broken in her chest.

It went very silent outside. She cautiously opened the door. On the lake shore a shining silver shuttle sat, and a boarding ramp lowered from it like a butterfly tentatively extending its proboscis. There was no one in sight and no animal noises.

"Hello?" a man called from the mouth of the shuttle. "Matthias Williams? Dr Robert Sounds?"

The door of the kitchen shed swung open and Matthias stumbled out. Blotches of blood and dirt stood out down his shirt front, and a length of filthy white linen hung over his shoulder. The kind of linen they used as a funeral shroud. He flung it away from him with a look of revulsion and Hepzibah clamped a hand over her mouth. The cemetery. It had all been dug up, and now she knew who had done it.

She drew a ragged breath and was glad she had nothing in her stomach to vomit up.

"I'm... Matthias Williams." It was half-croaked, as if his voice had been stripped from him.

"Kurt Conrad, Songheuser Corporation. Our accounting department caught our little shipping mistake." The man descended from the shuttle, smiling broadly. "We'd like to make it right with you."

"Food? You brought food?"

"Well, yes, we've got some of your supplies. Some has gone missing, I'm afraid. But we've drawn up a very generous reparations package that I'll need you to sign off on before I can make the delivery." The company man frowned. "Are you all right? You look a bit ill."

Doc Sounds came out of the kitchen shed, his face twisted with anger. "Reparations? My wife starved to death. How do you repair that?"

"We realize you people have had a rough time..."

Doc Sounds gave a sound that could have been a laugh or a sob. "A rough time." He scrubbed a filthy hand across his face. "A rough time!"

"Nineteen people have died," Matthias said. "Some of them children. It's been like hell."

"Now you have the power to change all that," Conrad said. "You just have to sign a few papers and promise never to tell anyone what happened here, and everyone will be well cared for. It's an extremely generous–"

"No!" Hepzibah burst out of the shed, coughing hard. "Your filthy money can't fix this. Not tell what's happened? Songheuser should be crucified for what they've done. All this is their fault. All of it. Even the Godforsaken things."

"I know it is, Hepzibah" Matthias said. "But they've got food, and we need it bad."

"If you make this deal, it's like you're saying the truth doesn't matter. That good and bad and morality and God's word don't matter. Animals put survival over what's right. Is that what you want to be? An animal?"

He gripped her by the forearms. "If you think I'm going to just let you starve to death when I've got a way to save you, you're crazy."

"Is that what you thought when you started cutting up the bodies in the cemetery?" She yanked away from his grasp. "You make me sick."

"You don't get to judge me, Hepzibah. That's God's job."

"He's judging you right now, Matthias."

He pushed her out of his way. "I'll sign anything you want, Mr Conrad, as long as we get those supplies." He put out his hand, and Hepzibah saw that his palm was as rough and dark as a dog's paw. Her legs went out from under her, and she began to sob.

Standish threw open Peter's office door. "Thank goodness you're out of that stupid jail."

He looked up from his desk tablet, revealing the gash across his cheekbone and his split lip.

"Jesus, what happened to you?" Standish hurried to his side. The cut added a gravity to his face she hadn't seen before. Peter had always looked like an irritable nerd, but today he looked like a warrior.

"I had a run-in with some folks who were angry about the mill." He flinched away from her hands, but she already had a good grip on his head. "Don't poke at it."

"Do you have a first aid kit?" She saw the box on the wall and got it down. She turned her ball cap backward and perched on the edge of his desk, then took out an alcohol wipe and began scrubbing. He gave a little hiss at the sting. "You should have left Canaan Lake, Peter. Whoever did this could have killed you."

"Hey, I've got a job to do. I'm not going to let the company poison the people who live here, even if they don't appreciate what I'm doing." He pushed her hand away. "Where's Hattie?"

"The dogs drove her away." Saying it out loud made it hurt more. But she described her adventure in the woods to him anyway. He had to know everything, especially about the dead zone. "And this morning I found out something about Joe," she added. "He has a wife with cryo sickness and feels like the company saved her life. He said he'd do *anything* for Victoria Wallace. *Anything*."

"Wow." He squeezed her shoulder. "I'm sorry about Hattie. Are you all right?"

She shrugged. "No? But what can I do until I can get my prescription filled? Do a rain dance?" She reached for the bottle of antibiotic ointment, unwilling to see the pity in his eyes.

"Hey, I learned while I was icing my head in the security office – Joe and Rob were both crack shots with an air bolt gun. Plus, they both liked hunting leather birds and know the woods like the backs of their hands."

"Joe's got the motive," Standish mused. "If the company wanted him to make sure no one knew about that dead zone, he'd make sure of it."

"Well, I think Rob would have done anything Joe told him. They looked awfully tight in that picture. And Rob was the one partying it up with those company biologists."

"I wish Rob hadn't gotten himself killed so we could ask him a few questions." Standish paused, feeling a connection forming in the back of her mind. The dogs had killed Rob. The dogs were stalking Joe. She wished she could just sit for a moment and think about all of this.

But Peter was talking. "Fuck! I just got a message from Mark. They're doing an aerial application of the degassing compound on a large test site I mapped out last week. It's scheduled for three-thirty this afternoon."

"Shit, that's… half an hour from now." Standish rubbed at her temples. Everything was moving too fast.

Peter stabbed his finger at his phone, his face going red. "He's not picking up. I think I'm going to have to go straight to Victoria Wallace. There's a spring in those woods and it feeds into the stream behind Jeff Eames's farm. I have no idea what it might do to his crops – or worse, his family."

Standish shook her head, remembering that UTV parked in the dead zone she'd found. "Do you really think it's lethal to humans or animals?"

"I don't know. Mark sent me the test results, but I'm still going over the more detailed breakdown, and I lost my notes. I thought they were right here in my desk and now they're missing. But I do know the compound gives off a fair amount of ammonia as it breaks down. If someone were sprayed with it, it could irritate their lungs, burn their eyes–"

Standish sat up. "Wait. Did you say Jeff Eames's farm?"

"Yeah, you know, its property line butts up against Sector 14. He's probably fine, but... Standish? What's wrong?"

She was already headed for the door. "Olive said she was going to look for butterflies in the woods behind Jeff Eames's farm today. I've got to find her."

"Standish!" he shouted, but the door slammed shut on his words.

Peter sat back down. He could chase after Standish, but that wouldn't help Olive Whitley. He needed to buy her some time. He picked up his hand unit and found Victoria Wallace's contact entry. His finger hesitated over it. The woman had threatened to have him deported. But then again, she'd do anything if she thought it would help the company's bottom dollar.

He almost put down the hand unit. But if he did, Standish would be on her own out there.

"Come on, dude. The sheriff cleared you. Wallace will understand. Probably." He jabbed at the screen.

"Wallace. What is it?"

Peter could see the basement hallway behind Victoria, her

hand unit's camera bobbing as she walked at a near-run.

"Ms Wallace, I know you think I'm crazy, but I need to talk to you about the degassing compound tests. I have reason to believe that the compound isn't as safe as the chemical manufacturer maintains. My own tests suggest–"

"Bajowski, even if I were inclined to believe an environmentalist nut like yourself, I've looked at your test results. I don't think they prove anything. Somehow your test site got contaminated with mildew spores, and that's got nothing to do with my compound. I've got a badly damaged mill that could be ready to run degassed lumber in a week, and I've got a stand of capralis ready for the compound. This test could save the company half a billion dollars at a time we're desperate for cash."

"But there's a major water source right there in that sector, and there are civilians in the woods this afternoon. We could be facing a major lawsuit, Ms Walla–"

"Look, Dr Bajowski, Sheriff Vargas swears you're innocent. But I'm not putting this test on hold. The local yokels aren't going to sue when they're the ones wandering around where they ought not. I've been working on this project too long to let something as trivial as trespassers stop it. Now if you'll excuse me, I've got a company to run."

She broke off the connection and Peter found himself staring at the blue background of his hand unit, the reflection of his face like an astonished cracked egg.

The bandage on his cheek didn't quite cover the ends of the gash. He touched it with his fingertips. This would be nothing compared to the chemical burns Olive and Standish would get from the degassing compound. He stood up. He had to do something. He had to find some way to stop the air drop.

He began to pace from window to door, thinking hard. Mark had told him to get hold of someone in the government, and Standish had been leaving messages for her friend Dewey.

Maybe Peter could reach her.

Peter paused in his pacing beside the terrariums. The flora-only tank looked worse than ever. Another fern had succumbed to powder mildew, and the patch of pseudo-club moss had shrunk, its edges gone brown. The tank beside it, the one with the tree scooters and the caterpillars, was surprisingly unscathed.

Something shifted in his mind. The connection, the irritating gap between his observations that had refused to close, snapped into place. He had built the tanks with nearly the same soil, the same frondy mix that covered the forest floor throughout Huginn, using nearly the same plants. But there was one difference.

"The mycelium. There's no mildew in the tank with the mycelium." He spun to face his desk. He had to write this down.

The door to his office swung open.

"Sit down, Peter. And don't even think about touching your hand unit."

The gun in Belinda's hand didn't waver even a bit. She just stood there, smiling at him, the gun – a real gun, the kind police officers carried – trained on his face.

Standish found the track Peter had cut into Sector 14 and stopped to look around. The forest stretched in a line along the ridge of the hills, with no breaks for kilometers in either direction. If she turned around, she'd see the long valley of the lake and the creek that fed it, Believer farms strung along the valley like beads on a necklace. Across from them, the peeled stripes of clear cuts stood out on Songheuser's land. But here the trees still held court, not knowing their term as supreme leader was coming to an end. Someday soon the cutting machines would sweep through, crushing the ferns and smashing the Christ's fingers, leaving the pale dirt bare for the first time since the forests had evolved on this bit of former volcano. This was the forest's last moment of peace, and any minute the drones would rush overhead to end it.

"Olive!" Her voice floated over the ferns, insubstantial and unwelcome. The girl hadn't been home when Standish had stopped at her house. She had to be out here somewhere, searching for her butterflies.

"Olive!"

Standish gasped as she ran, her heart pounding. It wasn't anxiety but ordinary fear. She checked her hand unit, strapped tightly to her wrist. Three twenty-five. The drones were on their way already. "Olive!"

Then she was at the first of Peter's test sites, the ground gray and dead, the trees like naked sticks. A stink like forgotten laundry and abandoned basements made her cover her mouth and nose. It was worse than Peter had described it. The effects looked nearly as bad as what she'd seen from the transmitter tower – if they'd reformulated the degassing compound since that test in Sector 13, they hadn't made enough changes to make any significant difference.

Then she was past it and glad to be back in the forest. She tried not to look at his second site, but only picked up her pace. She had less than a minute to find Olive, and no idea where the drones would spray. She slapped her hand unit. No messages from Peter. Why hadn't he gotten back to her?

Peter's track narrowed, leaving only a few cut branches to suggest a way in the woods. He'd charted most of this sector, hadn't he? She tried to remember what he'd said.

"Miss Kate!" Olive burst out of the ferns, her eyes luminous in her pale face. She seemed to nearly float over the bracken, like some kind of forest sprite.

"Oh, thank God." Standish ducked under a branch and knelt beside Olive. "We've got to get out of here. Come on."

"No, wait. Look!" The girl had uncovered something shiny,

some kind of plastic tucked under a squashed button fern. "Someone left this here."

Standish studied the canopy above. "Just grab it and hurry." She felt Olive get to her feet and stood, risking a glance at the sky. Her fingers curled and uncurled in the palm of her hand. She missed Hattie.

"I wonder who would leave their air bolt gun out here?"

Standish snapped her attention back to the girl.

"A hunter, I guess, although I don't see why they put it in a plastic bag." Olive began unzipping the top.

"Stop!" Standish grabbed the girl's arm. "Olive, let me see that."

The girl held out the bag but pulled it back when Standish reached for it. "There could be a reward. I need that money, Miss Kate."

Standish didn't know much about air bolt guns, but she did recognize Songheuser's logo stamped on the handle. This was it. This was the gun that had been checked out from Songheuser's ordnance locker and had never been recovered. It was the gun that had killed Duncan Chambers. The killer's fingerprints could still be on it. "You're right. You should leave it in the bag, though. I bet the reward will be higher if it's nice and clean."

Olive tucked the bag under her arm. "Good thinking. Come on, let's go. I didn't find any butterflies."

Standish reached for Olive's hand and tugged her toward the other sites. Or at least she hoped they were headed toward the other sites. Was that branch cut or had it just broken? Was she back on Peter's track?

"Shit," she whispered to herself.

"Did you hear that?" Olive sounded nervous.

"Olive, are we going the right way?"

"Ssshh," Olive whispered. "Listen."

Ferns rustled behind them. Standish let go of Olive's hand

and reached for the pepper spray in her pocket.

A low growl sounded to her right. Olive shrieked as a brown blur shot out of the ferns.

The dog hit Standish and she fell hard, smashing into the tree behind her and crumpling to the ground. The pepper spray canister disappeared into the ferns.

The dog bit down on her shoulder and she punched it in the side of the head, sending it sideways. Her head spun from hitting the tree.

The dog lunged again, going for her throat, the wet heat of its breath condensing on her tin necklace. It gave a shriek and shook its head, a red blister rising on its lip where it had touched the image of the saint.

Standish kicked the dog away from her, and another dog, black this time, burst out of undergrowth and leaped at her.

"Miss Kate!" Olive shrieked.

Something popped and whistled.

There was a terrible yelp and the black dog came down hard, its claws catching on Standish's jacket and skidding down her front. She grabbed it by the shoulders and shoved it away. The silver end of an air bolt stuck out from its side, the tiniest trickle of blood showing on the dog's coat.

The brown dog growled and took a step backward, its eyes on Standish's throat. She could see the purple and pink scars on its sides.

Without taking her eyes off the creature, she slipped the necklace over her head and thrust it in front of her. "Get back. Get back!"

The dog whined and took another step backward.

Olive lowered the air bolt gun, still in its plastic bag. "Kate, are you OK?"

Motors whirred above them. The acrid stink of ammonia filled the air.

"We've got to get out of here," Standish shouted at Olive.

She reached for the girl. "Give me the gun. Let's go!"

A yellowish cloud settled down out of the trees, and Olive began to cough. Standish took her hand and aimed them downhill. Her eyes burned. She couldn't see anything.

A sharp bark made her turn to her left. The black dog had gotten up. It took a lurching step forward and barked again. Standish caught herself on the nearest tree trunk. It was hard to breathe. She had to get Olive out of there, away from the cloud of gas.

The black dog barked louder, a long volley of barking, and a great crashing answered him as the pack rushed past. Standish felt a soft wetness on her hand and then a familiar soft ruff of fur. She blinked, trying to see if it was real, if this was really Hattie, but she couldn't see anything, her eyes were running too much, and then she felt the leather strip of a collar pressing against her palm.

She closed her fingers around Hattie's collar and let herself be pulled downhill.

I feel the best way to understand God is to think of Him as a kind of language. He is the tongue of all creation. His being transcends and includes the space between words, connecting and elevating the individual motes of creation.

For in the beginning was the Word, and the Word was with God, and the Word was God.

Can we even imagine the greatness of that voice?
— from THE COLLECTED WISDOM OF MW WILLIAMS

CHAPTER TWENTY-SIX

"We're going to go downstairs and find your boss. See, she's got to make a little announcement." Belinda stepped forward and grabbed Peter, snaking her arm around his neck to push the muzzle of the gun into his temple. She pushed him into the hall, squeezing the arm with the gun tighter around his throat. The smell of ferns came off her in waves, and for a discomforting moment, Peter felt as if he was gripped by a tree limb and not a woman's, as if Belinda's arm had turned from skin and bone into a tentacular horsetail limb, her Earthly human form transformed by her attachment to the forests of this world.

Her craziness was fucking with him. He forced a deep breath and focused his mind on the problem at hand. He had to keep her talking. That was his best chance to get out of this alive.

"Why did you come back? You already escaped."

"We gave you all a warning. You were supposed to stop killing the world, not redouble your efforts!" Belinda paused in front of the window looking down on Main Street. She had something in her free hand, he realized. He could see her clicking it, then caught a glimpse of a tiny red dot dancing on the street below. A laser pointer. She was sending some kind of message to someone out there.

"I guess you never worked for a major corporation," he gasped. Her grip was incredibly tight. Moving beer kegs had made her stronger than she looked. "All they care about is the bottom line."

"Nobody move!" someone shouted below. Something crashed and someone screamed.

Belinda marched him forward. A woman pressed herself against the wall, her mouth open in fear. "I want Victoria Wallace!"

The stairs were just ahead. Peter had no idea how they were going to get down two flights of stairs to reach Victoria in the basement. He was going to trip and fall and Belinda was going to blow his head off. She was that crazy.

"Careful on the stairs," she hissed, and she half-shoved, half-dragged him down. The homey smells of coffee and popcorn drifted out of the kitchenette as if this were any other work day. Peter ought to be walking into the kitchen right now for his third cup of coffee, and Julia from accounting ought to be coming out of her office with cookies, just like always.

But instead there was a gun pressed to his head and they were all going to be shot and killed and why? Because Victoria Wallace wanted to make it cheaper and easier to harvest horsetail lumber. This was all Songheuser's fault. The company never took no for an answer, never paid attention to anything besides their stockholders' earnings. They had screwed the Believers, rigged an election, covered up the death of scientists who were just testing a chemical they'd been ordered to handle, and yes, he was sure they had shot and killed the man he loved just so no one would find out what had gone wrong.

And now Peter would die too, and Songheuser wouldn't

give even half a shit.

"Put down the gun," a terse voice said. Brett Takas was creeping up the stairs from the basement, an air bolt gun in his hand and a Kevlar vest strapped around his chest. "My team has already taken out your friend on the ground floor."

"Where's Victoria Wallace?" Belinda shouted.

"I'm right here." Victoria stepped past Brett. She wore no vest. Her face was unreadable.

"You're not rebuilding," Belinda ordered. "Unless you stop this, we're going to wipe out every Songheuser employee in Canaan Lake."

"I see one woman with a gun." Victoria folded her arms across her chest. "I'm not very impressed."

Belinda jabbed the muzzle of the gun into Peter's temple. "I'll kill him!"

"What's one employee?" Victoria asked. "I can always hire more."

Belinda pulled the gun away from Peter's head and shot it at the ceiling. "Fuck you, you corporate whore!"

An explosion rocked the building and Peter staggered away from Belinda. The fire alarm began to scream.

Standish fell down, gasping, and a hot wet tongue wiped against her face. A stream gurgled someplace nearby, and someone tugged on her arm.

"Miss Kate? Miss Kate!"

"I'm OK, Olive." Standish rubbed her eyes and blinked. The air was clear here, but her eyes and lungs still stung. The skinny kid knelt beside her, mud and sticky sap and tears streaking her face. "Are you all right?"

"Yeah, the dogs helped me." Olive got to her feet. "Where did they go? There were so many dogs and now there's just Hattie."

Hattie barked. Standish put her arms around the dog's neck

and breathed in her unwashed stink. She never wanted to let her go, but after a minute Hattie wriggled uncomfortably, and Standish rubbed the dog behind her ears and then got up and looked around herself. They were in a field full of red clover, and the air smelled clean and vibrantly green. A fence ran just a few feet away, and a brown cow stood there watching them sleepily. Standish turned in a half circle and realized she could see a white barn about a hundred meters away.

Matthias stood between her and the barn, his hand clutched to his side. "Kate? Olive? Are you all right?"

She ran to him as he crumpled to his knees. "Matthias." She pulled his hand away. Blood ran from his side, and the silver air bolt stuck out just below his ribs. "Oh, God."

"You really shouldn't take the Lord's name in vain." His face tightened with pain. "Oh, this hurts."

She eased him to the ground. "How did you know where to find us?"

"It was the smell." He gave a little gasp. "We saw Joe Holder that night. He passed by us after we found Duncan. I couldn't figure it out then, but I put it together. He was hiding the air bolt gun. That was the smell."

"So Joe killed Duncan."

"He didn't do it alone," Matthias corrected her. "He didn't leave Duncan in the woods for us to find. That was the man in the boots."

"Rob McKidder." Standish looked over her shoulder. "Olive, go get Mr Eames. We've got to get Matthias into town."

"I don't want a doctor."

She stroked his cheek. His eyes were particularly gold at that moment, the blue circle around his iris like a piece of sky. "I've got to keep you alive long enough for you to tell Sheriff Vargas what you know."

He gave a weak smile. "Like she'd believe the word of a dog."

"You have to tell her everything. Not the weird stuff, but everything about Songheuser, and the election, and the agreement they made to keep you from telling everyone about their mistake." She kept her eyes on his face, because she didn't know where else to look. Her first aid training didn't cover gut shots. If she applied pressure, she'd only move the bolt deeper inside him and do him more harm than good.

"I swore I'd never tell." Matthias reminded her. "I made a deal."

"And Songheuser broke it. This new property tax was written to drive the Believers out of Canaan Lake." She squeezed his hands. "Don't you want to be a man again, and not one of Songheuser's dogs?"

Standish looked up and saw Olive racing toward them, her white hair streaming behind her like some beautiful free thing. Chameli's pink UTV was just behind her.

The building shook again, and someone grabbed Peter by the elbow. "We've got to get out of here!"

Niketa Shawl yanked him toward the far end of the hallway where the marketing and accounting cubicles sat. He remembered, then – the fire escape at the back of the building. He raced after her.

Julia threw open the window. "Come on! The building's on fire!"

Gunfire sounded behind them, but Peter didn't look back. He scrambled after Niketa, skidding on the metal landing outside the window.

Someone grabbed the back of Peter's jacket, reeling him back inside.

"Not you, Bajowski!" Joe Holder grinned madly, his blue eyes wide. He threw Peter against the wall. "You stay here and face what you've done."

"We've got to get out of here!" Peter shouted. "GreenOne's

setting off explosives!"

Joe's fist drove into Peter's stomach, doubling him over. The air went out of him.

"They're here because of you." Joe grabbed Peter's hair and jerked him upright. "I saw your notes. I know you want to bring Songheuser down."

Peter fought to catch his breath. "I just want... to stop... the test," he gasped.

"You're a fucking ecoterrorist just like your tree-hugging boyfriend." Joe's fist smashed into Peter's face and the gash on Peter's cheek split open with a hot spurt of blood.

Peter thought he might throw up from the pain. Smoke was beginning to fill the hallway, rising up from the floor below. The building rocked again, something vital inside it crumpling loudly.

Joe leaned in closer, an eggy stink coming off his breath. "I'm going to leave you here to die, Bajowski. I should have done it the night we took out Chambers, but I thought you'd have gone back to Earth by now." He gave one of his nasty chuckles and then shoved Peter sideways.

Peter hit the floor and felt his head spin. He could just see Holder squeezing out the fire escape. He had to catch up with him. The bastard had killed Duncan.

He pushed himself to his knees. The air was too thick to breathe. He could hear the siren at the VFD calling for help.

He grabbed the windowsill.

Below him, a dog howled.

"Bajowski! You've got to get out of here!" Brett Takas came out of the smoke, Belinda thrown over his shoulder and Victoria Wallace behind him. She squeezed past the security officer and climbed over the windowsill, her pumps clanging on the fire escape.

Peter pulled himself upright, coughing. Eyes streaming, he climbed out beside Wallace.

"Jesus Christ," she whispered.

"Help!" someone screamed, their voice so high-pitched that for a second Peter didn't realize it was Joe Holder. A big brown dog had him by the arm, blood running down its muzzle.

An explosion rocked the building, blowing out the window on the other side of the fire escape, the sound so loud the whole world went silent. Peter grabbed the railing, his head spinning.

Everything moved at half speed as his rattled head spun in the strange silence. The color seeped out of things; shapes distorted. The brown dog shaking Joe's arm became for a second a stocky man with a red-stained mouth and a cross burned purple on his side. A woman in head-to-toe green tried to run out of the parking lot but a gray and white dog leaped on her. Her mouth moved in silence; the dog ripped and tore without a sound; the woman squeezed off two silent shots at the sky in a dying reflex. The woman's blood was a cloudy white, the juice of a Christ's finger plant.

Peter couldn't move. The part of him that analyzed and measured had gone quiet in the blast, and his mind flailed to make sense of what he saw. Men became dogs, women became plants, reality twitched and struggled like a caterpillar resisting metamorphosis, like bread yearning to become body, like wine on the brink of becoming blood.

He squeezed shut his eyes, unwilling to see any more. He was hallucinating, his brain rattled by the sheer volume of the explosion.

There is no God, he reminded himself. *There are no saints. There is no magic.*

Then he felt a sensation grip him someplace deep inside, the kind of sensation his rational mind (which was stirring now and would certainly free him from this moment of insanity in a few seconds) would discount as a passing pressure on his vagus nerve, but which at this moment felt like the bass resonance of a cry vaster and greater than any he'd ever heard. The vibration spoke not in words but in crushing, painful certainty.

For a second, Peter knew that Huginn cried out and that its voice meant transubstantiation, and that if he believed that deeply enough, he'd change just as thoroughly as Belinda and her GreenOne friends.

A horn honked.

He snapped out of his trance with a gasp.

"Peter! Brett!"

"Who's in that UTV?" Wallace pointed to the red vehicle easing its way beneath the fire escape.

Peter shook his head in disbelief. "It's Julia and Niketa."

"Come on!" Niketa shouted up at them.

Despite his burden, Brett moved the fastest, but Peter was right behind him, his legs carrying him back into the world he understood.

"Holy crap," Chameli blurted. Six police cars sat in the street outside the office, while the Canaan Lake volunteer fire department worked to put out the flames bursting out the front of the building. A dog ran by, its muzzle streaked with gore.

"Keep going," Standish ordered from the backseat. She squeezed Matthias's fingers. "Hold on, Matthias. We're almost there."

Metal shrieked as the skybridge between the office and the mill snapped in half. Glass and wood tumbled down behind them, blocking Main Street.

Songheuser was being punished right now. But it wouldn't be enough unless the world knew the whole truth about the company.

"There – Sheriff Vargas!" Standish shouted.

Sheriff Vargas was leading a man in a green jacket to her cruiser. She shoved him inside and stopped to check her hand unit.

Chameli pulled up beside the sheriff. "Sheriff!" she bellowed. "We need you right away!"

The dull rumble of a chopper filled the air. Smoke rose up from dozens of spots along Main Street. The town looked like a war zone.

A UTV in Songheuser's white and blue skidded to a stop behind them. A handsome black man leaped out of the driver's side. "Bajowski? Where are you?" he shouted.

Peter stepped out of the crowd. "I'm here, Mark!"

"I got half the drones called off, but I couldn't override the others. If there was somebody out there–"

But Standish didn't have time to listen to their conversation. She let go of Matthias's hand and opened the door. "Sheriff Vargas! This man needs to talk to you. And he needs a doctor right away."

She glanced over her shoulder. Matthias had turned the color of fine paper, his eyes like holes in his cheeks. Blood poured down his side.

Sheriff Vargas hurried toward her. "Standish? You all right?"

"Yeah." She pulled the plastic bag with the air bolt gun out of her coat pocket. "I found something for you."

Vargas took it carefully and tucked it under her arm. She leaned into the car. "Matthias. Tell me what you need."

Standish stepped backward to give them room. Her knees wobbled beneath her. She didn't understand any of the madness around her, the people shouting, the crash and boom of falling metal. A part of her was still back in the woods facing those dogs.

"Standish." Peter squeezed her shoulder. "Is Matthias OK?"

His eye had swollen shut completely, and blood ran down

his cheek. She shook her head. She couldn't even talk.

"Get him out of here," Sheriff Vargas called out, and a paramedic rolled a gurney up and eased Matthias onto it. He gasped with pain.

Standish pulled away from Peter and grabbed Matthias's hand. "You'll be OK, right? You can't die, remember."

He smiled a pure happy smile. "I told the sheriff," he said. "I broke my promise to Songheuser. Hepzibah will be glad."

Standish grabbed his hands. "Don't leave me, friend."

"Do you hear that?" His eyes looked past her, the pupils vast. "Do you hear that voice?"

Then his face went slack and still.

My wife listened to God more closely than I did. She realized that God created not in individual words, but in great sentences and paragraphs. Each world is its own Good Book, its own wisdom text.

It is time to give Huginn a careful reading. Who knows what we might become if we only pay attention to the words of our new world?

— from THE COLLECTED WISDOM OF MW WILLIAMS

CHAPTER TWENTY-SEVEN

Hepzibah crawled away from the man who had once been her husband – the man who was no longer truly a man. She coughed again and again and a fine spray of red speckled the ground ahead of her. Something was really wrong with her lungs. She didn't think she had much time left.

She pulled herself upright using the shed door. There they were, her caterpillars and her bees. She had worked hard to tend them, but no one else had ever cared about her little project. If she died, they would, too.

She opened the latch on the caterpillar's case. "Time to find your own way, little ones," she said, or tried to say. She pulled open the gate on the nearest hive and then sank to the ground, gasping for air.

It was sunny out, she realized. For the first time since they had come to Huginn, the sun was shining. It filled the shed doorway, touching her legs and warming them.

A leather bird settled on a fern across from the doorway, holding something blue in its talons. She wanted to shoo it away, but it just sat there, its nostrils opening and closing at her. The scrap of blue in its grip looked almost like an orchid. The leather bird lowered the flower to its stomach slit and sucked it inside.

Hepzibah toppled sideways. Pink foam dribbled out of the corner of her mouth and she could no longer see the leather bird but only the tree branches above. They were full of flowers, beautiful blue and white and yellow flowers, and there were purple plant-looking things she'd never seen before, and some other leathery thing like a big-eared snake. There was so much up in the trees that she'd never noticed.

A leather bird swooped over a branch and bit off a flower, then flapped away at top speed. They ate flowers, she thought. Flowers, not blood. God had made them ugly, but there was more to their lives than their ugly exteriors. The ugliness and evil she saw, she had projected onto them from her own imagination.

"Hepzibah, please be all right," Matthias begged. She couldn't see him, only the sky and the trees and the creatures she'd never seen before today. He sounded like himself again, at least a little, and that gave her hope that he would not be a dog forever.

"I'm all right," she whispered. The fear and pain had dribbled out of her with her life's blood, and all that remained was a warm sense of goodness. She would be with God very soon, and all of this would make sense.

A little green caterpillar crawled purposefully in front of her face, its humble shape filling her vision. They had come to Huginn expecting Eden, but she saw now that God had other plans for them and this place. Even that caterpillar had a better sense of those plans than they'd had.

I'm going home, she thought, her chest no longer rising or falling.
No, I am home. I am.

And then the caterpillar was gone, leaving only the sky filled with branches, and flowers, blue flowers like butterflies, and a thousand unnamed members of God's creation.

"Standish! Wait up!"

Peter ran toward her and was glad to see her stop for him.

"Hey," she said.

The sun shone bright on the field of crosses and blue saints.

The dry season had arrived, and with it a kind of peace had settled over Canaan Lake. He had missed her the past few weeks. He understood why she'd gone, but he'd walked by her house every day, wishing she was there. "I didn't know you were back from Space City."

"I couldn't miss Matthias's funeral. Besides, my psychologist said it was important for me to get back to my normal life as soon as possible. I've got some new meds and I'm feeling pretty good."

He felt good, too, although he wasn't sure how he could explain that to Standish. They had set out to punish Songheuser, and yet the company continued on the same as ever. But somehow that failure didn't sting.

He opened his mouth and closed it again, unsure how to talk to her without their enemy to unite them. They walked slowly. People filed past them, headed for the grave site, but they were still early, and the day was too beautiful to be rushed.

"Joe Holder's in jail," Peter began. "The prints on the air bolt gun are probably enough to put him away, although his little confession to me will help. I wish Victoria was getting punished for something. It was all her idea, after all."

Standish shook her head. "People like her never pay for what they do. Songheuser will see to that." There was bitterness in her voice, but not as much as he had feared.

He stopped and put his hands in his pockets. The sun might have been bright, but the wind had a chill to it. "So what are you going to do now? I mean, you can't want to work for Songheuser after all this."

She stooped to pick up a fallen cross. "I talked to a lawyer. Sounds like I can get a share of that class action lawsuit money. That'll last a little while."

"But your visa. Victoria will—"

"Sheriff Vargas said she'd keep an eye on Songheuser, even

vouch for me. They won't kick me off Huginn too soon."
Standish pushed the cross back into place. Its crossbeam had
slanted in the process, and she patiently adjusted it.

He cleared his throat. "About Vargas. How did she know to
call for backup? She had all those cops and paramedics there
just when things started getting crazy."

"It was Dewey." Standish gave up on fixing the cross and
stood up. "I guess all my messages freaked her out, and she
called Sheriff Vargas."

"Thank goodness for Dewey," he said.

She looked down at Hattie, rubbing the dog's ears. It was
something he'd seen her do a thousand times, but he'd never
seen her look so casual about it. Maybe her new medication
had taken some of the tension out of her. "Yes, thank goodness
for Dewey. I thought about leaving Canaan Lake after all of
that. She reminded me that I didn't just come here because of
Songheuser. I came here to find a new life."

The words hit him hard, and he blinked away sudden
tears. After all, he'd come here for the wrong reasons himself.
Duncan had brought him here, had given him a reason to
stay, but Peter had come to the same realization that she had.

Huginn was home. He didn't understand the place, he
couldn't yet explain it, but he belonged here anyway.

"Peter," she said suddenly. "What about the degassing
compound? What will happen to the forest?"

"Mark and I are trying something." Her eyebrows shot up
and he raised his palms in self-defense. "I know, I'm working
with the enemy. But I can't just quit. The forest needs me."

She took a deep breath, and he braced himself for her
anger. It would be completely justified.

"So what are you trying?"

He blinked at her, surprised by her equanimity. "I found
this fungus," he said. "It's a terrestrial fungus, and it competes
with other terrestrial fungi, even powder mildew. It extrudes

some kind of chemical that impedes the growth of that stuff. It's a risk, of course – it's an armillaria species, and they can kill trees. But I've got a predator that eats it, so that's something."

He was talking too fast. She probably didn't understand a bit of what he said.

"A predator?" She leaned in. "But I thought nothing from Huginn could eat anything from Earth, and vice versa."

Her interest made him grin. "Well, the predator is a caterpillar from Earth. But somehow the tree scooters have found a way to milk the caterpillars for an additional food source, and they're all living together in this weird pattern. Like I said, it could all throw off the balance of Canaan Lake's ecosystem, but it's our best chance."

"Tree scooters and caterpillars, working together. It's like a message, isn't it? That we can find a way to work with Huginn instead of just paving over it."

"Yeah, I think so." He paused. "We keep forcing Huginn to be like Earth. We describe it like it's Earth. We name things like they're Earth things. But this isn't Earth. It's totally different. I feel like these organisms, this fungus, these caterpillars – they're part of a *new* story, a Huginn story. And if we can make sense of the story, then we'll find a way to fit into it."

Peter had thought about all of this a lot since the disaster at the office, but this was the first time he'd told anyone else about it. He couldn't shake the feeling that the stories they told themselves about Huginn, and about themselves, made a real, physical difference.

He kept dreaming about that vision he'd had when the explosion had deafened him.

Transubstantiation, a voice inside him kept whispering, a voice that sounded something like his grandmother's. Sometimes he caught himself wondering if Believers could really become dogs, terrorists really become part-plant neo-humans, wine really become blood.

He had downloaded several years' worth of scientific reviews to his hand unit for the nights when these thoughts woke him.

"A Huginn story." She gave a little laugh. "I like it, Peter."

He put his arm through hers. "Is there anything else making you look so happy? I mean, new meds and free money is pretty great, but that can't be everything. I kind of thought you'd be angry. I mean, Songheuser's not really paying for what they did."

She paused again. She looked from him to the big headstone marking off the Believers' graves from the others. They were very nearly to Matthias's burial site. "There is something. It was a big surprise."

"What happened?"

"Shane Vogel came to see me while I was in Space City. The Believers have talked it over, and they want to give me Matthias's house. I'm going there after the funeral."

"Do you think you'll be OK living there? I mean, won't it remind you of him?"

"Yeah, but that's the weird thing. It ought to hurt, thinking about Matthias. He was my friend, and now he's dead. But somehow, I'm not sad. It's not like denial, either. I feel like I skipped over the stages of grieving or something. That's impossible, right?"

Peter put his arm around her shoulder. The sun had baked her black jacket, and it felt comfortingly warm beneath his arm. "It's Canaan Lake, Standish. Impossible things happen here all the time."

They walked to the grave site and waited for the pall bearers to carry the coffin through the cemetery's twists and turns. Standish kept her hand on Hattie's head. This was the last time they would bury Matthias Williams. She was certain of it.

Standish looked up at the sky, which was cloudless and blue. She felt almost fine looking at all that space. Almost fine.

Of all the impossible things, that was the one that surprised her the most.

ACKNOWLEDGMENTS

This book could not have been written without the help of Maggie and Charlie, two of the best dogs I have ever met.

I am tremendously grateful to Robyn Lupo, who not only read the first draft of this book and caught my errors about assistance animals, life with dogs, and mental health (the errors that remain are all mine!) but who then encouraged me during the entire revision and submissions process. Robyn, you're a tremendous friend, and Huginn wouldn't be the same without you.

More thanks are owed to my extremely supportive writing group. Mask tips to all the Hucksters, but especially Dale and Jen, who beta read this book when it was a lot uglier.

More plot holes were fixed by my agent, Evan Gregory, who also found it a home with the wonderful crew at Angry Robot. Marc, Phil, Penny, Mike, Nick, Paul, and also Simon: thank you for taking such good care of my book!

Big thanks to John and Fiona for putting up with me while I worked on this project. I know I was a little extra nutty, and I'm sure you'll be glad to stop hearing about Huginn. Thanks as well to all the folks at *Lightspeed* and *Nightmare* who were neglected while I doted on my own work. JJA and Christie, you're the best.

But the biggest thanks go to Alice and Ico, fur-friends extraordinaire. I promise someday I will write a book about cats.

ABOUT THE AUTHOR

Wendy N Wagner is a full-time science fiction and fantasy nerd. Her first two novels, *Skinwalkers* and *Starspawn*, are set in the world of the *Pathfinder* role-playing game, and she has written over thirty short stories about monsters, heroes, and unsettling stuff. An avid gamer and gardener, she lives in Portland, Oregon, with her very understanding family.

winniewoohoo.com • twitter.com/wnwagner

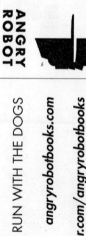

ANGRY
ROBOT

RUN WITH THE DOGS

angryrobotbooks.com

twitter.com/angryrobotbooks